I0822826

CONTENTS

The Investigation

The radiant midday sky was alive with the humming flow of traffic. The massive structures of a walled city stood tall amidst the green of the land. Aircraft circled the sky over it like a spinning halo at flux, as those who climbed to depart were steadily replaced by arrivals eager to land. With a wide turn, a small shuttle broke from the cyclic flow of moving vessels and began its decent for the busy port along the eastern wall of the city.

Thaut had been lounging in the luxury of his cabin, comfortably reclined as he prepared for the mission ahead. The details of his arrangements were fresh in his mind, but he continued his review despite the redundancy. He was ever the skeptic, experienced with age and wise enough to exercise caution over complacency. One could never be too careful, especially with the circumstance at hand. He sat up with a groan much like the creaking leather of his seat, as the shuttle slowed for approach.

High pitch voices chattered over the radio, the friendly voices of air control guiding the heavy traffic. Approach had always been Thaut's favorite part of flying. Nostalgia took him back for a moment, to a time when those voices over the headset broke the silence like the whispers of angels, reaching even the most forgotten of places.

Air traffic control hailed the shuttle. Thaut shifted to a more upright position in his seat, feeling somewhat stiff in his age. He heard clearance given over the radio and the rasping voice of his pilot, the seasoned Major Hapford, respond in acknowledgment. They had arrived at Paeon, Imperial capital of the Vanonia providence. His view was limited, but Thaut caught a glimpse of the outside world as he looked through the flight deck via the doorway that separated his cabin.

Thaut had seen the city many a time in his line of service, yet the bustling east docks of Paeon were just as impressive as the first time he had laid eyes upon them. The east wall of the city towered some three hundred meters in height. The docks themselves held level some seventy-five meters above ground, the ancient pillars that supported them weathered and dirty like the barren grounds below.

He shifted his gaze to his two man crew, taking a moment to appreciate the routine movements of Hapford and the young co-pilot at his side. As usual their movements were well synchronized. This would be a smooth approach. Within seconds the co-pilot turned in his seat, addressing Thaut through the doorway.

"We're cleared for landing, Sir."

Summers was his name, First Lieutenant Jakob Summers. Behind his ridiculous sunglasses, he spoke with the inflated confidence of a true novice. At twenty-four years of age he wore the stereotype of young ambition well. Thaut considered him a young fool but enjoyed his company nonetheless. He was close to making captain no doubt. His dark hair was crew cut, solidifying his fly-guy persona.

"Thank you, Lieutenant." Thaut replied with a smile, though it was more of a smirk. No doubt the years had hardened his demeanor. Fortunately, his social etiquette remained more or less intact.

Thaut had seen many a fledgling come and go over the course of his military service, having been one himself what seemed so long ago. Though he now held an esteemed position in the Emperor's council, his career had been anything but easy in the years that led to his appointment. He could appreciate the disposition of a young man playing bold.

The shuttle whined as the landing gear moved into position with an audible groan. Four rod shaped landing thrusters hummed into action, allowing better stability as the shuttle slowed. The engines sighed, power gradually reduced from the main thrusters to facilitate the transition. The stabilizers steadily gained more control, and the small craft began its final descent. Thaut had been correct in his assumptions, the transition was textbook as they hovered along the massive space of the busy port.

The surface was only a few meters below them, as they cruised along the strip. Various landing platforms lined the tarmac. Members of the landing crew zipped about like busy bees. Once they reached their approved sector of the dock, the shuttle groaned once more as the landing gear lowered. Four slender, segmented legs unfurled from the hull, their terminal points reaching for the pad. The shuttle looked like a squat, stumpy dragonfly come to land.

Smooth and steady, the shuttle took position over a landing platform. With a metallic clink the landing gear made contact. The shuttle settled gently to rest, centered and balanced. Textbook.

Once they had landed, Thaut watched the dock crew scurry outside the shuttle. The marshal stood a short distance from the nose of the craft. With its landing, she hurried off to aid the rest of her crew in servicing the small vessel. Thaut did not envy them their job today. It was afternoon, and the high sun was surely ripe with the heat of early summer in Vanonia's subtropical climate.

Major Hapford continued to run through shutdown procedures, flipping switches along various control panels. Soon the hum of the shuttle purred into silence. He removed his headset and turned to Thaut.

"You're cleared on the hatch, Chief. We'll be in hangar alpha one-three this time around. You sure you wanna go this part alone?" Hapford asked in his low rasping voice. With the exception of the corners of his bushy mustache, he somehow spoke without breaking the stern expression he bore. The graying dark stubble along his chin and cheeks added to his weathered appearance.

"I really don't expect much. Just going through the motions, Major. We'll see what happens. If nothing else, a little down time never hurt the cause." Thaut replied.

In truth he was not entirely sure what to expect with his upcoming encounter. As a precaution he had made arrangements to ensure the safety of his crew. He would go this one alone.

"The kid and I will keep it tight, just in case." Growled Hapford.

Summers continued to run through the remaining shutdown procedures, flipping at switches and scanning over monitors. The lights flickered as the shuttle was plugged into the power conduit on the landing pad and switched to external power. Shutdown was complete.

Thaut smiled. "No worries. We'll all be enjoying holiday by this time tomorrow. If all goes accordingly, I'll be joining you later this evening. Perhaps sooner if not."

There was no need to go over the rest. The details had already been discussed with Hapford and the lieutenant during planning. Hopefully there would be no need for contingency. Besides, a vacation was long overdue.

Thaut had reserved suites at the once luxurious Eden hotel. He hadn't been in years, but he had thoroughly appreciated his stays during previous visits. It was more of a tradition really. The hotel had long since faded from its golden age, but the greater appeal was its location. Not only was it within minutes of the departure hangars of the east wall, but it was close to district seven, also known as Rhiathan Cove.

One of the better local attractions, district seven was designed to simulate a tropical coast, though Paeon was far from coastal. It was really quite convincing in appearance, with white sandy beaches and crystal blue waters under an endless synthetic summer sky. Tropical plants and colorful wildlife flourished in the artificial habitat, completing the illusion. Thaut and his crew would most certainly indulge themselves on behalf of the Empire once the objective was met.

The lieutenant finished the last of his checks before removing his headset. He turned to peer through the doorway behind Hapford. "We're good here, sir. Good luck out there."

"Thank you, Lieutenant. First time in Vanonia?" Thaut asked.

"Yes, sir." Summers responded.

"Perfect. The people here are very generous hosts, plenty to see and do. We're in for some well earned R and R. For today, just make sure to be sober and ready. Not necessarily in that order." Thaut joked, though the lieutenant seemed to have missed it entirely. Humor was not his strong suite. "Stay sharp 'til then." Thaut rambled, as he adjusted the dark blue collar of his shirt back to a proper fitting about his neck and grabbed hold of his satchel.

"Chief." Replied the Lieutenant with a stern nod.

Thaut stood tall. Even hunched, his head bobbed along the top of the cramped cabin. He pulled at a lever to activate a door release along the side panel. Within seconds the hatch disengaged, and with a slight jolt it divided just below its center. One section of the hatch ascended overhead, another descended until it was even with the deck below Thaut's feet. In an instant, there was a portal providing passage out into the world.

The bright essence of summer spilled into the cabin with the hot rush of sticky air, humid and ripe with the aromas of Paeon. The high sun was blinding for a moment as Thaut stepped out from the silence and comfort of his personal shuttle and into the bustling chaos of the East Docks. A swift breeze caught the hem of his light jacket, causing it to ripple for a moment. The sky to the east hummed with shuttle craft, as traffic circulated from the city. The low thunder of massive cargo ships down below rumbled the grates at his feet.

The dock itself was a massive rectangular stage suspended by six columns that supported the platform along its outer edges. The western side of the dock was built into the great wall of the city itself, which was more than capable of supporting its share of the busy port's immense weight.

The area under the East Docks of Paeon was its industrial hub, and as the air stilled the smells that seeped up from below proved testament to its presence. The ground stayed cool and barren in the shadow of the docks, giving the place a musky odor year round. To top it off, foul smelling exhaust radiated from the relief vents of waste treatment facilities below the city, somewhere within the confines of the wall.

Exterior to the wall were the rail systems, used mostly to transport freight between the large cargo ships come to land on the packed musty soil beneath the docks. The massive ships hovered between the ground and the docks with a deep chorus of resonating hums. The amount of force required for the mobility of these aerial leviathans was immense, and as a result they appeared shrouded in eerie silhouettes like ghastly apparitions while in motion. They moved slow and steady at lower altitudes, easily spotted against the blue of the sky due to their size.

The area below the docks was also used for the inspection and processing of livestock brought from the more distant areas of Vanonia, usually by rail. The smell of death, feces, and sewage waste from the wonderful city combined to assail the senses, the stench of industrial achievement and the labors required to maintain civilization of such magnitude. Thaut was more than grateful when the perfumed breeze stirred the air once more.

As his eyes adjusted to the radiant world, Thaut stepped down from the landing platform with the click of his boots and looked out over the expanse of the docks. It was busy as always, traffic arriving from all directions and departing just the same. Of course, most of these craft landed on the south end of the dock. Thaut and his crew had landed in a smaller section on the northern most part of the dock, reserved for ranking officials of the Empire.

Thaut stood with his gaze locked to the east, the direction from which they had arrived. He was an older gentleman with close cut gray hair and pale thin lips that seemed as stern and cold as his icy blue eyes. Though he no longer dawned the uniform of a service member, he still carried himself as such, pride in his step. He stood tall and lean, prestige in the light blue fibers of his finely fitted jacket. A thicker dark blue material made the cuffs that folded back over his wrists. The same dark blue material lined the center of the jacket, where smooth gray stone buttons snapped up to meet a narrow collar.

The wind whipped at the corner of his jacket, momentarily revealing the silk wrapping about his waist where his simple white cotton undershirt met the more course, rugged ashy blue material of his trousers. The material did not necessarily compliment his fine jacket, but he had come to appreciate its durability over the years.

His trousers were bloused into his glossy black leather boots. The fine leather creaked as he moved. They were sleek in the light, metal rivets worked into the seams shining silvery bright. The same metal plated the back of each boot's thick heel and the ends of the toes as well, producing a metallic click with each step upon the metal grating underfoot.

Boots like these were customarily worn by commanders, a prestigious position Thaut had worked toward his entire military career. Yet, he had resigned to retirement shortly after his promotion, as he had felt the prestige of the title much diminished upon its acquisition. His ship and his crew had been lost in battle. It was only by a fluke that he had even survived. The details of that battle followed him long after the Empire claimed its victory.

He had gladly accepted his current title as Chief Investigator when it was offered. His majesty Emperor Haben Rashawn had called upon him personally, requesting his service beyond retirement. Thaut had found retirement to be boring anyhow. He was sure he'd have been driven into madness if he'd remained idle any longer, and he was glad to be of service once again. He hung up the uniform, but kept the boots. It would have been a shame to toss them out. Not to mention they could be outfitted with all sorts of nifty technological gadgetry, easily concealed within the intricacies of the bulky things. He was most fond of the metallic clicks made by his steps. There was no mistaking when a commander was on deck. No matter the circumstance, the sound unfailingly managed to catch the attention of an areas occupants upon arrival.

Thaut breathed deep of the passing breeze as he looked to the distant edge of the docks where the blue sky reigned. High in the distance rose a great tree, spanning over much of the open grasslands that encircled Paeon. Its massive branches reached far overhead, obscured by the distance. By night the large branches would be speckled with tiny lights, as native people still made their homes within the great tree.

Thaut turned to face the wall of the city just as his transport arrived. A young man wearing the standard white and red jumpsuit of the dock crew was behind the controls of a personnel cart. It hovered toward him. The bulky looking helmet worn by the driver wobbled when the cart stopped abruptly, making him look like a bobble head for a moment.

The cart was a mess. Black scuffs and scrapes from what must have been a lengthy history of hard use scarred the gray metallic exterior. The tan leather seats were torn and discolored, ripped and a bit stained in places from years of wear. It was designed to properly seat four occupants, though it was not unusual to see a cart loaded with as many crew members as could fit on the thing, barely scraping over the ground while in motion. It was quaint, but suitable enough. Luxury was hardly necessary.

A chime in Thaut's small earpiece sounded an alert, he was being hailed. He reached under his left cuff to his wrist communicator and entered a command with the tap of his finger, allowing a scan of his credentials. The driver's eyes were fixed on Thaut, as he waited. A blue light flashed momentarily across the driver's eyes beneath the clear visor of his full helmet. Protocol was met, and the driver had verified Thaut as his passenger.

The driver all but tumbled from the cart, his sleeve snagging on a broken metal ring where a safety harness had once been mounted. He scrambled his way around the cart to greet his passenger.

"Chief Investigator Thaut." He offered his hand. "My name is Rick Weldins. I'll be providing transport this afternoon. Welcome to Paeon, sir."

"Thank you, Mr. Weldins." Thaut responded with a firm shake.

Thaut made his way over to the cart and settled down into the seat next to Rick, shifting his satchel onto his lap. As the driver engaged the controls next to him, Thaut looked back to his shuttle. Hapford and the Lieutenant were visible within the flight deck. Hapford offered a lazy, non standard salute for luck. Thaut offered his in return. The cart made a wide U-turn, and with a groaning hum they zipped toward the city.

As they approached the east wall, Thaut ran his gaze up its spectacular height. Glass windows shimmered along the rough dark colored stone. Behind one of the more distant windows some two hundred meters above the docks was an abandoned conference hall Thaut had selected for the scheduled interview. It was isolated, secret.

The nature of Thaut's mission was curious enough, but the mysteries unfolding only added to his questions. He had been researching legends regarding a powerful entity of great interest to the Empire, more specifically his Majesty the Emperor. Following a lead he encountered in a neighboring providence, he had come to Vanonia to meet with an individual purported to be the very entity behind the legends of his study. A bold claim Thaut half hoped was false. And if it wasn't? His heart quickened and a smile crept over his face. It was possible he would soon be face to face with an ancient deity, a being who's capacities raised the concerns of the Emperor himself.

"Sir, the quarters have been prepared as you requested." Rick informed, as the cart began to slow. They were approaching a personnel entrance at the wall.

"Excellent." Thaut responded, pleased to hear things were going according to plan thus far.

He had arranged for certain modifications to be made to the intended chamber prior to the interview. If his source was genuine, danger was a very real possibility. The subject in question was to be approached with great caution. Thaut would be unarmed for the exchange, and if his guest had any decency things would go well. Regardless, the arranged modifications would allow for a most expedient exit in the event things got dicey. Contingency rules.

With a descending hum, the cart slowed to a halt in front of a closed shutter. Several guards stood nearby the entrance, armed with rifles and scanners. Two of them approached the vehicle. One rounded the cart slowly, scanning up and down with a handheld device that looked like a stubby toy gun. The other approached the driver side of the cart.

"Good afternoon. I need to verify your information, please." She kept her rifle at low ready across her chest.

The other two guards remained on either side of the shutters, eyes fixed on the cart from behind the visors of their helmets. The guard nearest reviewed their credentials, and called clearance over the radio. The shutters lurched and creaked as they began to rise.

"You're clear. Welcome to Paeon, Chief Investigator." She greeted, taking a few steps back from the vehicle as they shifted into motion once more.

The vehicle left the radiance of the sun baked dock and entered a dimly lit corridor. As they zoomed through the stone and metal innards of the wall, the hum of the cart reverberated within the narrow confines of the maintenance alley. The way the metal beams flashed by as the cart passed somehow reminded Thaut of flying through the dense forest he and his crew had visited in their last few weeks abroad.

A recent increase in combative incidents between Imperial forces and an unknown hostile entity left Thaut charged with investigating the more remote regions of the Empire. The anomaly in question was believed to be a strong celestial, an individual with abilities beyond the scope of normal human beings. Thaut had seen many a shaky poor quality video clip depicting incredible feats caught by flabbergasted onlookers. Entities such as these were considered a danger to the general public and were most often condemned, if not instead recruited to the cause of his Majesty's Holy Empire.

Those who sided with the Empire were known as the Ascended, the strongest continuing to become Knights of the Circle. These individuals possessed incredible speed and strength, serving as defenders of the realm. Esteemed commanders of the Vanguard, Imperial Knights were renown for their fierce loyalty to his Majesty's Holy Empire. Though there had been many cases documented, no subject on record thus far compared in scale to his Majesty Emperor Rashawn, who had stood peerless for countless generations.

Any disturbance in the lands protected under Imperial rule was met with the force of the Vanguard, led by a commanding Knight. As a result, many celestials avoided drawing negative attention at all costs, especially in those territories with heavy ties to the Empire. If ever such a disturbance occurred, it was dealt with discretely.

Aside from inhuman strength and endurance, recent reports indicated even further degrees of potential. The latest news footage offered a momentary glimpse of two unidentified individuals zipping through space at incredible speeds, perhaps even through time as some extreme theorists speculated. An immense impact had drawn a family's attention when something struck down near their farm on the outskirts of Vanonia. Two figures burst from the plume of dust and debris, the audio distorted by crackling pops and thunderous booms. The two blurry figures appear locked in combat for a brief instance, blades slashing with thundering movements before they vanish from sight. Similar bouts of thunder could be heard over the screams, growing more distant as the family ran for cover in the mere seconds covered in the footage. The media played the short clip on a loop for days following the incident.

Ahead the corridor met an intersection, where another corridor led west into the city no doubt. There was a small turnabout in a clearing at the junction with a small station built into in the inner wall. Above the door to the station a sign read "6B Level-23" in bright, bold red lettering to indicate this was the second in a series of maintenance stations for district six, which lay just beyond the inner wall.

District six was the unofficial heart of Paeon. The relatively narrow strip was only a fraction of the area compared to the larger districts, but its development swelled along its parameters despite that fact. The upper level was the city's central business district, a huge architectural complex of all fathomable designs suspended under a synthetic sky. On the base level of the district were the shops and eateries that attracted so many to the region.

The streets of district six were alive with the city's most luxurious squares and plazas, swarming with a ceaseless flow of people. It was magnificent in display, statues and fountains placed among the carefully selected vegetation. Somehow nature and technology came together, making a walk down the strip feel more like a walk in the park. A diverse array of flashing colors from innumerable signs and projections illuminated the metropolitan walkways. It was an awful crowded place this time of day, and Thaut was glad when the driver continued south along the innards of the wall.

It wasn't long before the cart came across another break in the corridor, complete with its own little station. The corridor widened, and the cart slowed as it entered the turnabout. The lettering above the station read "6A Level-23". This was Thaut's destination.

The driver brought the cart to a stop in front of the entrance to the station. Thaut thanked Mr. Weldins before dismissing him, and made his way to the entrance. The metal click of his steps echoed considerably in the hollow space of the roundabout drive.

He stopped for a moment, as the sharp echoes of his steps reverberated through the expanse of the corridors behind the fading hum of the cart. A strange feeling suddenly crept over him, as he looked over the gloomy grays of the concrete tunnel. The lights along the walls seemed to do little against the gloom, their bright electric glow locked in a constant struggle to hold back the dark. It was a good reminder of where he stood. He was well within the confines of the wall, headed for the belly of the beast.

Thaut's heart fluttered, as he raised his eyes to the concrete above. Was he really to meet face to face with a legend of old, a killer with god-like ability? He wasn't one for superstition, but the tales recounted did little to still his nerves as the moment of truth neared. Thaut felt the tingle of uncertainty rise like static across his skin, setting his hair on end. He set his resolve to press on, the click of his boots filling the space once more.

The glass doors of the station opened automatically, sliding to either side with a light swishing sound, releasing a rush of cool air. It was refreshing, fragrant with the scent of pine cleaner that lingered, mixed with the smells of an office environment. The pungent aroma of coffee was everywhere about him as he stepped inside the small, cramped station. A guard sat lazily behind a rounded counter staring at a network of monitors. A live feed droned on a screen high across the room, where chairs collected dust in a small empty lobby.

Thaut recognized the footage. It was a news broadcast, replaying the footage captured by the Higbey family for perhaps the hundredth time. The official report indicated that one of the whirling figures obscured in even the slowed footage was an ascended working in the services of the Empire, one of the twelve knights in his Majesty's private circle, known as Divinity Court.

The story on the news program still had little to offer in detail, of course. The whereabouts and identities of either figure were yet to be disclosed. The classified report, however, now officially stated the Imperial Knight Miguel to be deceased. His attacker, yet to be identified, was reported as missing and still at large. What would the media make of that? Thaut chuckled at the thought.

The footage recorded by the Higbey family had erupted in the media like wildfire, and it was no surprise to see it remained on the air here in Vanonia. Accounts like these had a long standing cult following, but nothing to this degree had made its way to the public eye for quite some time. As usual, the Emperor himself visited the family to apologize for the event, offering the support of the Empire but little in the way of answers for the bewildering phenomena. Though he was by no means sinister of character, his prestige alone was more than enough to silence most.

His Majesty had ordered a full investigation on the scene, though little was discovered by the standard preliminaries. It seemed the real task at hand was to be passed to Thaut. He received his orders directly from the Emperor in private, along with his first lead. Thaut's assignment was to uncover the identity of the unknown assailant. Sir Miguel had been deployed near the area by Imperial order when the unexpected encounter took place. Thaut's pursuit of the unknown assailant was only the beginning it seemed.

Another similar incident had occurred in the nearby providence of Irvahem, predating the attack at the Higbey farm by a questionable margin. Same scenario, an Imperial knight missing after a presumed encounter. This possible link snowballed the project into something far greater in implication. The connection between the two incidents lacked any solid evidence to indicate the same party as responsible, though it remained suspect.

Thaut had hastily assembled his crew and set out for Irvahem. He searched through the Imperial databases to find what information he could on the area, but was curious to find little to nothing on the history of the region. In fact, no information on the providence existed prior to the presence of the Empire. It was at that point that Thaut's interest was engaged, his curiosity winning the better of him. He had no choice but to seek out the myths and legends of the area directly. Together he and his crew spent weeks traveling the forests of the providence, searching for any leads connected to the powerful entity, designated in his report as Subject One.

The primary investigation was to be classified in secrecy. His mission was to begin in the less developed areas of Irvahem, where he was to thoroughly inspect the area and document any accounts of suspicious phenomena suggestive of celestial presence. Once he had successfully located the entity, the knights and the Vanguard would handle the rest.

Their search began in a small forest community near the site of the battle, where the first fatal encounter had taken place. The local lore on supernatural happenings had been a delight to sort through, but his further inquiries caught the attentions of the village elders. Before he knew it, his questions were shunned and dismissed by the same villagers who had initially shared so openly.

As he and his crew traveled from village to village, they received little more to go on than a tourist map of the providence with the capital city outlined. It wasn't until his search led him to a somewhat developed city located in the dense forest to the west that his luck changed. There he uncovered more interesting tales, told by the inhabitants of the oldest standing city in the providence, Verda.

Sorting through the myths surrounding his query had been an interesting endeavor, as accounts varied substantially in the region. Most people with relevant accounts told this entity to be a killer, a demon who laid waste to all in its path. Yet others told of a benevolent guardian spirit, a regal defender born of the natural world to maintain balance and peace.

Though the details varied substantially among the subcultures, the stories passed by the descendants of Verda told of the same event. Subject One was suspected of destroying the city before later attacking the Shem Koreem district. These events directly predated the arrival of Imperial rule to the region, before the logs in the databases began their record.

Demon or not, Thaut and his team had seen the scarred trees over Verda, standing as silent witnesses to validate the superstitious legends of the natives. There had been no other explanation, no evidence of a siege from an invading force nor had there been a civil revolt from within. Yet, Verda had suffered destruction in its history.

The guard behind the monitors took little notice of Thaut as he approached. He made no effort to offer a formal greeting. He merely grumbled the word "Clear" with the wiggle of his ludicrous mustache before pressing a switch that opened a second set of doors, allowing Thaut to progress through the facility.

Thaut offered a thanks as simple as the clearance given by the fat security guard, who hadn't batted an eyelash in his direction. Thaut may just as well have been a drone delivering the post.

Behind the door was yet another corridor, lined with many open doorways. A thin beige carpet covered the concrete of the floor underfoot. The barren walls were the standard off-white color found in most government facilities. As he walked the length of the hall, he heard chatter coming from the various offices among the clicks and beeps of staff and machines hard at work.

Thaut made his way further down the corridor to the nearest elevator, where he pressed a button to summon the lift. An electric hum through the shiny metal doors announced its arrival. The doors opened, and Thaut entered the lift.

The lift rose up and through the wall, as it accelerated to a moderate speed. Bright circular lights built into the concrete shaft flashed by as the lift rose higher still, carrying Thaut closer to his objective. His mind was clear, though he felt a tinge of anxiety. Something about the moment brought a smile to his face, as the lift continued its ascent with an oscillating whoosh, rising past each level as it climbed. He took a deep breathe and closed his eyes. There was no turning back now. The elevator slowed its ascent before coming to a stop at level fifty. With a ding, a set of silver doors opened to a dark reception hall.

As Thaut stepped over the threshold, the lights above flickered to life with a static hum. One of the lights flickered in the fixture overhead. Thaut imagined the hall looked more or less the same as it had on the day it was abandoned. He approached the counter of the reception desk. Monitors and various office supplies still littered the desk behind the counter, ready for use. Chairs stood positioned as if the previous occupants would return at any moment, though the facility had been empty for quite some time.

The utilities department once held its headquarters here, before relocating to a more 'accommodating' location near the heart of district six. The decision to move the department had been rather unorthodox, as the construction of this facility had not even been completed before the move was authorized.

As a result, here stood a facility outfitted to meet any and all needs for a bureaucratic chapter, complete with artificial plants and various works of decor. One might assume this space was a valuable asset to the state, yet it remained abandoned. Thaut ran his finger across the chalky surface of the dusty counter. The path he cleared in the wake of his finger revealed the smooth surface of the black marble counter top. What a waste it seemed.

He made his way down the corridor to the right of the reception desk. His steps echoed with the click of his boots against the dusty tile. He passed under another noisy, flickering light as he neared the end of the corridor. His destination was behind the last door on the left. As he neared it his heart skipped a beat. Time to go to work. Ready as he would ever be, he reached for the door.

The door opened, and Thaut stepped in from the brightly lit corridor and into the cooler atmosphere of the dimly lit chamber. It had been a conference room, barely used by the establishment for which it had been built. In the center was an exquisite table of smooth dark stained wood. Elliptical in shape, the smooth surface was covered in dust. Despite its fine craftsmanship, it simply lay to waste.

The abandoned conference hall was perfect in location, isolated and free of bystanders in the event things took a downward turn. While it lacked the greater luxury and grandeur of the newer estates within the capital, the chamber offered a more priceless feature, an actual view. In fact, Thaut had been particular in choosing the location for the interview for just that reason.

The east wall of the chamber was comprised entirely of glass from floor to ceiling, and the view overlooked a great portion of the eastern territories of Vanonia. From this height it was truly a spectacle. The smooth surface of the glass seemed like a portal to another world really, offering a glimpse into the realm beyond the crowded hustle and bustle of the technologically synthesized environment maintained within the capital. Walking the illumined streets of Paeon made it easy to lose touch with the world outside its walls.

A figure stood near the glass, fixated on the view as if lost in it. Thaut all but jumped as he noticed the man, hidden beneath a dark hooded cloak. A soft looking fur hung loosely around the stranger's broad shoulders. The cloak nearly reached the floor, and aside from the cloth bindings wrapped about his ankles, the individual's feet were otherwise bare against the dusty tile.

Thaut found himself unsure how to feel about the presence of his company. He made his way to the side of the table opposite the stranger. Typically he would consider it rude not to greet his guest, but this particular guest hadn't exactly shown for tea. Ever the skeptic, he tried to remind himself the deity he had been researching was yet to be established as real, much less to be standing in the very room with him. Regardless, he decided to exercise a little discretion nonetheless and kept his distance for the time being.

Thaut began setting up for the interview, making no effort to conceal his presence as he removed the recording device from his satchel and placed it on the table, activating it as he did so. It prompted him to interact with a projection device centered in the tiles above the table, which could be used to direct holographic displays and other imagery information during a presentation. It was all rather nifty tech, but pointless in today's meeting. He dismissed the prompt, silencing the gentle hum in the tech above.

Thaut pulled out a chair to make himself comfortable, the wheels rolling over the dusty floor beneath. How magnificent they were. Neutral blues and grays accented with reds and gold lined the fabric of the resting surfaces. The fabric itself had been well selected for the long tedium of delegation. They could talk for hours in relative comfort. He couldn't have asked for better.

There were nine chairs total seated around the oblong table, eight of which had fabric comprised of interwoven dark blue patterns. Thaut had selected a moderately dusty blue chair located across the table from the stranger in the room, to whom he now shifted his focus as he took his seat.

The back of the chair was slightly taller than Thaut's profile, perfect for placing emphasis on the faces around the table during a conference. The four legs of each chair were convexly curved so that each joined at the same central point, just above the rail fastening system at the base of the chair. The only exception was the chair at the head of the table, which had a slightly taller, broader profile than the others with much more red integrated into its color scheme.

Each chair was a perfect compliment to the table, and the one Thaut selected offered a welcoming comfort as he eased into the fabric surface that lined the beautifully finished wood. The room itself extended only a short distance around the table, its squared corners offering a nice contrast to the rounded table.

The device was ready, the time was 1325. Thaut set it to record and commenced the interview. He spoke clear and direct.

“Good afternoon, my name is Thaut. I serve as Chief Investigator on behalf of his Majesty's High Council."

Thaut paused for a moment. He liked to leave an opening after dropping his name and title. It was a good way to break the ice, as he could usually tell how an encounter would go based on the exchange during introduction. No response came. Thaut continued.

"I appreciate your time. Thank you for granting me the privilege of an interview. I must warn you, it is my duty to play the role of the skeptic, a role I inhabit quite naturally. Especially when an opportunity seems almost too good to be true. If you are who the young sergeant claims you to be, and I have no reason to doubt you, sir, then this is quite the lucky break. For social etiquette as well as for the record, how should I call you?"

"Subject One is adequate, for now." The stranger replied casually.

Thaut's eyes widened at this response. Flustered, he leaned forward to examine the recording device. The screen was a blank white glow, save for the few lines transcribed thus far. Thaut scanned the text. There were no indications of the designator for this report, yet there it was in the final line of text. Subject One.

He had been careful enough not to expose the nature of his research during his investigation, nor had he any reason to believe he or his crew had been under any kind of surveillance. Yet there it was, the first two words spoken by his guest. The entity known as Subject One had yet to so much as turn from the window, and already Thaut was a bit unsettled. He eased back into his chair and collected himself, eyes still fixed on the recorder.

Was this a breach in security or a subtle display of power? Finally Thaut decided neither to be particularly relevant and commenced with the task well at hand. He would discover the answers along the way he was sure. He lifted his sharp chin slightly and smiled, even stifled a nervous chuckle despite himself. Anticipation was beginning to swell under his skeptical demeanor. Was he losing his nerve? Never. He adjusted in his seat and reset his focus.

"Subject One it is then." Thaut hoped his reply had been eloquent enough not to expose his mild frustration. He didn't appreciate being toyed with, nor did he have time to waste on silly games. "And I would call it rude to snoop, but that would seem a bit hypocritical given the nature of my work. At the very least, introductions are out of the way."

Perhaps it was the prestige of his title that had bolstered his ego beyond its measure. Or maybe it was his health in his old age, caution and fear well diminished by the certainty of death. He had delivered his retort so readily to a bringer of ruin, a harbinger of destruction. He felt a tingle rush through him as if all the adrenaline in his body was eager for a trigger. What a rush it was, something he hadn't felt in years.

Thaut focused on his breathing. His nerve had been solid when he made the arrangement, agreeing to withhold his findings from the Vanguard for the time being. The immediacy of the circumstances had set him on edge despite his iron gut. Heightened and alert, he focused on the large window to calm himself. He managed to steady himself in a few regulated breaths, regaining his composure as if he had never lost it for a moment in all his life.

"Magnificent view..." Thaut sighed aloud, fixed on the sun baked green of the land and the bright blue of the open sky beyond the glass. No response came.

No amount of adrenaline or militant experience would save him from such a foe should confrontation arise. This reality pressed down on some deep part of him that still knew fear, some part of him that must have sensed that any truth he may find could threaten more than just his skepticism. Yet this only sparked his excitement further. He found it all rather enjoyable, but knew it foolish not to keep his wits in the forefront.

With a change of tone, Thaut decided to start things off more smoothly. "May we begin?"

"Yes." This time Subject One responded in a more welcoming tone, much to Thaut's delight. "My apologies, I hadn't meant to be rude. And I agree, the view is magnificent. Perfect for the occasion. You chose well, Chief Investigator Thaut." The stranger remained standing only inches away from the glass of the large window, obscured behind the fur cloak.

Thaut's expression brightened at the response. "No trouble at all." He admitted earnestly. It really hadn't been. "You should know this isn't a witch hunt, I'm not here to accuse or make any speculations on behalf of the Empire. I'm here to collect whatever information you are willing to share regarding the details of this investigation. For the record, of course." He leaned back in his chair with a creak and folded his hands in his lap.

“Of course." Subject One agreed. "I have met you here to do just that, Investigator. This is as grand an opportunity for me as it is for you, a chance to share my journey to becoming. More important, it is a chance to offer the people of the world much needed answers." He paused as if he could feel the questions swelling in Thaut's mind.

"To becoming who or what exactly?" Thaut asked, hoping his smile softened his inquisition.

"We'll get to that in time." The stranger's voice replied. "I feel it's best to begin my story long before the destruction of Verda, before the legends. I'd like to recount my story to a fullness worthy of record. You have come here after hearing of the terror and ruin left in my wake, already suspecting that I am an adversary. Over generations, stories lose much of their finer detail. You heard of the terrible misdeeds of a monster, but nothing of what made it so. There is much more to be told.”

Thaut raised a brow at this. “So this is to be the legend retold through the eyes of the monster? Should prove insightful. And the term used in Verda was demon, I believe.”

Thaut felt himself flush. He was prodding, attempting to elicit further response with passion, but suddenly felt he should be more tactful in his terminology. Demon had been perhaps a bit forward in projection.

Subject One responded, no aggression or anger in the soft rolling timber of his voice whatsoever. “Such terms are relative, simply a matter of perspective. What are you to an ant but a marvel, a wonder obscured beyond the scope of its limited comprehension? It wasn't until the moment I became a threat that I made that transition in the minds of the people. Splendor turned to terror in the eyes of those that had cheered for me as their champion. A monster, or demon, was thus identified in the harsh moments of my wrath. Gods and devils, heroes and villains. Terms based on the perceived influence of power. Though my influence at times has most certainly fallen under villainy, I would by no means call it evil.“

“Well if not evil, what would you call it?“ Thaut asked.

“Unfortunate, perhaps.” Subject One replied solemnly. He hesitated for a moment as if to gather his thoughts, then continued. “My capacities were not known to me in my youth. Back then, my struggle was to know peace. It was accumulated heartache that brought out the worst in me. Before my blunders, prior to my first steps into legend, I was only a boy.”

“That's how it starts, I suppose. A boy grows to be a man.” Thaut added. His breathing had steadied, his nerve settled.

Subject One turned his head slightly, the shift beneath the cloak's hood the first notable sign of movement since the interview began. “Yes, but few ever truly grow to be known as men. Most become something else entirely.”

"And what's that exactly?" Thaut asked, taking the bait with bitter sweet anticipation.

"Fools..." Subject One replied coldly. This last word lingered with a sting of condemnation.

Thaut brimmed at the response, a grin widening his face. "Indeed they do." Thaut agreed, then repeated once more. "Indeed they do." They were going to get along just fine.

Subject One turned from the window, revealing his face. He looked nothing like Thaut had expected. Beneath the hood of the cloak was the face of a man who looked to be late of age. His hair had slight hints of gray woven into the wild dark locks that peaked out from the cloak's golden seam. His brows were thick and bushy, his eyes a radiant green. An unkempt beard encompassed the outline of his face, it too bearing slight hints of gray speckled throughout. He bore no sign of opposition, and a calm aura seemed to flow all about him as he slowly approached the table.

Subject One sat in the chair across from Thaut, the soft ruffling of his unseasonably warm cloak the only sound. He pushed back the hood of the cloak, revealing a full mane of long dark curls, unkempt and messy.

"This is much more appropriate for conversation, I think. Yes?" He smiled as his gaze met Thaut's for the first time.

His eyes were deep and foreboding, but otherwise void of hostility. Whatever mysteries were held there, Thaut couldn't be sure of their nature. Thaut agreed at once with near childlike enthusiasm, feeling like an idiot as he nodded his head.

Subject One began. "As you've gathered thus far, I am from the region known to the Empire as the Irvahem providence. You are familiar?"

Thaut was dazed with disbelief. What luck had landed him an audience with his query. He shook himself from his stupor, regained his composure and responded rather eagerly.

"Yes of course, quite a lovely territory, for the naturalist at heart anyway. I left with a newfound appreciation for it myself, having spent a deal of time there recently. Easy to get lost in the trees." He suspected his company was already aware, but felt it worth mentioning. He decided to pry a bit more. "And if I may, Do you know it by another name than that given to it by the Empire?"

Subject One smiled softly and responded. "No, Investigator. When I was a boy in the village to which I was born, the Empire had yet to establish itself in the area and unite it under its cause. The region was not unified under one name, though many called it home. Back then the villages were fewer and scattered, isolated from the advancements seen elsewhere. The land had no unified code of law nor a central ruling power to govern it. A man lived by his ability to defend that for which he cared in a world that could be perilous at times. Because of this, few ever ventured from the security of their respective communities. In fact, it wasn't until I ventured out that I learned of the many settlements and cultures beyond the few with which I was familiar."

Thaut was all the more intrigued, but he attempted to remain skeptical just the same. "That was quite some time ago. Unless of course, you mean to say you are from one of the outer, more distant settlements of the territory. Where are you from exactly?"

Subject One appeared content with the exchange thus far, much to Thaut's relief. He allowed only a short pause before replying. "My village was to the northwest of what is now considered the capitol of the providence, the Imperial city Aeritrou. Open grasslands cover much of the northern territory. These grasslands range from the walls of the city to the banks of the Veylspring River that runs along the northern border. Following the river west, the grasslands meet with the dense forests that encompass most of the territory. I belonged to a small tribe that once lived to the west along this northern boundary, where the fields met the soft leathery trunks of the Arching Forest."

"Ah, the western forests." Thaut exclaimed, being somewhat familiar from his recent travels. "I've had the pleasure of seeing the area myself. The view from Aeritrou did it little justice. The forest up close was something else, towering green flourishing in all directions. Truly awe inspiring."

He spoke with honesty, it truly had been a spectacle. Thaut and his team had been speechless as they approached the towering mass of vegetation, standing like a breathing wall soaring over the open plains that spanned the gap between the great forest and Aeritrou. From the moment they departed the city's high peaked western wall, the dark greens of the deep forest loomed in the distance, growing sharper and more massive as their vessel drew closer. Despite all his experience and prestige, Thaut had indeed felt as small as an ant when he stood at the base of a great tree, fathomless in size and towering into the canopy beyond sight, as some of these giants could reach nearly a kilometer in height.

He continued. "I didn't see much on the flight in. Once I entered the forest it all became a flashing barrage of green. Got to see plenty of it though, I spent about a week in Verda, another few days further west in Emtsa Aur, and another week rummaging around the forest south of the Stone River Valley. Quite a legacy you left behind, might I add. I'm eager to hear if any of it was true. But we'll get to that I'm sure."

He followed his words with what he intended to be another warm smile. The stark features of his face did not particularly compliment such an expression, but it was authentic nonetheless. Though his interest was specific regarding this conversation, he was more than willing to sift through the details in the meantime.

"Yes, we'll get to that." Replied Subject One with his own faint but warm smile hidden beneath his beard. "My home was a small village known as Reisenbough. It was well north of Verda, nestled in the wood line near the Veylspring River. I spent the greater part of my adolescence there with my father and adopted brother. The name given to me by my mother and father was Kael."

History of Reisenbough

At the heart of the Irvahem providence lies the Imperial city Aeritrou, forged from the ancient ruins of a forgotten age, much like Paeon itself. Unlike Paeon however, the structure that provided the bones for Aeritrou had been much degraded and weathered with the passage of time. Long was it revered as a forsaken place, and few among the indigenous peoples dared to enter the monolithic structure before the coming of the Empire. These ruins were believed by most to be a tomb, haunted by the vengeful spirits of the sinister gods of old.

Whatever race that built the colossal structure was long gone, but spirits were said to curse any who ventured into the tomb. Its towering walls loomed on the horizon as an ill omen, standing high at the top of the plains to the southeast. In my youth the stories of the tomb were among my favorite, tales of men who had braved its mysteries only to have ruin and terror follow the rest of their days. Though the details varied among the tribes, all the stories I encountered told it to be a forsaken place.

As children, my brother and I would climb high into the canopy above Reisenbough with the early evening, when the view was best. Light from the setting sun would strike the towering mass on the horizon, lighting it like a beacon. The distance added to its ghastly appearance, as the shadows of evening crept upon the land. We would contemplate the legends and boast of someday braving its dangers, or simply brood in silence as the days passed.

Of course this all became nonsense once the Empire arrived. They had discovered structures much like the tomb all across the known world and studied the mysteries within, proclaiming these ruins were the remnants of an ancient race of giants they called 'The Architects'. In fact, it is this line of study that led to the rapid advancement of technology within the Empire.

With a vast collective knowledge of the world and its long forgotten histories, the technology harnessed by the Empire has truly reached incredible potential, revitalized from the ancient designs left by the Architects. Even in my time, the Empire arrived to the lands with marvels the people had never seen, floating ships that traveled the skies with all the ease of birds, soldiers armed with equipment that allowed them to defy the laws of nature. And of course, the Emperor himself..."

Subject One trailed off for a moment, silhouetted against the bright blue sky of the window behind him. His gaze had shifted, and he now stared into a corner of the room as if he could see his memories there. "I'm getting well ahead of myself."

"I can only imagine. Please, take your time." Thaut reassured.

Subject One seemed a little warmer with the gesture. A smile rose beneath his scraggly beard. He continued his story.

"My home was just within the northern boundary of the providence, a good distance northwest of the ruins that became its capital. I will refer to these ruins as I knew them, as the Tomb of the Shadjah.

By modern standards, the distance between the tomb and my village is easily traversed. In the world of my youth however, such a distance required days of travel, even with the luxury of domestic beasts. Life was much different then, in what would soon become part of the Empire.

I was born to a proud tribe, known as the Dóvai. Our people had lived near the Veylspring River for a mere seven generations at the time of my birth. Of course, growing up I was completely unaware the Empire existed, or that the world would prove so vast a place. Life was my adventure, each day a blessing.

Our ancestors hailed from deep within the great forests to the west, having once belonged to a prosperous civilization. In size and wealth it dwarfed all others known to the time. Hathlanda had been the name of that glorious city. It was built high above a powerful river known as the Purge, along the sheer cliffs forged by its churning currents.

According to legend, the city of Hathlanda was built by the very hands of our forefathers, carved from the trunks of the great elder trees that stood along the face of the cliffs. Its beauty was said to be unparalleled in its splendor, a place where the forest met the sky, high above the deep rolling waters of the Purge. Beyond the north bank of the river were lush open plains, rolling green hills as far as the eye could see.

Legends of that wonderful city, rich in both wealth and culture, were told again and again. By the dark of night, it was said to shine like a beacon atop the cliffs of the bend. By day, the waters below were alive with the traffic of trade ships come to barter goods from various regions along the river's path.

Unfortunately our forefathers had not been as rich in foresight as they had been in commerce. They had built their city on the cliffs formed by the fury of the massive river that chewed at the earth below, tearing at the land over the years with its relentless churning. The cliffs themselves were the result of a sharp bend in the mighty river, where its flow was forced west from its northern origins. As a result, the waters pealed at the base of the forest, exposing a wall of soil and sediment held together by the massive roots of the elder trees that towered high above.

When tragedy befell Hathlanda, it was quick. Prolonged heavy rains caused the river to swell far beyond its normal boundaries, flooding the plains to the northwest and tearing hard at the earth along the bend. As the rains persisted and the waters surged higher and higher, the purge became a ravenous force with such power that the massive roots of the great trees could do little more than groan and crack against its pull.

History inevitably repeated, as the Purge finally grew strong enough to consume more of the land. Not even the might of the great elder trees was a match for the raw power of the flood waters. The helpless giants toppled into the swift waters to be dragged away, carrying Hathlanda with them.

The once great city was swallowed in an instant. The southern most part clung to the mainland just long enough for my surviving ancestors to flee into the forest. As the river swelled further, the last remaining elder tree of Hathlanda and its corner of the once great city slipped from the mainland and sank into the depths of the raging waters.

As the rain continued to fall, my ancestors fled further into the forest to the southeast, fearing the Purge would grow so massive it would consume them entirely. Not far into the journey they came to another river swollen beyond its banks, and the forest was flooded there as well. This was the Stone River, typically little more than a trickle and rarely flowing enough to even fill the basin within the Stone Valley. Yet, it too had grown massive from the relentless heavy rains of the season. Its waters pushed ever westward toward the Purge, feeding the already monstrous force. Our ancestors could travel no further south, east was the only direction left in which to seek refuge from the waters that threatened to consume the land.

As they followed the Stone River to the east, they encountered a tribe known as the Ireah. They too had been displaced by the unprecedented flooding, though they had suffered no casualties to the like of Hathlanda. The Ireah were a simple people in comparison to the once proud and materialistic culture that had been Hathlanda, and this chance meeting in turn became the hope of our people's survival. Our ancestors had mastered civilization, but they were in no way prepared to survive beyond its collapse. Without the Ireah, they too may have fallen from existence.

Typically the Ireah settled at the base of a gorgeous waterfall that rolled in a sparkling cascade down the rocky cliffs of the Stone River Valley, crashing into the crystal waters of a natural lake below. On the banks of this beautiful lake they made their homes, where they constructed simple mud huts that could be easily rebuilt. They had little concern in the way of material wealth, holding a value to the natural world that no amount of coin or precious metal could rival. It was this respect and awareness of the natural world that had allowed them to avoid a catastrophe like that suffered by Hathlanda.

The Ireah lived in perfect harmony with nature, reflected in their abilities to utilize the forest as if all the land were their domain. They had simply relocated when the waters began to rise, already possessing the skills necessary to sustain while they waited for the waters to subside.

Luckily, the Ireah were a peaceful race. They took pity on the helpless refugees from the once great city, taking it upon themselves to teach them how to utilize the land to meet their basic needs. They traveled with our ancestors for the remainder of the wet season as teachers and guardians, offering lessons in philosophy as well as survival.

When at last the rains subsided, it came time for the Ireah to return to their ancestral home in the Stone Valley. They bid their farewells with warm wishes of prosperity, asking nothing for their patronage to our people.

It was this encounter with the Ireah that divided the people of the once proud city of Hathlanda. Those whose hearts had been open to their new teachings now sought to avoid the sins of the past, electing to follow the ways of the Ireah. Never again would they place such value on material possessions or call themselves masters over others held as servants, a practice that had no place in the natural world.

Of course, there were also those who remained entrenched in the ways of old, and their hearts were closed to the teachings of the Ireah. They elected to build a new city, bigger and stronger than ever before, claiming it to be within their divine right to seek power over all they desired. As a result a schism occurred, dividing the people of Hathlanda in three directions. Some decided to live among the Ireah, seeing promise in their ways. The rest were cleaved in two by differing ideologies.

One group followed a man known as Dóv, who led the more enlightened minds of Hathlanda further north, where they came to the northeastern edge of the forest near the Veylspring River. The others who elected to retain the ways of old traveled further to the east, where they established a new civilization, nestled at the edge of the forest where it met the open plains near the heart of the territory that would become Irvahem.

Thus, two tribes emerged. My ancestors, still weary of nature's fury, settled atop a great stone mountain known as Mount Yerok. Well hidden in the confines of the Arching Forest, Yerok served as a cradle for the people that would come to be known as the Dóvai. In the years that followed, they descended from the mount to build Reisenbough at its northern base.

The mountain stood between the Dóvai and our estranged brothers of old. In time, the dissidents erected a new city, roughly two day's journey to the south around the base of Mount Yerok. Reminiscent of the erroneous ways of Hathlanda, their city came to be known as Verda.

As I'm sure you could imagine, the differences between the two tribes eventually led to adverse relations. The people of Verda were considered lost, viewed as greedy and corrupt. This proved to be most true in the years that came, though my people did not foresee the depth of that corruption or the hate Verda cultured for them. Time would attest they were not to be trusted as brothers. To Verda, my people were tragic simpletons, far below them in stature by their very nature. Our people were considered little more than ignorant savages.

In the early years of my grandfather, Verda mounted an assault against our tribe, eager for the rights to the territory the Dóvai called home. There were precious metals, gems, and minerals of interest hidden within the stone of Mount Yerok, a place of sanctity to my people. They would not allow the land to be stripped, least of all by those working under the lash.

Tensions mounted. Verda could only work at the mountain along its southwestern face. Reisenbough stood to the north, the Dóvai firm in their convictions to maintain their home. The eastern face of Yerok was steep and unforgiving. The southern face closest to Verda was to remain untouched. It was the nesting ground of the Malekaur, ferocious predatory insects.

These beasts grew to be heavier than two men, but maneuvered about the air and the canopy as easily as the tiny songbirds they silenced with the thundering hum of their ornate, membranous wings. It was a splendor to behold their shimmering metallic bodies, every armored section as reflective as a mirror and covered with tiny hairs that bent and scattered light into all the shades and colors of the visible spectrum.

Festivals were brought to life by the harvested bits of their bodies, as movement added a hypnotic effect by the light of the fire, the same captivating effect that made the Malekaur so formidable. The colors and patterns changed seamlessly and with whatever fervor the object moved, portraying a rhythmic display of color and light.

As ornate as this phenomenon made for costume and decor, it was most terrifying in its natural display. These insects were masterful killers. The mechanical precision in their grace was second to none. The quickness of their movements and the fluttering patterns they created with their wings weaved a hypnotic exposition of sound and color, so intricate as to bend the boundaries of light and sound.

In the beginning, even the most skilled hunter stood little hope of besting their talent for murder. Mesmerizing in display, beauty and majesty hid the true horror of its intentions, for its sting was not fatal in itself. Death came slowly.

Within an instant, the victim would slide into a mindless state, never again to rouse from the terrible spell of the insect's poison. They did little more than breathe until they simply breathed no more. In earlier years, neither tribe dared disturb the perilous southern face of the mountain. It was the uncontested territory of these powerful insects, the Malekaur.

Fortunately the Malekaur had a relatively small hunting zone, as they did not stray far from their little ones. The Dóvai kept their distance, studying the creatures from afar and brooding over the occasional dead specimen. Our people continued to collect the attractive shells of the Malekaur, using them for crafting elaborate costumes and jewelry. Eventually, my ancestors learned to best the Malekaur, utilizing the strength of these magnificent predators against them. The potent venom they produced was eventually used to coat the tips of special darts, arrows, and spears.

The discovery of this natural weapon combined with tactical knowledge of the environment saw the Dóvai become masters of the land, silent killers that stalked the canopy of the Arching Forest. This later gave my people the advantage necessary to repel the attack mounted on Reisenbough during the years of my grandfather. Eager for the resources within the mountain and unable to operate along its southern face, Verda had sought to take the area by force.

That is the history of my people leading to my beginning memory, paraphrased of course." Subject One broke from his dictation.

"Interesting. Sounds like the region has changed considerably over the years. Have you seen it more recently?" Thaut asked, sincere in his curiosity. The forest had been much reduced in the northern most regions of the territory near the Veylspring, and Thaut hadn't taken notice of a mountain north of Verda. Records could most likely verify, but somehow Thaut felt he had little reason to doubt the possibilities in the instance of Subject One's testament.

"Yes, most unfortunate. The mountain has been stripped down to the ground, and even lower at its core. The forest has long been cleared along the Veylspring, its current now utilized to produce power for the modern technological city that occupies the once beautiful home of my ancestors. Indeed, the world has changed." He trailed off again.

Thaut tried to imagine what it would be like to witness such a dramatic change, the indigenous peoples of the land long forgotten since the establishment of Imperial rule. Modernization had reshaped the region considerably, as it did for all the lands assimilated under the Empire. The unified advancement of mankind was the driving force behind it all.

"Well, you've certainly taken it better than most would I suspect." He offered, then added with a bitter tone. "Wish I could say all change is for the better."

Subject One smiled. "Change is natural, it is certain. Without it, life would not bear the tenacity to reach ever greater heights. I admit, at times I too have wished certain changes had been better in my favor. Yet, I also know it was through the darkest circumstance brought by such unfavorable change that I became aware, both of my potential and that of the world around me. Many times has it been tested, my light burns true."

For an instant it seemed that an eerie radiance reached out from the twinkle in his eyes. Thaut swore he could feel an energy emanating from across the table, pulsing like the wake of the tide as it ebbed and flowed, exploring the parameters of the chamber like an icy draft creeping in through an open window... But the sensation was gone as soon as it had come, and Thaut nearly shrugged at how silly he felt. How he loved the way a good story could toy with the imagination.

"Yes..." Thaut cleared his throat. "Well, the Empire takes great care in preserving the various cultures and histories within its territories, keeping detailed records of each providence in the archives. Although I must admit, the archives had little to offer on the culture and history of Irvahem predating the arrival of the Empire. Sparked my intrigue to say the least. Kind of embarrassing to have an incomplete file in such an impressive library. If nothing else, you could help fill a few gaps in the timeline, much as you already have." Thaut confessed.

Of course there was more to this inquiry, and he suspected his guest knew that just as well. Already he had established that Subject One had indeed been to Irvahem, perhaps recently enough to have been involved with the incident there.

"It would be my pleasure, Investigator. Oral tradition carried the histories through the generations. As you might expect, not all things are told as accurately with each generation as perhaps they once were. The members of our tribe were skilled storytellers, and though their stories were not always qualified in fact, they were truthful in nature."

He paused for a moment. The green of his eyes was radiant in contrast to the dark unruly hair that framed his face. His gaze remained fixed on the device on the table. His shaggy unkempt beard hung just above his collar, his simple hide tunic open to reveal a peek of his chest. He looked a mess, even for a vagrant.

"Rest assured Investigator, I will keep my account historically accurate to the best of my knowledge. It is only fitting to share their story in this way. " Subject One assured. He fell silent again, as if to gather his thoughts before he continued.

Thaut however had not lost sight of his intentions in the slightest. The time on the record rolled, the numbers climbing. This was his prompt to nudge things along. With the patience of an ironclad saint, Thaut broke the silence as he pressed for more.

"Please, indulge me further. Share with me the history by your account. Lead on, Kael." He had spoken sincerely, and his smile brightened ever so slightly at the positive response that followed.

"Of course. My thanks." Subject One spoke warmly. "Long has it been since my recollection has strayed this far into the past, and for the first time, openly.

The descendants of Hathlanda that settled the lush grove between mount Yerok and the Veylspring River were the Dóvai. Together the members of the tribe established a simple community of huts built into the sloping terrain under the Arching Forest. Her people were children of nature, both wise and strong. Though they could be fierce in battle, they valued peace and brotherhood above all else.

The Dóvai were indeed my people, and I was never so at home as I was in that wonderful place. Mud, stone, and various debris fallen from the canopy were used to construct the homes of Reisenbough. Each hut was as unique as the hands that built it, yet the proximity of the huts portrayed the sense of family that gave such strength to our people.

Reisenbough was located at the edge of the forest, but was well hidden despite that fact. The grasses grew tall and strong along the river basin, obscuring any view of our crops along the Veylspring below the village.

Across the river to the north was the face of a sheer cliff that rose to a barren plateau. The southern banks were gentle and gradual in their slope, leading up the ridge formed at the base of the great fruit bearing trees that comprised the Arching Forest, known as the Allichene.

The Allichene were a symbol of love and prosperity to the Dóvai. These massive beauties by no means reached the towering heights of the elder trees, but rather grew to fill the lower canopy with an interwoven network of limbs branching out in all directions. Together they created a dense canopy that expanded high above Reisenbough and its people. The lower branches arched over the town, reaching over the fields. The forest itself stretched well to the south.

The ends of their great branches curled skyward during the colder seasons, but the blooms of spring would give way to hundreds of lush reisen berries. These spherical berries, deep blue in color, grew to be the size of a man. During the harvest season, the berries added such weight to the great branches that they would hang low over the fields, indicating time for harvest. The reisen berry was of significant importance to our village, as with it we produced the finest wines, jams, and sweet breads for survival and barter alike.

In the outer forest the Allichene grew crowded, often even fusing to one another, leaving little space to traverse the forest floor where they grew thickest. Their many roots knotted through the soil, creating a most uneven terrain around their clustered trunks.

The Allichene were far more broad than tall, with leafy branches arching out in all directions, twisting and interlacing to form an intricate environmental system within the dense canopy. Much like the creatures that lived there, to the aspiring youth of Reisenbough the canopy was home.

The ground sheltered by the great arching branches of the Allichene grew less of the tall grasses of the open plains, allowing for the more leafy specimens to flourish. Known as the shaded fields, this terrain was the preferred hunting ground of the Dóvai.

Reisenbough stood along a small, crescent shaped ridge nestled at the base of the Allichene, its many structures silhouetted against the trunks of the great fruit trees. The branches of the arching trees provided shade from the heat of summer and shelter from the bitter cold that swept the plains in winter, as these gentle guardians did not shed their broad leaves with the coming of fall.

The ridge itself was littered with ferns and decaying materials fallen from the massive vegetation, the soil beneath rich and dark. The rounded huts were topped with light colored wooden shingles, cut from the bark of the Allichene. Scattered along the ridge, the huts blended with the natural decor. Constructed of stone and mortar, each dwelling complemented the earthy colors of the gully.

Snug between two ridges in the center of the village was an open area, reserved for fire circles and social festivities that often lasted well into the night hours. The dark colored stone and the greens of moss and lichen provided natural beauty in that cool place that smelled of earth and fire. This was Reisenbough, my home.

We were simple in our ways, even for the era. While other civilizations had flourished into crude cities elsewhere, our people elected to live in ways that differed greatly from their forefathers. They had witnessed firsthand the corruption of civil progress and the destructive power of greed, as it had inevitably turned an entire tribe of their brothers against them.

These were the tales I heard most as a child, warnings of the nature of greed and the virtues of awareness and unity. Lessons I took to heart, as did every child huddled around the warmth of the fire to hear what stories might be told each evening.

The history of the tribe was passed in this way, through the aged voices of the elders. By day they usually did little more than watch over the youngest children of Reisenbough while their parents tended the needs of the day. The watchful elders provided care, entertaining the young with stories of epic journeys and battles passed down over the generations. Their stories were tales of adventure, teachings of bravery, courage and endurance.

Fueled by the exciting world promised by the words of the elders, children grew all the more eager to find adventures of their own. Almost as soon as a child learned to walk in Reisenbough they ran through the foliage with the others. The elders did little to intervene aside from keeping the peace when necessary.

It was a respected role and one I greatly looked forward to fulfilling in my late years, though many others most certainly did not. The youth of Reisenbough were called wildlings for good reason. Even the beasts of the land seemed more willing to engage one of our brawny hunters than a frazzled wildling pup.

When the children were old enough, they would spend less time with the elders by day and join their parents stalking the fields or working the crops along the river. However, the elders would ever remain the warm centers of wisdom, their value growing all the more precious as their days passed.

No matter how full I was from the matters of the day, my evenings belonged to the fire circle of my kin. My father was not one for telling stories, as he said very little in his later days. Yet he was always there next to his father, much as I sat next to him. What was left of my closest elders sat adjacent to us and their living children around them. With the dark of nightfall came the warm light of the circle, and the members of the circle spoke openly about all things mentionable.

Once conversations began to subside stories were shared, whether newly told or retold for yet another time around the circle. Stories were always told best around a fire it seemed, or perhaps that was due to my interest in the more foreboding tales. Nothing was more exciting to me as a young wildling than hearing the tales of mighty warriors and the dreaded beasts they faced, like the Trickler- a creature most dreaded.

The Trickler was a worrisome creature. It had a long serpentine body of armored segments carried by a legion of soulless marching legs. At each of the terminal ends of its body was a pair of long tendrils that waved and reached through the air, as if groping for the very souls of men. The tendrils at the lead end were slightly larger, and beneath their junction to the body was a gruesome set of jaws, fed by a ruthless pair of razor sharp talons opposed to form a wicked vice which no armor could withstand. This creature meant death.

The Trickler had been a nightmare for the village, much before my time. Once it began feeding on our people, it seemed reluctant to stop. It started by attacking groups of hunters, but once it found the village matters grew worse.

According to the stories, it killed nearly a dozen before it was stopped. Blades, axes, and arrows were useless against the thing. Injuring the Trickler was not only difficult, but foolish as it turned out. When wounded, the creature thrashed about wildly with immense speed and strength, turning to deliver its vengeance through toxic evisceration. It killed only what it intended to devour, and it devoured most entirely. It did not take long for the Trickler to grow bold enough to enter the village once its ferocious appetite developed.

As the village was under siege, the elders elected to relocate the inhabitants to sanctuary on Mount Yerok until the creature was vanquished, leaving a small band of the Dóvai's strongest to confront the beast upon its inevitable return. When they first settled the area, my ancestors took residence within a series of small caves high on the mountain. Thus over time the summit was made into a refuge for our people. They would not risk another disaster like that of Hathlanda.

Yerok's peak rose high above Reisenbough, obscured by the forest. Located just south of Reisenbough's center was a pass between two great trunks of the Allichene. The rich fragrant soil of the well trodden path was smooth and dark, contrasting with the light colored, leathery trunks of the Allichene. The pass lead along the leafy floor of the Arching Forest and up the mountain's less steep northern face.

Around the base of the mountain the soil gradually became more rocky, and the Allichene grew less in number. The mountain rose abruptly to reach its pinnacle, the rocky contour perilous to traverse.

Caverns and tunnels were numerous, as were the creatures that inhabited the dark unknown recesses within.

The high caves of the refuge were a perfect place for the tribe to take shelter. They were far from the reach of any flood water that might rise, and the terrain offered a natural defense against predator and enemy alike. The caves were well maintained, stocked each year with enough provisions that the Dóvai could survive, quietly hidden on the mountain for months if necessary.

The location was remote and difficult to reach, and there was very little reason for anyone aside from the Dóvai to venture the treacherous heights. Yet, my elders were surprised when they climbed the mount to discover a man already taking shelter in the refuge.

His name was Terk, a runaway slave escaped from Verda. Terk claimed that he had once been a servant to an ill tempered lord. He and a few others had attempted to escape their bondage but failed to make it out of the city. The others, according to Terk, had been sent to Verda's coliseum, where they had surely met death in the arena. Terk had been sent to work the mines along Yerok's base, a fate his overlords considered far worse than death in the arena. He explained the harsh conditions under the lash in the deep dark confines of the mountain.

Terk managed to break free of his bindings and escaped, climbing the steep face of Yerok. He happened across the sanctuary of the Dóvai and hid while he regained his strength, living off the provisions he found in store.

Relieved when the Dóvai did not greet him with hostility, he told them of the many things he had heard during his transport to the mines. Verda was expanding around the mountain, and they had no intentions of negotiating the northern territory. The troops that escorted Terk and the others bound for the dark depths of the mines were buzzing with the news of Verda's advance.

The elders had long been suspicious of their neighbors to the south, but even they were appalled at this. Could there be truth in these words? Could Verda really mean to destroy the peace between brothers?

When the hunters returned with the news of the vanquished Trickler, they did not meet the praise and celebration they expected. My mother's father, Darius had been among the brave that stood against the beast when it returned that very evening. With little time to boast upon returning to the rest of the tribe, they aided the elders in responding to this new threat at once. Two teams of scouts were sent from the top of the mountain to see if Terk's claim was true.

One team carefully worked its way to the western face of the mountain. There they witnessed Verda's progression, as they had already began to dig further along the mountain towards Reisenbough. Slaves worked under the lash, as a legion of armed guards patrolled around them, just as Terk had described.

Their forces were well armed, each armored troop wielding a spear in hand if not at work with a whip. Finely worked blades and shields, and even metal plates fitted into studded armor suggested Verda had long aspired to build this militant force. Each of the metal chest plates bore the same symbol boldly, a wreathe with a V pointing skyward through its open crest.

The second team ventured around to the south side of the mountain from the east. They had set out for Verda, seeking news of this alleged assault. Scarcely had they made it around the south bend of the mountain when they encountered a large militant force marching north along the shaded fields. The numbers of Verda's army was staggering in comparison to the warriors of the Dóvai. They were no doubt set for Reisenbough. Within a day's march, the main force of Verda would be upon the village. The scouts knew they had precious little time to waste and returned at once to the refuge on Mount Yerok, braving the perilous southern cliffs to do so.

The elders gathered the reports from the two teams, leaving them with heavy hearts. The forces marching on Reisenbough were as well if not better armed than the slavers of the mines, Verda's symbol upon their armored chests. The tribe delegated among themselves until a decision was made. A clean escape was hardly an option, with barren cliffs north of the river and Verda's forces to the west. There was little hope they could flee east to the open plains either, as the army marching north through the shaded fields would most likely cross their path. For the first time, the Dóvai armed for war.

All able fighters took their best weaponry in hand. Hunting knives, spears, and arrows laced with the deadly poison were readied, and two bands of warriors descended down the sides of the mountain. One band headed east to meet the main forces advancing through the shaded fields. The other group headed west to engage the troops along the mines, hoping to clear an exit to the deep forest should it become necessary for the Dóvai to flee.

The group that left to engage Verda's main force had a brilliant strategy in place for the conflict. The Dóvai had long adapted to hunting large game in the shaded fields, ambushing their prey with arrows from the canopy. One group of hunters would stalk the open plains, herding game under the canopy where the other hunters waited to loose their arrows upon the frantic creatures from above as they dashed for the safety of the forest. This method had been successful in hunts for decades, and with a little modification it held just as well in battle.

Thus the troupe to the east divided, some took to the canopy while others stalked the grass of the field the same as they would for a hunt. They worked their way south along the shaded fields to meet the advancing forces. Once they met Verda's army, the two teams lay still, waiting for the moment to strike. As the first formation of troops marched under their position, the canopy team loosed the first round of arrows upon the unsuspecting troops.

In an instant the entirety of the first formation of armed men was brought down by the deadly procession of the archers. Poison tips struck their mark by the dozens, the hissing sound of arrows flying was soon followed by the woozy cries of the wounded.

Before the soldiers had time to react, the ground team quickly attacked their right flank. The hunters were a flash of flesh and fur as they broke through the ranks of the armored men and slashed at unprotected legs and throats before quickly disappearing back into the tall grass.

The forces of Verda were no match for the wild spirit of the Dóvai. Within seconds, two units of forty men each had been leveled to the ground. The wounded lay screeching among the dead and incapacitated, clutching at gushing wounds. The next unit broke away to foolishly pursue the ground team into the tall grass. They met their fates perhaps without ever seeing the proud tribesmen. The hunters of the Dóvai were like ghosts in the tall grass of the plains, long since learning from the predators that hunted there. The soldiers might as well have marched off a ledge. Forty more lost of Verda.

The Dóvai archers continued their onslaught, sending the forces below into a panicked frenzy. Desperately they struggled to try and make out their attackers from the lush chaos of the canopy. Verda's archers did their best to retaliate, though their marksmanship was dreadful compared to the Dóvai. Aimlessly they fired into the canopy at random in hopes of hitting something.

With the arrival of the archers, the Dóvai broke off their attack to regroup. They had suffered no casualties in the first attack, while Verda had lost many. The forces of Verda did not retreat, but they had been dealt a devastating blow. The shaded fields were littered with armored bodies, and as they tended their wounded the soldiers discovered many locked in a catatonic state from which they could not be roused, even those with the slightest of wounds.

The forces of Verda marched onward, but with a growing reluctance in their step. The Dóvai repeated their attack twice more before the forces of Verda began to withdraw to the south, away from Reisenbough and her savage defenders. The day following, the Dóvai mounted one final attack on the shaken army of Verda. Two Dóvai hunters had fallen during the previous battle, and the soldiers had desecrated their remains out of spite.

While the army slept, the Dóvai crept into the camp bringing death in the night. Using poison tipped darts, the hunters silently killed one for every two men they counted. When morning came, the war was over. Suffering utter defeat, the forces of Verda withdrew south of the mountain, remaining silent and distant for years to come.

Our brothers on the west face of the mountain had not fared so well. They managed to overcome the armed guards that controlled the mines, but suffered a considerable amount of casualties by the end. The terrain around the mines offered little cover from arrows, and our people were by no means seasoned in the arts of war. What they lacked in skill, the Dóvai made up for in spirit and tenacity. They were defending all they held dear, their very way of life.

The battle turned once those held captive in the mines rose up as well, overwhelming their former masters. With the help of those freed from bondage, our hunters gained the advantage and turned the tide against Verda. In the end the battle was won, Reisenbough had endured.

Kael

Peace and celebration filled the years of our tribe in the wake of victory. Reisenbough had triumphed over two great perils of the world. The dreaded Trickler was no more, and the forces of Verda had been defeated utterly, the odds a staggering forty to one. My mother and father were of the first generation born in the wake of Verda's assault, what was to be the golden age of the Dóvai. I was born at the peak of this golden age, in the days following the festival of harvest.

My mother was a true maiden of our people. Slender of build, she was fair-skinned with thick locks that swayed from her frizzled mass of jet black hair. Her eyes were a radiant golden brown and glowed around the fire as if they were distant embers themselves. Her smile was thin and wide, especially when she was furiously engaged in a spar with my father.

She was the daughter of Darius the Great, who had fought bravely against the forces in the west mines, having also fought to slay the dreaded Trickler. The oldest of three daughters, many joked that she was Darius' only son. Meriam was her name, but my father called her Little Raven.

Darius had fought alongside Kraegar the Proud, my father's father, during the battle against the slavers of the west mines. The two had survived the ordeal together, and a strong kinship between houses ensued. As a result, my mother and father spent their youth playing together as frazzled wildlings. The two were fated it seemed, paired long before the coming of age.

From their first steps as wildlings the two were said to be inseparable, a most troublesome duo. They were fierce competitors, especially when it came to sparring. Combat efficiency became an integral study among the Dóvai, and my mother prided herself on her ability to match the youngest son of the proud Kraegar, who in his own time grew to be known as Krayton the Mighty.

My oldest memories recall what little I knew of my mother from my earliest years. I remember her dark hair, and the sweetness of her voice. When we woke in the early mornings, my father would playfully pick at my mother and me as we huddled together under the furs of our simple bed. After he had his fun picking at us, he would spring from the low lying bed of straw stuffed hides to ready himself for the hunt.

Waking was my favorite part of the day. There in the comfort of her arms against the soft furs, I would gaze into the fire pit at the center of our simple domed hut. The coals burned low sending a gentle torrent of warmth through the crisp morning air. We were always together and warm with the first light each morning. I would lie there with my mother for a little while longer while father readied himself. Then, we too would rise and greet the day.

Once we had all risen, mother would prepare a quick breakfast while I battled my father just outside the hut. Even as a young man I wouldn't have stood a chance against him, but as a wildling I knew no limits. I gave it my best, charging the hulking giant that was my father with little stick sword in hand. No fear.

My father was a good sport, putting up just enough fight each time that I felt victorious in my lessons, as though I had faced the monsters of legend. My ego as a wildling was as big as it would ever be. Humility would bring growth in the years to come.

Once she finished inside the hut, mother would partake in the fun as well. Whatever battle we were enacting, she would join the fray before we gathered for breakfast. Swift and diligent in her offensive, my mother was just as formidable an opponent as my father, known for her skill with knives.

Breakfast was usually a tasty grain porridge of sorts, flavored with jams and sweet bits of dried fruit, served steamy and warm. Once we had our fill of play, we took our seats around the fire where our clay bowls awaited, brimming with delicious steamy goop. As we sat around the fire pit enjoying our meal, my father would boast to us of the hunt ahead and the kill he was sure to make later that day. It was always something outlandish, usually along the lines, "I'll kill ten leagues of hatual with my fists alone and bring back the most beautiful furs you've ever seen!"

There was little in the way of wrestling beasts or collecting colorful pelts on his day to day, but he and the other hunters rarely came home empty handed. My mother and I would antagonize him, playfully calling his bluff. He would jokingly growl his rebuttals, promising his word held true as 'Krayton the Mighty'.

After the meal, my father would retrieve his massive bow from where it rest in the rafters. He was tall and broad at his shoulders, brawny even in his youth. The rafters were low, hanging just above his head. In some places they brushed the unruly locks of his dark hair that frizzed out in all directions each morning. Before the hunt it would be lazily bound to hang at his back.

His bow was a true work of mastery. It was robust and a bit heavier than most, but in power and beauty it was unparalleled. My father was gifted in his abilities with a carving knife, and he had artfully crafted many intricate works into the bow's sleek wooden surface.

With warm wishes and affections bared, he would leave to join the hunting party. Usually the parties would rally at the southeastern edge of the village, where the great boughs of the trees loomed high above the ridge like a low sky of vegetation. Once the light of day reached into the shadows under the canopy each hunter would speak a blessing, wishing his brothers both safety and success in the hunt ahead, accented of course with banter and playful quips. Then off they went, vanishing into the lush green of our world.

My mother and I would depart as well, walking hand in hand along the narrow path that lead to the center below the ridge. Other huts lined the path, the homes of friends and family. Other children shared the same routine journey, as well as a few late rising elders. The older children blazed about the trail, bursting and rampant with boundless energy. All were on their way to the village center, where the elders chatted amongst themselves as they awaited the arrival of their children's children each morning.

The aging faces of my grandparents were brimming and warm when they greeted us around the fire circle each day. My mother would exchange about the latest happenings before bidding us farewell to join the others tending the crops along the river. Many a family circle gathered between the ridges, more children spilling from all directions into the social trough at Reisenbough's center.

The smell of smoke and food permeated the air, as leftover bits of meat roasted on skewers along the blackened stones of the fire. Baskets of bread were kept near the sitting stones around each fire pit, snacks to carry us through the day. Later there would be fresh fruit as well.

Wildlings spent their morning hours in the watchful eyes of the elders. Fortune smiled upon me, as I was blessed to have many years with great aunts, uncles, and grandparents. There was my grandfather Darius, grayed and slightly hunched. He was humble and wise, as he had seen much in his time. He was usually in the company of his old friend Kraegar the Proud. In age they were years apart, but they may as well have been brothers.

The two old men argued philosophy relentlessly to pass the time. Some conversations became somewhat redundant over the years, but were never the same twice. From them came lessons of the mind, and stories of the brave hunts of their youth. Stories of war were saved for the oldest sons and daughters, to be told by the late light of the fire. These lessons grew far more somber in nature with the coming of age.

There was also my grandmother Dialah, my mother's mother. She had dark silver hair that had been much like my mother's in her youth.

She was a frail looking woman, with soft leathery skin and deep eyes that hinted at her wisdom. A black shawl draped about her slumped shoulders to hang down just below here knees when she stood, which she did only out of necessity.

She offered sweet breads and stories of romance and adventure, told in the comforting sound of her soft aged voice. She rarely entered the debates brewed between Darius and Kraegar, but when she did things got wonderfully entertaining. She was a healing warmth, and Darius was proud to have her at his side all his years.

My father's mother was Helena, and she was every bit the female equivalent to Kraegar. She was a larger built woman, broad at both her hips and shoulders and just as loud and boastful as any of the men. She prided herself on keeping a watchful eye on the wildlings running amuck, claiming to know each and every whelp by name and family. Quite the bluff, but one no wildling dared to test. The thudding stomp of her flat foot on the packed earth and her deep rumbling voice were more than enough to put a stop to any unruly behavior. She was the wildling authority on the east side of the gully.

Of course there were plenty other wildlings my age in the kindred circle. There was Kori, the son of my father's older brother Raethos. He was wiry and wild in his youth, with a mouth as large as his face it seemed. His was a warm and vibrant spirit, and in time the sun itself became his symbol.

There was also Pol and Cas, twin brothers of my mother's sister Raikel. The two were really one unstoppable force divided between two thick haired, brown eyed boys. Where these two were found, mischief was soon to follow. They were adventurous and fun, despite their meddlesome nature. Though we were reluctant to participate in most of their endeavors, Kori and I were rarely far behind them, enjoying the fun from aside and stepping in to help whenever they met trouble.

As a wildling, if I wasn't running through the gully with the others I was intently listening to the words of the elders. By way of stories they shared valuable teachings and lessons, though most were told simply to entertain. My grandfathers made sure we were well exposed to philosophy and reason, thinking up new riddles and puzzles for us to solve before our parents returned each day.

The women of Reisenbough were the first to return from their labors, arriving in the early evening, bringing with them fruits, vegetables, and grains. My mother returned among these members of the Dóvai, carrying her basket perfectly balanced upon her head. She wore it like a crown, grace in her step.

I was never late to greet her upon return, running to her side excitedly. The hunters would return soon after, with fresh kills cleaned and ready to be prepared for the evening feast. My father would stomp up to us, boasting of the bounty. Raikel often teased him that his symbol should have been a cock rather than the bear.

With my parents return came time for more play and exciting stories of what we saw out in the world that day. Mother would tell of eagles swooping down and plucking shimmering fish out of the Veylspring. Father would tell of the beasts of the field and the thrill of the hunt. My stories were those of a wildling, telling of the many colored birds and insects I'd encountered in the day's adventures.

Play was an essential part of life in the village. Eventually my parents would grow tired of stick fighting and the like and take their leave to have a rest with the elders. I would eventually run off to join the other wildlings playing all sorts of fun games, wreaking havoc throughout the brush. With the wildlings away, the center of the village was readied for the evening feast that would end each day in Reisenbough.

Everyone contributed to the evening feast in some way or another, even the youngest. The oldest wildlings would be given the task of collecting fruits and berries along the edge of the village. It was a simple task, more for keeping wildlings busy than anything else. But it was a task that inspired envy among the younger wildlings. They willfully tagged along, eager for the day that they would be given the woven baskets to return them, brimming with squished berries for all.

Once it was time to return, a horn was sounded. The older children of Reisenbough would filter in from all directions it seemed, from the fields, the forest, and even the canopy. They too were summoned by the call of the horn, and helped collect and guide the wildlings to the center along their way.

The evening feast was truly wonderful. All manner of roasted meats, vegetables, breads, fruits, and even sweet cakes were passed between the circles of families. The smell of food saturated the air, churning tiny stomachs everywhere. The entire tribe was present, making the center wonderfully crowded with family. The sounds of warm brotherly voices and laughter filled the village, as the fires burned into the night.

At the heart of the village was a great open area with a large stone circle, where a great pyre burned during tribal gatherings. Once they had eaten their fill, people of all ages would gradually make their way to this center. There was song and dance, as the light from the large fire lit the night every bit as bright as the sounds of laughter that flickered above the music. Sometimes the elders would speak here, for all to hear. They would also present any newly born, name and house for all to celebrate.

When it became late, we would bid our farewells for the night and return to our hut. There by the light of the fire, my father would give in to my pleas for more stories and tell of the various figures and creatures depicted in the etchings of his bow. We always sat close and warm around the fire, bathed in its soft light as he spoke.

Story time was my favorite time, and my mother loved it just as well. My father thrived on the attention, though his art of storytelling was nowhere near the caliber of the elders. New stories would come, and his etchings grew to cover the bow entirely over the years, though some of these stories were not so kind to memory.

I would ask to hear another and another until I woke to a new day. I recall waking early one chilly winter morning, and as we lie there my mother shared a lesson through the soft glow of the waning coals. They were remnants of a strong fire that had kept us warm and safe through the cold winter night. Though it lay weak and all but burned out, its strength could easily be rekindled to its former glory. It was a symbol of purpose and endurance, as it would soon heat our breakfast and warm our home.

Her words came soft from just behind my ear, as I lie on the soft furs with the smell of her hair all around me. "The flame in you is just as strong, my son. And just like the flame, you will rise with the morning light to greet each new day, with all the strength of Reisenbough."

These words became a mantra for me, held dear to my heart and soul. No matter the darkness, I would rise. Such was my life as a wildling, a life of love and plenty. I was born on the fruits of victory, an age of great prosperity for the Dóvai. In the years that followed, however, it seemed I would grow into an age of great loss.

Mother died around my fifth year, in the winter that followed the festival of harvest. A plague struck when the pride of our people was at its peak. Reisenbough had endured. They had bested the odds, overcoming the forces of Verda. Yet it seemed nothing could have prepared our people for the sickness that came. Death crept its way into even the strongest hearts of the Dóvai, sparing neither pride nor beauty in the random victims it claimed.

I fell sick as well, so I don't remember much from the time. It was a blur. Reality was obscure and distant, and though I wanted to wake I was lost in a deep dreamless sleep, lost between fleeting moments of consciousness. I never got to say goodbye to my mother, and perhaps that was for the best. One day the darkness simply left me, and I awoke to a world without her.

It all seemed like some terrible dream, and I wanted so badly to wake from it. But each morning I woke alone, my father crouched over the coals with wide staring eyes. He slept little, if at all. So many times I clenched my eyes and hoped to hear her words from just behind my ear, but her voice surfaced only in memory. Rise and be strong, she had said.

I took these words upon myself as a vow. Each day I would rise stronger. My goal was to push myself to be the strongest I could be. To honor her. To honor my people.

Though grief was far from over, it would not fold our home. I did my best to help my father in that place so haunted by memory. Whenever tears swelled or his voice began to tremble, I made sure he knew he was not alone. We had one another. The remaining hearts of the Dóvai still beat as one. We would face the world together, strong in the love that remained.

Indeed loss was felt in all the hearts of Reisenbough. There wasn't a home that hadn't lost a member of their family. Some had lost much more. Grief was everywhere, but as time moved on it seemed few were as lost to it as my father. His proud boasting and cheery personality fizzled, and many began to call him Krayton the Solemn.

Many years passed, and in time the growth of the remaining Dóvai saw prosperity and strength return to our people, as together we did our best to move beyond the pain of loss. After all, our loved ones had returned to the Great Mother, their ashes carried upon the gentle currents of the Veylspring to meet the churning depths of the Purge. Surely it met with some distant sea, as surely their spirits met with peace knowing their legacy lived on. The Dóvai would endure.

Together, father and I worked harder than ever. The pain of grief became fleeting, buried beneath the weight of duty and purpose. The labors of our days became the central focus of all. Reisenbough was unified in this service. United, we shared in filling the tasks left behind, and in time the void became less obvious, less painful, the days more fulfilling. Our people grew stronger still.

My training intensified, as play had lost much of its appeal. Instead of role play and games, I now sparred with my teacher in what little spare time we found. I quickly became the most formidable wildling in the gully, though I had little time to exhibit my skills.

With fewer hands to work the fields, the older wildlings were welcomed help tending the crops. I considered it a great honor to tread so close to the footsteps of my mother, and my contributions to the evening feast helped restore some warmth to Reisenbough as well as to her memory, warm as the sun at my back each day. Her spirit rested with the divine, her legacy remained with her people.

Life gradually evolved beyond sorrow. My father and I were finally getting along better in the wake of tragedy. Neither of us were the same, but we managed better with each day. We had found the strength to heal. Yet, fate would change our lives once again.

During my ninth year, the hunting party encountered an unusually aggressive beast. A ferocious and capable predator known as the hatual stalked the tall grasses of the plains, uncontested as the apex predator of the field. These large sleek, cat-like carnivores could easily overpower a man, with sharp fangs set in crushing jaws and razor sharp claws powered by solid, rippling muscle.

These formidable creatures stalked the plains in small family units, typically shying away from and avoiding people altogether. Yet this particular beast stalked along the edge of the shaded fields, alone and brave in the presence of our hunters. At first it kept its distance, snarling and pacing just out of the range of their arrows, as if it recognized the weapons. The intent behind the creature's unusual behavior unnerved the party, but they continued despite the ill omen.

As usual, the hunters split into two parties. My grandfather Kraegar led a team of three into the tall grass of the fields. He took with him his two sons, Raethos his oldest and my father Krayton. They were weary of the beast, mindful and armed with the deadly poison of the Malekaur. But as they stalked the fields, the beast was nowhere to be seen.

Continuing with the hunt, they managed to herd two large doe toward the waiting archers. Kraegar rushed for the clearing of the shaded fields, waiving his spear and screaming to give an edgy doe one final push into the trap. Just as he neared the clearing, the beast sprang from behind, biting hard into his right leg. It pulled him deeper into the tall grass, horribly mangling his leg below the knee.

He struggled to fend off the creature. Having lost his spear in the attack, he reached for his knife. As he moved to stab at the creature, it quickly backed from his reach and in a snarling rage turned to Raethos, the first to arrive at his father's aid. The beast met him with a powerful offensive, overtaking him in an instant.

My grandfather watched the beast easily avoid the hunter's weapons, as if it were all too familiar with them. This was no natural beast. Scars covered the flesh beneath the dirty shine of its smoky gray fur.

My father had not been far behind, and he met the beast with his spear ready. He struck true, driving his weapon deep through the creature's left flank as it mauled his older brother. The beast toppled to its death, my father's spear piercing it through.

The beast lay dead, a snarl baring its grizzly teeth. Scars in the shape of stabs and slashes covered the creature's body. It had known hunger, depravity, and the lash. Metal bindings ate into the flesh around its ankles. This creature had been subjected to cruelties unfathomable to our people.

Tragic as it was, there was little pity for the fallen beast. My uncle was gravely wounded and passed shortly after the beast was slain, as my father tried desperately to aid him. By this point my grandfather was fuming in a delirious rage. My father and the others did what they could to save him. He survived the ordeal, but lost his leg below the knee. His wounds would heal, but the loss of his oldest son so soon after losing so many to the sickness was more than his mind could bear.

With the passing of Raethos came another wave of grief to our household. Raethos too had lost his wife to the sickness, leaving his son orphaned with his passing. This is how Kori, the son of Raethos, came to live with my father and me. In time broken hearts would heal as best they could. Kori and I became as brothers.

We rarely spoke of our dear departed. Instead we focused on our training, growing stronger with my father as our guide. Kori had little trouble advancing in combat, and eventually it became quite difficult for me to match him. Our competitive spirits kept us striving to be faster and stronger as the days went on. I would not have been half as accomplished if not for the extra challenge of his rival.

Kori and I were trained with short swords. The combination of a small rounded shield and a shorter blade had shaped the technique passed down to the descendants of Kraegar. Kori's father had began his training in this style, as my father had elected to do with me. I however, did not care much for having the small shield and preferred to fight without it, much to my father's dismay. I felt lighter, faster, and more maneuverable. It felt natural.

Eventually my father relented, allowing me to train how I saw fit. He pushed me harder to make up for the lack of a shield. I was to be stronger, faster, and more versatile in my abilities to compensate. I trained to use both hands, together and independently. Ambidexterity added to the fluidity of my movements. I had even given my best attempt at using a twin dagger set, though I was more distracted and clumsy with two blades it seemed. Nevertheless, I was well on the path to mastering my own way. By the year of sending my father couldn't have been more proud.

Kori and I were equals in a spar most days. He used his sword and shield well, and together we grew to be bold young warriors under the tutelage of my father. Soon the day came when my father could no longer best the two of us, though I doubt either of us would have truly stood a chance in a real battle against the brawny son of Kraegar. His pride grew with each passing day. The booming sound of his voice rang with his excitement as he called out things like "Excellent!" or "Wonderful form, that's the way!" over the snapping sound of the wooden replicas crashing together.

By the coming of our fourteenth harvest, my father could scarce keep up with his star pupils. His lost pride seemed to return upon seeing the fruits of his teachings. We were strong, quick, and sharp of wit. We were natural hunters, capable trackers, and novice craftsmen. Kori and I dreamed ourselves to be skilled warriors more than prepared for the journey ahead, ready for our first steps as men in the eyes of the Dóvai.

Our grandfather Kraegar couldn't have been more proud of his two grandsons, shaping into fine young lads. By this time, he was a grizzly old man with a troubled taste for wine. His beard was gray and haggard, splashed with bits of purple from his drink. The hide of his tunic was worn and musky like the earth. He was a weathered hulk, and after a few drinks of wine he would pivot about on his crude prosthetic, roaring like an ogre as he moved to playfully scare what few wildlings dared venture near.

He never missed an opportunity to brag on the children of his house, telling all how bold and skilled they were becoming. He was ever so proud to boast that only the sons of his sons could rival those of his sworn brother, Darius.

A bold eagle marked the symbol of the family crest for many generations before it passed unto Darius. Cas and Pol were proud to wear the symbol of their house, displaying the eagle at every opportunity, incorporating it in all their works from the time they could scribble. The headbands that kept their wild hair at bay had rather square shaped, proud eagles shakily embroidered into the centerfold that the twins had etched themselves. The duo represented their house well, well enough that all in Reisenbough knew the bushy haired mischief makers by name and family.

The two had grown to be tall and lanky, but were strong and quick despite their scrawny appearance. This jittery double act was unmatched save for Kori and me, and only rarely did we manage to best them. No matter the challenge, as a team the twins were unstoppable.

Kori had grown to be the shortest of the group, but even as a young lad he was already brawny like our fathers. He had a short mane of ratty, sand colored hair he kept bound back by a scarlet headband, passed from his mother. The tethers that held up his waist cloth were bound to an iron buckle in the shape of a burning sun. It was a symbol of light, a reminder of the house to which he was the sole surviving member. The master metal worker Balthar had helped Kori fashion the buckle not long after he lost his father to the hatual.

I was tall and broad at the shoulders like my father, but lean like the twins. My thick dark locks were those of my mother, as were my talents for speed and agility. The radiant green of my eyes was a trait of my own it seemed. Nevertheless, the best of both my parents could be seen in me. My heart and mind were open to the world, and my body and spirit strong enough to endure it.

I studied under my father alongside my brother Kori. Much to my father's dismay I struggled in archery, what my father considered his master skill and craft. I excelled at the crafting portion, quickly honing my technique for shaping a well balanced and powerful bow. I could chisel stone into fine points and edges, work them into lethal arrows and knives, but it seemed I couldn't shoot an arrow from a bow in hopes to do well by anyone. It made for good laughs if nothing else.

My father was patient and supportive through my struggle, trusting that I would better develop my skill in time. Kori, Cas, and Pol often practiced with me in secret along the river. Kori was of much better help, as the twins often spent their time bickering over one another's advice which typically ended in a scuffle, cutting the lesson short. Eventually my skill with a bow improved well enough, though I was nowhere near the caliber of my peers. What I lacked in archery was more than compensated in combat.

The four of us had grown strong, well learned in the lessons of our fathers before us. It was all in good reason. Once a boy came of age in Reisenbough, he would leave on a pilgrimage to earn his right as a man within the tribe, braving the elements of the four seasons to travel deep into the great forest and back again. It would soon be our time to embark on this journey to rise as men, the sacred sending known as the Allioht.

With the arrival of autumn came the festival of harvest. With the festival came the return of those who had embarked on the Allioht the year prior, welcomed home as men of the Dóvai. From the dark of night they would appear, aglow in colorful paints and festive costumes fashioned from the colorful shells of the Malekaur.

Young maidens of age would approach from the river, dressed in similar garb and fashion. The new generation of men and women were united and celebrated to begin the festivities, lasting well into the early hours of morning. It was an honor shared by all.

Eventually, the year of sending came for my generation. During the festival of harvest we would be recognized before the tribe, honored and celebrated before our departure. The morning that followed my age mates and I would embark on the Allioht, wearing only our simple garb and taking only a few simple gifts bestowed by our loved ones.

Oh course, the youth of Reisenbough were more than ready for the event by the time it arrived. Each father mentored his sons, teaching the necessary skills to hunt and survive off the land. Self defense and weapon training were also heavily integrated into the curriculum, for there were many hardships to be faced out in the world. The Malekaur of the mountain, the hatual upon the plain, giant arachnids, and the serpents of the marshlands were all fond of an easy meal. Though an encounter with any of these creatures could prove deadly, we were warned that it would be other people who posed the greatest threat. We were to remain a mystery, avoiding contact with any rouges we might encounter in the wilds.

My brothers and I had broken it down to a science, our life study at this point. The first day of the journey would be spent gathering supplies for crafting tools and equipment. Once we reached the refuge atop the mount, we would use the oldest of the supplies stored in the caves there, which we were to replace upon our return before the next festival.

By the first nightfall, we should have constructed the tools we would need. Bows, arrows, knives, and axes ready for use. We would sleep the night in the safety of the refuge atop Yerok where we would pay homage to those gone before us and call upon the guidance of our ancestors for the journey ahead.

On the second day we were to descend the mountain to the west along the old mines, the battleground where our grandfathers had fought against the slavers. From there we would head deeper into the elder forest to the southwest, avoiding the marshlands to the north where the Veylspring met the rough terrain of the Arching Forest. At the western edge of this great forest is where our duties would begin. The first trial was to survive the chill damp of the rainy season in the ruins overlooking the purge, the last remnants of Hathlanda.

A full year would pass before our return. Much lay ahead on this great journey, the stories I hoped to one day share with my tribesmen and descendants alike. The Allioht was to be an adventure truly like no other.

Well do I remember the day of that final harvest. It was a time of celebration, and all the Dóvai looked forward to the grand festival that lit the season each year. It offered a momentary reprieve from the toils of the day to day, a chance for the village to celebrate the fruits of the garden. Together we would praise thanks for our blessings and the bounty of the land. The fires would dance well into the night with music and song.

There was much work to be done before then, however. By midday the people of Reisenbough were scattered about, all so merrily at work that it seemed like play. The hunters had already returned with an easy bounty, fresh fish and venison. Produce had been collected and gathered the same, heaped in baskets at the village center.

While some worked to prepare within the village, others gathered under the distal ends of the weighted branches to harvest the plump reisen berries of the Arching Forest. There were cutters, who climbed the drooping boughs of the Allichene and hacked the stems of the lush berries ready to fall. Using ropes they would secure each deep blue, succulent berry. When the stem was cut, the berry could be safely lowered to the ground.

The pullers would release the berries once they met the ground, allowing the cutters to recover the rope. Each berry was then rolled by a delivery team to one of several work stations, where it would be squished into juice for wine and squashed into jam for preserves.

Most of the other boys had jumped at the chance to be on a roller team. Each work station had a press, where the berries were diced and tossed in to be squished under the tender feet of the maidens of Reisenbough. The young ladies were spectacular, as they stomped and giggled about covered in the rich blue nectar. Rolling the berries was hard work, but the delivery teams were well motivated.

Our ancestors had been clever in arranging this tradition. Near the press were several mashing pits where the wildlings squashed chunks of berry into mush for jam and sweet breads. As tantalizing as the young ladies might have been, the obnoxious goop covered wildlings were more than enough to prevent any flirtatious lingering. A delivery boy not busy was a delivery boy free to play, and a likely recipient of a face full of berry goop.

Cas and Pol naturally took to hacking away at berries in the canopy. Kori and I had been challenged to "try and keep up" as their ground team. There was little choice in the matter. It was far better to meet their challenge at a loss than to listen to their nagging.

Our trial began under the distal end of a drooping branch of the Allichene, so heavy with fruit that it touched the swaying grasses of the field. The twins wasted no time scurrying up the branch, heckling along their way. Large coils of rope were slung about their shoulders and torsos, making them appear far more robust than they were.

"May the best team win... No hard feelings, yeah?" Cas bolstered.

"Remember, there is no failure. Some of us are just better than others." Pol added.

"Yeah, yeah." Kori waived them off. "Just get up the damned tree, will ya?"

They began hacking down berries at once, allowing those close enough to the ground to drop the short distance. The branch shook and bobbed with each release, the twins rising higher with each cut.

Kori and I simply stood by and watched for the time being, waiving to a curious group of rollers. The confusion on their faces was obvious, we were cutting a bit far from the main group. Shenanigans were at hand, no doubt they suspected as much. Smile and waive, that was our part.

The twins were covered in spatter from hacking at the thick stems. The leaves shook and rattled with the thudding whacks of their hatchets, as they climbed higher. Eventually a berry dropped down with a squishy thud. After a few more, they had climbed high enough that the next berry sent down split open when it struck the earth. It was game time.

Kori yelled up to the twins. "Oui! Tie off!"

"You sure?" Giggled Cas, a brimming grin spread across his face as he looked down at us. "Maybe it'd be more efficient to cut and squish in one go."

Pol added a follow up as usual. "Innovative. Direct."

"Not to mention it'll make things much easier on the ladies at the press. We're just lookin' to help, yeah?" Cas chattered back to his brother before the two chuckled.

"Like two chittery little birds, peckin' away at berry stems. I've got half a mind to send an arrow up to get you moving!" Kori yelled back in idle threat.

"Half a mind, he says!" Pol giggled as he removed a coil of rope from around his shoulder.

"Leave the other half with your bow? Or you gonna have Kael flick arrows at us with that wicked tongue of his, cousin?" Cas teased as he grabbed hold of the rope his brother wrapped around the base of a branch. He slipped down a stem holding the other end of the rope and began to wrap it around the girth of a plump berry.

Kori wasn't sincere in his anger, but he chucked a small rock up at them anyway. It glanced off the soft bark of the branch the twins were working from, not but an arms length away from either of the boys. They jolted with the thudding knock of the impact. He had caught them off guard as they toiled with the rope.

"Oui! Good shot! That tongue of yours has really got some bite to it, Kael." Shouted Pol, sounding legitimately impressed.

"That's our Kael, marksman extraordinaire." Cas teased, as he finished up a tension knot along the side of the berry. He lay on his stomach, his legs wrapped around the stem.

"Don't make him mad, brother. He'll cough another pebble up and at us in an instant." Pol warned playfully before the two erupted in laughter. They were always happy to pester and tease.

The banter never ceased. Rarely did I have anything to add while they verbally prompted one another, leaving the twins' only option to poke fun at my silence. In truth, I had little talent for quick witted insults or retorts. It was hopeless against the twins anyhow.

My stoic defense worked well enough, even though the twins made light of this as well. The two made a point to playfully interpret my silence or react dramatically in the event that I did speak up. It was as if I spoke in revelation the way the two of them carried on sometimes. They were actually quite gifted at improvising, and their performances were well entertaining. It was good fun and rarely led to discourse, but if ever tensions mounted peace wasn't far behind.

"Is it going to take all day for this one berry? Silas and Gregor have already lowered two berries in the time you lot have spent on this one, and none of theirs have gotten split or squished!" Kori called up to the twins.

Silas and Gregor worked on the team closest to us. The two had indeed lowered two berries, having started about the same time. They were a few years older and more experienced, but Kori enjoyed goading the twins anyhow.

Pol stood atop the thickest part of the branch, one hand clasped to the rope secured around the berry. He had wrapped the rope around a smaller branch close to the berry and secured an end around its base, allowing the slack in the rope to dangle from the side of the main branch opposite.

"Aw, you hear that Cas? He says we aren't moving fast enough." A sly smirk crept across his face.

"Well then brother, we best pick up the pace. No more wasting precious time..." Cas replied.

He bounced up onto the branch to stand next to Pol, who pulled down on the rope to ready himself. Cas pulled his ax and in two solid strikes cleaved the stem in two.

Next was the part Kori and I had been waiting for. As the berry fell, Pol waited for it to swing under the main branch. When it was at the peak of its swing he did the unthinkable and released the rope entirely, sending it down at a near free fall. Just as it seemed the berry was doomed to smash into the ground the rope snapped tight, and the momentum of the berry was suddenly redirected to jerk and spin wildly.

Kori and I were speechless. The berry swung back and forth like a juicy pendulum. At its lowest point it was at my chest, suspended and still very much in motion. Laughter exploded from the twins, as Kori and I attempted to wrangle the wayward berry.

"Well, seems like you two have this under control. We're off to setup the next one." Pol called down, delighted to see their mischief at work.

"And don't keep us waiting, we'll need that rope back." Cas chimed in, as the two raced further along the swaying branch to the next cluster of berries.

After many attempts, the berry slowed significantly. I grabbed hold of the ropes along side and pushed my heels hard into the ground. No good, it just dragged me across the dirt in its wake. The berry slowed further, allowing Kori to grab hold. Together we managed to steady the thing, but getting it to the ground was to be a task all its own.

Kori and I worked at the ropes. With the berry suspended, the tension knots that held it were secured by the full weight of the berry, making the task of releasing the ropes far more difficult than it need be. Had the twins followed tradition the berry would have been slowly and safely lowered to the ground, and the ropes would have been a cinch.

"Lift together!" Kori exclaimed.

Grabbing hold of the soft girth of the berry from either side, we heaved at the thing. It lifted a bit, then a bit more. The rope loosened as one by one we tugged at the knots, balancing the heavy fruit as best we could.

"Got it!" Kori shouted, as he released enough to free his side.

Another berry came crashing down to swing just as wildly as the first one had. This was to be their game. Kori held strong, squatted under the weight. I tugged at the ropes a few more times before the thing came down with a thud. We stepped clear of the grounded berry and set off toward the next.

"Kael, take point!" Kori huffed as we closed in on the second swinging berry.

It had a little more momentum than the first, making it dangerous, making it fun. I followed the berry as it passed through the lowest point. On the return swing, I ran along side it and jumped to grab hold when it came close enough. In an instant I had pulled myself onto the berry, causing it to spin. I held tight against the force of the swing, my hair moving with the rise and fall as I whooshed through the air clinging to the berry.

Dizzy and a bit disoriented, I fumbled with the ridiculous rope work of the twins. I all but wanted to reach for my knife, knowing well it would lead to discourse. Kori grabbed hold of the berry to try and steady its movement. Being of heavier build, he fared much better at gaining control of the rouge fruit. Once he stopped the spin, I managed to loosen the ropes. Keeping up with the twins was not going to be easy, but Kori and I were more than capable.

As we continued to work on the second berry, there came not one, but two crashes. Two more berries came down within seconds of one another. The twins had certainly been well prepared. They had carried two ropes each, all four were in use. Even with a double drop, Kori and I were soon to close the gap.

At last, the second berry hit to the ground. Kori and I raced toward the third. Pol was running the opposite direction along the branches above to retrieve the ropes Kori and I had freed. He took a moment to call down a few taunts as he hoisted up the first of the ropes, but neither of us paid him any mind. Kori and I were already well at work on the third berry.

"Looks like we aren't keeping them busy enough, brother." Cas pointed, as Pol returned along the branch with two hastily coiled ropes.

"Then we should pick up the pace! Wouldn't want them to get bored down there." Pol responded, dropping a coil of rope into his brother's arms.

The two set to roping another berry. We released the third in half the time it took to release the first. As we moved for the fourth, the twins dropped another. Then another, and another... They must have hidden more rope in the canopy, or perhaps some of the berries had already been tied off, the cheats. There was no telling what else the two scheming brothers had in store.

I looked to Kori, shaking my head in dismay. We scoffed to one another.

"Cheating devils." He grumbled.

"Shall we then?" I smiled.

"Might as well." Kori groaned. "If we don't, they'll never shut-up about it."

"Oh they'll not shut it regardless, brother."

We shared a laugh as we dashed into action once more. One by one, we worked through perhaps a dozen berries altogether, continuing to improve along our way. At last we reached our mark, where the momentum of the final berry had dwindled to a sway as it dangled in wait.

Kori was winded, and I wasn't far behind. We had managed to catch up to the twins well enough. The last berry was all that remained, and it still had a little swing to it. They were but a step ahead of us now, having exhausted their supply of preset berries. Finally, Kori and I released the last berry only seconds after closing the distance. We had done it.

By this time we were well under the canopy, nearing the peak in the arch of the bowing branches. This was as far as we were to go. The twins were somewhere high above, obscured by the large spade shaped leaves of the Allichene.

I dropped to the ground to catch my breath. Kori heaved the same, sweaty and gasping. The twins were hidden somewhere in the green above, their snickering indicative of their approximate location.

"Looks like your challenge has been met, you cheating devils! Is that all you've got?!" Kori shouted up into the trees.

He huffed as he bent over to catch himself on his knees. No response came from above. Maybe they didn't hear his words, or perhaps they were up to something more. Suddenly the answer came crashing down, four berries in rapid succession. This was the big finish we had come to anticipate from the twins.

Kori and I looked to one another, wide eyed. I was finished with this game before the last berry was wrestled to the ground. Discretion to the wind, I pulled my stone knife from my waist cloth. Kori smiled and took his knife in hand as well. Ropes still dangled behind us like markers along our trail. The twins had these ready to drop all along, waiting for the finale. Clearly we were free to improvise as well.

We raced into action. Kori grabbed hold and swung onto the closest of the four berries, slashing at the rope suspending it as I ran past for the second. I jumped at it, catching the ropes that bound it with my free hand. I fumbled for a better grip as the berry continued swinging through the air. I lunged my knife into the berry to pull myself to the top, soaking the hides of my tunic and waist cloths in the sticky sweet dark juices of the reisen berry. This was a blatant foul.

I climbed up to my feet and slashed the rope, which popped with the release of tension. I tucked and rolled to dismount the berry, rising to my feet and dashing for the last two.

Kori was already mounting one of them, and as he did so it crossed paths with the last remaining berry. The ropes began to intertwine, sending the berries spinning round on a collision course. They accelerated as the spiral gradually narrowed.

I made for the other berry, this time clenching my knife between my teeth to free both my hands. I caught hold of the ropes, the momentum slinging me high and pulling hard against my grip. The berries were a moment away from colliding when Kori and I cut the ropes in near unison. We both dropped free, rolling away in opposite directions. The berries touched, dropped to the ground, and jolted away from one another. The game was finished.

Cas and Pol cheered from the canopy, as Kori and I stood before our efforts. A trail of berries reached out to the distal ends of the drooping branches. We had left our competition far behind, as those close enough to witness our shenanigans were most distracted from their work by the sight of us wrestling flying berries across the shaded fields.

"You're covered. What happened?" Kori asked through heaving breaths. Surely he had already noticed the oozing gash along the crown of the berry I had stabbed.

"I cut one. Sorry, brother." I responded, scratching at my head in embarrassment. The berry juice smelled both fruity and sweet. Delicious, even for shame.

"I wouldn't worry about it, those two cheats already busted one anyways. They can't base a victory on a lesser blunder. Its a clean cut, not smashed to bits like the one back there." Kori reasoned.

The berries were meant to be brought down intact so that they were easy to move. Round berries rolled nicely across the soft dark soil of the shaded fields. Damaged berries tended to rupture further when rolled, or simply could not be rolled at all.

One by one the ropes dropped down from the canopy. Kori and I helped gather them, neatly displaying the ends of the ropes we'd sliced on top as we awaited the twins. Eventually the two made their way down the broad trunks of the Allichene.

The soft leather skin of the trees split in the dry season, leaving large fleshy scars when greener new skin developed to heal the wounds. The Allichene were perfect for climbing, and we had been climbing along the gentle contour of the Arching Forest for years by this point.

The twins came scuttling down the arched trunk adjacent to the tree in which they had been working. The two were already snickering. My right side was splashed and spattered with dark blue, a clear indication of my offense. The worn gray hide of my tunic took the brunt of it and was most certain to keep a shade of color to it. It didn't matter to me in the slightest. I was actually kind of proud to have it, the symbol of a challenge met.

The twins made their way over to where Kori and I stood. One of the berries still oozed from an obvious slash. The two of them took notice immediately.

"Looks like you've got a little something on you there, Kael. Could that be juice from a reisen berry perhaps?" Pol teased with a sinister grin. They clearly assumed to have gotten the better of us.

"You know, I think it is. One of these berries is bleeding out, Pol!" Cas gasped as he kicked at the wounded berry. "And it looks like they cut a few of the ropes as well! Tisk, Tisk..."

They were clearly having fun with us. Neither of them really cared about the challenge nor the ropes it had taken days to make. It was all play, as was everything to them.

"What's gotten into you two?" Pol teased. "Slashin' ropes, stabbin' helpless berries. Honestly, to treat the sacred fruit in this manner, you should be ashamed." He stomped about playfully as he spoke. "Kael, is it safe to assume you are the slasher then?" He asked with a raised brow.

"Aye. That one there." I responded, pointing to the wounded berry. "Two of the ropes as well."

"Noble as always, Kael. Thanks for your honesty..." Cas nodded with a stern face and serious tone before bursting with a jubilant smile. "Well, looks like Pol and I win this round. As you know, damaging a berry counts against you. A blatant foul."

"A foul indeed. Sorry kids, guess you'll have to try again next season." Pol agreed. A smile crept over his smug face.

Kori had been ready for their nonsense and wasted no time setting the twins straight on the matter. "Damaging a berry is a foul is it? Then what about the one you squashed at the beginning, you oafs?! You were disqualified from the start if that were the case." He growled.

The twins wouldn't concede that easily.

"We didn't do that bit." Cas denied.

"Nope, not responsible. All we did was cut the stem. After that, it squashed all on its own." Pol agreed, crossing his arms and shaking his fluffy head.

Cas quickly added. "And that's just nature's way. We were simply aiding the will of the Great Mother in a very natural process. If anything we should receive a bonus for that."

Kori was on the verge of fury. "Bonus?! Ha! You hacked at it with an ax, you twiggy twit. How is that natural?"

"Whoa, now! There's no need for name calling, brother. We only hacked the stems, and there's nothing against that in the official rules. Neither Cas nor I laid an ax to any fruit today." Pol offered, happy to prolong the squabble.

"Indeed, he's right. Best to leave the berry slashin' to the pros, right Kael?" Cas teased with a wink.

I gave a nod, bringing a fist to my chest in bravado. I took pride in my ability to deliver a good slashing, berry or not. It was good fun, and I counted it as a victory nonetheless.

Kori however, was not willing to concede so easily. "Official rules?! What a load of horrah! And what about all the extra ropes? The unconventional, not to mention dangerous, practice of letting them fall rather than lowering them like you were suppose to, huh? How is that for 'respecting the sacred fruit'?" Kori railed, eyes growing large with passion as his spittle flew.

The twins were rolling with laughter, one of them quite literally. Cas now lie on the soft earth, lost in a dense patch of leafy vegetation near the base of the bleeding berry. One foot kicked from the green that shook with his laughter. Pol was laughing too, despite his attempts to remain focused on pestering Kori, the latter of whom was beginning to transition into true anger under his frustration. The fun was over.

"A draw." I offered in compromise.

The twins would agree. They knew when enough was enough. Pol had a scar on his left cheek to remind us all should we forget, a scar for which I was responsible much to my regret.

It happened the previous year, during a spar. The four of us often sparred, for fun as well as study. It was good practice, essential to honing combative skill.

Kori and I struggled to keep up with the twins. The two devils were fast, both wielding twin daggers and moving together with remarkable precision. They were incredible opponents, and we both thrived on the challenge of besting them.

Humility was as much a lesson as combat efficiency, a lesson that would have saved Pol the nasty blow that left him that scar. Kori and I had foolishly engaged the twins in a 'friendly' spar without the watchful eyes of the elders to interfere. The two were obnoxious as usual, but on this particular day they were notably more deviant.

Their form and etiquette were fine enough in a spar, but their tongues were another matter altogether. The two were unmatched in their prowess, and they made sure to rub it in at ever opportunity. Again and again our wooden replica weapons were parried and answered with a quick jab to the ribs or sharp poke to the gut or throat. All the while the twins would rail us with taunts and insults. This was nothing more than juvenile fun, until it became personal.

On that day tensions escalated, and the competitive spar turned into a nasty scuffle. The twins fought back to back, splitting Kori and me apart. Kori was being forced back, further away from me as he desperately attempted to break free of Cas. I was left to face off against Pol.

I was managing my own well enough, but gaining no ground one way or the other. Pol was barely trying it seemed, playfully poking at me with a childish tongue. As another of my strikes missed wide.

"Oh dear, poor Krayton. He's two duds for students!" He lunged at me following the insult.

I quickly jumped back to clear his initial attack, and back yet again with his next two swipes. I lost my balance as I narrowly escaped the last jab and stumbled over a mass of vegetation. I fumbled for a solid step to regain my footing and fell back. I rolled to recover, landing on my feet with my guard ready.

Pol laughed outright. "Are you sure you want to do this? There are some wildlings down the way, maybe they are a bit more on your level."

I ran at him, replica raised over my head. I brought it down to my right and swung wide when I got close, hoping to get lucky more than anything. He dropped to my left, kicking my legs out from under me and laying me flat on my back.

Winded, I slowly moved to recover. Before I could stand, the end of a replica dagger poked at my cheek. Looking up, I peered into Pol's eyes. They glittered with a sinister joy.

He snickered. "Too bad your mom isn't still around to show you how it's done."

It had been a compliment really, but instead it had reached a hurt within me. Before I fully realized, I had grabbed hold of his wrist, and with a strength unknown to me flung him to the ground before bringing my replica down across the left side of his face with a thudding crack.

I was instantly horrified at what I had done. Pol's face was already bloodied when he cried out in pain. I had wounded my sparring partner, my brother and friend, Pol.

I fled from the ordeal, climbing high into the canopy. I wanted to be far from the faces that looked to me in horror, wondering why I had done it. I hid in the silence of the high canopy. To wound a friend during training was shameful enough, but it was the surprise of it that had shaken me. I felt terrible.

I returned to the village when I was ready to face what I had done. My father was waiting for me, but there was no lecture. Not then anyway. The next day Cas and Pol arrived with their father Archon. The two fathers had arranged for a hunting party, an overnight trip in hopes of opening hearts under the stars.

Trips were common, typically focused around some of the more serious aspects of our training. It offered a chance to teach and practice the various skills that would serve both to keep us alive during the Allioht and care for the people of Reisenbough in the days beyond. This trip was different, however.

There was an uneasy tension, though no one seemed angry with me in the slightest. The tension lessened over the course of the day, but followed into the evening after we made camp. By the light of the fire, the four of us were silent as our fathers pushed us into confronting the dilemma.

At first, not a word was spoken. Not even the banter of the twins, which was highly unusual. At last, my father broke the long and awkward silence.

"I miss her too, son."

He had caught me off guard. I was expecting a serious talk, but not about her. The tears swelled in my eyes almost instantly, and I looked down as if I were ashamed to have it seen.

"It's okay, Kael. None of us are here to judge, we are here because we are family." Archon spoke reassuringly with a soft rumbling voice. "The Dóvai have come to be strong warriors, but it is not the discipline of the sword nor the precision of the arrow that gives us our strength. The strength of Reisenbough comes from the heart. No warrior stands stronger than the one who stands with his brothers and sisters, his sons and daughters; no warrior is stronger than one who fights for this love. Share your heart with us, young brother."

I wept in silence. Listening to their words around the warm light of the crackling fire.

"Emotions can be tricky. How you feel will reflect upon your perception of the world. If you allow that perception to become clouded, you lose your ability to navigate the world around you. Memories of your mother are powerful for both of us, son. Remember, that is the power of love, deep and everlasting. Don't hold it back, share it with the world. For love is so much greater than any one of us, and it's only when we forget this that it becomes painful."

His voice broke a bit at the end. The fire crackled in the brief silence that followed. I looked up to see he had been crying for some time now, though he did not sound like it as he spoke. Even with tears shimmering down his unkempt beard, he still looked powerful.

"You cannot hope to overcome your feelings by ignoring them, Kael. Especially ones as complicated as grief or love. Only hearts that have known great joy can know great sorrow. You have to face this within yourself, find the strength that lies beyond your sorrow."

"But you're crying, dad." I sniffled out in a squishy, nasally voice before I had time to catch myself. I was all but sobbing and only half thinking at this point. It was really more of an open thought wrapped in emotion.

My father burst into a deep burly laugh. It was so vibrant and uplifting that one by one the rest of us began laughing as well.

"Oh my boy, I didn't say it would be an easy practice. It will take great will and concentration. There will be good days as well as bad. It's up to you to decide what each day will be. And remember, you aren't alone."

I knew I wasn't alone. Family was everything to the Dóvai. I just didn't like talking about her. Perhaps it was true, I had to overcome a darker part of myself.

"I lost my mom too, you know." Kori spoke, his voice warm and low like the fire. "It's only been a few years since I lost dad as well. When I found out about my father, I lost my ability to feel anything it seemed. I had already been as sad as I thought I possibly could when mom died. When my father's pyre was lit, I couldn't be sad or angry. Everything seemed so impossibly far away. I just went numb..."

He trailed off for a moment before continuing in a more cheery tone. "Luckily when I snapped out of it I was well into living with you and Krayton, and I still had you two misfits about to keep me entertained as well." He shot a playful fist into Cas's shoulder.

"Touching." Cas responded.

"None this way. Had enough, thanks." Pol teased.

Kori continued. "I don't know what I would have done without all of you, honestly. I am grateful to have you as my brothers."

Suddenly I felt ashamed, realizing again the loss Kori had suffered. We all had lost loved ones. I wasn't the only one fighting to stay strong it seemed.

"Ah that's very sweet of you, Kori." Came Pol in his most endearing tone. A smile half formed on his bruised and battered face. It was almost as if he had already forgotten about it.

"Yeah, we like having you around too, stumpy." Cas teased. The twins carried on like he was a squat troll, but made sure to do so sparingly.

"Boys!" Archon's voice boomed at his two whimsical sons, cutting their giggles short. Their eyes widened a bit, as they snapped to attention. "This is a lesson for all. You are to be men of the Dóvai. You must learn to help one another, depend on one another. Each of you are only as strong as your brother next to you. Be strong for one another, be strong together. Iron sharpens Iron."

The twins offered squeaky apologies.

"Yes, father."

"Sorry, dad. Just keeping it fun."

"Was it fun then, getting knocked hard on your arse?" Archon asked as sarcastically as either of the twins would have.

Pol responded in a voice that sounded like a young Archon. "The best of fun, sir."

"A real good time it was." Cas added. It seemed impossible for one to speak without the other chiming in.

"Bull! I've scarcely heard a wildling carry on the way you were. There were tears and everything." Archon teased with a smile.

"Those were tears of joy, dad!" Pol fibbed. "Cas and I have been working with these two for a long time. It felt so good to finally see some progress that I just couldn't hold 'em back."

"Yeah dad, it was a real shocker. We really didn't think Kael had it in him." Cas added.

"Well it seems like you got a good look, but that wasn't progress." Archon scolded. "Wounding your partner is not the intent during a spar. Neither is intentionally pushing your opponent beyond the point of self-control. The goal is to work and become stronger together, not pit yourselves against one another."

The smiles faded from the twins' faces along with the confidence of their sarcasm. It was a relief to know I wasn't to take the brunt of the blame for the incident, though I was embarrassed to hear the twins lectured. Even if Pol had antagonized me outright, I had no right to batter his face over it. What a mess I'd made.

Archon continued. "Let this be a lesson in itself. That wound will be sore for awhile as it heals, and it will likely leave a scar. Consider yourselves lucky it wasn't worse."

I cringed at this. If it scarred, I would be reminded of my guilt each time I saw it.

"Hopefully it'll serve to better remind you all of your teachings and prevent this from happening again. Your training is to prepare you to defend your brothers and sisters, not maim one another in trivial contest."

He stopped at this. There wasn't anger in his voice, only passion. He felt he had spoke enough, but the length of the silence beyond suggested there was still much to be said as we sat around the fire.

Finally I spoke, breaking the silence. "I am sorry, Pol. It was wrong of me to do what I did."

It took a lot for me to look at him, the left side of his face bruised across the cheek. A deep red blot marked a cut along his cheek bone. His father's words were true, we had indeed been lucky.

Pol's face formed into the best smile it could, half of it swollen and discolored. "You're alright, Kael. A face this pretty makes even a scratch like this look good. If nothing else at least people'll be able to tell me from Cas now." He joked, looking to his brother.

Cas was not as accepting. "Ah, but that was our best act! Now what will we do to keep things fun for everyone? And worse, now mum'll be able to tell us apart!" He flung his arms about as if this were detrimental to continuing his very life.

"Oh, I'm sure you two'll make due. Mischief comes natural wherever you are." Kori piped. He smiled at the twin brothers from across the fire.

"Thanks for believing in us. You're a regular sweetheart. " Pol offered, sounding genuinely sincere. It was always difficult to tell when the twins were joking or being serious, assuming they were ever serious.

"You've got a right way with words, Sir. Almost teared up on that." Cas added. He brought a fist to his chin and bit down on his lower lip in an exaggerated expression as if he were truly touched by Kori's words. "You'll be breaking hearts in no time."

We all erupted in laughter. Kori flushed a bit, but he too couldn't help but laugh.

The remainder of that night was spent sharing embarrassing moments and warm stories until the fire waned. The next day we woke early and hunted with our fathers before leaving for the river. Along the southern bank of the Veylspring we spent the morning reviewing proper sparring technique and discussing tactics and execution.

When the afternoon came, we finished the leftovers from the small game we had caught. After we finished lunch, the twins left with Archon. Kori and I remained with Krayton to learn a new technique, one for clearing the mind and assessing the body. There along the clear rippling waters of the Veylspring, we learned to meditate.

My father had us sit in the soft leafy vegetation that grew near the water's edge. We were close enough to reach out and touch the water, but far enough that it would not distract from the lesson.

"The mind and the body are one, but it is easy to forget this when the mind is overwhelmed or the body is broken." My father's words came low and steady. His teachings were stern with passed wisdom, but gentle and easy like his warm spirit.

"Sometimes to solve the puzzles of the mind it is helpful to let go for a moment, pull the mind out from that which burdens it. Remember that the two components are one. The easiest way to do this is to passively explore the world around you. Perceive of it with all the senses. Begin with your eyes, look around you."

The rippling waters of the Veylspring lapped at the rocky soil of the bank. The water was calm and flowed more gently in the shallows, but grew increasingly moody and even turbulent along the rocky cliffs to the north.

The rocks were mostly sandstone on the levels nearest the water. In the heat of the midday sun they were all colors of red, orange, and yellow. High above the river to the north loomed the gnarled black stone of the dead lands.

I gazed across the heights of the rugged black stone. Further upstream to the east random bits of color began to emerge along the otherwise barren features. These bits of color were ribbons tied to the tails of arrows.

A dense thicket of cane grew along the bank adjacent to the multicolor mural of arrows. The growing fields were just beyond the cane to the east. From there the older children would fire arrows up at the blackened terrain, hoping to set their arrow higher than those before them.

It was a contest as old as our tribe. A bow had to be strong to send an arrow high enough, and the arrow perfectly crafted to stay true on course, the tip hard enough to pierce the crumbling wall.

Kori and I sat to either side of my father along the bank of the Veylspring. Green encircled us in all imaginable shapes and sizes it seemed. Behind us was the arching forest. We were well beyond the reach of the distant tips of its branches.

Further down the river, the banks were covered in thick wild grass. The grasses grew taller, and more dense along the river's path into the wetlands. Here the grass was tame like the flow of the river, gently swaying in the breeze that blew. This was a place of peace.

"Now I want both of you to close your eyes." My father's words came again. "Try to visualize your surroundings, recall as much as you can."

I heard my father begin to stir as he spoke. Half bored and hardly meditating, my eyes opened before I'd realized. I saw my father standing over Kori, tying a blue band of cloth around his head to cover his eyes. Centered on Kori's face was the symbol of a blazing sun.

"Kael! Eyes closed." Came his voice as he noticed he was being watched.

Kori didn't seem to stir at all. I quickly closed my eyes and redirected toward the splashing sounds of the river bank. Soon my father's footsteps came close behind me. I heard the soft rustle of what I assumed was another headband like the one Kori had been given, as it was pulled from his waistband. I struggled to keep my eyes closed, as a soft cloth wrapped gently over my eyes. I felt a slight tug as my father secured the blindfold in place behind my mass of dark matted hair.

"As you imagine your surroundings, seek to connect to them as well. Listen, breathe, and feel the world around you. In time, one can learn to master all the dimensions of perception, strengthening the bond between mind and body." He sat between us again.

"Breathe in of the world, breathe out to the world." My father coached in a soft low voice, grinding just above a whisper before slowly fading to silence.

The fresh smell of the river was aromatic and powerful. It smelled of life, and a bit fishy. It seemed to punctuate the other scents, as the crisp smell of vegetation mixed with the rich smell of the soil.

The trickling sound of the river was almost overpowering. The ripple of the waters edge was crisp, and behind it was the deep roll of the current rushing past a few large rocks fallen from the northern ledge. The more distant sounds echoed off the stone wall, adding a magical rolling depth that drew my perception of my surroundings even further.

Soon other sounds began to emerge. A groaning sound came from the tall shoots of cane, as the stalks rubbed together in the breeze. The soft leafy blades of grass made flapping sounds here and there when they caught the occasional gust. Birds chirped in all possible directions it seemed. The croaking of frogs sang throughout the foliage along the river.

We sat in silence for some time. I had stopped trying to picture everything and simply sat in the warm sunlight, the breeze from the water to keep me cool. The experience was incredible. It was as if I had forgotten the beauty of my homeland, the very awe inspiring phenomena of the natural world and all the life that thrived there.

Suddenly my woe was melted, and tranquility eased over me. I forgave myself for the incident with Pol and silently promised that it would be the last time my actions would scar one of my own. I would protect the peace between brothers.

"Do you feel it yet, the connection with the Great Mother?" My father's voice came low, but it broke through the prolonged silence like a crashing symbol.

I all but jumped out of my skin. Kori had been startled all the same, as a hearty "Sons alive!" burst from him. My father's thunderous laughter seemed almost unbearably loud, and soon we were all laughing.

The moment passed, and my father's voice became serious again. "Meditation is a tool, helps to keep a warrior in tune. Remember you are connected always, just as we are each connected through the Mother. What burdens one can grow to burden many, if simply ignored."

"You have to face the negativity within yourself. Only after you accept the truth in your heart can you hope to conquer your hurt, your anger. Learn to channel your emotion, make it your strength instead of weakness. Let the brighter part of the past be your strength to face today and your reason to wake tomorrow. Pain and sorrow will pass, but only if you let go long enough to see beyond them..."

His words rang with the depth of experience. Kori and I uttered not a word. What was there to be said?

"Thank you, father." I said finally, not knowing how else to respond.

"Thank you." Kori repeated, his voice deep and quivering. He sounded like he was on the brink of tears, if he hadn't shed any already. This lesson was heartfelt for each of us, as it seemed the pain of loss still lingered from years past.

"Now," my father spoke in a lighter tone, shaking us free of the somber moment, "you two are ready to take your training to the next level. Rise to your feet, and make your way to the water's edge."

As I shuffled to my feet, I heard my brother and father do the same. The water was only a few careful steps from where I had sat for so long. My feet were a bit numb, and it took a moment for my legs to regain their strength. Slowly but surely, I blindly wobbled to the water's edge.

The water was cold on my waking feet, sending a rush through my body as my toes touched the icy ripples. I waited on the bank for our next instructions. Kori must have made his way to the water as well, as he let out a surprised "Oosh!". The feeling was mutual, as was the laughter that followed.

"Ah come now, its not that cold." My father teased.

He splashed with his steps, sloshing icy drops of water all over Kori and me as he entered the water. He laughed merrily at the cringing gasps that came.

"Now I want the two of you to step in further as well, take care not to trip. The water's a bit chill."

He bellowed with laughter. Kori and I carefully made our way into the water until we were as far in as my father.

"Good, now take your training weapons in hand." My father directed. I fumbled to take hold of the wooden replica thrust at me through the darkness. "Today we will train without our sight."

"Blind?!" Kori blurted, as if it the concept were ludicrous.

I too was less than keen on the idea of fighting blindfolded. I had already managed to bludgeon one of my brothers in the face and felt no need to experience it all over again.

"This practice will help you learn to use all of your senses more readily, increasing your awareness not only of your surroundings, but of yourself as well. Kael, you and I will go first." My father instructed. "Begin!"

The icy water rushed at my knees. With a gulp I readied my guard, gripping my weapon with both hands and holding it steady before me.

In an instant came the tap of my father's stick at my left shoulder. I didn't move. This was going to prove most difficult.

"Well we've started now. Remember, you can't see, so focus your efforts in other ways. Why did I strike where I did?" Came my father's coaching.

"I left myself open." I replied, feeling slightly belittled by such a novice question.

We had been training for the entirety of our lives, any wildling could have told him that. His point was met though. This was more an exercise in focus and discipline than of performance.

"Yes!" he roared, and another tap came to my left side.

I moved to counter, missing it entirely as another tap landed on my right. The challenge was motivating, but frustration began to build. I had grown adept in the ways of the sword, yet it meant little without my sight.

The experience was humbling to say the least. Perhaps one of my father's greatest teachings, passed from his father before him; perception is far greater than sight. One who is willing and ready to push beyond what is known will journey well into the true depths of understanding.

Such were the teachings of the elders. From our first days, life brings its lessons as play. This is how the children of the Dóvai were taught, to see all life as play. In truth, the training was good fun. The depth of these long standing lessons were lost on me in my youth, though time would make them precious to my heart.

I smiled wide, reveling in this new trial of becoming. I hadn't missed his last strike by much. It was simply a matter of practice, putting all my skill to new use. Like the rushing currents of the river, move with the flow...

I heard the water slosh but an attack did not come. I moved to counter nothing. The sound had been my father turning to face Kori. He simply laughed.

"Excellent form, my boy. Steady for a moment, let your brother have a go at it."

Kori had been standing in silence as he blindly witnessed my blundering first attempt. I was glad he hadn't seen it, and hopefully no one else had either. They'd have thought me hopeless for sure.

"Your turn Kori." Came my father's voice.

I heard the slosh of the water with each movement, as their footing changed or shifted against the lapping pull of the current. Suddenly there was a familiar clank, the sound of wooden replicas slapping together. Kori managed to block an attack.

"Excellent!" Came my father's praise.

"Hold onto that thought, Kori. Lets see if Kael can catch wind of it." My father turned back to me. "Okay, your turn."

This time I was steady. I left an opening to my left again, hoping he would repeat the first strike. The water moved, and I shifted to counter left. The tap came to my right, however. I missed the first strike. Instead of allowing myself to fluster, I focused and calmed myself. I could almost hear my own heartbeat in my ears it seemed, steady and throbbing.

The water stirred again, this time my counter met with a solid impact and the same clank heard from Kori's success. Another strike came, and once again I diverted it and even sent an attack of my own. I caught only air, but my father's gentle laughter was that of delight.

"Good! You boys are picking this up quick! Took a little longer when my father showed me."

My round was over. He turned back to Kori. There was a clank with nearly every slash my father dealt. What didn't meet with a clash was avoided in a splashing shift of heavy feet.

Next it was my turn again. This time my father threw in a few dirty tricks, splashing water at my face and even advancing, forcing me to stumble through the thick pull of the water as I struggled to keep my balance. The water was cold, but I no longer felt it.

After a few rounds there was a disturbance on the bank. Footsteps approached. As I listened, I made out what sounded like three pairs of feet, though two of them seemed to move in time. Suddenly there was a commotion, as someone stumbled and fell hard near the water.

"Ummff!"

"Ah, this was suppose to be a stealth mission, brother. Now they know we're here. Hopefully you fight better than you walk, or you'll end up with a face like mine."

"I already have a face like yours brother, only mine's a bit prettier now, thank you."

"Not for long if you keep falling on it like that."

Cas and Pol. The twins were back on the scene. The third set of footsteps were most likely those of their father, Archon. Soon his voice came to verify.

"So much for the surprise."

"Well what did you expect, dad? We suggested holding off on the blindfold bit. You said you'd guide us. Didn't see that rock there?" Cas teased his father.

"You were doing well enough. Besides, now you know it's there don't you? That's the path to discovery. You'll be all the stronger with the experience." Archon shot back.

"Tough love. That's the way it is then? Come 'ere, dad. Let's hug it out." Came Pol's voice, followed by what sounded like a playful scuffle.

Archon's voice followed. "Get off, you mongrels! Make your way to the water, and try not to drown before today's lesson."

"Why would we drown, dad?" Came Cas's response.

"Yeah, we're only wearing blindfolds. Unless today's lesson is how to swim with our eyelids." Pol added sarcastically.

He followed his comment with a torrent of wet flapping sounds, and the two erupted in laughter. How Archon managed the patience to deal with the two of them was a mystery all its own.

They made their way to the water with the wet sloshing sounds of their feet dragging along the muddy banks.

"Are the others here?" Pol asked, knowing well the answer was yes. "Kael! Kori! You two there?"

Neither of us responded.

"They can't hear you, brother. They're under the water, chasing fish around, lids flapping. Kael leading the way with Kori hot on his trail, no doubt." Cas teased, hoping to catch a nerve.

His efforts were rewarded as Kori's voice came in response. "Yeah we're here, you idiots. And the only thing flapping is your mouths."

"Oh, feisty! We're off to a good start." Cas teased as the twins splashed their way into the water in the direction of Kori's voice.

Their reaction to the icy cold water was hysterical. It was worth a good laugh, but I didn't feel ready to spar with the twins in the slightest, especially not blindfolded. Whether I wanted to or not, it was happening. Archon intervened before the two reached Kori.

"Hold on, lets ease into it. Its no wonder with you two. This is training, a degree of discipline is required. You can work on getting your faces clobbered on your own time."

Our fathers set us into position. One of the twins was guided upstream to my left. I turned to face the direction, taking a one-handed stance, my weapon centered and ready. Quick reaction was most necessary. I didn't have to see to know I would be facing Pol.

Archon and Krayton centered themselves between their arrangements, the way my father had stood between Kori and me. The coaches were ready, and the command came from both of them simultaneously.

"Begin!"

I did all I could to remain as still and calm as possible, hoping to avoid the endeavor entirely if I could. Pol however placed no efforts in concealing himself at all.

"I know you're there, Kael. Easy on the face, yeah?"

I remained silent. He continued.

"No hard feelings about what happened. You can totally get over it and fight me now. Honest..."

I remained still, frozen in place, hardly a breath.

Pol sighed. "Well then, so much for a clean fight."

Suddenly a splash saturated me in a wave of icy droplets. A startled gasp escaped me, leaving me little time to recover from the cold shock as two wooden daggers glanced off my guard.

I retreated from his advance, leaving him a noisy trail to follow in my wake. He drove me back, as again and again I somehow managed to evade or block his aggressive offense. The hollow clanks of the wooden replicas reverberated through my being. It was luck more than skill. I couldn't remain on the defensive. I had to advance, shake free of his offensive. Otherwise, he would surely drive me further back to deeper water.

Finally, when the cold water reached my groin, I mustered the courage to send a strike his direction. He managed to defend, but only just barely. His guard was sloppy. It had been a terribly weak strike even for a blind spar, but it gave me all the confidence I needed to overcome my fear.

Again I struck towards my opponent, this time with a downward slash. My weapon struck his full guard with the double clank of both his daggers. He would attempt to lock or redirect my weapon before diving in for a strike. He always fought this way. The impact vibrated through my wooden weapon, and where hesitation once left him the chance he needed, I left no opening.

I knew what was coming next, and instead I responded with a few horizontal slices his direction. It was working, I was driving him back. After a few steps, he swept my weapon hard through its swing, stepping in to drive his shoulder into me as he did so.

He barely nudged me, but it had been enough in my contorted position to set me off balance. I fell into the icy water, completely submerging for an instant. I came up quick and gasping. Pol was already laughing.

In a panic, I reached up and pulled the cloth away from my face. When I opened my eyes, the world was a blinding blur of light and color. Pol stood over me. He too had removed his blindfold and now extended his hand to help me to my feet.

"Oh come now, it's not that cold." Pol said with a smile as I reached for his hand. "Good to have you back, brother." He pulled me to my feet.

"What's all the ruckus about? Has someone been clubbed again?" Cas's voice came from across the way.

The others stopped to free their vision as well. I was drenched, cold, and heaving. The lesson was complete.

I looked down to the cloth now draped about my neck. It was not what I had expected at all. I pulled it free to have a closer look at it. The cloth was soft and durable, a deep golden color like that of fallen leaves. At its center was a shimmering black, finely stitched raven.

I would have expected to find the symbol of my father and his father before him, that of the powerful bear. The Dóv, as it came to be known, was a symbol of strength and tranquility, power and versatility. This wonderfully stitched raven before me had been a symbol unique to my mother, a tribute to her memory.

"Cas and I had mom run through several designs for the raven before we felt she got it right. The first one looked more like a stork." Pol giggled. "Your mom was amazing with a knife. Her performance at the festival, the Dance of Blades, that's what inspired Cas and me to take up the study ourselves. The way she flipped about and slashed with lightning speed. That's why she was fresh in my mind. I guess I did get kind of carried away. Sorry, Kael."

I felt great joy as he smiled the warmest, most sincere smile I had ever seen on either of the two. It had truly been a heartfelt gift, wrapped in truth.

"Thank you, brother." I said in the strongest voice I could muster, hoping the water draining from my hair hid any tears that might be there. "I am sorry too."

The moment didn't last long. Pol broke away.

"Alright then, so can we go again? This time don't hold back, yeah? Your defense was atrocious." He teased with a wink, readying himself for another round.

"I think that's enough for today, boys." Came my father's booming voice as he made his way to us.

Pol moaned as he shrugged away in exaggerated disappointment. I was well drenched and ready to leave the icy water. As we made our way to the bank, an excited Kori approached.

"Kael! Did you see? They've made us official headbands! They're every bit as awesome as the ones the twins wear, look!" He pointed to the emblem securely placed across his hairline.

It was magnificent. The sun was a vibrant golden yellow. Around its central sphere were interwoven tongues of flame, reaching out in gold and red.

"The two colors of the sun represent both my mother and my father. Yours has a raven then?" He asked, still very much excited and fidgeting to fit his comfortably. He didn't even bother mentioning how his spar with Cas had gone. I displayed my headband for him, holding it taught with the raven full center.

"Whoa... Raikel really went the distance." Kori remarked, still giddy with excitement from the entirety of the experience.

That she certainly had. The headbands were magnificent works. It must have taken her weeks to make, and so far I had shown my gratitude by scarring one of her sons. I must have flushed with embarrassment.

"And she was glad to do it." Came my father's voice again. His broad shoulders stood proud, a smile visible at the center of his wild beard. "You boys be sure to extend your thanks. She worked hard to make these. Wear them proudly." His eyes moved between Kori and me as he said this.

"Yes, father." I replied.

Indeed, I was proud to wear this symbol. I took a deep breath and stood tall, as I pushed my hair back and fitted the headband into place with the swoosh of the knot sliding tight behind my head. I brought my arms down to my sides, feeling the cool rush of the wind as I stood there by the river. I breathed deep of it, my chest swelling with pride, the crest of the raven like a crown.

"I am proud of you, my sons." He embraced Kori and me for a moment, before turning to join the others headed for the village.

Cas and Pol were already a ways up the grassy bank with Archon. The two couldn't leave without saying anything.

"Don't forget, you owe me a rematch tomorrow, Kael!" Pol turned and shouted back. A sinister smile flashed for an instant before he disappeared into the green.

"Try and not lose your shield next time around." Cas called back his bit as well, a remark obviously directed at Kori.

"You got lucky is all! Don't count on it happening again!" Obviously Kori had fared about as well as I had. It didn't matter. Win or lose, we were all the same at the end of the day, all family.

I had never felt like such a fool, nor so honored. I was glad for these gifts, and the gift of my brothers and sisters as well. The Dóvai were my people. It was there in the year before the coming of age, that I decided I would do nothing less than honor them to the fullest. Reisenbough was all I would ever need, my blessings as plentiful as the stars.

A year made it all seem so far away. The scar on Pol's face was small and fading, but it was enough to remind me of my greater role. I was my brother's keeper. We were a team, a family. I no longer looked away from his face, the sting of shame faded like the scar. I couldn't help but wonder what the year held in store, as we stood near the slashed berry beneath the canopy. Cas had recovered from his laughter and climbed to his feet.

"A draw it is then." Pol agreed, his smile reaching just below the light pink scar on his cheek.

"A draw." Kori repeated, though he didn't seemed less than enthusiastic about the idea. He would cool his temper soon enough.

"But only this time, yeah? We can't have anyone thinking we've met our match." Cas sneered as he passed by Kori and me.

He bent down to pick up a large coil of rope, fitting it snug over his head to rest across his left shoulder. He reached over for another coil before looking back to Kori and me.

"Well are you gonna help or just stand there?"

"And why would we do that exactly? You two carried it out here on your own well enough it seems." Kori spat grumpily, even as he reached over to pick up a bundle of rope.

"Yes, but it took us all afternoon yesterday to set that up. The looks on your faces were well worth it though." Pol explained before pausing for a short laugh. "The sooner we get this rope back, the sooner we can sneak off before anyone asks us to do anything else."

"And what's so important that you two can't help prepare for the festival like everyone else?" Kori asked rather impatiently as he struggled to pick up a fourth coil of rope. There was really no need for him to try and carry so much at once, but there was no use in trying to convince him otherwise.

"Why our costumes off course!" Pol exclaimed rather excitedly.

"We have to make the finishing touches, work out our body paint. Maybe run through the routine a few more times, things of that nature." Cas explained, his brows raised and head nodding as if to express the importance of his words. "Its a big deal. We will be taking stage in front of the entire village!"

He finished with a wide gesture, as if he were on stage and opening his arms before a crowded audience.

The two of them had been going on about it for what seemed ages in anticipation of their debut at the festival. Whatever they had been practicing was a secret they kept carefully guarded, not that anyone ever went looking for them when they disappeared for practice. The early afternoons were nice and quiet without them for a bit, and had been for many moons since their approval was met.

"Well it had better be damn good for as much time as you two have put into it." Kori poked.

The way he figured, it didn't matter what the two had in the works. They'd likely treat it as a joke anyhow. He was more concerned that the two of us didn't get pulled into any possible shenanigans. We'd all look like fools on our big night.

In truth, we were both eager to see what routine the two had put together. This was to be our last festival as adolescents, and the twin brothers would be performing on the stage of the elders. This was a huge deal to us all, though neither Kori nor I would admit it around the twins. Their egos were menacing enough without our support.

The twins had talked their way into performing at the festival of harvest. Typically only adult members of the tribe were allowed the privilege to take the stage at the village center, and only after the approval of the elders. The boys managed to arrange an appearance before the council of elders after months of nagging Archon. The elders had been inspired by their appeal and decided to allow them an exception in light of their skill and tenacity. They would be performing a knife fighting exhibition no doubt.

At first I had mixed feelings regarding the upcoming performance. I was happy for them and anxious to see their skill displayed before the entire tribe, for Kori and I bragged on our abilities to hold our own against them. This would only boost our reputations as well as that of the twins.

Yet, at the same time I was bitter about it. My mother was renowned for her prowess with a knife, which she exhibited boldly against a most intimidating opponent; my father, Krayton the Mighty. I found myself afraid of what would happen if their performance was better than hers, would she be forgotten? Would I be forgotten one day as well?

Even in my moments of despair, I knew these were foolish thoughts. Thoughts of this nature were not heard among the Dóvai, so I kept them to myself. Her legacy lived on through the skill of the twins she had so inspired, and through the hearts of her loved ones, through me. My headband was a reminder of that devotion, and I wore it every day. So long as her symbol rested above my brow, she would not be forgotten.

I decided I too could live on even after my time had passed, if only I grew to be strong. Perhaps I could grow strong enough to leave my mark not only in the time of my peers, but in the time of our descendants as well. Like the stories told around the fire, someone could tell of my adventures one day. I kept this goal in secrecy, as my motivation to climb to ever greater heights. I would rise to honor her memory, to honor the history of my people. One day, my story would be legend.

The twins were reaching for greater heights too, and with the upcoming performance they were well on their way. I would not allow silly thoughts to narrow my vision, and I did all I could to replace it with pride knowing Cas and Pol would represent the best of the Dóvai.

"You two could tag along, help out if you like. It's still kind of tricky getting into costume, even more so to paint ourselves up. You could have the honor of being our assistants! What do you say, Kael?" Pol teased.

"No thanks." I replied with a smile.

"Not a chance." Kori spat, now loaded down with several hefty bundles of rope.

Cas had been delighted to help in this. He approached Kori with another coil to be sent away.

"Oui! I've got enough! You lot can handle the rest, you chuckling buzzards."

Cas broke out into another laughing fit, as Kori shifted under the weight and began awkwardly hobbling in the direction of the village. Soon he gathered a decent pace beneath him and was well on his way. He was strong as an ox, and likely to make the entire distance without a moment's rest.

Cas turned to me with the bundle of rope still in hand. "Well, looks like your turn now, Kael."

"No thanks. I'll take these two." I declined, as I picked up a second bundle of rope. I could easily carry twice the weight, but I meant to catch up to Kori and take a few off his hands.

"Ah, but that leaves Cas and me with three each! That's an odd distribution. You know we prefer even numbers." Pol teased, already comfortably fitted with three. Surely the twins knew what I meant to do.

"Now, now. No need to get whacked upside the head again, bro. Some of us are a little more scrawny than others. It may not be equal, but it's fair enough." Cas playfully poked at his brother.

"Fair it is." Pol agreed.

Before I fitted the second coil of rope over my shoulder, a barrage of thudding stomps announced someone's hasty arrival. I turned in time to see two sticky blue feet come to a stop before me, as a confidant young female voice called my attention.

"Hi, Kael."

It was Sarah. She smiled wide as she greeted me, her wild hair tousled about her delicate face. She was only a bit younger than me, and growing into her own all the same. She was the second daughter of Balthar, the finest metal worker in the village.

If not in his forge, he was with his family, a proud father of three beautiful daughters and a new baby boy. Balthar and his family lived just across the village, on the ridge adjacent to my father's hut.

Sarah had taken a liking to me as wildlings, affinity turning to affection with the coming of age. Lately, she was finding any reason to talk it seemed. I said as little as possible without seeming rude whenever she came around in hopes of inspiring her to do it less frequently. In truth, she made me nervous, and I didn't want to hear of it from the twins.

"Your father sends for you. Finding you was easy enough. That looked like fun." She nodded toward the berries, her arms crossed behind her as she spoke. Blue goop colored her legs below the knees. Her vibrant blue eyes almost seemed violet when the light hit them just right.

I didn't know how to react as she stood there smiling at me. It came as no surprise to hear the ruckus we made had caught some attention. A mob of lecturing parents sure, but I hadn't expected Sarah to appear. Flustered and looking for an exit from the situation before the twins noticed, I cut straight to the heart of the matter.

"Where is he?" I asked. My voice shaky, and lacking the slightest hint of confidence.

I heard the twins begin to snicker behind me, stifled giggles escaping them in snorting bursts. She didn't seem to mind them in the slightest.

"I'll take you, come on."

I would have much rather made the trek alone, suspecting he would most likely be found near the press at which she had been working. Before I had a chance to avoid her company, she turned with the flash of a smile and ran for the tree line.

"Keep up, if you can!" She called back as her hair flailed about behind her. I didn't feel much like chasing after her, but it was much better than hanging around Cas and Pol.

"Ah, what's this about?!" Pol exclaimed, as I set down the rope I meant to carry. I didn't know what I was setting into, but I preferred to set into it without the rope.

"Sorry." I offered sincerely.

"That's cold, man." Cas said, shaking his head with his arms crossed as if he were actually disappointed. "Shrugging your responsibilities off on someone else, so you can run off with some pretty girl. We'll remember this."

"And we have the next year with you." Pol called out.

I had already began running in the direction Sarah had gone. While the twins were having their fun, she had disappeared into some brush at the base of the Allichene.

I made my way across the short distance and entered the brush. As I rounded the broad base of one of the Allichene, she sprang out from behind some vegetation to my right. I slid to a halt just in time to avoid a collision. She laughed and gave a playful shove.

"We aren't running the whole way, silly. I just wanted to get you away from those two clowns." She said with a grin.

I didn't respond. Honestly, I was still a bit winded after chasing the berries and glad to hear we wouldn't be racing around. We continued in the direction of the village, making our way down one of many paths worn through the dense green.

"The festival tonight is going to be extra special, aren't you excited?!" She exclaimed, as if she were floating. She seemed excited enough for the both of us.

"Yeah." I responded, trying not to sound as nervous as I was. I knew where this was going.

It was obvious what was happening. A wildling could have just as easily delivered this message. My father had given the task to her with the intention of having us spend time together. We were heading in the opposite direction of the pressing stations. I could imagine his burly laughter, as he sent a wildling off to deliver this task to Sarah and set the whole thing in motion. He was playing his hand as matchmaker, as this festival marked the coming of age. It was a role typically reserved for the mothers of Reisenbough, and if it weren't for the sting it would bear I might have reminded him of that fact.

"So you'll be leaving come morning then?" She asked, knowing the answer. I was becoming slightly annoyed with the situation.

Conversation had only recently become awkward, as the expectations of our houses encroached upon us as surely as the coming of the festival. I cared for her dearly, just not for the roles desired of us. Not yet learned in how to deal with such things, I was glad that the morrow would deliver a swift escape.

"You know I will." I responded, trying not to exhibit my frustrations. "At sunrise tomorrow, I'll depart with the others as is tradition."

I attempted to sound cool about the whole endeavor. In truth I couldn't have been more anxious. There were many perils beyond the sanctity of the village, and my pride hungered for the honor I would attain upon my return. I felt ready to brave all the challenges the world could throw at me. Yet my spirit stirred with the idea, as if something were still amiss.

I would take the mark of the Dóvai upon my chest and be recognized as a man, the same as my father before me and his father before him. With it came the freedom to choose one's way in life, the right to build a home and start a family or freely travel the land. I longed for this freedom, for there were many things I wished to see, many things I wished to know. I had my reasons.

"It must be a wonderful adventure. I wish it weren't only for boys, seems less than fair." She said, kicking at the soft dark earth with a foot covered in dirty blue goop. Dirt squished between her toes as she trotted along, a jolly rhythm in her step.

"It's dangerous. Some of us may not return." I responded, regurgitating the age old explanation.

As a male, I hadn't put much thought into her perspective. Women faced their own rights of passage, rights as old and sacred as the Great Mother herself. I wasn't about to discuss this with Sarah, however. I'd sooner run.

"But that's what makes it exciting!" Sarah exclaimed. "Facing the elements, braving new unforeseen challenges, banding together to do whatever it takes to return to your people who eagerly await and celebrate your return. I would like an adventure like that someday..." She gazed up through the canopy above as she said this, longing in her eyes.

"Careful what you wish for. Danger and adventure are real enough." I warned, once again simply regurgitating the lessons of the elders. I was beginning to think I was the only member of my generation who truly listened to the wisdom they shared.

She laughed. "Same old Kael. Must you always be so serious?"

She reached out and gave another playful shove to my shoulder. She liked a good scuffle, exploiting every opportunity to spark play or prove her endurance in a grappling match. As small a frame as she had, she could hold her own well enough.

I had my fill at this point. "Whatever." I snapped in a flat, subdued tone. "If you find me less than tolerable, you are welcome to seek company elsewhere."

She stopped in her tracks, responding in a broken whisper. "Maybe I will."

I turned to see the tears welling in her eyes. I felt myself flush with embarrassment. Once again my temper managed to get the better of me. I tried to think of something to say to undo my words.

"Sarah, I-"

"You'll find your father at the mill. May you enjoy your last day as an angry child alone, son of Krayton." She barked in a voice wrought with condemnation and hurt. She turned and disappeared into the brush.

I felt simply dreadful at the slip of my tongue. Surely I was a fool. She was my friend, and I enjoyed her company more than I would admit. With the shame of self defeat heavy in my heart, I turned to continue the rest of the way on my own. Father would not likely be pleased to see me arrive alone if he had in fact meant to see us together.

We had nearly reached the village before Sarah fled my company, and I was at the very least grateful that no one had witnessed my blunder. Hopefully nothing would come of it, but somehow I doubted it. I could already see the disapproval on my father's face.

For once I found myself in need of the cryptic advice of the elders. My late grandmother Dialah would likely have offered the wisdom needed in her warm soothing voice. Unfortunately she and Darius had passed within a fortnight of one another, leaving a chill void around the fire that it's flames could not hope to warm. Instead, I was likely to meet with a good scolding from gran Helena, a far less desirable outcome.

I made my way through the village by way of the winding path that lead down toward its center. Wildlings ran amuck, already painted in all manner of color for the celebration ahead.

As I neared the stone steps leading down to the fire circles, a shiny object came crashing down to shatter at my left, giving me quite a start as I lumbered along deep in thought. I jumped clear and looked up in the direction from which it came just in time for someone to call down in apology.

"Sorry!"

They were hard at work hanging ornate bulbs from the canopy above the village center, crafted from bits of Malekaur shell. The colorful ornaments were dazzling by the light of the fires come nightfall. They shone like lanterns when the light hit them, suspended by lengths of rope that allowed them to sway and dangle in the breeze, creating a floating sea of color over the celebration that would take place below them come nightfall.

I continued through the busy village center. The place was buzzing and very much alive with the Dóvai hard at work. Heaps of firewood were stacked throughout the center to keep the fires burning deep into the night, as more was wheeled in by the cartful.

The air was a perfume of roasting meat mixed with the sweet aromas of breads and pies baking in clay ovens. My stomach churned and my mouth watered at the smell of it all. The festival was a time of warmth and celebration for our people, and this particular festival was to be unforgettable.

As I walked through the center, I was surrounded by friendly chatter and laughter as the village worked away towards a common goal. Suddenly my spirits brightened, and the fallout with Sarah seemed distant. There was so much more to look forward to on this day. For my generation, this was a once in a lifetime experience. This was my last festival as a child, a celebration of the coming of age before all our people. We were one; we were strong. We were the Dóvai.

With a new perk in my step, I picked up the pace and raced toward the river. The mill stood visible in the distance along the bank, somewhat obscured by the sea of gently swaying grass that covered the slopes leading to the water. I ran through the tall grass as it scratched and whipped at my legs. The pungent citrus smell of the field moved with the breeze, as each wonderful breath filled my lungs to carry me further.

At last I arrived at the mill. A massive wooden wheel lay on the bank, as several of the Dóvai's strongest men worked at it. They had pulled a large branch fallen from the Allichene down to the river's edge and were hacking and sawing to produce slats and planks to repair the broken wheel, where my father stood.

As I neared the work site, his eyes found me. His booming voice called out above the sounds of hacking and sawing.

"Kael my boy! Just in time." His beard bounced as he called out warmly. His smile faded a bit as he asked. "Where's Sarah?"

My heart skipped. I had thought of everything on the way except an answer to this question. I felt myself flush with embarrassment but decided to face the truth and get it over and done.

"I think I upset her." I offered timidly, averting my eyes and scratching my head as I spoke.

My father's smile returned, and he simply shook his head. "Oh boy. Sounds like you've taken your first steps into romance, and by the sound of it you're a natural like yer old man."

The men who were listening burst into laughter. He was indeed playing matchmaker and wasn't the slightest bit uncomfortable with admitting it, so openly at that. I thought of jumping into the river.

Defeat must have been evident in my expression. He chuckled, placing a hand on my shoulder. "Don't fret over it, son. You've got your whole life ahead of you. It's not the last time you're likely to meet the scorn of a woman. Its best to let her cool down a bit, trust me. You can make it right in time if you so choose. She has her mother's temper, count yourself lucky you haven't got a black eye."

The men erupted in laughter again.

"Now, I need you to pick up about a dozen pins like this one from Balthar. Run 'em back here as quick as you can." My father instructed. He handed me a heavily rusted iron pin, roughly the size of a finger.

"The damned wheel broke away from the shaft again. This time we mean to fix it good. Take this to carry 'em." He handed over a leather pouch along with the rusty pin.

"Father." I responded in acknowledgment before I turned to run back in the direction of the village.

As I ran up the grassy slope toward the village, the same wind that whipped through the grass seemed to flow through me as well, returning the pep to my step and making the climb easy. My father hadn't been the slightest upset by my blunder with Sarah. Better yet, I had been handed an opportunity to visit Balthar's shop.

Returning from the river offered my favorite view of Reisenbough. The lengthy, intertwined branches of the Allichene towered over the village, adding a majesty to the soft billowing smoke that rose to dissipate through the canopy. Balthar's shop was attached to the third outermost dwelling on the lesser western ridge.

Closer to the village the grass was well trodden and maintained by free ranging goats. The smell of them was somehow sweet mixed with the rich smells of the land, the healthy green grass soft and plush beneath my bare feet. I made my way up a worn dirt trail carved by hoof and foot alike, playfully shooing a few carefree grazers from my path as I walked.

In no time I stood before Balthar's shop. It was a crude open shack built into the side of the stone hut he called home. Two stone pillars held a roof of mud and sticks aloft at one end, the other rested atop the domed hut. A single wall lined the rear of the shop, constructed of the same stone and mortar as the hut to which it was attached.

A fierce heat radiated from a large blackened stone forge. A rhythmic clanking sent sparks of yellow and orange hissing through the air, as the hulking beast of a man that was Balthar pounded at a glowing length of metal.

Balthar was Reisenbough's finest metal worker, not that he had much in the way of competition. As a young man he had traveled the lands in hopes of besting the trade of forging metal. His journey had led him to the Tomb of the Shadjah. Within the ominous confines of the tomb he had studied under a surreptitious tribe of metal workers, known as the Salvek.

Before his ambitions sought them out our people knew nothing of the Salvek, though we had unknowingly traded for their works many times, unaware of their origins. They were the finest metal workers in all the land, as Balthar came to discover. They lived a reclusive existence deep within the confines of the forbidden tomb, trading only with the peoples of the White Hallow.

Balthar had chased rumors to discover the hidden trade routes in hopes of locating the masters he sought. He had succeeded in this task, only to be shunned in his initial attempts to gain their tutelage.

Eventually they granted his request for apprenticeship, but only after he demonstrated his intense desire to learn the trade, an endeavor of which Balthar never spoke. According to rumor, he had been sworn to secrecy by the Salvek. Balthar himself only laughed at such accusations. He alone knew the story of how he earned the right to whatever knowledge the Salvek had bestowed. Whatever had transpired, a heavy limp suggested he had earned his trade well enough.

When he returned to the Dóvai, he brought with him an invaluable trade. His skill was mastery, and with it he supplied Reisenbough with all manner of tools, ornaments, and perhaps more notably, weapons.

Balthar looked up from the radiant yellow-orange length of metal, his deep brooding eyes appearing huge through the crude goggles of stained glass that clung tight to his pudgy round face.

"Kael, my boy! What brings you to my shop? Come for Sarah have you?" He asked in a rather squeaky voice for such a large man.

His arms were bigger round than my torso, and his gut was as large as a reisen berry. He lumbered toward me as he pulled the goggles back from his face and landed a warm slap on my shoulder that left me jolted, though I weathered it well enough.

"Actually sir, I've come on behalf of my father to deliver a request. He and the others need more pins like this one to repair the mill." I explained, as I produced the rusted metal pin my father had given me.

"Ah, I see." Said Balthar, turning to look uneasily over his shoulder toward the back of the workshop. I couldn't see around him to know what it was that drew his attention, but thought nothing of it.

"And uh, how many is he asking for?" A smirk rose within his scraggly light colored beard. It was patchy, scorched in places below his chin.

"A dozen should do." I answered.

"A dozen?!" Balthar blurted with a laugh. "I suppose it should. That old rickety thing falls to pieces more and more with each passing year."

He made his way over to a work bench where he bent to sort through various wooden bins stacked rather sloppily beneath. The tinkling sound of various bits of metal clanking together soon filled the shop.

"I should have a few like this somewhere under here..."

As he sorted through the bins I looked around the place. It was always interesting to see his various works, proudly on display along the racks that lined the workshop. Along the wall that joined the shop to his hut there were several axes of various sizes and a massive hammer that I couldn't hope to lift. On the workbench adjacent to where Balthar crouched were four shiny new blades, resting as if on display atop a well stained wool cloth. I ventured closer to have a look.

There atop the cloth were two sets of twin daggers. They had been polished to a sleek finish, and looked to be deadly sharp with wicked fine points. The blades seamlessly formed into wings at the handles, the regal stare of metallic eagles at the end of each. I didn't dare touch them. These fine works were undoubtedly meant for the twins. Lucky devils.

A repetitive motion caught my attention from the rear corner of the shop. The awe drained from me, as my eyes widened. A rather miffed looking Sarah sat atop a wooden stool, dirty feet casually kicked up on the end of a weapon wrack. She rest her weight on her left elbow, back against the outer wall of the workshop. The motion had been a knife she stood on its point with her left index finger and set to spin atop a wooden work bench with the flick of her right. She silently glared my way, though it felt more like her searing gaze shot through me.

As our eyes met, she drove the knife hard into the bench. She left it there, jabbed in the wood, as she rose to her feet and marched her way by me without breaking a rather contemptuous stare. She left the shop without so much as a word. I watched her go, unable and unsure of what I should have said, if I should have said anything. I stood there with her hulking father, a man that could swing that same hammer I couldn't hope to lift.

"She's been in a ripe mood since she came in." Balthar explained.

I turned to face him. "It's my doing, sir. I apologize, I meant no disrespect." I offered most sincerely. I felt foolish again.

Balthar's laugh came light and airy. "She'll get over whatever it was in her own time. No use in fretting over it, boy. Believe me, between a wife and three daughters I'd have worried myself into an early grave by now. You'll never know what you did, and she'll never quite be able to explain it. Just gotta move along. Besides, she won't likely stay mad for long, not at you anyway..."

I didn't know how to respond, nor what to think on the matter. It was awkward at best. Balthar too seemed suddenly uncomfortable and moved to change the subject, clearing his throat.

"Hrrm, so you like my latest work? Them's a couple of little beauties there." He said excitedly, pointing to the daggers I had been gawking over.

"I've had them ready for a few days now." Balthar went on. "I don't usually put so much into the detail work, makes it hard to keep the balance just right. Well, that and I'm not much of an artist." He chuckled a bit. He knew they were splendid in design. "Here, feel for yourself."

He picked up one of the shiny daggers and presented it. I took the dagger in hand, and instantly felt the mastery of his work. It was slightly heavier than it appeared, but well balanced and undoubtedly strong. The point looked sharp as a razor. The thought of what these could do in the hands of the twins was terrifying.

"Wow..." The compliment came naturally as my eyes moved over the sleek surface of the blade.

Balthar chuckled, pleased to hear what he already suspected. His work was splendid. The regal birds stared down the length of the blade, wings spread for the quillon. The grip was soft to the touch. The fine leather creaked pleasurably against my palm as I squeezed tight. These were indeed works of mastery.

"Balthar sir, these are amazing." I complemented. I offered the blade back to his charge.

"Why thank you kindly. It's always good to see my work appreciated. They are going to love these." He smiled wide as he marveled once more at the blade before setting it to rest with the others.

"The pins you need are in the box atop the bench here." He said as he moved back toward the workbench opposite. "Take what you need, not sure there are quite a dozen there. Leave the box on the bench. It'll be my reminder to make more. Now, I'm gonna get back to working on this last little project before I call it a day. The festival is nearly upon us."

He placed his colored glass goggles back on his face and reached back into the forge, taking hold of a glowing metal bar with a set of iron tongs. He positioned the bar into place, grabbed hold of his mallet and set to work. Once more torrents of sparks shot through the air, cooking it with each pounding swing of the mallet.

I retrieved the leather satchel and filled it with dark metal pins like the one my father had sent. The pouch was heavy, and I heaved as I lifted it from the bench. Balthar continued to hammer as I waived my farewell, nodding in affirmation.

"See you tonight!"

With the boom of the hammer, I fitted the pins over my shoulder and stepped out from the heat of Balthar's workshop just in time to meet Nisha, Balthar's oldest daughter.

"Hello, Kael." She greeted. "I hear my sister is in a bit of a spoiled mood. Wouldn't know anything about that would you?"

She shifted her weight with a bounce, adjusting her grip on the child on her hip. The wildling that clung to the soft gray rabbit furs snug around Nisha's full breasts was Neeko, her youngest. She shyly peeked at me with watery eyes that suggested she had been sobbing moments before.

"Aye..." I responded, unsure what to say and eager to move on with my objective.

Father said to be quick. I went to casually make my way around her, but politely stopped when she continued.

"Hold on, Kael. She's upset, but she'll be alright. If you're looking to cheer her up she really likes the lilies that grow near the spring north of the pass. They grow big and red, surely you know the ones?" She asked, shuffling the weight of the child across to her other hip. "Might do to pick up a few to go with an apology." She suggested warmly.

"Yes ma'am. Thank you."

I was beginning to suspect everyone in Reisenbough was involved with arranging the two of us, but the flowers were a good idea nonetheless. It felt strange to have her upset with me, and I was ready to be over it. I bid farewell to Nisha and continued down the path from Balthar's shop. The air was growing crisp with the onset of evening settling over Reisenbough, warm and rich with the scents of late summer. A cool damp still lingered from the rains the day before. I breathed deep of it, feeling lifted as if the very air was latent with energy. What a perfect day for the festival.

The great branches gently swayed overhead, their large spade-like leaves softly rustling in the breeze, accenting the golden beams of light along the edge of the fields with added hues of green. Night would soon slip over the grove. The sky was already giving way to the shades of early evening, leaving just enough time for me to both deliver the pins and travel to the spring before dark.

I looked to the other ridge across the village center, toward home. My father's hut of gray stone stood dark and empty across the distance. I lingered for a moment to savor a gentle breeze as it eased over me and listened to the sounds of rustling leaves and the hustle of the Dóvai wrapping up the preparations for the festivities ahead.

I took another deep breath and let the moment go, the sweetness of it filling me once again. I secured my package and dashed toward my goal, racing past warm faces and a few chalky textured homes of cut stone. The green of the leaves above was radiant in the light of the waning sun, soon to disappear far beyond the giant trees of the elder forest.

I ran through the open field, feeling weightless as I made my way down to the river. In no time, I arrived back at the work site near the mill, where my father and the others stood chatting. The new parts were arranged and ready to be fitted with the pins I brought. I handed them to my father as I caught my breath.

"Whoa now lad, no need to tire yourself out before your big night." My father teased. "The last thing you want to do is spend such a nice day working. Bwah-ha-ha!" His spirits seemed unusually good for this time of year.

He turned and handed the pins to the others. They set to work fitting the new pieces around the center of the wheel, hammering away with crude mallets to secure them into place.

"Thanks, my boy. We will have this finished up just in time for the party, if we can manage to get the damned thing back on the axle well enough." His tone made this sound like it was to be the real chore at hand.

I was hoping to dip out before he asked for my help in lifting the massive thing. No request came however. Instead, my father placed a hand on my shoulder.

"Go get yourself ready for tonight. Your cousin Tori made plenty of paint this season, all manner of colors. Stop by if you like. You and Kori can ready yourselves for the festival in style. That's if the wildlings haven't made a mess of it all by now. They have four now, bless her heart."

He looked over toward Prov, the proud father. He had overheard, smiling wide as he called out.

"Aye! Four lovely little angels they are."

"Little devils is more what I hear." My father teased. He chuckled to himself.

"We're expecting our second any day now." Pek added, as he reached for another pin.

"Just wait until number three comes around. One wildling is enough, two are a handful, but three..." Added one of the older men.

"Me and mine are happy with two, but likely to end up with a third if tonight goes well." Teased another, followed by a wave of laughter.

"Oh, now look what I've started. Best run along, Kael. They'll talk about their pups til nightfall if you don't get a move on. Fathers love to brag." Father scoffed playfully. He was perhaps the most guilty of this. "See you tonight, son."

He waived with a warm smile, a gentle light in his eyes. He turned to aid the others in finishing the wheel.

"Alright, let's get this over with. That wine's not going to drink itself."

I made my way through the village once more, this time through the bustling center and past the stage where the twins would give their performance after the words of the elders. A few members of the tribe were busy setting the reflective casts around the torches along its base. When they were lit later this evening, all would be able to see the events as if the sun itself shown on the stage. I felt a rush of excitement, and hurried on toward the mountain pass.

I made my way through the dense vegetation that grew in the loose dark soil of the Arching forest, the feel of it soft and cool beneath my feet. The smell of the lower forest was rich and earthy. The red of the lilies popped through the deep greens, letting me know the spring was just ahead. The smell of fresh water permeated the air as I neared.

The surface of the small pond was calm. Not even a ripple disturbed the crystal waters of the spring, making it seem as if the few bits of plant matter along its surface were floating in midair. The lilies flourished in bushels around the spring, lining the swollen trunks of the Allichene.

Their vibrant red petals were a beautiful contrast to the smooth milky gray bark of the sacred trees. I knelt down near a cluster of the delicate red flowers. It seemed a shame to harm such beauty, but I drew my knife and severed a few select flowers for my cause.

Night wasn't far, and the colors of twilight were beginning to seep down from the canopy into the deepening blues of the lower forest, adding a dreamlike quality to this place. I wanted to linger a bit longer, rather enjoying the solitude of the moment. I breathed a sigh and made my leave. With a little luck, I'd have just enough time to get ready before joining the others. Small red bouquet in hand, I returned to Reisenbough.

Next, I made my way to cousin Tori's hut. She had married Prov, son of Raemon, and the two lived further south along the same ridge as my father. I arrived as three of their four children ran screaming and screeching around the hut, all spattered in vibrant shimmering colors where they had painted all over one another.

Tori appeared in the doorway, pushing the hide flap aside to peer out. Colorful little handprints were smeared along the bottom of the hide. She clutched her youngest by the hand. He stood at her side, looking to me with curiosity.

"Ah Kael! Good to see you. I was beginning to wonder if you would make it before I set out. Kori already came by, seemed to be in a bit of a rush. Come in!" She gestured for me to enter.

I made my way through the door. Their hut was a bit larger than ours, comprised of two domes joined together. It smelled of flowers and soot. The shimmering colors of paint were smeared everywhere, little handprints telling a story. She released the young boy's hand.

"Go play with the others, Kev."

The boy hadn't taken his eyes off me, a sparkling weaver spider artfully drawn along the right side of his pudgy face. He scampered off through the door without a word.

Tori made her way to the other side of the chamber where some high shelves were built into the sloped wall of the hut. She reached for the highest shelf, having to stand on her tiptoes to do so.

"I saved your favorite colors, though I didn't have much red to work with this season." She retrieved three small clay vesicles. "Here you are; green, yellow, and a little bit of red left in this one here." She explained, as she waived one of the containers.

She offered them over. I carefully placed the stems of the small bouquet of lilies in my waistcloth as not to mangle the delicate petals before I got them to their moody recipient.

"Ah what a lovely bunch of flowers you've got there, Kael! For someone special I take it?" She asked warmly.

"Not really." I responded, as I reached for the paints.

"No?" She smiled. "Well that's too bad. They sure are lovely."

I pulled one of the flowers out from the rest and offered it to her. "Here, have one."

"Oh why thank you, Kael!" She exclaimed.

Her smile brightened as she took the flower and began working it into her hair. It complimented the yellow, blue and green paint smeared across her arms and shoulders. Clearly the children had aided in painting their mother as well.

"That's very sweet of you. Whoever she is, she'll be happy to have them."

I tried not to think too far into the matter. "Thank you for the paint, Tori. See you at the festival."

"Anytime." I heard her call sweetly after me, as I took my leave.

I hurried home along the ridge. The center below was already brimming with my fellow tribesmen spattered in all colors of iridescent body paint. Elaborate costumes accented the crowd, as they danced about. The music had already begun with the sounds of woodwinds whistling over the thumping drive of the drums. The gully was soon to be alive with the hearts of the Dóvai.

A light shown from inside my father's hut, and as I entered the door I saw Kori struggling to secure a set of glittery wings over his shoulders.

"Kael! Just in time. Can you help me finish with my costume?" He pleaded in frustration.

I set the paints I had brought on the stones around the hearth and went to his aid. He had managed to acquire a set of Malekaur wings and worked them into a makeshift harness to wear. The large insect wings shimmered along the dense fibrous frames that encompassed the soft membranous segments, each larger and slightly different than its smaller predecessor from joint to tip. They would no doubt look splendid as he masqueraded about the festival. It didn't take long to secure the drooping wings at his back.

"Thanks, Kael. Gotta rush. I'm meeting Tiahla, she's probably already there waiting for me. She accepted! We are to attend the festival together, can you believe it?!" Kori exclaimed, happy to boast he had apparently caught the attentions of the young maiden he fancied.

It was no surprise at all to anyone other than Kori. He was always too focused on winning her favor to realize he already had it. She swooned and giggled whenever he came round.

He had certainly put more effort into the detail of this year's attire, painted in broad finger width stripes of yellow and orange from his ankles up to his shoulders. He had managed quite well, his look both colorful and cohesive.

Each of us had our reasons I suppose, that which drove us through tomorrow. His intended was a robust young beauty with soft brown eyes that sparkled as if she wore a smile, even when she didn't. She was a warm and caring soul, and Kori was like a blissful child when he had her attention. She also had the fullest breasts of all the young maidens, a point the twins constantly teased to be Kori's true motive.

"Wonderful." I said as warmly as possible, though my excitement was nowhere near his own.

He stood tall and proud of his work, two stalks of grass fitted to stand like antennae from his headband.

"What do you think?" He asked, placing his fists at his hips and puffing out his chest.

He wore nothing but the headband, the wings, and his waist cloths spattered with paint from where he had apparently wiped his fingers between colors. I smiled at this.

"Well done, brother." I admitted. I had no such costume planned. I hadn't the faintest idea what I would do, and time was running out.

The evening was growing chill, and the waters of the Veylspring would be colder still. I planned to wear my tunic, maybe even bring a fur along. Honestly, I didn't feel inspired to paint in the slightest, but

I would look silly appearing before the entire tribe as if I had forgotten the festival.

As Kori made a few final adjustments to his wing harness, the hide flap over the doorway moved aside. It wasn't father as I had expected. Instead, Sarah appeared in the door. A wonderful array of rippling blue and chalky white covered her exposed skin, outlined with a smooth, deeper shade of violet. Her face was lightly dusted with the chalky white paint, a thick band of violet across her eyes. The contrast made the blue of her eyes appear all the more radiant. They were calm, where anger had been.

"May I come in?" She asked politely.

In a panic, I fumbled for an excuse. "This is my father's house, I can't-"

"Of course, come on in!" Kori interrupted. She entered, letting the deerskin fall closed behind her.

"You aren't ready?" She asked, looking most extravagant in a way I'd never seen.

Her hair was neatly braided and bound back, revealing more of her delicate features. She too was coming into age. Shimmering blue dots traced the curve of her brow that crossed through both the violet and the white. The same blue lightly traced the soft outline of her lips.

"No, not yet." I stated the obvious. "Is it okay if I work?" I requested, gesturing to the paints along the hearth.

"Of course. Would you like some help?" She offered, stepping into the center to stand next to me.

I felt my eyes widen in panic. I hadn't expected this in the slightest. "Uh, n-no thanks. Kori is here. He can-"

"No can do brother, I'm outta here. Running late, remember? This is my big chance, I can't miss it for the world, let alone to rub paint across your greasy hide. Sarah's already offered, she can fix you up. If you're not too fragrant for her... At least the parts of you covered in berry got a rinse today." Kori laughed.

He had a fair point, I hadn't bathed that day or perhaps the day before either. I'd been far too busy running around the village. I comically sniffed myself for their amusement and stood proud and strong in my musk. Kori and Sarah laughed.

"You smell nearly as strong as your grandfather." Sarah joked.

"Thank you." I responded rather proudly. "He'd love to hear it."

"He'd tear up for sure, from pride as well as the stink." Kori teased with a brimming smile as he made for the door. His spirits were certainly high. "Fix him up nice, Sarah. Leave it to him, and he'd just go as he is now."

He sputtered merrily as he disappeared through the doorway with the shuffle of stolen insect wings. As soon as Kori was gone, Sarah came close.

"Now, let's get you ready. Lose the top."

"I'd rather keep it. It's chill out." I responded, knowing she wouldn't take no for an answer.

"The fire will keep you warm. Besides, you'll look brave and strong without it." She insisted. "Now come on, arms up."

I didn't need to go without my tunic to prove myself, nor did I require her assistance in the slightest. Not willing to risk another fallout I lifted my arms. She slid the worn hide tunic up and over my head, getting it caught around my unruly mane of dark hair as she did so. She tugged a few time before relenting.

"I'll let you work that out." She laughed, reaching for the paints along the fire pit.

I pulled the tunic free of my hair, my headband pulling free with it. I held onto the headband and tossed my tunic at the cluttered lump along the southern wall of the hut that was my bed. I felt ridiculous, and my frustration began to rise at my predicament.

"Those are really nice." She said, nodding toward the bouquet of red lilies still stuffed along my waistband.

Instantly I felt like a fool, having all but forgotten. "Yeah," I spewed as I carefully retrieved the flowers and presented them to Sarah. "They're for you."

She placed the small clay pot of red paint back along the hearth with the others and took hold of the small bundle of flowers. She was glowing and content. I hadn't botched the gesture too badly.

"Thank you, Kael! These are my favorite." She brought them close to her face and closed her eyes as she breathed deep of them. The bouquet was well battered, a few of the flowers had already begun to wilt...

"You're welcome." I responded, glad to see she was happy to have them despite the poor presentation.

Out of the small bouquet I had assembled, only two of the flowers remained intact. The other few flowers had been mangled and crumpled, petals missing.

She selected the best two flowers and brought them up to her hair. She closed her eyes with a smile, as she skillfully worked the vibrant red flowers to rest slightly above and to the left of her soft, colorful face.

As I watched her do this, I noticed for perhaps the first time that she had bloomed much like the lilies she adorned. Her slender frame was strong and capable, but appeared soft and delicate in every way. She had blossomed into a fine young maiden of our people without my realizing, and tonight's festival was just as special for her as it was for me. How shortsighted of me that I hadn't noticed before, so narrow and selfish had my attentions been.

This realization did little to still my nerve, as her eyes suddenly sprang open with a radiant burst of blue. Their sparkle glistened as a smile returned to her lips, the deep red lilies ablaze in her thick dark hair.

"You look lovely..." I finally managed.

She brightened. "Why thank you, Kael. You actually said something nice. Any stoic words of wisdom to mark the occasion?" She asked rather sarcastically, cutely shrugging to one side.

"I think gran might have a few." I teased, and together we laughed.

"Let's get you ready." She rose from where she knelt over the paints and moved closer to me. "I think we should start with red." She said, dipping two fingers into the small container of red paint before she brought them to the center of my chest. The paint was cold, and her touch was soothing. Chills rippled across my skin, as she ran a thick stripe of red down my sternum.

Her fingers came to rest on my waist cloth just below my naval, the lingering weight of her touch pulling at the snug fit of the wrap. Her words came soft and low.

"I spoke with my mother at the return ceremony. You missed it. All four returned."

"Ah..." I responded. Indeed I had missed the ceremony. It was good to know the last troupe had fared so well. "Blessed news."

"I was mad at you, you know. For missing it. I mean, I was mad at you anyway." She laughed. "Mother asked me why I was upset, and I couldn't really answer."

She stopped for a moment, as if contemplating her next words.

"Turn around." She directed, as she dipped her fingers again in the red paint.

I turned away from her and felt the slick cool of her touch return to my skin, this time leading down along my spine. Another ripple of chills washed over me.

"I'll spare you the finer details of her lecture, but she said it would be a shame to waste a day on something as useless as a grudge, especially a day as important as this..." She reached again for a dab of the dwindling red paint.

"I see." I said, having nothing better with which to respond.

Her fingers continued to work the paint across my skin, bringing waves of chills each time she did so.

She finished with the paints in no time. My arms and legs were covered in banded stripes of green and yellow. She rummaged through the paints Kori had used and found a shade of blue she liked and used it to trace along my ribs and face. The remaining red she used sparingly, shadowing around my eyes with the leftover blue. With the last of the red, she coated the palm of her right hand and placed it over my heart, a moment that made it skip in my chest.

I couldn't see the finished result, but I felt ready. I tied my raven headband proudly to rest again at my brow. With a new found appreciation for her company, I took Sarah’s hand in mine, and we departed for the festival well underway.

The Dóvai

The village center was a writhing blur of sound and color. The drums thundered, as generations of sons and daughters danced like the flames that lit the night, vibrant and filling the hallow with life. Sarah and I made our way to the heart of the nearest fire circle. Colorful bodies moved and glittered in refracted light, as bright leaping flames chased shadows to the rhythm of the drums. The many shell lanterns hanging from the canopy wildly reflected the light over the happy throng. The amount of color was surreal, the village both aglow and alive.

As we made our way into the crowd, painted faces greeted us with blessings from all around.

"Saiyu!"

My grandfather was already well drunk on wine and laughing hysterically, as several colorfully painted wildlings wrestled at him. He all but stumbled off his seat as yet another of the wildlings pounced upon his back, and he likely would have were it not for one of the little scamps hanging from his outstretched prosthetic leg like a counterweight. He seemed to be having as much fun as they were.

"Kael!" He called out merrily, his smile brimming through a multicolored beard. "Get over here, lad! Who is this lovely young flower you've got with you?"

"Grandfather, it's Sarah." I responded.

The disbelief on his face for a moment was as genuine as my own had been. That or he was poking fun. His aged old face crinkled as he looked her over.

"Balthar's girl? No!" He all but fell back in disbelief. "Last I saw she looked like one of these scrawny boys running about, and just as mean too. This here's a young lady, looks to me."

His words slurred. He swayed a bit as he shot a wink my direction. His smile was every bit as warm as his spirit.

Sarah stepped forward to playfully engaged my titan grandfather. "Oh none to worry old timer." She widened her stance, placing both feet firmly on the Earth and raising her guard. "I'm only a lady for tonight. I'll get back to running them boys like sheep come tomorrow."

Kraegar burst into laughter. His deep bellowing startled the wildlings, sending them to scurry for cover. Indeed his deep laughter caught the attentions of many, rising above the rhythmic drive of the music.

"Bwar-har-har-har! Ah, there she is. Looks like a young woman sprouted under all that hair and dirt."

His brimming smile returned. He reached out a hand, and she met it with both of hers. My grandfather looked from her to me and nodded with approval, as the wildlings moved back in around him.

"Take care of one another. That's all it takes..." He sniffled a bit. "And have a drink or two while you're at it!" He laughed as he reached for a much depleted wine bladder. "Now you two go have some fun! This old man is where he is tonight."

His attentions returned to battle as the wildlings ambushed, climbing over him once again. The oldest of them had an impossible mess for hair, swinging from my grandfather's massive arm as it lifted the wine bladder to his mouth.

For a moment they had my envy, for I had spent many a festival in this very way when I was a wildling. When at last he tired, my grandfather would gather their attentions with epic tales, told with the slur of wine by the heat of the fire. He told them but once a year, for the best stories are reserved and told sparingly. They were tales of terrible beasts from the past, of war, of triumph and brotherhood. As a wildling, my favorite stories came from my unruly grandfather, Kraegar the Proud.

As we made our leave, I heard him begin the tale of Keamett, the demon hatual that claimed the life of his late son. I knew this story well, as did all members of my house. This particular story had touched the hearts of my kin, and though I loved my grandfather's stories I did not care to hear this one again. It was a tale that most certainly marred my memories, preventing complacency during my father's lessons. Krayton the Mighty had slain the beast of legend, one of the many icons carved into his powerful bow.

Soon he had them gripped with his tale. Every year his stories grew more fantastic. The beasts grew larger and the battles more fierce, as if the details somehow became sharper with time. As each new generation heard Kraegar's words, the emotion in their reactions rekindled my own. The experience became grim with age, for the older children grew to understand why he shared such stories.

Sarah and I bumped our way deeper into the crowd toward the village center. The drums beat faster, a new energy rippled through the people in a wave of excitement. All manner of costume and painted patterns decorated the bodies of my tribesmen, bringing even familiar faces together under exotic anonymity.

The energy reflected in my heart, and the music had me. Sarah seemed to feel it too. We had found our place among the Dóvai. She turned and began to dance with the music, her movements rattling the beaded tendrils that hung loosely from her hips. I began to move with her, lost in the flashing colors reflected in all directions and the relentless drive of the drums.

The bouncing crowd resounded with whoops and cries, dancers jumping high in the air around the raging fires that lit the village center. The excitement swelling in the village seemed to drive the players, and the music became more and more lively, evolving freely as the night pressed on. All worries melted. Fear and sorrow were not in this place, not on this night.

Even the lashing tongues of the flames seemed to move in time with the powerful harmony, celebration surging through the throbbing pulse of stomping feet and beating drums. Bursts of color flashed wildly about the writhing mass of elaborately painted bodies, all moving in time, the drums the heartbeat driving them on.

Soon we were both soaked in sweat, glistening like the colorful paint. The smell of wine permeated the air, mingled with the smell of fire and a hundred dancing, sweat covered bodies. My senses were overwhelmed with the splendor of our people, as Sarah and I danced our way around the inner fire circle in progression, leaping and jumping in time with the music. Every now and then a celebratory call would sound over the crowd to be passed and answered in time, reverberating through the village.

Eventually the drums slowed, the melody softened, gently reducing the energy from its roaring din. I looked to Sarah, feeling more content than ever. The glittering paint shimmered across her skin, making her eyes seem like two precious blue jewels.

The enticing smell of roasted meats, breads, and sweat pies crept through the crowd as it began to thin. I felt my stomach rumble at the smell of the delicious feast. I took Sarah's hand and pulled her through the crowd. She held on tight, as if by some chance I might slip away.

We broke through the sea of painted bodies, arriving at last to the source of the delicious aroma that led our way. Along the base of the western ridge were makeshift tables loaded with all manner of fruits and vegetables. There were salads of greens from the shaded fields, roasted venison, and a massive carved boar on the center most table.

Breads, cakes, and pies lined the outermost tables, with both roasted and fresh vegetables heaped between. My mouth watered at the sight of this bounteous harvest. The seasons had been kind to us, and the village viewed this as a good omen for passage through the coming winter.

A tiny growl rumbled, and a giggle escaped my companion. It seemed both our stomachs were churning. Like two ravenously hungry feral youths, Sarah and I rushed to get a place in the shuffling line of costumed bodies come to feast. When at last we reached the delicious bounty, whatever caught our fancy was scooped into a shallow clay basin hugged at my waist.

Once we gathered a heaping pile of food we headed for the main stage. It was set at the heart of the village, where the two ridges met. We navigated through the crowd to get as close as we could, shuffling past those already gathered on our search for a place to sit.

We found a nice spot not far off the northeast corner of the stage and settled down. I placed the hefty tray of food between us. She wasted no time, tearing off a large chunk of glazed sweetbread. The fruity smell of berry preserves rushed the air, as the soft bread was stretched apart. She took a bite and chewed slow. Her eyes eased closed with the experience.

"Mmmm, so good." She said through a mouthful, nodding in approval. "Worth the wait. I reckon after you leave I'll gorge myself nice and fat on what's left and just sleep the winter through." She joked, stuffing another bite of sweet bread into her mouth.

"Find yourself a nice cave as well then?" I teased, picking at a tender cut of roasted meat. My mouth was more than ready for the savory rush. It all but melted on my tongue, seared and well flavored by the heat of the flame.

"Oh most certainly!" She laughed, as she sorted over the heaping platter to make her next selection.

"Well I suggest you stay clear of anything south of the mountain. Not the friendliest of neighborhoods, and I hear there's a nasty bug problem." I took another bite of the scrumptious meat.

Her jaw fell slack in a devious expression, as if a smile were waiting to follow her next words. "And who better suited for advice on the matter than a son of Dóv? Lucky me..."

Her eyes raised in time with her smile, rising with the corners of her pretty, blush lips. I stammered clumsily, choking on a bit of meat. I had reached for something clever, but my mind was still processing her implications, and I stammered something blatantly agreeable instead.

"Th-the Dóv is the symbol of my father's house..."

Much to my relief, the deep thump of the drums drew the attention of the people. Sarah and I looked on, as the village elders took the stage in ceremonial procession. Each was accompanied onstage by a torch bearing escort, sons and daughters from the various houses they represented.

The elders stood center stage, as the escorts lit the lamps around its edges, where the Dóvai anxiously gathered. The drums pounded. The escorts left the stage in a similar procession and extinguished their torches. Bursts of brazen whoops and cries arose throughout the crowd, as the tribe recognized the symbols of their houses and paid homage. All waited to hear the words of the elders.

Master Yani was the first to step forth, elder of the house Ariae. The symbol of this house was that of a proud lion, named after the founding father Ariae. Those who shared kinship under this symbol roared and cheered before Master Yani, who bowed in acknowledgment and raised a frail weathered hand to bring them to silence.

"Welcome! Brothers and sisters all, we are once again blessed by the Great Mother. Another bold year, the Dóvai honor the fruits of the land with the festival of harvest. Let us celebrate our years, as we remember the time of our fathers, and most importantly, honor those who will inherit the years still to come."

The tribe shook the night. Sarah and I added our own cries to those of our people. The elder's hand raised to return the silence.

"A fruitful year indeed, three little blessings born to the house of Ariae. We welcome two sons and a sweet little girl. Tamus, born of Yeheli, daughter of Waegrah the Wise and Yakov, son of Daeyron."

Yani found them in the crowd, presenting them with an outstretched hand. The family stood proud, lifting their young one high for all to see. Together we all cheered.

"Trevon, born of Shaela, daughter of Adriena and Moish, son of Vren." Yani presented another family from among the crowd. Cheers followed.

"Rael, born of Driana, daughter of Krav and Remos, son of Leos."

The family stood to be recognized, their little one giggling merrily as she was hoisted aloft. A single tooth poked from her smiling gums.

"What little blessings they are." Yani smiled. "Now let us recognize those who will soon leave us to undergo that sacred pilgrimage, those brave youths destined for honor and manhood. Tonight the House of Ariae recognizes the coming of age for three sons."

Those of the house Ariae rocked and cheered loudly, as the three made their way onstage to be recognized by all. There was Devin, aloof and arrogant. Already full of himself, the kind words of his great uncle did little to stir him. He stood in pose, chest out where the mark would be.

Kris and Nattan were far more engaging. Each emboldened by the warm words of Master Yani. Each bowed in respect as Master Yani concluded his blessings. Both were well received with the warmth of the Dóvai replying in turn.

"May your journey bring you home, my sons." Master Yani bowed deeply, grace had not yet left him in his age.

"Saiyu." The prayer rippled through the Dóvai.

The tribe yipped and cheered as the sons of Ariae embraced Master Yani and bolted from the stage to be greeted by teary eyed loved ones. Love, pride, honor; family was everything.

Cheers turned to chatter, as a stoic figure took center stage next to Master Yani. He stood tall, elaborately painted and bearing the mark of the Dóvai upon his chest. Yani raised his hands, the drums began to roll. The chatter died instantly.

"Brothers and sisters! May I present before you all, a man risen of the house Ariae, Aldus of the Wind!"

Sarah and I jumped and cheered, the power of the Dóvai shaking through the village. Aldus stepped forth, raising his fists high. We yipped and cheered in honor of his return, in reverence of this great symbol of passage.

"Indeed a blessed year. Thank you One and All." He bowed before the Dóvai. "Elder Mildrah, the stage is yours."

Master Yani waived with a smile before turning to shuffle toward the back of the stage where the other house elders stood. My grandfather was among them, napping on his feet it seemed.

Mildrah stepped forth, taking center stage. Her unkempt silver hair was bound into a frazzled mess behind her. She was known for her wild spirit and unconventional methods. Blue and white patterns covered her body in ceremonial art. She was the house elder of Geenah Vesh, represented by a lotus blossom with a flame at its center, typically depicted in blue. The heritage of Geenah Vesh was curious, the knowledge of medicines and herbs passed along their lineage for generations.

"Thank you, Master Yani. Well spoken, old friend. Tradition holds strong, your words honor us all. I'll spare everyone the effort on my part, you all hear plenty from me as it is." She joked.

A chuckle rattled through the crowd.

"Now if someone could bring me a drink, that would be just lovely."

With a hand on her hip, she raised the other in anticipation. In no time, someone stumbled on stage with a sloshing goblet of wine and handed it to the eccentric elder of Geenah Vesh.

"Thank you, my boy."

She took hold of the wine. He ducked off the stage and dropped back into the crowd with a yip. Elder Mildrah turned to face the tribe, raising the drink high in offering.

"To the Dóvai!! To another wondrous year!"

The tribe yipped and cheered, Sarah and I calling out with our people. Mildrah drank deep of the wine before flinging the empty vessel off stage and back to its original handler. She nodded in thanks with a worn grandmother smile, as he fumbled to catch it. He bowed in return.

"The harvest is plentiful this season! A fruitful year indeed for the Dóvai. The Great Mother has blessed the house of Geenah Vesh with three daughters and a son. Careful critters of the valley, the garden grows strong..." Mildrah teased. Whoops and laughter followed her gist.

Animal totems stood for three of the four houses of Reisenbough, Geenah Vesh unique with its lotus. As such, those of Geenah Vesh playfully referred to those born of other houses as critters. They in turn were known as blossom babies.

Mildrah called the names of those born, each family recognized and celebrated following introduction. When the four little ones had been recognized before the tribe, Mildrah called the names of those to depart on the Allioht. Geenah Vesh offered two this year, Ian and Jake.

Ian wore a broad fuzzy mane of rich dark, curly hair. He was short and broad about the shoulders. One day he would be full like his father, belly big and round. He wore a kind smile. If he ever grew a beard, he would look more like the Ariae.

Jake was taller, less full, and far from talkative. He bore a soft smile to the world, tagging along with his shorter, more vibrant fuzzy haired cousin. Jake carried a reed flute with him most everywhere he went, which he played quite well.

The two stood proud before the tribe. Honored by all, they bowed in gratitude before breaking from the stage. No doubt the two would be essential companions on the journey ahead.

"Brothers and sisters all! This day marked the return of two strong sons, sent from us as children, returned as men. Before all the Dóvai, stand with me and be recognized, for you are of the people. Saiyu!!" She summoned those returned.

"Saiyu!!"

Called the people in turn, as the two sons returned of Geenah Vesh leapt onstage to stand alongside Mildrah, bold and hard as stone. Their armor was the same shimmering metallic plates forged from the rigid exoskeletons of the Malekaur, hunted and constructed for the third and final trial. The mark upon their chests was that of the Dóvai. Hunters. Warriors.

"Welcome home, sons of Geenah Vesh, brothers of the Dóvai. Aidyn and Ulrick!" Mildrah bowed deeply.

They stood to be recognized, fists raised before the tribe. Yips and cheers echoed into the night. She lightly embraced each before they too slipped from the stage to disappear back into the crowd.

"Kraegar! You're up!" Mildrah called over her shoulder. "Blessings and tidings all!"

Cheers and whistles followed her from the stage. My grandfather Kraegar was standing elder for the house of Dóv. He was well drunk, but somehow gathered his wits about him well enough. He bobbed his way center stage, the thudding tap of his prosthetic leg sounding with every other step. His voice boomed, as he called.

"Alright lads, no reason to make me call you out. Come on up here, I want to stand with you as I boast before all the houses. Karoo-ah!" He roared as he flexed a body like aged stone, shaking the stage with the stamp of his foot.

The numbers of the house of Dóv were few now in comparison, but our return came full and evenly spread throughout the center. I too rose to roar in turn, new courage waking a thunder within me.

Excited, I bolted for the stage, eager to stand at my grandfather's side. As I vaulted onstage, Kori popped out from the crowd as well. We reached our grandfather at roughly the same time, both wearing cheeky smiles under painted faces. Proudly we stood at either side of the hulking house elder to be recognized as the sons of Dóv.

"I present Kori, son of my boy Raethos, a noble hunter for his people in his time, and Undine, daughter of Pultas and maiden passed. Their spirits rest with the divine, but their legacy stands here before us all!"

He paused for the cheers that followed in reverence of the departed. Yips and cries roared, the experience far different from the perspective onstage.

"He is strong and bold like his father, reminding me much of him. That temper is more like his mother's, even catching fire from time to time like her's did. Bwar-har-har!" Kraegar bellowed, his laugh echoed through the crowd.

"He is a bright and rising star of his people. Good call dressing like a firefly, lad. It suits you."

He slapped Kori on the back. Laughter again rattled the crowd at my grandfather's light humor. I managed to stifle a chuckle, as Kori's fierce Malekaur was mistaken for a harmless firefly in front of everyone.

Kori wasn't shaken in the slightest. He stood firm and proud, simply smiling with the laughs of his brothers and sisters. He appeared happy as could be, honored in the moment. His eyes peered dreamily into the crowd, fixed hard at whatever it was that held him. I followed his gaze to find Tiahla, warm and giddy as if she were living that same dream.

I didn't bother to stifle a scoff as it rose. Good for them, terrible for the promise of adventure beyond our return. This turn of events led me to suspect he was most likely to settle his roots instead of braving new lands with his brothers.

"Laughs aside, Kori, you're a fine lad." Kraegar boasted, his tone sincere with his words. "You bring pride not only to the house of your family, but to all the Dóvai. May the Mother bless your passage; may you find the strength within you to become the man you are meant to be... Saiyu."

"Saiyu!!" Burst the Dóvai.

Kraegar bowed best he could, the tip of his beard gliding across his gut. Kori bowed gratefully for his honorable words in turn. Kraegar embraced him.

"I'm proud of you son."

Kori returned his embrace. "Thank you, Grandfather."

The tribe erupted in cheer once more, the sound of it shaking the wooden beams of the stage. To feel the energy of friends and family united, to feel the spirits of the people... What an honor it all truly was. How silly it was for me to be any kind of bitter. His path was his own. Through our common heritage we were to stand united regardless of the directions we should choose.

"Now go enjoy that sweet young honey you can't peel your eyes from."

Kraegar slapped him gently on his back again, sending him off with laughter. Kori's pride swelled with the words of our grandfather. He looked to me, smiling wide and toothy before making his way back into the crowd. I brought my fist to my palm to show my respects. A lesson had been learned without his ever knowing, a blessing passed to honor the freedom of his spirit. My brother. Kraegar turned to me with a pivot upon his peg leg, a proud smile on his beaming face. His beard was a chaotic mess of dried color and beads. It looked to have a twig or two lodged in it as well. He spoke, voice booming deep like the dark depths of his aged old eyes. The power of his words moved through me, as they were meant for all to hear.

"The lad standing before you, painted like a blue skeleton with a heart of fire, is my grandson Kael. Son of Krayton the Mighty, and Meriam the Swift." Kraegar began.

The moment seemed to last forever, as I looked out into the colorful faces of the Dóvai. It was difficult to see them clearly beyond the blinding light of the lamps, making them seem ghastly, lost in the distant dark beyond the flickering light of the stage. I was a bit nervous, standing before all the eyes of my people. Long had I looked forward to this day. More than anything, I felt pride.

My grandfather continued. "The prodigy of two fine houses, the great eagle-dragon of the sky, Shemah Yen, and the powerful beast of the forest, the Dóv; the perfect balance between his father's strength and his mother's agility. Unfortunately, the poor lad got both their brains and twice the ego."

The crowd laughed, some whooped and cheered. I didn't mind in the slightest. I felt as tall and strong as any of the men before me. My path would be that of legacy. I need only live it first. They would see. Tales of my adventures would be told around the fire for generations to come.

My grandfather now turned to me, as he had to Kori. "Kael, you represent the best of both your parents, in strength, focus, and will... But it is your heart that represents the true strength of your people. Listen to it always, that you be both mindful and courageous. May the Great Mother bless your passage. May you find the strength you seek within, and better yet, may you know what to do with it when you find it."

He embraced me, the smell of wine and age clinging to him. I embraced him in return, my arms unable to fully encompass the old titan of a man. I lingered there for only a moment, heart swelling with the power of his words, trying desperately not to cry in front of my people.

As I released him, he spoke. "Stay strong son, and greatness will follow." He bowed.

"I will, grandfather." I promised, returning his bow.

I stood tall before the Dóvai, as cheers ignited once more. With pride in my steps, I turned and made my way off the stage, finding Sarah in the crowd. She was bouncing on her feet, ecstatic and cheering.

"Congratulations Kael, what an honor! What did he say to you at the end?" She was almost as excited as I was.

"He told me if I continue to be strong I will achieve greatness." I confided.

His words held a caution as well, a lesson that would weigh heavy on me in days to come. Though on this night I was far too young, far too involved to give it much thought. I desired strength and honor above all else, surely this is why he chose his words. The idea that I would ever lose touch with myself was unthinkable, yet a dark foreboding began to stew at the back of my mind.

Sarah giggled a bit, bringing me out of my brooding mind and back to the moment at hand. "Your grandfather is wise." She responded, smiling softly. Her eyes seemed to sparkle.

The final elder took center stage. This time it was Beatrice, house elder of Shemah Yen. She was Archon's aunt, risen to the position of house elder with the passing of my grandparents, Darius and Dialah.

Beatrice was pretty in her old age. The years had only added to her delicate features, making her all the more warm and inviting. Long silver hair flowed about her delicate frame, neatly hanging down to her knees. Blue was the only color used in the intricate designs painted down her arms, as she opened them as if to embrace her people. She spoke with a sweet voice, deepened by her years and just as easy to hear as my grandfather's had been.

"Brothers and sisters, together we celebrate the fruits of yet another glorious year of peace and prosperity."

Cries of celebration rose, as the Dóvai jumped and whooped throughout the hollow. Sarah and I too were leaping and shouting our own cries into the canopy. Beatrice smiled humbly and bowed her head ever slightly, as she waited for the silence to return.

"Today we celebrate life, and give thanks for all that is. Saiyu."

She offered her praise, raising her hands to meet above her head as she looked up through the triangle made by her outstretched thumbs and index fingers.

"Saiyu." The Dóvai responded in a chorus of soft voices.

Beatrice's arms fell back to her sides, and she stood boldly to address her people. "Let us first recognize a life returned." As she spoke, a brawny painted warrior took the stage. "Son of Gaz, born of the summer fields; the warrior known as Ardos the Bold!"

Ardos beat his chest with a fist before raising it high with a mighty roar. The Dóvai roared in turn. Next year I would stand there much the same, adorned in the armor I would carve from the Malekaur.

Beatrice continued, as Ardos left the stage. "Together let us celebrate new life, the gifts of the Mother. There are two born to the house of Shemah Yen this year."

Cries and cheers erupted throughout the crowd from those representing Shemah Yen. Beatrice continued.

"Primus, son of Kean, and Taylah, daughter of Mina welcome a new daughter, Leah."

She pointed the family out from the crowd, as the tribe cheered for them. Taylah wore a glowing smile, as she peered down at the infant nuzzled in her care. "Welcome, daughter of Reisenbough."

"The house of Shemah Yen welcomes a new son as well. Levi, son of Katav, and Ziala, daughter of Balka welcome their new boy, Yekav. Welcome, son of Reisenbough."

Cheers arose once again. This time the parents were out of view, but Sarah and I cheered loud for them anyhow.

"We are honored with the fruit of seeds sewn, now let us honor those who will sow the seeds of tomorrow, our brave young men to be!" Beatrice called over the crowd, ending with her arms outstretched as if she had truly released her words to the cheers of the people.

"This year the house of Shemah Yen sends five on the journey to becoming." She announced with pride in her voice.

She began introducing the boys one by one. There was Trev, son of Valtis and Marni. He was tall and lean like his father, with a broad face and a flat nose. His hands were balled into huge fists at his waist, as he stood proudly before his people. I didn't much care for him, but I cheered nonetheless. Like it or not, I would see more of him on the journey ahead.

There was also Yuri, son of Laz and Pina, and Vren, son of Kar and Esta. Yuri was a short frazzled looking character, with wild dark hair and golden eyes. He was always happy and vibrant, wearing a smile wherever he went. He loved to talk more than anything.

Vren was a bit shorter than me, with close cut blonde hair and a round face that made his chin look both pudgy and pronounced. He was a friendly sort, but didn't much care for the company of the twins. He didn't look the least bit comfortable taking center stage with his age mates, fingers twitching about at his sides, eyes wild and weary. After Beatrice's words, Vren dashed off the stage, all but tripping on his way.

Beatrice addressed the Dóvai. "Tonight the house of Shemah Yen offers a remarkable pair of twin brothers to embark on the Allioht as well. Cas and Pol, born of Raikel, daughter of Darius the Great, and Archon the Healer."

As she spoke two figures emerged at either side of the stage. Each wore an elaborate headdress decorated in golden brown feathers like those of the great eagle that represented their house. Hooked beaks protruded down over their carefully painted faces. It was near impossible to distinguish the twins through the feathery costumes.

More feathers covered their chests and shoulders, some even dangled from ties along their arms. Their extremities had been painted with a feathery texture leaving one twin mostly blue and the other white. It was difficult to tell which was which, though I was quite sure Pol was the blue.

"These brothers represent their house well, now standing as the youngest members to take the stage. The two have worked tirelessly in their preparation, offering an exhibition of skill to honor tonight's festival with an age old tale retold. Brothers and sisters all, I present to you; The Battle for the Heavens!"

Beatrice announced, arms swinging wide in presentation before she bowed and stepped back from the stage.

The drums came to life, thumping a steady rhythm as the twins took their positions on the stage. Once the two were in place, the thumping of the drums rose to a crescendo before dropping to an abrupt halt. Each twin was approached and presented with a set of daggers, real daggers. The silvery sheen of the blades glistened as they hissed through the air upon demonstration. The awestruck reactions from the audience reflected my own. All of Reisenbough was watching. The twins of Shemah Yen held the full attention of the tribe.

The drums picked up once more, this time accompanied by the faster, higher timbre of the full ensemble, creating a lively drive in the air. The rhythm beat from the drums carried into the stomping movements of the twins as they danced and moved in time. The melody rose above the rhythm, as the two eagles circled in opposition.

As they moved round, they began to tighten their orbit, winged arms spread, daggers in hand. When the two met, they at once began exhibiting their skills, twirling and slashing at one another before all of Reisenbough. They moved in perfect sync with the music. Skill and precision were on point, the two narrowly avoiding the bite of the blades that nipped at the feathers along their chests.

Already they had won the crowd, as gasps and wonderment accented each flurry of swipes and dives. The two met one another with a kick just as the cymbals crashed. Each staggered back, putting distance between them as the music carried like the wind beneath their wings.

The two approached one another, feet dancing about and feathered arms held wide like wings at flight. They circled around the center, squared for battle. The drums were accented with cries from the drummers, adding to the climactic tension of the scene.

Suddenly, one of the twins lunged his blade hard at the other, sending feathers free into the air. The audience gasped, as the other narrowly dodged the blade and delivered his own attack. He sent his opponent back with a series of lightning fast slashes and jabs. The stage was a colorful flurry of flips, feathers, and silvery slashing blades.

I was on my feet before I realized. With each bout of slashes and narrow acrobatic escapes, my heart skipped. I knew they were skilled, but it was still nerve-wracking to know these two clowns had been trusted to perform with real weapons. They were fantastic, and as I watched the two of them it reminded me of a similar display I had witnessed years before.

For a moment my memory took me back, as the figures moved across the brightly lit stage. Mother was dressed in similar garb as the twins, except her feathers had been black and she wore no such headdress. Her flowing black hair had been decorated with black feathers that glinted in the light, as she flipped about slashing at my father with wicked precision.

My father was the embodiment of the Dóv, wearing thick fur about his arms and torso, the head of the creature resting atop his own. He would take great swipes at her with his short sword, as she eluded his attacks and fluttered about him in a flurry of silver swipes. The two moved across the stage in all manner of slashing acrobatics, sending the crowd into excitement just as the twins were doing now. The performance of the twins was an honorable homage to those before them.

As the drums pounded, the white eagle lunged toward the blue. The blue countered and avoided three dizzying slashes before sending a few of his own. The white pushed the blue off balance and down onto one knee. The white used the bent knee of his opponent to step up and flip back through the air as an incoming slash from the blue shaved a few golden brown feathers free of the headdress.

The white eagle landed safely on his feet, guard ready. The blue had risen and was readied as well. The two continued to dance about the stage, circling one another, as the crowd cheered them on. The anticipation had most everyone on their feet now. The twins were really putting on quite a show. With every bout of slashing theatrics the crowd reeled.

Suddenly the drums changed rhythm, picking up furry for what was surely to be the finale. The twins changed their dance, circling once more with stamping steps before parting to either side of the stage. They turned to one another. The blue eagle raised its wings high, standing on one leg. A bent knee aimed for the white eagle, poised to signal the impending attack. The white eagle crouched low, wings splayed and daggers readied at the blue.

In a flash, the two charged together, leaping high into the air as they met, daggers out. I nearly fell forward, resisting the urge to race to the stage as they clashed past one another midair with the zing of the steel blades. Each landed where the other had been before the jump, turning on one another in a wild slashing fury that left the crowd silent in awe.

The drums pounded with their strikes. Cries rose from the drummers, accenting the slashing blur of white and blue.

Just as it seemed they might destroy one another if it continued, the two shot apart and the drums slammed to a finish. The two eagles turned to the audience and bowed, as cheers erupted around the stage. The two had simply been amazing. I felt proud to call them my brothers, as I too raised my voice in celebration.

Sarah was jumping up and down next to me, jubilant and slightly flushed from the wine she had drank.

"Stars in heaven, that was amazing!" She blurted. "I had no idea those two could do something like that. You and Kori train with them?"

"All the time." I all but gloated, though our sparring sessions were never as flashy as what the twins had just performed. In truth, their display had been just as new and exciting for me as it had been for her.

"Come on, lets go see them!" She reached for my hand and pulled me toward the stage.

We made our way to the twins, the two already surrounded by praise and compliments. Now that we were closer, the blue eagle was revealed to be Cas. He was still dancing around like a bird, squawking at random as he bobbed through an excited crowd of friends and family. Pol stood proud with his fists on his waist, chest out. He seemed ridiculously tall with the eagle head above his own.

"Ah, Kael. What did you think of the show?" He asked, not waiting for a response before changing the subject. "Oh, and who is this young beauty with you? She's even holding onto you! Brave thing that, holding onto this one."

"Cut the nonsense, Pol." Sarah snapped. "We came to congratulate you two numbskulls. That was... stupendous."

Pol laughed. The white of his teeth and red of his mouth appeared eerie in contrast to the white paint that obscured his face beneath the stern expression of the eagle.

"Why thank you, Sarah. That's mighty sweet of you."

Cas reappeared from our left in a flutter of feathers and blue. "Kael! Did you see us?!"

He was still bursting with excitement. His wide eyed expression and toothy smile terrifying as he peered from the throat of the eagle.

"I did. Exceptional performance, you truly honor your house and your people." I bowed my head ever slightly. I felt warm from the wine.

"Well of course, but didn't expect to hear you say it outright." Cas responded, shocked by a compliment so readily given. "Usually your brother has to nag at us for a bit before you speak your peace. One day with your girlfriend here and suddenly you're a sweetheart. I don't know if I can get use to this side of Kael." He teased, obviously more aimed at Sarah than me.

"Oh grow up!" Sarah barked, though she seemed somewhat flattered by the comment.

Sarah sent a slugging fist, but Pol ducked away easily enough. She missed wide, and the twins burst into laughter.

"No need for violence!" Pol mocked. "I only mean to congratulate the two of you. A good match, really. Stupendous even..."

He looked pleased with himself, as he and Cas chuckled like a couple of goofy bird men. Sarah looked to me in defeat, blue eyes sparkling from the fun of it.

"How ever do you manage?" She asked, her words drenched in sarcasm.

"Ah come on, Sarah. We aren't so bad. I mean, did you not just see what we did there?" Pol asked, as he pulled the large bird head off his shoulders.

"Of course she did, brother. Everyone saw. In fact, I see a few misty eyed young maidens who clearly enjoyed our performance." Cas prattled, nodding from his brother to a group of splendidly painted girls. They were practically swooning over the twins.

"Well lets not be rude, brother. Ladies mustn't be kept waiting." Pol responded behind a ridiculous smile. He shot a wink toward the gaggle of trouble. "Later, Kael. We'll leave you with princess sucker punches."

"Whatever." I retorted, as per the usual.

The twins wandered toward the group of colorful maidens. Cas pulled off his headdress as well, calling out to the girls as the two approached.

"Ladies!"

The amount of giggles that arose following his call suggested they would be well received.

"Those two are more like a couple of prancing cocks than eagles." Sarah quipped.

We watched the two flirt with the girls, attempting to dazzle them with more theatrics. Their banter would inevitably scare them off. As much as I wanted to see how it worked out, I decided it was best if Sarah and I made a break for it just in case the twins decided we were more fun.

"We should go." I suggested with a nod in my intended direction.

We moved through the thinning crowd. She merrily followed, catching up to wrap herself around my arm. She certainly didn't mind getting close, and I was minding it less and less.

We made our way back through the village center. Music returned a lively melody to the air, and the colorful bodies resumed dancing around the large pyre still blazing. The festival was far from over.

On our way through we joined in the central circle that moved around the fire, merrily dancing and stomping alongside our brothers and sisters. I considered staying there, as Sarah seemed to enjoy dancing. Instead, when we made our way to the north end of the circle, I took her hand and we fled further.

"Where are we going?" She asked, chest heaving from jumping around the fire and yelling into the night.

"Almost there." I responded.

When at last we broke free of the dancing mob, I turned to Sarah and pointed to a group of elders gathered around a small makeshift stage. Wildlings clambered about onstage, armed with stick swords and wearing fun little costumes. Parents and elders were gathered round, laughing at the hysterical antics of the young entertainers. It was a nice little gem nestled in a corner along the eastern ridge, a welcomed change from the intensity of the dance circle.

"Come on." I urged, and together we found a place near enough to see.

The jubilant young characters were reenacting the battle with the dreaded Trickler. The wildlings with toy swords scrambled about yelling, belting tiny war cries. A long segmented body of stitched fabric lumbered about on many tiny feet. The wildlings inside the long costume moved without the slightest synchronization. Tiny voices growled monstrously from within the fabric facade, as the drunken beast attempted to do battle with the warriors.

The pincers at the beast's bobbling head were controlled by the wildling in front. He roared as he dashed for the toddling warriors, the pincers sloppily groping through the air. The other segments had no idea where they were going or when they would move next. The creature bounced and jerked about as the segments bumped into one another, stumbling to keep up with the wayward head.

As the Trickler's head changed direction to catch a warrior by surprise it tripped, pulling free of the rest of the body. The look on the wildling's face playing the segment next to the head was priceless, as they struggled to rejoin the head to the body. Sarah was all but rolling with laughter.

Again and again the great monster would fall apart or bump into a warrior wildling and send them to the ground. It was chaos, wonderful and fun.

"Of all the stories they had to choose from, your grandfather's were the only ones they were interested in doing. We settled on the story of the Trickler, though it was not their first pick." Came a soft voice from my right. It was Nisha. "Nice to see the two of you together."

Her hair was tied back similar to Sarah's. She wore blue and green paint across her face and white banded stripes with blue and purple shapes around her wrists.

"Hey sis." Sarah responded. "Little Koda up there?"

Nisha rolled her eyes and sighed. "Of course. He's near the tail somewhere. I think he's the second to last one there."

She pointed. Two tiny feet shuffled about as the segments in front of it all but dragged it to and fro.

"Oh, how fun." Sarah laughed. "How much longer you think he'll last?"

"Oh it should be wrapping up soon." Nisha explained. "They tend to get caught up in this scene. Eventually they'll get tired and work it out."

The grand finale was wonderful. The tail of the Trickler finally broke away, and Nisha left us to aid her teary eyed toddler. A few of the warrior wildlings had lost interest in the beast and began battling one another instead.

As the warriors still fighting the creature went to deliver the final blow, the boy leading the party tripped. The boy behind him stumbled over his fallen partner to fall as well, landing them well short of the beast. It split in two as if they had met their mark anyhow, by fate it would seem. The two arrived moments later to deliver the triumphant swings that would surely have done the trick.

The segments ran about, as the wildlings within screamed before tumbling over, feigning death. The warriors cheered, and the parents and grandparents watching cheered as well. I looked at Sarah just as I felt her hand reach for mine.

"Thanks for sharing this with me." Her voice warm like her smile.

As the wildlings emerged from the Trickler costume and ran to the arms of loved ones, a low thumping pulse began to sound from the northern edge of the village, where the light of the fire did not reach. It was slow and steady.

Thump... Thump... Thump...

The other drums and instruments in the heart of the village fell in time with it, creating a lulling rhythm, a sacred song. Next the reeds and flutes joined, adding a somber melody to the air, changing the mood in the gully. The dancing bodies stood still, and voices one by one fell in time with the music. Chanting unified the people, adding a soulful chorus to the music. It was time to honor those to be sent and to pay homage to loved ones departed.

The music descended through the gully, the ensemble leading the way north. A line of colorful bodies followed, still united in the woeful chorus. Sarah and I would need to follow suit. This night, my peers and I were to be honored. We were those to be sent. I moved for the precession. Sarah was about to tag along, when Nisha caught her.

"Sarah! Would you be a darling and hang back to help me look after a few of the little ones?" She all but pleaded.

Sarah looked back to me apologetically. "Sorry." She said, as if she expected disappointment.

"Don't be." I responded with a smile. She smiled back, blue eyes sparkling through the magenta paint that encompassed them.

I turned and made my way into the procession. The woeful chorus traveled the length of the crowd, as we made our way down to the river. This night the Dóvai would honor those who would depart with the rising sun, that great journey to becoming, known as the Allioht.

The drums and woodwinds led the way through the night, fields lit with the light of the harvest moon. The sky was clear, and the air was cool and crisp. The moon was swollen and bright, still hanging slightly to the east.

Two torches held high in the front of the procession guided us through the night. The silvery landscape was crisp in the moonlight. The Song of Sending added a dreamlike quality, making the experience all the more surreal. The earth was cool beneath my feet, and a fog had begun to creep across the fields.

I breathed deep of the cool night air, the lingering smells of the summer mingled with those of early autumn. The chill, moist air somehow made the scents more vivid, more invigorating. I held it there for a moment, relishing a feeling of peace as the song of my people washed over me. My spirit in tune, I sang out as well, adding my voice to the song and feeling it resonate within me.

At last we reached the waters of the Veylspring. The river was dark as the night, reflecting the light of the torches off its smooth, glittering surface. I touched the edge of the water with my toes and wished I hadn't. The waters were frigid, as always.

One by one the others set to depart joined me at the water's edge. Ian and Jake arrived to my right. Ian was shorter than me, and broader too. He looked almost menacing, a stern look on his face as he glared over the water. Jake was slightly taller than me, a curly mane of hair pulled back from his painted face.

Yuri and Trev arrived next, the twins hot on their tails. The twins of course came to stand at my left, cheesy smiles on their faces from their excitement. Even though I could tell they had plenty to say, they dared not utter a word during ceremony.

Kori was the last to arrive, Tiahla at his side. He seemed more interested in his new companion than in the ritual taking place. He nudged his way between Pol and me, all smiles, drunk with the night. His face too became hard, the icy water lapping at his feet rendering his focus to the moment at hand.

Finally, all twelve to embark on the Allioht were at the water's edge. All the village gathered around us, united in the rhythm of song. The music from the instruments reverberated from the rocky cliff face of the northern bank. The echo that returned added an eerie depth to the somber notes, as if the song of the Dóvai were being returned in time by those beyond. The thought of it made my hair stand on end, or perhaps it was just the chill of the night air reminding me of the brisk dip I would soon take.

Suddenly, the music stopped. A delayed echo rippled back over the silence, and as it passed those of us in line turned to follow it, facing the tribe. The torches gathered in the center of the wide semicircle formed around us. In line with my brothers I stood rigid against the chill, letting my eyes wander over the faces of Reisenbough.

Some stood with eyes closed as if connected in their hearts. Others knelt at the water's edge, offering their prayers to be carried to loved ones passed beyond. My father was among them, sending his regards to mother no doubt. This was not an act of woe, but a moment of reverence for those loved beyond life. Ancestors be praised, their spirits with us always. This was the way of the Dóvai.

Mildrah appeared between the two torches. She wore flowing robes of emerald green, ceremonial paint highlighting her face. A vertically oriented eye was painted at the center of her brow, glowing in shimmering magenta against the light of the torches. A line came down from either corner of the painted eye to cross her nose and end at either cheek. She stood firm before the Dóvai, addressing all as she spoke the traditional prayers of Sending. Her voice came full and strong, as she opened her arms and spoke toward the moonlit sky.

"Great Mother, we praise you for the gift of life that fills this world, the life that fills our village and makes our hearts strong. Saiyu." "Saiyu."

Her last word rippled through the crowd in turn. Those of us standing in a line before our people remained silent.

"Great Mother, we offer our thanks for the precious time spent with the dear departed. May all our journeys end in your grace that our spirits remain united. Saiyu."

The prayer was once again answered in turn by the Dóvai. Now Mildrah took a commanding tone, speaking to the line directly. I felt myself snap to attention.

"Chosen youth of Reisenbough! Before you are the sacred waters of the Veylspring. These waters have carried your ancestors to the afterlife for generations, flowing to the Purge and to the sea. With it are carried the prayers, the hopes and wishes of your people. May your dreams, your passions carry eternal in this flow, for you are the legacy of the Dóvai."

She gestured to signal it was time for us to enter the water. At once the line moved into the icy pull of the dark river. It was indeed cold, but it didn't stop any of us in the slightest. I all but winced when the frigid water hit my groin. I turned to face Mildrah and the Dóvai once more, wading against the tug of the frigid current.

"Be cleansed in it, let the waters still your hearts against the trials ahead. May it carry the prayers that bring you home to your people, no matter how far your journey... SAIYU!" Mildrah cried out, her arms shooting up and over her head.

"SAIYU!"

Came the cry of those gathered round, and the line to be sent plunged into the water.

The cold rush was paralyzing for an instant. My breath escaped, and I sank against the muddy bottom. I remained there only for a moment, but it felt like an eternity.

There came a rippling sensation, much like that of the chilling cold or static build. Everything was different. It felt as if every bubble around me lingered with a tickle across my skin. The pull of the current became sluggish, less intense. I felt like I could fly up and out of the water, fly higher than the great Shemah Yen. I felt unstoppable...

Just as quick as the sensation had come, it was gone. Feeling that I had been submerged long enough, I shot up from the icy waters expecting to be among the last to do so. To my astonishment I appeared to be the first. I wiped the chill water from my eyes and looked around me in shivering disbelief.

The next to spring up was Yuri, who hooted and hollered from the cold water. Cries of celebration and laughter rose up in turn, as one by one the rest emerged from the icy darkness and made for shore.

Shivering, I stumbled through the water, making my way to the colorful smiles that lined the river's edge. My father stood tall and proud on the bank before me, Sarah next to him holding a large fur draped in her arms. His beard and face were painted in a similar manner to my grandfather's, tiny hand prints and dried globs matting the hair together. His smile was the brightest I'd seen in years.

Kori splashed through the water alongside me. He let out a victorious roar and thrust his fists into the air, as we stepped out from the river.

"You honor me, my sons." My father's words came low.

"Thank you, father." I responded, hoping Sarah would soon offer the warm looking fur as I tried not to shiver too badly in front of everyone, my breath heavy in the chill air.

"Was it cold, boys?" My grandfather teased, his thunderous laugh warming the night.

It took a man under each arm to steady him. His laughter shook them off balance, and all three swayed as they righted to catch him.

"Not at all, old man. Have a dip while you're here!" Kori teased.

Kraegar rumbled with laughter. Kori quickly shifted his focus to Tiahla. She offered him a similar thick brown fur, which he accepted and gingerly wrapped around himself.

Tiahla was vibrantly painted in blues and purples, her hair braided nicely with stones and beads. Her full breasts were all but spilling out of her soft fur top, which looked tiny by comparison. Kori opened the fur and pulled Tiahla into his arms, wrapping her in the fur with him. She giggled and squealed about how wet and cold he was.

"You must be freezing." Came Sarah's voice with a bit of a slur to it.

She came close and wrapped the fur around me, her hands lingering at my collar. She was flushed and her breath smelled of wine. Her eyes were wild and blue, as her gaze pierced my own.

"Careful, lad. Looks like someone means to make a man of you tonight.... Bwarhahahahar!!" My grandfather rocked with laughter, stumbling as his two escorts struggled to keep him standing.

I felt my eyes widen in shock. I didn't find his words funny in the least. Sarah was either comfortable with the idea or paid little mind to the wobbly old timer's gist. I looked back to my father. He shook his head and smiled.

"I'll leave you kids be." He placed his hand on my shoulder, his face sincere. "Take care of her, son. To honor her is to honor your people. Remember this."

A smile peaked out from beneath his colorful beard, but sorrow lurked behind the sheen of his eyes. He turned and walked away. I all but called out for him to stay, as much from concern as from the terror of my grandfather's implications.

"Come on." Sarah said, grabbing tight to my hand and pulling me toward the tall grass to the west.

"Oui! Don't get so wrapped up that you forget, lover boy!" Came Pol's voice.

"Same place, yeah?" Cas backed him up, arms crossed.

"Yeah, yeah!" I replied, as I was all but dragged away from the crowd and into the grass.

We rushed through the tall grass, the smooth leafy blades cool to the touch as we brushed past. Wrapped in the thick fur I no longer felt cold, nor afraid in the blue and silver shades of night. The moon shone high above, bright and full through the tops of the green tendrils that reached toward the sky as if in praise of her majesty.

I breathed deep of the night, the power of it kindled a flame within me. Sarah looked back as we breached into a clearing, a smile on her lips as she asked.

"You up for it?"

We had emerged in a familiar clearing. Sarah and I had come here to spar on occasion over the last few years. I had never seen the place by night, though with the bright moon overhead it was little different.

While the scenery may not have been much different, the atmosphere had certainly changed on this occasion. She had never looked so delicate, far from the usual wiry angry faced combatant. On this night, she was dressed and painted like a young maiden of the Dóvai, hair still neatly back. Usually we were both a mess, even more so by the time we were finished flipping around in the dirt and grass.

"Not really." I answered honestly after a lengthy pause. I wasn't in the mood for a fight, nor anything else that might have been on the agenda.

"Why not?" She asked, delivering a playful shove that was a bit harder than perhaps she meant.

"It's late." I said, knowing it wasn't much of an excuse on the night of the festival.

"I see..." She swayed a bit as she laughed. "Its probably best we not, just in case. Wouldn't want word getting out you got beat down by a girl right after your manly ceremony."

She moved to shove at me again. I deflected her hand away, opening the warm fur I had kept close around me. She swung wide with her other arm. When I moved to block it, she rounded her footing and spiraled into my arms.

Her skin was freezing despite her warm appearance, so I decided she could stay close. I wrapped her in my arms, her soft skin nice against my own. Her icy nose tickled at my chin, as she giggled. The smell of wine was fragrant.

"Thanks for sharing, neighbor." She joked, shivering a bit. She wrapped her arms about me beneath the fur. "You're warm!"

"You should have brought another for you." I suggested impulsively, my tone cold like the water that beaded from my hair.

Her eyes closed as she rested her face against my chest. "I like this better, but I'll keep that in mind... Jerk." She bit me.

I flinched. "Hey!"

She giggled again. Her blue eyes peaked up at me, the dark fur tickling at her neckline. "Something wrong?"

We laughed. Silence followed, as we stood in the open night wrapped in the warmth of the thick fur. She was well warm now, and the softness of her was welcoming. I held her to me, but only just a little. A pack of wolves called from somewhere in the night...

"So... You're likely planning to set off on some crazy adventure, like my old man did right?" She asked suddenly, as if she could see my thoughts clearly.

"Yes." I responded.

"And why is that exactly?" She asked, running her fingers lightly along the skin of my back. The tingle of her touch brought chills.

"I want to know what's out there, to see what lies beyond what is known. To brave the world and return with great stories to honor the house of my fathers..."

I confided. I trailed off for a moment, but she waited patiently for my words to return.

"Of course it's deeper than that. Something pulls me out toward the world, as if there is a purpose calling to me from some faraway place I have yet to discover... Please don't tell the twins that part."

She snickered.

"I'm at a loss to explain. Maybe I'll find something extraordinary, or perhaps nothing at all. I don't know... Which is why I have to go." I concluded.

She allowed only a brief moment of silence to reflect. "Before you even ask, yes I'd love to come along." She volunteered. We laughed together.

"I'm serious, you know." She continued. "You'll need looking after. Kori's likely to be settled down before he even leaves tomorrow, and there's no way I'd send you alone with the twins. I can only imagine what trouble they're likely to find, set to freely roam about the land."

She was right about the others, but I didn't like the idea. It simply wasn't the way I had envisioned the journey.

"Truth is," she continued with a more serious change in tone, "I too long for adventure, to brave challenges unknown, to come home with wild stories and to brag about what lies beyond the lands beyond."

I considered her words. It hadn't dawned on me that such a thing would appeal to her too. Of course it would, it wasn't difficult to believe. Her father had done the same, the very dreamer who inspired the dream in me.

"They say there is a palace that floats high over the land, higher than even the peak of the Tomb. They say the only way to get there is to climb a mighty tree that holds it within its branches... Wouldn't that be exciting to see?" She asked.

"A palace built in the heavens?"

I hadn't heard of this.

"You know what else is exciting?" She asked.

"What?" I asked, curious to hear what other crazy marvels she had to share.

"The thought of us."

Her lips reached up to meet mine as she pressed against me. Her hands became far more adventurous than they had ever been before.

I panicked. I drew away gently, and thought of escape.

"I still have to meet the twins, I promised." I quickly explained.

She blinked, a dreamy look in her eyes. "Must you really now, Kael?"

"I gave my word." I responded boldly, as if it had been a blood oath.

"Why don't you wait for me? My bed is the one with the darkest furs, along the east wall." I suggested softly, in what I hoped was a seductive tone. This had not been in my plans for the evening at all.

She smiled at the idea, her blue eyes peering out from the magenta which had begun to bleed down onto the patchy white along her cheeks.

"I'd like that..."

She came in for another kiss. Her lips soft and invigorating this time. Her touch lingered as she turned back the way we came.

"Here take this with you." I wrapped her snugly in the warm damp fur. "I'm warm enough now."

I smiled at her, and she brightened.

"Don't be too long, Son of Krayton." She called back, as she scampered away through the tall grass.

My blood was on fire from the new experience. My heart was pounding, as she seemed to linger all around me. I let enough time pass for her to get a good lead before making my way back to the village.

The number of lively bodies that had filled the village center was far less with the late hour. The music was gone, save for a small group that still danced and carried on around the large dying fire at the center.

I passed a fire circle where several bodies still gathered around a low lying table dimly lit by candlelight. Balthar sat among the small group, peering over the contents of the squat table. Many unique figurines were placed on a decorative game board, and the group was now disputing how best to defeat a monster their characters had encountered in the game.

This was Balthar's favorite hobby, and his youngest daughter Fae Lee had managed to join the group. She was all but asleep with her head resting on her father's leg, as he argued with the man next to him as how best to deal with the giant arachnid threatening their party.

Further along, I saw a hulking old man hunched and alone around a dwindling fire. As I drew closer I recognized it to be my grandfather, Kraegar. Instinctively, I went to him.

His eyes were all but closed, his cheeks rosy above his haggard beard. I called to him as I placed a hand on his massive shoulder. His eyes slid open, as he smiled.

"Kael my boy." He paused to wet his lips with a wet smacking sound and the shuffle of his beard. "It's gotten late hasn't it?"

"Yes it has, grandfather. But never too late." I smiled and offered my hand.

He reached out and grabbed hold. "Oh yeah? Need your ole grandfather to help you home for the night, eh? You've drank a little more than you're use to."

He chuckled. We both knew he didn't need assistance, drunk or not. It was the initiative that mattered.

He shifted his weight onto his left leg, stretching the prosthetic out to his right. He stood to his feet as easily as any other drunk man with one leg, the prosthetic sliding up and under him as he rose. He was standing, but not ready to walk it seemed.

"Whoa now!" He groaned. "The world's got a mighty spin to her tonight, don't she?"

He held onto my arm for balance, swaying with a chuckle. His smile was as wide as his crazy beard, battered as much with color as with age. To me, he would always be that warm guiding spirit, a spirit that inspired my own.

"Doesn't she always?" I teased.

"Always? Well that's a long time, lad. So far so good, might be the one consistent thing shared by all women. Now listen close to this little gem of wisdom, one to buzz for generations. Hold onto it and pass it along... The Great Mother is always spinning, and there's a mighty good reason for it, my boy. Ladies love to dance. Remember that. Keeps 'em happy."

He chuckled again, not quite set enough in his wits to take the next step. He dipped only slightly as he brought the prosthetic around.

"Ah, progress! We've got 'er now, lad! Only forty-three more to go..."

"You've counted them?" I asked, finding it possible, though unlikely. "No, just a guess." He said, followed by a cheeky smile and burly laughter. "I'll either get there in less and sleep off the difference, or in the least be forty-three steps closer. Sooner or later... Though I prefer sooner than later."

He chuckled again, as I walked beside him. The small shuttered windows of the huts around us were aglow with low burning fires that warmed the sleeping families within. These were the homes of the Dóvai, brothers and sisters all, winding down with the late hours of darkness.

Finally we reached my grandfather's hut. It was far less well maintained since Gran had passed, but it still held the same familiar comfort. My father's hut was the next one over, so I didn't mean to stay long. I wasn't ready to face Sarah just yet.

"Thanks for seeing an old man home, my boy." Came my grandfather's words.

"Good night, grandfather." I said with a smile. I bowed before turning to go about my way.

"Hold on, boy. I've got something for you."

My grandfather called after me, as he reached into his hut and produced a shiny bottle containing a dark liquid. The cork was finely wrapped with twine.

"A little goes a long way. That's a bottle of my finest there."

"Thank you, grandfather." I said, as I accepted his gift.

The glass was clear and smooth, truly fine in quality and rare. I held the bottle by the neck and looked through it. Thick and heavy, it would be of great use on the journey ahead.

As I made to leave my grandfather's voice came once again, this time heavy with concern.

"Be careful out there, son."

"I will, grandfather." I promised. He disappeared behind the flap of the door he could scarcely fit through, and I was off toward the canopy.

When I reached the trunks of the Allichene I tied the bottle secure at my waist and climbed a rope ladder that hung along the soft leathery bark of the tree. The climb was a bit treacherous in the dark, but it was familiar enough that muscle memory all but led the way. The twins would be found in the branches of the adjacent tree.

Cautiously I navigated through the treetops, my sight much limited in the dark foliage of the lower canopy. The dwindling lights of the village glowed far below, as I hopped across a short gap between branches. There was a light flickering through the leaves marking my destination, letting me know the others were still waiting. The bottle bumped and beat against my thigh, as I closed the distance effortlessly.

From the moment we were old enough to climb, the four of us wandered the canopy. We climbed higher and more bravely as time and experience progressed. The peaks of the Allichene above Reisenbough became a safe haven from chores and lectures. There we would discuss the things we were learning as peers. Each family had unique teachings for similar lessons it seemed, and we spent the last hours before sunset discussing and sometimes arguing over various methods and techniques. In the heights of the canopy we were free, usually to do nothing more than lounge on the large, deep green leaves of the Allichene.

High in the canopy, we had found a cozy spot to hideout. An unusually level branch met the tapering center mass of the tree, creating a decently sized platform. There we spent many an afternoon lazing in the shade of the canopy. During the daylight hours, a lone great tree could be seen standing far in the distance to the southeast, its great mass towering in the distance. A forest of similar great trees obscured the sky to the west beyond the mountain, forming a greater canopy high above that of the smaller Allichene.

I arrived to see Cas and Pol sitting around a small fire set in a rather large, heavy clay basin. We had hoisted the thing up for use as a fire pit. During the process, the first one had fallen to shatter rather close to one of the eastern most huts below, an unexplained phenomena that left our clique under suspicion.

"Ah, well look who it is!" Cas called from where he sat around the fire. He sprang to his feet.

"At least one of you showed up, better late than never. We were about to give up on you." Pol added. He stood leaning against the tree where it joined the branch.

"What's that you've got there?" Cas wondered aloud as he approached to check out the shiny glass bottle.

"A gift." I responded, offering it over. "From Kraegar."

Pol quickly pranced his way over as well. "From Kraegar you say? Damn good stuff then, from what I've heard anyway. Let's give it a try."

I handed the bottle over to the two, who in no time pulled the cork and began swigging. Cas was the first, while Pol impatiently waited with groping hands ready to snatch the bottle.

"Whoa!" Cas cried, making an awful face. "That's dreadful strong."

Pol took a swig. His face went through similar changes, but he seemed to handle it better. Or at least pretended he did. "Right good stuff, you got here. Burns like it's meant to."

He didn't have a clue what he was talking about. He took another great swig before passing the bottle to me. I didn't need to try it to know it was terrible, but I did so anyway. My grandfather had wanted me to have it. After tasting the stuff, I couldn't help but wonder why.

I passed the bottle back to the twins, glad to see it go. Kori never showed. As a result I got to hear the twins bicker back and forth over the matter. It wasn't long before they were tipsy from the drink.

"All I'm saying is, if he'd rather spend the evening with her than with his mates, it would have been nice to at least hear it." Pol ranted before taking another swig from the shiny bottle.

I poked at the fire with a stick pulled from a stack of firewood. I didn't understand it either, how my brother's new found love interest superseded his dedication to the pack, but I respected his freedom to do as he pleased. He was my brother, and family was sacred. Who was I to deny his pursuit of happiness? He would be leaving with us come morning anyway.

Cas tossed an armful of wood into the basin with a clunk. Embers shot up from the impact like a thousand shooting stars, a few lasting to drift lightly up and away.

"Yeah, but can you really blame him? I mean, really?"

Cas asked, his hands reaching at his chest to clutch handfuls of imaginary breasts each time he said really. He then shrugged.

"You know what brother, I suppose not." Pol said, stopping short of another swig. "Do you think it's jealousy perhaps?"

"You? Jealous?" Cas asked as if the question had been absurd. "Ridiculous. Besides, she's only got him for tonight. We get him for the next year. Ha!"

"Right you are, brother. Right you are." Pol smirked. "I still say he should have at least dropped by, eh Kael?"

He finally took the swig he had started to take before his words.

Might have been nice. He has his reasons." I responded, looking back to the coals. In truth I was a bit disappointed that he hadn't come. It was quite late, the special night drawing to a close.

"Only one reason I can think of." Pol joked, as he nudged Cas with an elbow.

I laughed along with them. Kori had my respect, but the thought was still quite funny. Silence followed our laughter, as the fire crackled low in the basin. Light reflected off the tree, casting shadows along the base of the great branch on which we sat. Above was a black sky, as the moon had disappeared behind the great forest.

There came a rustling along the branches, and the sound of nimble feet coming closer. For a moment I thought it to be Kori, but to my disappointment it was not. Two girls came giggling into view. Cas and Pol moved at once to greet them. I rose to my feet as well, but to take my leave instead.

"Whoa, Kael! Where you going?" Cas called as I walked away.

I stopped and turned back to the twins. Already they had set to entertain the giggling duo with drink and banter around the fire. I had no desire to be there for their antics.

"It's late." I replied. "Keep up with that bottle."

"What? Ah, fine."

Neither of them were particularly concerned about my leave, well distracted by their flirty guests. I carefully made my way back across the branches. It took much more time to get back. With the moon hidden behind the greater forest, the world was darker.

When at last my feet were back on the ground, I traveled down the length of the eastern ridge toward my father's hut. Sarah would be there, but it didn't matter. I was tired and empty. I had longed for this day to come, but now that it had I didn't know how to feel about it. I was ready for sleep.

The air had gotten much cooler, all the more crisp under a clear sky. The stars were visible beyond the distal branches of the Allichene. A sky with stars felt better to have overhead. I eased my eyes shut the last few steps to the doorway. I breathed deep of the night one last time to say good bye, for it was never the same twice, and stepped through the door with the whip of the leather flap.

Inside the fire burned low and warm, welcoming against the chill of the night outside. On my bed lay Sarah, nestled in the fur and fast asleep. An impossible snore rose from her small frame. Across the fire from her sat my father, who looked to me with warm eyes.

"Welcome home, son." He smiled. His voice sounded like he had been silent for some time.

"It was quite a shock when I came in and found her instead of you. Startled us both I think." He laughed softly. "I hadn't been ready for that one. Didn't take note of much, just went out for a walk. She was snoring as bad as you when I came back."

I sat down next to him and watched the rise and fall of her breathing beneath the fur of my bed. A dirty foot peaked out from the bottom corner.

"You did a good thing, son." Came my father's words. "I'm proud of you. I'm sure she'll appreciate you as well come morning." He continued.

"I hope so. I'll not be going for any more flowers." I smiled.

"Well at the very least Balthar can sleep sound, not that he's the least bit concerned with the idea." My father teased.

"He and everyone else, it would seem." I responded, sounding more cold than I had meant to. I was still not privy to the concept, regardless of what was expected. Not yet anyway.

My father laughed low and soft. "We just want you to be happy. Your path is your own, but don't let pride blind you to the obvious. In time, you will find your way."

There was a long pause, as the fire crackled low in front of us. Sarah breathed deeply as she slept, each breath like a sigh of relief. I was ready to sleep just as sound.

"You and Kori are more than ready." My father spoke encouragingly. "You will do fine."

"I know." I responded, realizing he was reassuring himself more so than me. "You've taught us well. We won't go hungry or lose our way."

"I certainly hope not." He smiled wide, his bushy beard making him appear warm and fuzzy by the soft light of the fire. "If nothing else, you lot can certainly fight well enough."

I couldn't help but smile at this. He was proud and confident in his pupils, both as a teacher and a father. The father seemed to worry a little under his pride.

"The sun will rise soon. We should get some rest, huh?" He said, shifting into his bed.

"Yeah." I responded, more than ready for sleep.

I looked over to Sarah, a pretty mess sprawled across my bed. What remained of her body paint was smeared and blotchy.

"Don't worry lad, she won't bite. She's fast asleep, and I'm right here." He teased. "If nothing else, your brother's bed is available for the night it seems."

I considered using Kori's bed, but decided against it. I didn't like his stink well enough to wallow in it. Besides, his bed was a mess now, and it hadn't been before.

"That's fine." I said, as I moved to sneak into my own bed without disturbing its current occupant.

She didn't stir in the slightest. As I laid my head to rest and pulled the corner of my favorite fur over me, I heard my father's voice from the other side of the fire.

"Good night, my son."

"Good night, father." I whispered back as not to disturb Sarah.

She sighed gently next to me with the rise and fall of the shaggy dark fur. It was strange having her there. I hadn't shared a bed since I was a wildling. At the very least, my bed was warm and inviting, and I drifted fast to sleep.

The Day of Sending

I woke well before the light of day, despite the late night adventure. The world was quiet, and the cool mist that blanketed the morning world crept into the hut through the wooden slats of the windows. The only sounds were those of a few early rising birds, practicing their songs before sunrise.

A gap in the shutter above my bed let the cool scents of the waking world flow into the warmth of our small home. The glow of the coals still existed deep in the fire pit at the hut's center. I simply lay there, indulging in the moment, knowing on this day I would rise to embark on a sacred journey.

Next to me Sarah began to stir, limbs still heavy with sleep. She rolled to face me, eyes opening for a quick peak before closing again. She lay her arm across my chest and stretched a leg over my own, nestling close and warm against me. Her skin was soft, and her scent was sweet. A hint of wine lingered. I returned her embrace, placing my arm under her and bringing her close. A smile crossed her lips as she lay there against me.

She must have fallen back to sleep, and as I lay there I wished I could do the same. I would need all my energy for the day ahead. Yet my mind remained alert and awake, too excited to listen to good sense.

I closed my eyes and focused on the sounds of the world, letting the silence wash over me in hopes sleep would follow. I heard my father breathing on the other side of the hearth, Sarah's soft sigh next to me. Small tweets from early rising birds came closer outside. Dawn would break soon, if it hadn't already. I heard the heavy tread of familiar footsteps approaching...

I opened my eyes and waited. Sure enough, the flap pulled aside and Kori stepped into the hut. The bright grays of early morning spilled into the chamber with a blinding flash. Perhaps he had returned for a quick nap, I hoped in silence. No such luck.

"Brothers!"

He burst as he came through the door, a triumphant grin wide on his face. His paint was gone, and he was well groomed despite the early hour.

"May the blessings of the Mother be upon you this day. I tell you, her gifts are well bestowed upon me. I feel amazing!"

He hopped gallantly about the hut, bright as could be in the early morning gloom. My father chuckled as he sat up to face the exuberant Kori, eyelids still clinging to sleep.

"She's blessed me with you lot, and that's well more than enough. Especially at this hour." He groaned with a warm smile, his eyes still not quite able to remain open.

As Kori rounded my bed on what must have been his fourth trip around the cramped confines of the hut, he stopped dead in his prancing tracks. The female presence in our cozy home had finally caught his attention.

"My apologies, I wasn't told we had a guest. Where are your manners brother?" Kori scolded playfully as he stood over my bed, face brimming wide.

Sarah pulled the dark shaggy fur away from her face, her glittery blue eyes peaked out followed by a sly smile. "Good morning."

"Good morning, miss Sarah!" Kori responded, shooting a suggestive wink and a smile between Sarah and me.

I felt myself flush. Sarah and I shot up from the cozy confines of my bed. We were both suddenly ready to move on with the day. The tiny hut seemed impossibly crowded, the four of us all but filling the domed structure. Sarah made for the door, I dawned my tunic and followed after her. She turned to my father before exiting.

"Thank you."

My father simply nodded. "Young lady."

Outside the hut Sarah and I listened to Kori rail my father in his excitement, jubilant to share the details of his magical night with Tiahla. His intended had indeed accepted him in turn. We laughed, knowing well enough already.

"Good to know someone is feeling it this morning." Sarah joked, looking a bit faint as she belched. "I feel rough."

"Yeah..." I all but sighed, not having much else to say on the matter.

"Well, I best be off. Father is likely still asleep. That game lasts long into the night most times they play. Mom will be up and around though, and probably in a ripe mood if I had to guess." She laughed. "Thank you for a wonderful evening, Kael."

She kissed me gently before she turned and hurried along, running across the open stretch of field to the adjacent ridge where Balthar's house and workshop stood. I watched her go, feeling the new appreciation for her company grow in depth and meaning. All of it was more confusing than anything, but the idea was growing on me despite my intentions.

The door flapped open, and my father ducked through it to stand next to me. His eyes moved over the village.

"Beautiful place to call home isn't it?"

Sarah had disappeared into Balthar's hut. I looked over the village following my father's words. The huts lined the ridges, smoke rising here and there were fires burned. The Dóvai had already begun to move about in the early morning light, now bright and golden as the sun crept over the fields.

The canopy above swayed ever so gently. A few broad leaves reflecting light down into the village in bright rays of yellow and green. Color reflected from the sparkling lanterns still hanging, suspended overhead.

"Aye." I sighed, knowing full and well the depth of what he meant. I would not see the village again until my return.

"If you think you miss it now, just wait." He chuckled. "You'll miss it well enough. Believe me, the seasons go quick out there. You'll be back and full of yourself before you know it, son. Of course things'll be different then. You'll fall in love with this place all over again, more than ever if you end up with that one."

He pointed to Balthar's hut. A warm, hearty laugh followed his words. It seemed to bring new life to the fresh morning air.

"How was your night, brother?" Kori popped out from the hut, a silly grin on his face.

"Good." I responded, knowing he was looking for details of my time with Sarah.

He was in for disappointment, but there was no need to reveal all that just yet. We would talk eventually, I was sure. Avoiding the subject altogether would have been fine by me, but with Kori and the twins around to nag it was far from likely.

"You two knuckle heads make me proud every day, come 'ere!"

My father shouted as he scooped us up in a bear hug as if we were still just wildlings. He all but crushed us against his chest for a moment before dropping us to the ground. We scuffled about, warming the morning with the hearty laughter of family at play.

My father stretched with a groan, as Kori and I recovered.

"Its about that time now. No warm breakfast today, lads. Better off rummaging through leftovers on your way, if the birds haven't beat you to it. Go on ahead. I'll meet you at the gate."

I was reluctant to leave, but he was right. It was time. Kori knew as well, and together we set off through the village. Our loved ones would gather at the pass that led to Yerok and see us off with warm wishes and blessings.

The path squeezed between two massive trunks of the Allichene where it met the village. It was referred to as the Spirit Gate, the singular point from which we would leave the village to begin the Allioht. We would step through it to begin our journey this day, and again upon completion on our return.

The world was fresh from waking. A chill caught in the mist that lingered promised gentle passage into the heat of midday. Families groggily stirred within the warm confines of their domed huts.

The village felt distant, as Kori and I walked the path along the ridge. From my first steps the soft earth underfoot had led to the heart of Reisenbough, and it seemed all the more appropriate that it should lead me on this day.

Autumn wasn't far. The chill would vaporize with the mist, cooked by the radiant morning sun. It had already risen to shine bright along the ridges as it crept higher into the sky, the warmth of its light welcomed across my skin.

To the north the grasses whipped over the fields with the breeze. The Veylspring flowed against the shadowy face of the bluffs. Festival and ceremony, the experience had been incredible. Father was right, I would love it all the more when I returned.

The forest was alive, as if it too were ready to honor this day. Overhead, the shady greens of the canopy stirred like the village. The slow gentle sway of the great branches seemed playful, as the leaves tussled about in the gentle breeze. Birds called, scattered like their songs, fluttering colors in the green.

This would always be my home. I lingered in the moment, breathing deep of it as if it were my last. The air carried the smell of Reisenbough, rich with the scents of a world preparing for summer's end.

It seemed Kori was caught in the same wave of nostalgia, shaking his head as he reflected.

"Hard to think we are really leaving today... I mean, all these years I knew it was coming, but now it's here. Do you feel any different than any other day?"

"Not sure." I responded earnestly. "I'm not even sure how to feel about yesterday just yet."

Kori laughed. "Yeah, I think I know what you mean. Last night was amazing." He smiled wide. "So you and Sarah?"

The question arrived. "No."

"Oh." Kori responded, surprised to hear it. "Well did you two at least get along well enough?"

"Well enough. Had you not been so involved yourself, you may have noticed." I responded shrilly.

Kori shook off the quip with triumphant laughter. His happiness was unshakable and contagious it seemed, as cheers erupted from those who had emerged from their homes to see us off. Word of his union with Tiahla had spread no doubt. Kori was ecstatic, spinning around to bask in the celebratory cries of the people. Young love was the promise of tomorrow for the Dóvai, and little was celebrated more than the bond of kinship my brother had made between houses. He was happy, happy to honor his people.

"Come, brother. Breakfast is served!" He all but sang as we neared the ravaged tables that held the leftovers from the night's feast. "Hope you brought your appetite."

We made our way to a table topped with a few leftover helpings of fruit and bread. I grabbed a chunk of bread and dipped it through some berry spread. The sweet flavor of the berry went well with the wholesome bread, pillow soft and chewy.

"A full year... You think we'll be able to handle the 'twits' for that long?" Kori teased.

"I think we'll find out." I responded between bites of sweet preserve and bread.

We finished our breakfast quickly, eating as much as we could stand. There was no way of knowing when another big meal might be. More of our age mates were coming through as well, heading for the gate at the pass. A few of them sorted through the leftovers as we did. More cheers sang out, recognizing and honoring the others as they had for Kori and me.

I waived to Kris and Nattan, who walked just ahead of Devin and a rather groggy looking Yuri. Judging by the crowd already gathered around the gate, the majority of the others departing were already there waiting on the rest of us. Kori and I made no effort to hurry on our way to the pass. By the time we arrived at the gate, we were the last of the departing to do so.

The pass stood at the south end of the village, where it lead into the forest. The snaking pathway would take us to Mount Yerok, winding its way through the dark belly of the Arching Forest where the Allichene grew thickest. The two trees that marked the path formed an arch high overhead, where two branches crossed and twisted together. This was known as the Spirit Gate.

Crossing through the Spirit Gate would complete the sending. Farewells would be given, prayers would be offered, and my brothers and I would embark on the Allioht. Most of the village had already gathered. The faces of the Dóvai were cheerful, some still painted, some refreshed anew.

Mothers stood teary eyed next to proud and beaming fathers. Their pride seemed warm like the golden morning sun, mingled with a parting sorrow like the chill that lingered in the early autumn air. It felt as if the hearts of the Dóvai were preparing to change with the seasons.

As we made our way through the crowd, I looked up to see the peak of the gate where the two large branches intersected. The branches became pinched tightly together where they first met, twisting a bit where they broke free of one another. Each continued to grow into the intricate workings of the other's crown. These great beings grew together with such harmony, it was no wonder our ancestors had decided to settle here.

I looked over the village. The world was well lit with the morning light, and the fields to the north were bathed in a golden radiance. The stone huts that lined the ridges would still be there much like our people, awaiting our return. The sound of familiar voices brought me back to where I stood.

"Kori!"

"Kael!"

Kori and I turned to the sound of our names. It was the twins.

"Glad you could finally make it. Late night?" Pol teased, landing a friendly fist on Kori's shoulder.

Kori said nothing, only smiled brightly and nodded like a fool. The twins erupted in congratulatory praise instead of their usual banter.

"Boys!"

Came a haggard, thunderous voice that could only be that of my grandfather. He caught our attentions, startling half the crowd around us as he did.

"You hear what I called you? Boys! Today's the last day I get to call you that. Make sure it's the last time you answer to it as well. Bwar-har-har!" Kraegar laughed merrily with the rocking of his gut. His laugh spread throughout the crowd.

My father stood next to him, a thick fur draped over his broad shoulders. He looked almost as large as my grandfather, a somber look on his face despite the smile he managed. Sarah stood next to him, all but hidden behind the end of the thick bushy black fur. She was back in her simple tunic and waist cloth. Her paint was gone, the braids in her hair all that remained of last night's maiden. She smiled brightly as our eyes met, and I realized I was smiling back.

To my grandfather's left stood Tiahla. Her delicate features seemed especially vibrant, her eyes fixed on my brother. He had already started toward her.

I met my father first. His dark eyes were glittery as if he might cry. A gentle smile hid within his dark tangled beard.

"Every father dreams of this day. Now that it has come, I wonder if I have dreamed long enough."

His words came much stronger than I had expected. He presented a sword. The leather bindings that held it had been worked into a rugged sheath. My father held it forth, tightly gripped with both hands.

I reached out to receive the gift, gripping the finely crafted leather tight. I felt the hard steel within the sleek confines of its case, my heart pounded in my chest.

"Only." He spoke, awaiting my response.

"Only when. Only then." I responded. He released his grip, and I brought the weapon close.

The leather sheath was recently finished, the strips that wrapped and bound it still soft to the touch. My eyes traced the bands of dark leather to where they met the broad silver guard of the blade. Similar leather bindings wrapped the grip, leading to a decorative end piece at the bottom of the hilt.

A polished black stone was fitted into the center of the handle, showing at either side, clutched in the powerful jaws of the mighty Dóv. The shiny metal smoothed where the hilt flared into the guard, the image of a raven intricately etched into the dark surface. Its wings were agape across the guard, its beak raised to point down the length of the blade.

Grabbing hold, I pulled the blade free with a metallic ring and ran my eyes down the wonderful work of weaponry, sleek and shining in the light. The blade was tapered on one side, the edge looked sharp as a razor. It was more wedged on the other, dull and rigid, a fine and wicked point at its terminal end. It was sleek and well balanced, as I felt it in my grip for the first time. I slid the blade back into its sheath, letting it fall to rest at my side and faced my father.

"You honor me."

"As you honor me, my son." He smiled brightly.

"Now its only plated, so don't go smashing it into things at random!" Came my grandfather's booming growl, as he coached an excited Kori.

Kori had received new armaments as well, a sword and shield. Steel plates were bolted to the flat round face of the shield. The light color of the wooden base meant it was most likely featherwood, a light and durable substance rare to the western forests. His blade was a bit shorter, with a less pronounced guard in comparison to my own. It too was a work of mastery.

"These are amazing, grandfather!" Kori exclaimed, as he gripped the shield tight against his forearm and moved it about to get a feel for it.

"You're welcome, lad. It's the least we could do. Well, Balthar and Krayton did most of the doing. I held my end with the least part." My grandfather chuckled.

I couldn't help but smile, as I slung the newly acquired sword and sheath over my head to rest across my back. I reached to grip the handle above my right shoulder, readying my stance as if I might draw. The steel was cool to the touch, the textured handle porous and gritty between the weaves of soft leather bindings stretched over the grip.

I seized the handle with the creak of leather, and in a swift graceful motion brought it up and out of the leather case with the hushed zing of steel. I brought it down before me to marvel at its craftsmanship.

"Love at first sight." My father laughed as I gawked. "Careful with that, lad. Balthar at his finest there. It's the real deal."

Kori drew his blade as well, and began twirling it about as my grandfather continued to coach him on his newly acquired gear. I held onto the sword with both hands, facing an empty section of the path, blade readied for an imaginary battle. It was perfectly balanced, but the weight and mechanics were not yet familiar. Instead of swinging it around foolishly, I carefully lifted it over my head and slid it gently back into the snug fit of the case. As anxious as I was, practice could wait.

"What do you boys think?" My grandfather asked, a grizzled smile brimming within his messy beard.

"I think this will be the longest season ever." Kori said jokingly, as he pulled a rather giggly Tiahla into his arms.

Her giggling intensified as he kissed at her neckline where a shell necklace hung loosely. A smooth, polished stone of deep blue hung down at its center. Carved in its face was the symbol of her house, Gina Vesh.

"I made this for you." Came Sarah's voice, low and sweet. She offered a round wooden shield, completing the traditional melee arsenal of a Dóvai warrior. "I know you prefer to fight without one, but I made it for you anyway."

"Thank you." I responded, grateful for her gift.

It was sturdy and solid, comprised of several colors of wood bound together. There must have been three or four different kinds of tree worked into it, yet it held. She had learned well under her father, her work barely distinguishable from his own. A handprint marked the center of the shield's wooden face. It was Sarah's, without a doubt.

"Maybe it'll come in handy. If you ever learn to use it." She teased. "At the very least, it'll cover your back while I'm not around."

I felt the multicolored face of the shield, pressing her handprint against my own. She had done a fantastic job crafting it, well studied under her father's tutelage.

"A fine job."

"Yeah, well..." She flushed a bit, her voice quivering ever slightly as she kicked at the dirt. "I put it together using the best pieces I could find lying around the shop. It may not look like much, but it'll hold just as well."

"Its perfect, Sarah. Thank you." I said, moving to fit the sword and sheath through the grips of the shield. When the two were snug together, I slung the gear across my back. "With any luck, I won't need either."

The shrill call of a horn sounded, letting us know it was time to go. A numbness crept over me. I wanted to say something memorable, something to let her know, to let them all know. But no words came to mind.

"Be careful out there, Kael." Her words came softly. Tears were soon to follow, twinkling as they gathered across eyes as blue as the heavens.

Before I could respond, she threw her arms around me and pulled herself tight against me. Her lips pressed hard into mine, her kiss deep and ferocious. She hugged me tight once more, whispering at my ear.

"Come back to us, son of Krayton."

Once again, I had no words. Somehow it didn't seem I needed them. I returned her embrace, her sweet fragrance filling my breath. We lingered there but a moment before she pulled away, tears streaming from her angel eyes. She turned and ran for the village, disappearing into the crowd.

"Well, time to head out you two lovebirds." Came the rather cheery voice of Pol.

He was dressed in his usual garb, only he now had a nice warm looking fur draped about his shoulders. At his waist were two daggers, the same presented at last night's festival, the same I had seen in Balthar's shop.

"Time to let him go, he's ours now. No worries though, we'll bring him back." Cas teased playfully, as he meant to pry Kori away from Tiahla.

He too adorned a new fur. His was slightly darker in color, a similar set of daggers at his waist. He made little effort to actually come between the two, allowing Kori's shoves to push him back.

He was right though. It was time, and she knew this. Tears lined her soft rosy cheeks, as she removed her necklace and fit it around Kori. His neck seemed incredibly broad in comparison, as the necklace clung to him as if it were the very extension of Tiahla's embrace.

"Come back to me, son of Raethos. You have children to father." She said before kissing him deeply. Cheers erupted all around, as their union was one most accepted.

"He's got to become a man before he's any good for that, lass." Kraegar teased.

Laughter erupted. Tiahla herself laughed through her tears.

He turned to Kori. "You best get going before you end up weepy eyed as well. Better she doesn't see that part." He chuckled, slapping Kori on the shoulder to console him. He did look to be on the verge of tears. "She'll be here waiting for you when you get back, lad. Now get goin'!"

"Remember, the forest is safest come winter." Archon's voice came. "Until then, be wary. Creatures of all sorts are on the move, the worst of them storing food for the cold ahead. Avoid anything that looks to be a den or burrow. Chances are, it is."

"They can handle it." My father said, the sound of concern latent in his voice despite his reassurance.

"No need to worry, Uncle. You've taught us well. We are well practiced in all your teachings, especially him." Kori said, nodding in my direction. "You'd swear it was his job to recite the lessons he hears."

"Its true." Cas added, nodding in concurrence.

"Always brooding and stoic." Pol contemplated aloud. "He's like a regular prince of proverbs."

They laughed as if they had expected the men to do the same.

"It's good to know at least one of you value the wisdom of your people." Kraegar spat.

With that, the twins were off. They delivered their final farewells to their teary eyed father and their rather bubbly mother, excited to see her boys grow into men or perhaps happy for a break from them. Either way, they didn't linger, all but skipping away through the gate.

"You have to go now." My father instructed. "Show the world what you are, see the world for what it is. Return as men."

"Yes, father." I responded, pride swelling. I used it to turn and chase after the twins. I didn't dare look back.

"You lot best come back next season, you've got that fathering to do! Bwarr-harr-harr!" Kraegar teased, his thunderous laughter rattled at our backs as if to push us along the forest path.

As I passed through the gate, my courage seemed to leave me. I ran after the twins. There was no turning back. Not ever. Kori caught up as well, running at my side. The day had finally come.

After we rounded a few turns, the village was far enough behind us that we slowed. For a few steps we remained silent, catching our breath in the chill damp forest. We followed well behind the others on the path, winding deeper into the shade under the Allichene.

As we rounded another bend, the twins popped out from behind some brush, brimming with excitement as if they had been eager for the ambush. With cheesing smiles Cas and Pol dropped in line to walk alongside Kori and me.

"Wait until you hear about last night..." Pol said, smiling even wider somehow despite the limitations of his face. He placed an arm across my shoulder as we walked.

The energy changed with the four of us reunited. The somber chill of goodbyes began to subside, as we walked deeper and deeper into the forest along the path. Once again we were unstoppable, ambitions burning strong enough to last well beyond the trials of manhood. Together we set out to face the world with all we were. There was no reason to look back. I would return, and I would do all I could to ensure my brothers returned with me.

The trail through the lower forest was difficult to discern at times, as we continued toward Mount Yerok. Vegetation grew heavy among ages of debris fallen from the Allichene, making the forest air rich and alive as the sun grew stronger somewhere above the canopy. The chill damp gradually became warm and steamy.

The twins prattled on in their usual manner, telling Kori and me all about their latest adventure. After I had taken my leave, the twins and company had finished the bottle of wine, leading to what the twins considered to be 'a right good time'.

The four of them had been dancing about in the canopy when one of the girls nearly fell, a fall that would have most certainly been fatal. The twins had found this brush with death to be most entertaining. The young ladies had been quite shaken by the event and found the laughter of the twins offensive enough to retire from the evening's festivities. The twins couldn't have been more tickled to tell the story. Cas laughed so hard I thought he might collapse, gasping for breath.

Kori was no more shocked than I was, though he at least had something to say on the matter, letting them know how ridiculous and irresponsible they had been. The twins continued their banter. I barely caught a word. Instead, I simply enjoyed the company of my brothers.

There was little to be said anyhow. My mind was preoccupied with the journey at hand, a welcomed distraction from the complications of age. We would reach the summit before nightfall, but there was still plenty to do along the way.

As we continued, I took time to reflect. The smiling faces of Kori and the twins reminded me that I was not to face anything alone. For a moment I eased my eyes shut to feel the dense forest around us. I felt my heart beat to the rhythm of my step. We had taken our first steps, wandering boldly into the savage world that awaited, the promise of an adventure like none before.

The Allioht

It was well beyond midday when we reached a small clearing near the base of Mount Yerok. The sun shone brightly through breaks in the canopy, lighting the leafy shoots of green vegetation that grew in the small meadow. The forest had become less dense near the mount, and the brush that grew was well nourished by the increase in sunlight.

My age mates worked along the narrow path we followed, stripping the skin from the stalks of green leafy shoots that grew in great numbers along the clearing. These tall shoots were known as the Kefari. The fibrous skin of these plants was perfect for making powerful rope and cords, the latter of which would serve to make a much needed bow.

"This looks like a good place to gather supplies." Kori said, taking his knife in hand and grabbing hold of one of the tall leafy plants. He squatted and began scraping down the length of the stalk.

"Excellent form, you're doing fantastic!" Pol teased with a grin, passing Kori by as he worked.

"When it comes to rubbing stalks, he's a natural." Cas teased in concurrence as always.

"We'll need a strong bow as well." I interjected.

There was little time to waste. It would take much of the remaining daylight to reach the top of the mountain. There was still much to do before making camp.

"Whoa, slow down Kael." Pol replied. "We've got time to spare. Cas and I can take care that."

He was confident in his words, following with a thumbs up. Cas seemed to disagree with the suggestion.

"Oh can we now?"

"Of course, brother." Pol replied. "With ease."

No doubt mischief was to follow, but such was to be expected. As long as they did their part, it didn't matter. With that, the two were off.

I made my way into the nearby thicket to work alongside Kori. One by one Kori and I shaved the skins from a dozen or so of the Kefari. Before we knew it, we had a decent sized collection of fibrous tendrils, bundled and ready to be worked into fresh new lines.

We set to work carefully weaving the deep green fibers together while we waited for the twins to finish their part. The green of the plants stained our fingers as we worked. The smell of the injured plants was potent, adding a pleasant aroma to the smell of sun cooked vegetation.

The twins made plenty of noise along their way, singing a rather humorous number as they moved along. A few of the others still working in the area laughed occasionally, as one twin sang out a clever line or two to be answered in time by the other. The two lived to entertain, and as I laughed along with my brothers I couldn't have been more grateful for their company.

It was fun to hear them carry on as they worked, even better to know where they were. It didn't stop their mischief by any means, but at least a direction of origin could be determined. It was no surprise when a reisen berry came crashing down with a great splat so near the path that some of the juicy blue fallout spattered the plants where Kori and I worked.

"Heads up!" Pol called down after the fact, followed by a duet of maniacal laughter.

"That does it for our end of the foraging then."

Cas teased as he appeared from the brush, a ridiculous smile upon his face. He carried a perfect bough precariously tossed over his shoulder, freshly cut and ready to be shaped into a deadly bow.

"Well met." Kori responded, his words lacking any real enthusiasm.

He barely even shifted his eyes from the bundle he was looping, his focus on the task at hand. He was unshakable, even for the twins. He moved with a new motivation, evident in the smile that lingered through the day.

"So, which of you would like the honor of carrying this thing the rest of the way?" Cas asked, sounding somewhat serious as he dropped the beam of light colored wood to crash into the leafy vegetation at his feet with a thud.

Kori said nothing, he simply continued working the freshly cut fibers into lines while they were still wet and pliable.

"We'll take turns." I resolved.

"Oh good then. That concludes my turn." Cas replied. He made his way to the splattered berry Pol had cut free and began hacking at it with a stone knife.

"For now."

Kori spoke, his hands fast at work weaving the frayed threads of plant skin into a single, tight thread. He worked with diligence, a purpose beyond the immediate. He had found his resolve, his devotion.

I too set to work weaving threads, while Cas cut and pealed four large circular flaps of skin from the berry. He snacked on the sweet innards of the fallen fruit as he worked.

Just as Cas severed the last of the four bowl shaped flaps of thick dark blue skin, Pol emerged from the brush. He appeared giddy with excitement, eyes wide with bewilderment. He was heaving and out of breath, leaving him frantic as he tried to form his words.

"Took you long enough, brother." Cas teased as he looked up from his task to greet his brother. "Wha-"

He uttered only a syllable of his intended message before stopping short. The smirk he wore faded with his words. The sight of his brother so shaken left him serious with concern. Cas quickly recovered from his stammer.

"Brother, are you alright?"

Cas stopped dead from his task and listened most concernedly for his brother's response. His concern seemed to grow in the span of silence, as he waited for Pol to gather his words. Indeed, he had caught the attentions of many in his excited state. We gathered around Pol just as he caught breath enough to speak.

"After I cut the berry, I decided to climb higher. Thought maybe I'd scout ahead, got a great view of the mountain by the way."

"How is old Yerok standing these days?" Cas asked.

"Tall and strong, brother. Tall and strong."

Pol replied, and the two laughed. It was safe to assume there was no danger. A few of the other onlookers lost interest and returned to their chores.

"So you found a lovely view of the mountain then?" Kori asked. His words tinged with sarcasm at such an anticlimactic reveal. "Well that's great, buddy." He returned to his work.

"How much further?" I asked.

"It'll be a good walk, but not too much farther. Looks to be clear skies too." Pol responded quickly before calling out to Kori. "But that's not all I saw. I saw this!" He pointed to the symbol on his greasy headband, the mighty Shemah Yen.

"Yeah right!" Kori shot in response, ripe with skepticism and spittle. "Even among the house elders, only two such claims exist. The deity of the sky doesn't appear to just anyone."

"Well it didn't just appear, silly. It flew overhead. While I was up there a great shadow passed over, and that's when I saw its mighty wings spread wide, high over the canopy. Maybe even above the elder trees!" Pol exclaimed, rather believable in the grip of his passion.

"You sure it wasn't just a fallen leaf from one of the elders, tossing about on the wind?" Kori suggested, not bothering to look away from his work.

Pol released an exaggerated sigh and rolled his eyes. "Hmm, I don't think so. Not unless the symbol of my house is NOT the mighty eagle-dragon, but instead some giant winged tree petal with a mind of its own."

"Kind of puts a new spin on some of the legends though." Cas said jokingly.

The two laughed.

"I must say, Kori. Your ability to confuse a dragon with jungle fodder 'leaves' me baffled." Pol teased.

Kori flushed with anger, though he said nothing.

"Come now brother. Just 'leaf' it at that. Personally, I find it a re-leaf that no one got eaten." Cas added.

This time I couldn't help but laugh along with them. Even Kori cracked a smile despite himself. With Pol returned, we fashioned the cuts of berry skin into makeshift bladders to gather water at the first opportunity. The days were still quite warm, and we would need plenty to drink along our journey.

Our errands complete, we set off once again. We had fallen well behind the others, tailing them at a distance. Though this was favorable, no one said it aloud as we trotted along the trail. In fact there was little more than the usual whimsical conversation between the twins, leaf puns now the running joke.

Together we collected firewood in bundles, bound by the cord we'd fashioned. Between the three of us, it didn't take long to collect enough for the night. Kori had resumed his unshakable calm, his head high as he led the way along the path. It had become more winding, as great boulders were scattered about the massive trunks of the thinning Allichene. The brush grew thicker as the canopy thinned above, soft broad leaves and green tendrils tickled at my sides with each step along the increasing gradient of the land.

Many times along the way I stopped to fidget with the straps of my equipment and readjust. Carrying it was still very new to me, and the weight and feel of it was awkward at times. When my turn came to carry the bough, I handed my gear off to Kori to free my shoulders.

Eventually we arrived at another small clearing near the base of Yerok and stopped for a much needed break. I rolled the bough off my shoulders to thud in the dark green, leafy grass that covered the clearing.

"Hey now! Careful with that!" Cas barked playfully. A short drop onto the soft, damp grass that grew here was far from damaging.

It was the perfect place for a rest. A small stream trickled down from the moss covered stone. Green algae flourished in the clear cold water that flowed into the dark confines of the forest. A light breeze seemed to find its way through the trees, as the forest met the sheer rocky face of Mount Yerok.

I dropped to one knee in the deep green leafy blades of soft grass to drink of the stream. The water was cool and refreshing, as it trickled through me by the handful. The day had grown warm with the heat of the sun, and I had grown quite thirsty along the way. As my hands brought a serving of the chill elixir to my lips, a dark blob plopped into the grass at my side.

"You don't have to drink it all in one go. Save some for later, yeah?" Kori stood at my side. The blob was a newly finished bladder, assembled from a few threads and a hunk of berry skin.

"Thank you, brother." I responded. He had been kind enough to work on it for me when my turn came to carry the bough.

"Glad to help." He responded, plopping down in the grass next to me. He produced another crumpled bladder and plunged it into the stream. "Honestly, I just hope these things hold up as well as grandfather says."

"I guess we'll see." I said, watching water flow into the fettered mouth of the bladder as I held it in the icy stream.

It took only a moment to fill, becoming bulbous as it swelled with water. I tied the mouth closed with a bit of cord and held it up to inspect it more closely. The smooth blue skin of the berry didn't seem the least bit stressed by the water sloshing within.

"Seems rugged enough."

"Oh does it now?" Came the excited voice of Pol.

The twins arrived right on cue, their timing impeccable as ever. The two had been flipping about in the clearing, practicing with their knives when last I'd saw them.

"Nothing like a nice rugged sack, eh Kael?" Cas teased with the nudge of an elbow.

The twins burst into laughter. I tried to retain my composure, but lost it completely when Pol slipped on the wet grass and fell into the icy stream with a whoosh and a reel from cold shock. Cas was barely breathing, gulping mouthfuls of air between giggling fits. It was always good to share a laugh, worries forgotten with the sound of merriment.

A playful scuffle ensued. The twins splashed about in the icy stream, but were quick to catch up once Kori and I started toward the path once more. It was Kori's turn to haul the branch, and I was glad to hand it off for the time being. The mountain path was steep and unforgiving in places, winding up the rocky face of Mount Yerok.

Kori tucked his water into his waist cloth and handed me his gear. Once he situated himself under the weight of the branch, it was time to move again. With our bladders full, we set off along the mountain path.

As we ascended along the northern face of the mountain, the dark earth underfoot became lighter, more red in color. Great boulders and sheer cliffs outlined and shaped the winding trail leading to the summit. Moss grew heavy on the exposed rock faces, adding a healthy green to the reds of the sandstone.

The twins took it upon themselves to provide whimsical conversation to pass the time. They continued their puns, inventing a new game as well. Kori had inspired them far more than he'd have hoped when he vocalized his skepticism. Whether or not Pol had legitimately witnessed the mighty Shemah Yen was beyond question at this point.

"Is that a leaf or a dragon, you reckon?" One twin would ask, pointing into the canopy off to the side of the mountain.

"Oh, well now that is a leaf, silly." The other would respond.

"Oh, right. I see it now. Well what about that one there then?"

The two had great fun with the new game, pretending to be stumped at times and reaching out to either Kori or me to resolve the vexing dispute.

"Hmm, I'm not sure on that one. Best to ask the expert."

Their banter was amusing enough at first, but eventually it began to bore. When it came time for Kori to hand off the branch to Pol, I thought he might bash him with it. He didn't though. Instead, he rolled the weight of it onto Pols shoulders with a soft thud against the back of his head.

"Whoa, now. This thing is heavier than it looks, passing it off must be quite the re-leaf." Pol smirked, even after the conk to the head.

Cas chuckled at his brother's wit despite the same pun used for what must have been the hundredth time. Kori had simply shook his head and laughed. What would our journey be without them?

We had traveled most of the distance up the mountain, when the smell of rain crept into the dusty air...

Clear skies he'd said. Time was of the essence now, the rocks would no doubt be slick under the cold rain soon to fall. We picked up our pace, climbing over the rocks and dirt, catching up with the others just before they reached the summit.

Cas whistled merrily when it came his turn to carry the branch. His tune was cut short with the crack of thunder. The terrain was steep, the rain would make it treacherous. We scrambled up the crest of the mountain, careful not to lose any supplies along our way, especially the firewood. It would be much needed when the oncoming storm hit, providing heat as well as light. At the very least, thirst wouldn't be a problem.

The sky to the west was dark and sinister. The great elder trees swayed at their towering heights as the turbulent skies drew near. We didn't have long before the storm was upon us.

At the summit of Mount Yerok was a large crevice, shaped by many great stones that jutted up along the eastern and northwestern slopes. These great stones provided shelter atop the mount, and our ancestors had built a refuge within the natural contours of the rocky terrain. Several open doorways led to shallow caves, each with an elder symbol carved in the stone above it.

At the center stood a large cistern atop a natural stone basin, which lay snug between two great rock formations. It would collect any runoff that trickled down from the smooth rocks, already a quarter filled and soon to be spilling over with fresh rainwater.

The wind began to stir in violent gusts, sending tiny bits of dry earth and dust to scratch across the rocks. The sky above whirled with angry darkness, as the smell of rain filled the air. A sensation rippled in the chill breeze, much like the static effect of the flashing heavens.

The rain came down all at once it seemed, just as we reached the shelter of the refuge. The twins had selected a cave, and hurried inside with two large bundles of dried stalks and twigs. Kori and I were saturated by the sudden torrential downpour before we made it inside, leaving us shivering as we quickly ducked into the cave to escape the chilling rain.

The cave was dark, as the many sounds of its occupants reverberated back from the domed confines of the chamber. Now and then, sparks lit the dark, allowing a flashing glimpse of the cave as the twins worked to build a fire. Lightning lit the world outside in spontaneous bursts of brilliant white. Under the fury of the storm, it was as dark as the inside of the cave.

Eventually one of the flashes from the twins was followed by a low glowing light. In no time, the cave was alive with light and warmth. There were seven of us all together, huddling around the small fire. Kori worked at removing his gear and pealing off his soaked clothing across the fire from me. The twins continued to build the fire, gradually feeding it larger pieces of firewood as it grew at the center.

Around the fire opposite sat Ian, Jake, and Vren. The others spilled in when they discovered we already had fire. They had taken refuge in another cave, but their efforts to build a fire had been in vain it seemed.

The twins continued to stoke the fire as the rest of us made ourselves comfy around the glowing warmth. Ian and Jake wasted no time on formalities, and set to eating on what little food they had managed to bring along. Vren was silent and fidgety for the longest time, but eagerly accepted a chance to assist the twins with tending the fire.

I slipped out of my soaked tunic. When I removed the shield and lay it next to my sword, I found a soft braid wrapped about the grip. It was a lock of Sarah's hair, bound with ribbon and tied in place. I smiled with the discovery, keeping the memento in secret.

While the others set to swapping stories, I sat around the fire in silence, working with the plant fibers in hopes of making a cord strong enough to string a bow. A few of the others worked as well between chatting and storytelling. It was well entertaining to have their company, the cave filled with the young aspiring hearts of the Dóvai. There were smiles, and everyone seemed to be getting along well enough, despite the sudden storm that drenched the evening.

Ian and Jake got along with the twins well enough. Kori perched in the middle of them, already set to working the bough into a weapon with long shallow cuts from his stone knife, running down the length of it. I watched the familiar motions, as Kori shaved and shaped the bough, his movements rhythmic as he worked. Indeed we had learned well.

The confines of the cave were warm and welcoming against the cold rain falling outside. The light of the dancing flames flickered over elaborately painted murals that covered most of the lower surfaces of the smooth walls. Each seemed to tell a story, though the characters and happenings portrayed in the images were unknown to me. I gazed over the various figures, recognizing a few of the landscapes depicted.

Old tools lay scattered about at the back of the cave, left by those who had been there before us, perhaps even generations before. Large clay pots stood neatly stacked to the high blackened ceiling along the back wall, most likely food stores. There was plenty to eat within these large clay pots, but we would take only what was needed before continuing on our way. When we returned to the mount for the third and final trial, we would restore that which we used for those to come.

Above the doorway there was a symbol carved into the stone, the etchings painted a vibrant blue. The symbol was that of a feather edged, conical flame with a strong, swirling base. It marked the Order of the Blue Flame, one of three prestigious houses that had survived Hathlanda in ages past.

I knew very little of the once great organization marked by this symbol, as it was not the house of my direct lineage. The same symbol was carved into the worn stone above the door outside, where the rain that had raged for some time sobbed in anger.

The night moved on, laughter and stories filled the air of the cave much like the warmth and light of the fire. The bow's construction was well underway, and it was my turn to continue the work in progress.

As the hours passed, tales of hearts wooed and future ambitions were at last losing their luster. Silence gripped the cave once more, but just long enough for us to realize the storm had subsided. It was well into the night. The slicing sound of my stone knife sheering at the bough was eventually accompanied by the sound of Jake's flute.

It nearly gave me a start when he first sounded it. Laughter followed an initial harsh note. When next Jake blew into the instrument the sound was right for the cave, and a soothing melody soon held its lofty sway over those gathered. The cold and dark of night meant little, the world distant against the dreamlike ambiance of flame and song. In that moment it seemed all the more right to hear his song here in this place of our ancestors, the song of their descendants reverberating over the murals, inked images of their legacy. The same legacy lived on, dancing through the notes of Jake's song.

Ian took notice of the image that again held my attention, the mysterious blue flame above the doorway. He too had been silent under the sway of the melody, but found the time right to speak.

"It was a respected symbol among the Elder Houses." Ian began, his voice soft and confident as he began to share his knowledge of this mysterious relic of our ancestral history.

"My forefathers were of this house, the Order of the Blue Flame. They were alchemists, well scientists really. Well prided in their studies of the elements. At one time their libraries had been the greatest house of knowledge known to the era, collected and shared from all areas connected along the Purge. When the city fell, the sapphire tower of the order and all its precious archives went with it."

"What little was left of the order elected to further their alignment with the elements, continuing the pilgrimage that led to the foundation of Reisenbough. It is through the residual knowledge and practices passed down by the order that an antidote to the fearsome poison of the Malekaur was derived, the same antidote carried in small blue vials entrusted to each of the house elders. Blue was the color of the order, and that is why blue is still used to mark potions and elixirs of healing..."

Ian's voice trailed off, and it became apparent that he held the attention of all in the cave. Jake's flute came to a graceful stop, as the last note faded. The fire had died to a low crackle.

"Well that's interesting." Pol nodded. He reflected for a moment and set back to poking at the embers. "I heard tale they were a bunch of ninja assassins."

Laughter erupted around the circle. Pol fed the fire just enough to keep the cave warm against the chill grip of the waning storm. I closed my eyes to get some much needed rest. The warm glow was soothing against my face, the smooth dirty stone beneath me cool in contrast.

Sleep came easy, but my mind refused to stay at rest. My dreams were flooded with ill omens, shaking me from sleep many times as the night passed. I dreamed that we couldn't complete our journey, for the forest had no end. Reisenbough and all her people had vanished, and the village was empty when we returned. Worst of all, I was utterly alone, alone and lost in a world most unfamiliar to me...

The others didn't stir a bit it seemed. Each time I woke, I tended the fire to keep the cave warm against the cool air and listened to the world around us, allowing its peace to flow over me, returning my own. As I lay there, the sounds of a world at rest guided me back to sleep. The snoring of my brothers around me, the crackling of the warm glowing fire, the gentle trickle of the soft rain outside...

When sleep finally came, I held tight with a deathlike grip. The next morning I was the last to rise, waking to an empty cave. The fire had long since expired, and the bright light pouring in from outside suggested it was late morning. Had the others already gone?

I rose quickly, perhaps too quickly. The cave seemed to spin for an instant, as I bent over to collect my belongings. My tunic was still damp. I piled it on top of my shield, slung my sword across my back, and stepped out into the bright golden sunshine.

The air was warm and muggy, the earth and stone a shade darker with the water that trickled down the rocks to collect in puddles. The sun above was warm and radiant, not far from high noon.

At first I thought I might have been alone, until I noticed a commotion at the cistern. Kori and the twins were gathered at the great basin. I made my way to them, toes squishing in the cold mud as I walked right through the heart of a large puddle.

"Ah, at last he is risen! You almost had us worried, you know." Pol blathered upon seeing me.

He collected water as it trickled down from a nozzle on the cistern. A lever on the side of a bulbous stone nozzle moved a bolt that ran through it. When the lever aligned a hole in the bolt with the one in the nozzle, a stream of water was released.

"AND we missed out on a fresh kill this morning." Cas chimed in.

"A kill?" I asked, my astonishment suppressed in my groggy state. The others had already finished a bow.

"Yeah, a doe from what we've heard so far." Cas continued. "Trev's the one who got it."

Of course he is. I thought to myself with an audible scoff.

"The others ran off to check it out a long time ago." Pol added. "We've been stuck here under the charge of Master Kori, working our gifted hands to the bone..."

Pol paused as if to gauge Kori's reaction, smiling wide before continuing.

"He did most of it actually. He may not know the difference between a leaf and a dragon, but he knows how to craft a decent bow. Check it out."

Kori had been sitting on a stone just beyond splashing range of the spout. He rose now, clutching hold of a newly carved longbow. It was tall like a staff, having a singular curve shape that led from each tip down through the broad powerful body, twine wrapped to form the grip. It would last, feeding us well in the seasons to come.

"It didn't take long with the three of us working together." Kori said, standing proud as he spoke, marveling at the work. "We got through the brunt of it last night. Once we have a cord that can hold, it'll be ready."

He shot an accusative glance at the twins.

"What?" Pol asked, as if unaware of his implications. "So it didn't hold, not my fault it snapped."

"Could have happened to anyone really." Cas argued, sounding matter-of-fact. "At least no one lost an eye, I think we can all find some releaf in that."

Kori simply shook his head. "You should count yourself lucky you didn't wake up in a flood. These two nearly brought down the cistern earlier. I had to show them how to work the nozzle."

At this, Pol jumped down from the stone step under the spout and offered an explanation on the events, defending his actions.

"Whoa, now. Neither of us have used this old thing before. How could we have known it worked like that?" He asked rhetorically.

"Besides, it took you a bit to figure it out as well." Cas chimed in, backing his brother.

"Yeah, but I figured it out didn't I? And I did so without bashing an ancient relic of our people with a rock. They were going to smash the pin out! Could you imagine?" Kori bellowed.

"Nah we weren't!" Defended Cas. "We were just getting it all loosened up, so you didn't have to muscle it as much. That's all."

"Yeah, you really should be thanking us. It was a team effort!" Pol pleaded mockingly before they burst into laughter. It was good, waking to their light humor after a long night of dark dreams.

Kori came closer. "Is all well, my brother?"

I felt silly with my response, but I gave it with honesty. "Restless night. Just a few bad dreams, brother. Sorry to keep you waiting."

Kori accepted this response, though he seemed ready to hear more. We would surely revisit the topic around a fire later this evening, hopefully with a fresh kill and full bellies. But not now.

Pol scoffed. "You thought we were waiting for you to wake from hibernation? Ha, nah. Truth is, there's more than enough of that doe to go around. We just let the others rush into doing all the work while we sit back and enjoy the fruits of the labor. It's genius. You got your beauty rest, we finished the bow, and defeated the cistern all while the others were off preparing our lunch... I'd say that's a win on several accounts."

"There are some bits of dried meat here for you as well." Cas added, pointing to a small stack of seasoned meat strips atop a rather battered leaf. "Someone left a cache of it wrapped in a hide. Found it tucked away in one of the caves. The others shared it this morning. Someone else claimed the hide though. We found this leaf a suitable replacement."

"You sure it isn't a dragon eagle?" Kori asked in a growling voice, ripped with sarcasm and indifference. His eyes looked about ready to set fire to the leaf in hopes of burning the joke with it. I decided to grab my share just in case.

"Of course it's not, silly." Pol chirped merrily. "Don't be ridiculous."

I rolled the soft leaf around the spicy strips of dried meat, and tucked them into my waist cloth, keeping two of the larger pieces out for breakfast. They were every bit as delicious as they smelled.

My tunic was dry enough to wear finally. Once I got my gear situated well enough to continue, I filled my water supply like the others. Together we set off down the steep, slippery path to the west, carved by the runoff as it trickled down between the great rock formations wedged into the sides of the mountain.

Eventually the path ended at a sheer cliff face, where water spilled over the long fall to the ground, splashing through the vegetation that clung to the wall of the mountain face. From there we proceeded down through a narrow cave, lit only by the light that spilled in from the entrance through which we came and the opening to a path at the bottom. The cave was incredibly dark in places along our decent. The steps grew narrow where openings created shafts that lead down into the deep dark unknown recesses of the mountain. A fall would leave one lost in the vast innards of Mount Yerok.

I was beyond relief when at last we stepped into the light of day once again. The blue sky was obscured by towering vegetation, as the secret pass had led us down under the steep cliffs of the summit. We now stood along Yerok's rocky crest, on the western slopes of the mountain.

We continued west, the journey down the less steep western slope was much easier than the previous day's climb. The earth underfoot was chill from the cold rain, the vegetation thick and wild. The forest was alive. Birds sang all through the canopy, deer gingerly nibbled at leaves before bolting at the sight of us. It was no wonder the others had managed a meal so easily.

There was plenty left of the small doe when we reached the kill site. A fire still crackled, roasting a few skewers of meat. Ian, Jake, Vren, and Yuri sat around it, finishing their meals and stocking food for the trail ahead.

The twins surrounded Vren, nagging him for details on the kill. Kori and I joined the circle as well, picking at the remains and setting bits of meat to roast over the small hot fire. All the best parts had been claimed or taken for later, leaving little for us to carry along after the fact. The twins had been right, however. This was an easy meal and there had been plenty. While we prepared our food, the others filled us in on the latest happenings.

"The mines aren't far ahead. A few of the others found a skeleton." Jake explained between mouthfuls of water.

"Yeah, I was totally there." Ian was excited to share, his eyes wide over his gloating grin. "When we split off for the hunt, my group stumbled across the mines. We had to check it out, you know? Not worth it."

"Whoa.."

I pondered his words while Cas and Pol prodded to hear more of the mines. We would no doubt pass through the area, ruins of the atrocities known to our ancestors. As a result of my wandering attentions, I overcooked my food. It was tough like the dried meat, but a welcomed treat all the same. Ian and the others finished their lunch, stashing their future rations in leaf wrappings and tucking them away for later. They bid their farewells and hurried along, disappearing into the forest.

Lunch was rushed, as the twins were eager to see the mines. We finished our toils at the kill site and set out to carry on the voyage. I roasted a few more cuts of meat for later, wrapping them in waxy leaves and tucking them into my waist cloth with the dried meat from earlier. With bellies full and spirits high we set off to quell our shared curiosity, to see for ourselves what lie in wait hidden within the green blinds of the forest.

It didn't take us long to reach the first of the mines, those highest along the mountainside. They were like dark portals, empty and foreboding. The area was mostly younger growth, smaller trees and brush where the forest had reclaimed the site after its abandonment. The mines were like lamenting mouths protruding from the mountain, choked with vines.

"What do you suppose is in there?" Pol asked, as he stood recklessly close to one of the dark portals.

Vines hung lazily down over the entrance, further obscuring the deep dark secrets within. Whatever curiosity I held wasn't nearly enough to compel me to venture further. Strands of arachnid silk lined the forest floor, leading to a few of these openings. They could keep their secrets.

"I'd rather not know." I replied with all honesty, pointing to a strand of shiny rigid silk stretched across the forest floor, my finger tracing its length to the vine covered entrance.

"Good eye, Kael." Cas complemented. His smile faded. "On the bright side, this is better string than anything we could ever weave!"

He then turned, yelling to his twin. "Brother, it's probably best to step away from that endeavor. I love you dearly, but I don't do spiders."

He then turned back to Kori and me. "In fact, might I insist that we carefully collect what we can use of this substance in a hurry, and I do mean hurry, and be on our way?"

"Indeed."

"Yep."

Pol cautiously stepped away from the mine, avoiding the strands as he stepped. With our efforts regrouped, we collected what we could of the more distant strands and departed with a new awareness.

As we descended Yerok's western slope, the mines grew more and more frequent. There were queries, where great chunks of the mountain had been removed and reduced to towering heaps of rubble. Many old roadways remained discernible along our way, making our path easier to traverse. Though they were well overgrown with vegetation in places, it helped to navigate the area encompassing the mines. Some of these roadways were even made of cemented cuts of stone.

Old worn carts and strange gadgetry lie scattered about the place, half hidden as the forest had slowly reclaimed the area over time. There were indeed skeletons among the debris, remains of those fallen, testament to the histories spoken. This place was a blight upon the mountain, a grim reminder of what happens when man looses himself to greedy ambition.

As we walked through the ruins, few words were spoken. The threat of the arachnids was behind us now, as our surroundings had been clear of traces for some time. The ruins seemed completely lost in the grip of years passed, the forest healing as it silently buried this dark past. The purpose of our journey became all the more clear, for to see these things brought life to the stories told around the fires of my childhood.

"What a dreadful place." Pol muttered once we were clear of the mines.

The laughs that followed broke the gloom completely. With the change in mood it almost seemed funny that we so casually trotted through an ancient battleground where so many had perished. Peace was restored to Yerok and the forest, sin but a fading scar upon the land.

When we had at last reached level ground, we decided to take a break at a stone roadway that crossed the path we followed down the mountain. The road was broader than the rest, providing a travel route leading north to south around the base of mount Yerok. There was a small trickling stream just north of where these paths met. We took the opportunity to refill our water and have a quick chat about the day's adventure thus far.

The twins, thoroughly excited by the experience of the mines, engaged in horseplay to vent. They went from scuffling about, to drawing their shiny new daggers and practicing their forms and stances side to side. They looked so serious with actual weapons in hand.

It inspired me to practice with my own, as I had yet to really get a feel for the blade. Balance was everything. The zing of a blade pulled free let me know Kori had come to the same conclusion. He stood ready, blade in one hand and shield gripped tight in the other.

I drew my sword. The metallic sound of its pull to freedom cleared my mind. Once again I was in awe of its mastery. The powerful head of the Dóv stared back at me, the dark jewel clenched hard in its teeth. The wings of the raven flared wide across the guard, driving its way forward with the length of the blade. I felt my pride swell with this weapon in hand, and set it to motion, slicing though the air to get a feel for it.

We lost ourselves for quite some time, running through familiar drills with new focus and improvising where inspiration struck. Our favorite game had gone to the next level, as we took turns facing off against hypothetical enemies and discussing form responses and move executions. The idea was to be as ready as possible should the need ever arise. Strange that in our efforts to ready ourselves against any possible threat, a great lumbering creature of the forest had managed to sneak its way near the stream during our lessons.

Kori had been the first to notice the creature, jolting with a start and yelling like he meant to charge into battle. His reaction startled the rest of us, and we turned to face the hulking reptilian beast. Our war cries faded to laughter upon the realization that this creature was far from threatening, aside from maybe getting trampled. It was a large terrapin, a great shelled reptile with a gentle nature and a healthy taste for leafy green vegetation.

The hulking shelled beast was more interested in the stream than us, as it cautiously approached the water, its great glossy eyes lazily fixed on us. The pupils were large and soft, surrounded by vibrant red irises at either side of its honking beak. The dark leathery skin of its face was smooth, accented with vibrant gold and yellow patterns around its bulbous, beak shaped mouth.

Two great nostrils flared as the creature huffed at us. Finally, it decided we were no threat. With the arching of its massive scaled forelegs, it let its great shell rest against the stones of the road with a heavy scraping sound. Its toes terminated in long, powerful claws caked in dirt. It sighed as it stretched the length of its wrinkled neck, lowering its head to the stream. Its mouth gulped at the water, revealing glimpses of its pink fleshy tongue.

The twins began circling the creature, touching the rough battered exterior of the deep green shell. Pol was the first to take the liberty of mounting the poor creature, which took no notice of the fluffy haired boy stomping around on its back. It simply continued to gobble down mouthfuls from the cool stream.

This encouraged Cas to hop on as well. The two of them danced around atop the creature's back. Kori and I had circled around to the terrapin's wrinkled hind quarters where the twins had scaled their way onto the shell. The creature's saggy, wrinkled bottom protruded from the shell slightly, and its stumpy tail dragged lazily to the left.

"You guys! Just hop up her bottom, she won't mind a bit! Come on!" Pol all but screeched at us before we had a chance to tell them to do the opposite. "Glenda says she'll give us a ride."

"Glenda?" Kori asked, most confused.

"That's her name, the terrapin." Cas explained as if it were silly he was having to do so. "Who else?"

"How do you know it's a girl?" I asked.

"Cause her name is Glenda, silly." Pol responded, sounding impatient. "Now don't be rude, climb up and get cozy."

As Kori and I stood at Glenda's bottom pondering whether or not to climb, she shifted and began to move. Her steps were powerful thrusting motions, heaving her massive body forward along the stone road.

Kori and I dashed to catch up to bulky reptile. We each hopped up an outstretched hind limb as it pushed and climbed up to the twins. In an instant, the four of us were riding atop Glenda's back as she dragged along the clearing made by the road. She was headed north, while our destination was due west.

"She's taking us the wrong way." I pointed out the conflict in our heading.

"Oh relax, Kael!" Pol all but slurred in his indifference, throwing his head back dramatically. "She's heading slightly west. And it's not like she's moving all that fast. Enjoy the fun for a change, we can make up the time and distance easy. You know we can."

"Yeah, Kael." Cas nagged. "Come on, it's the first day of our big adventure! Why not have a little fun?"

He smiled. Admittedly it was difficult not to indulge in such an opportune experience, as the gentle beast lumbered through the forest, shuffling over the smooth stones. Now and again she paused to nibble at the stems and roots of plants, crunching them down her smiling beak. In truth, it was indeed fun.

We rode on Glenda's back for some distance. After a while, the rocking motion of her movements became soothing, and we simply lounged atop her smooth dark shell and watched the forest. Idle conversation passed the time, as talks of the festival inevitably led to girl talks once again.

I had little interest in discussing my experiences, dodging any attempt to gain details of my evening. It was better left to their imaginations. As far as I was concerned, they could believe whatever they wished. Such matters were confusing to say the least. The lock of hair came to mind, still wrapped around the grip of the shield.

Glenda trudged into a clearing of thick grass, as the road ended. The canopy was flooded with sunlight and the chirping of birds that sang overhead. A thick mist hugged the forest air with the heat of late afternoon. It had been long enough, not much daylight remained.

"We should go."

We had reached the end of the stone roadway. We were well to the north now, and it would likely take us the rest of the daylight hours to make up the lost ground even with the ease of following the road. Kori noted this as well, and sighed long and audibly before he reasserted my concern.

"Well, it's time to bid our farewells to Glenda." Kori said in a light and cheery voice, as if he were talking to wildlings.

"But it's too soon!"

"We just met, it's not fair!"

The twins groaned mockingly. I gathered my things and prepared to depart. As I did so, a great shadow passed through the canopy. I caught only a glimpse of a silhouette as it slipped through the trees, what looked like a giant feathery wing. My hair stood on end, as my mind frantically tried to put reason to scale.

Glenda must have sensed it too, for she stopped dead in her tracks and lifted her head as high as her scrawny neck would extend. Her eyes were wide and alert, scanning for the threat she sensed. The others hadn't seemed to notice, continuing to argue over the best materials and techniques for crafting arrows along our way.

"It's time to go." I demanded, speaking over them.

The forest itself had changed, the birds were silent. Danger...

"What's wrong, Kael?" Kori asked, alerted by the concern in my voice.

There was little need to explain, as Glenda suddenly dashed for the dense undergrowth of the forest at full turtle speed. She violently ripped her way through the brush. The four of us clung low to her shell, doing what little we could to avoid a thrashing from branches as they scraped by in her wake. She carried us deeper into the trees. Saplings cracked and snapped against her bulky weight. Once we entered a clearing, the four of us took the opportunity to abandon ship, sliding down and off the terrapin's back.

Just as she reached the other side of the clearing, the canopy above whirled with a shattering disturbance, branches snapping to fall. As I looked up, my breath left me. Two great golden brown wings spread agape dropped through the canopy. Below them were two massive clawed feet, open wide in an impossible deadly vice. The great spirit of the heavens, Shemah Yen, descended.

Its massive body loomed behind its gaping claws, as it dropped into the clearing from the heights of the great canopy. With the flare of its wings, it landed hard with the thunderous crunch of debris under its great talons. Powerful gusts whipped at the forest floor, tearing through the vegetation.

The sight of the sacred creature was unbelievable, its sharp beak gleaming at the towering height it stood. The feathers of its body were a deep brown, almost golden in color where they lightened along their edges. Its wings folded in close, its head ducking low as it leapt forth to close the distance on the terrapin.

Glenda made a break for escape, but it was no use. With a swift kick and another gusting thrust of its powerful wings, it reached into the brush and pulled her back into the clearing, tossing her with ease. A great cooing sound hummed from the Shemah Yen, as if it were gloating over the meal it had found.

The chaos of the assault had prompted us to take cover, cowering in the knotted roots of a nearby tree. Debris continued to sail through the air, and the ground moved with the impact of Glenda's landing. She lay on her back, limbs flailing, struggling against defeat.

With a quick turn, the long fanned tail feathers whipped around, as the Shemah Yen leapt up and over the helpless terrapin. It held her there with one foot, its talons pressing down with a piercing scrape against her shell. She continued to flail, attempting to right herself in a fruitless effort to escape.

The terrapin struggled in vain. Realizing defeat, she closed as tight as she could inside her shell. The great Shemah Yen simply examined her, as if waiting to see if she would emerge. The moment seemed to last forever, as the piercing eyes of the Shemah Yen peered about the forest floor. One of the great golden eyes fixed in our direction before losing interest.

All at once, the great beast of the sky bowed its head, opening its great dark wings. With a storm of powerful gusts, the great hunter took the terrapin in its mighty talons, gripping her hard about her midsection. Its wings released another torrent of powerful gusts that nearly ripped the forest floor apart, sending large chunks of debris and dead vegetation sailing through the air, bringing a branch down near where we cowered beneath the roots.

With the mighty thrust of its powerful wings, the great beast shot up, dragging the terrapin along in its grasp. The force sent another maelstrom over the forest floor. I struggled to watch against the wind and stinging debris. Its wings beat again, and again, each as powerful as the last. Higher it climbed. It all seemed so impossible. The wings beat once more, and the two were gone into the recesses of the canopy. A shrill screeching roar reverberated down from somewhere in the distance...

The forest was quiet again. For a moment all was still. The silence was maddening, as the four of us listened. The only sounds remaining were the cooing sounds of a few smaller birds, calling an all clear in the wake of the action. It was safe to emerge.

"Wow!! Can you believe that?!" Cas jumped and yelled, all but punching at Kori in his excitement.

"Ha! Told you!" Pol barked, though he seemed just as surprised as the rest of us. He looked shaken even.

"Fine, maybe you did see something after all." Kori spat. "But that's enough adventure for today. We should be able to catch up to the others if we hurry."

"It must have been fate, right?" Cas reasoned. "The guardian spirit of our house? Ha! Most go their entire lives without seeing so much as a feather!"

"That's twice for me now, thank you." Pol corrected brashly.

"Your guardian spirit is eating Glenda." I teased with a smirk.

"He would never!" Cas gasped, as if the suggestion were absolutely ludicrous.

"Being a guardian spirit can work up quite an appetite. It's just the natural way of things." Kori added, shooting a wink my way.

"No way!" Pol dismissed. The twins didn't seem to like the idea in the slightest.

"And who's to say he's gonna eat her anyways? Maybe he's helping her get where she's going, gave her a lift so she didn't have to walk is all." Cas suggested, knowing well that was far from likely.

"Well, where 'she' went, faster is the better way to go." Kori insisted. "And fast is the way we should travel if we hope to catch the others, thanks to our little detour to peril."

"As if you didn't just have the time of your life!" Pol challenged, his face contorted in vulgar disbelief at Kori's rigid demeanor.

"Yeah, that sensation that rushed through you just then, that's called life brother. Enjoy it. Whoo!!" Cas shouted into the canopy sending the birds to chattering.

It was not often I found value in anything offered in the words spoken by the twins, but in this instance I did. The day had indeed been both exciting and eventful. We were truly fortunate to be alive, a reminder that life itself was the grandest of adventures, the greatest of gifts.

"Ah, just wait 'til the others hear about this!" Pol exclaimed.

We backtracked along the stone road. Once we reached the stream, we refilled our water and started west in search of the others, traveling deeper into the forest.

The trees were larger in the deep forest. The familiar soft trunks of the Allichene remained present, but here they grew fewer in number. The forest was older, and the ancient trees grew taller and larger still, the canopy becoming a vast world between earth and sky.

I had been born of the forest and lived in the trees. Yet, even I was awestricken by the sheer magnitude of the elder woods. The great broad leaves fallen from the obscured branches above were large enough to construct a shelter the size of a small hut. The concept was appealing, as evening began to fall. Night was another realm, and the forest of that realm did not belong to us.

Each step was soothing, as the rich dark earth underfoot was damp and cool with the rains of the night prior. The day had been warm with the sun, obscured by the canopy it lighted. The moisture trapped under the forest made it steamy with late afternoon. The same lingering moisture that offered cool relief during the peak hours of day would become a chill mist with nightfall. Shelter was needed.

Our pace was slowed greatly by the change in terrain. Indeed it had been most foolish to follow the terrapin. The growth and debris of the forest floor were much more difficult to traverse than the rolling hills of the land. The elder trees stood further apart than the clustered Allichene, but the terrain was obscured by leafy greens. We trudged along, staying to higher ground as best we could on top of what must have been ages of leaf litter.

As we climbed to the top of a large root, a burst of light broke through the canopy high overhead. It lingered about us in the humid air, illuminating the forest with columns of evanescent light that beamed from the distant sky.

The other three had climbed ahead of me, standing atop a large root for a better view of our heading. Cas and Pol both looked back with a shared expression of awe on their faces. Eagerly, I cleared the top to see what it was that fueled their excitement. The same golden rays lit the gloom of the elder forest, beams shining down through the green. The distance was far, but beyond the blinds of the forest was the blue of sky...

"Wow..."

The expression escaped me, as I looked out over the landscape we were to challenge. It would take at least another full day to even try and clear the distance we surveyed. Smoke rose not far from where we perched.

"Look!"

I pointed in the direction. Two cheeky smiles looked back to me.

"Good eye."

"Well done, Kael."

"If it's the others, we could rejoin them by sunset." I calculated aloud.

At the top of the root where it branched from the tree, Kori had stopped. He nodded in approval, facing the direction of our heading. For a moment I thought perhaps he had missed the thin column of smoke, but as I watched I understood. He had stopped to acknowledge the moment.

I eased my eyes closed, as I breathed deep of the forest air. Each breath was filled with the rich scents of summer's belated passing, the smells of drying vegetation and the damp earth, a world preparing to shift into autumn. I opened my eyes just in time to see Kori turn abruptly, a groping hand about his collar and an expression of panic on his face.

"I've lost it!" He cried out, as his hands continued to feel about his neck for the missing trinket. "How could I be so stupid!? I took it off at the stream; it has to be there."

He started down the length of the arching root much faster than he had climbed, passing the twins in a hurry. They spun after him with confused looks.

"Say what?"

"You really must be joking..."

"I have to go back." Kori cried in devotion. "It carries her blessing."

He passed me by despite my gesture for him to wait. My eyes followed after him, half in disbelief at what was happening. Surely he knew better, even in the grip of an emotional response. The twins came crashing down after him. I followed after them. The forest had already begun to dim, evening well upon us.

"Hold on there, we haven't got much daylight left. You really think you can make that before dark?" Pol asked, sounding legitimately concerned for once.

"I can try. It'll cost some ground, so I'll understand if you go ahead without me." Kori dismissed his warning as he continued down the root.

"Leave without you?" I grabbed him by the arm. "Have you gone mad, brother?"

"Let me go..." He all but growled.

If I had to throttle and drag him the rest of the way, so be it.

"Whoa now!" Cas interjected. "No need for all that. We're in this together yeah?"

"I know it's less than sensible, I'll understand if you go ahead without me." Kori stammered apologetically.

"No worries, you'd do the same for one of us, right?" Pol offered with a change of heart. "Besides, our journey has shown promise thus far. What's the worst that could happen?"

"There is plenty that could happen." I declared. "It is foolish to fall any further behind the others."

"I know, brother. Please forgive my carelessness." Kori muttered in defeat. "I must do this. I must."

Kori looked saddened by my words. I had said them in my frustration, and now I was sorry I had done so. This wasn't a joyride on the back of a slow moving reptile; there was purpose and dedication behind his action. There was love. I still didn't like it, but my support meant more than being right, especially if it would keep him alive.

"If we hurry, we can reach the stream before dark." I offered with a barely managed smile. Another misadventure awaited.

"Thanks." Kori breathed.

"Well, you're welcome I suppose." Cas chimed. "Guess I'm along too then."

Each step became less reluctant than the first, as together we backtracked through the forest. I was the only one ruffled by the idea, and ruffled I certainly was. Cas and Pol chatted merrily away, even playing one of their favorite games despite Kori's radical pace. They struggled to hop from rock to rock, ran along root systems, and swung through low branches, anything to keep from touching the ground as they sped along.

As wildlings, we would pretend the ground was sky. Missing a step meant falling without end. It was a child's game, but the increase in pace added a new dynamic and the twins met the challenge well enough. Now and then one of them would fumble, resulting in a silly acrobatic recovery.

It looked to be good fun, but I still considered them too aloof in the moment for my liking. As gold fled the canopy, it gave way to shades of blue among the ascending shadows. Night wasn't far, vigilance was necessary. As much as I wanted to join the fun, I kept my wits about me instead. One of us had to. When we once again neared the stone roadway, night was all but upon us.

"We should make camp." I announced sternly.

"Agreed." Cas was the first to say. He turned to look about the forest.

"Now would be better than later, agreed." Pol huffed between breaths. He didn't stop until he had caught up with Kori.

Kori stopped once Pol's hand touched his shoulder, but only his head turned to us. His body remained poised to continue his mission. He sighed.

"Yeah, night is nearly here. Not much time left." He paused for a moment, his eyes moving to Cas and me. "Setup camp. I won't be long, it's just up the way. I'll be fine."

He turned and set off again. I didn't like this reckless change in him. His passions emboldened him to foolishness it seemed. At the time I didn't understand, but somehow intervention was less than conceivable. He said he had to, and so I did my best to trust him to his task.

"I'll go with." Pol readily volunteered. "Here, take this. You might find the time to finish it up."

He tossed the bow to Cas, and with a wave he too was off.

I didn't bother looking after them. I was beyond frustrated with the events of the evening. We could have been eating with the others around a fire, telling of the encounter with the Shemah Yen. Instead, we were well behind and stressed to make camp before dark. There was very little light left with which to find adequate shelter, and at once I set to climbing above the brush to have a look around. Cas climbed up after me, as I scanned the area.

"Looking for something?" He asked.

"Shelter." I responded flatly. "Unless you'd rather sleep up here..."

"Nah, shelter sounds good." Cas responded. "So, you see anything?"

"Trees." I responded flatly.

Cas laughed. "Stay sharp, brother."

He climbed down. I scanned through the dark foliage, all but giving up as I assessed the fading light. So what if we spent the night in the trees? Foolishness.

When he reached the ground, Cas called up after me. "Oh, I found a nice spot down here by the way."

"What?" I all but fell from the tree.

"Oh, yeah. Its not much. There's a small cave along the roots over here." Cas stood at the base of the tree below me, pointing to a shelter I couldn't see.

I was too relieved to be angry about his silly games. I made my way down and followed him to the shelter he had found. There was a small alcove worked into the earth under a great gnarled root system. It was well guarded, tucked away in the wild roots of the Allichene. It was quaint, but there was room enough for the four of us and a fire.

"See, told ya." Cas said. "We can start a fire in no time. Pol and Kori should find us easy enough. Then we can just prop this up to close it up for the night."

He squatted and grabbed hold of a fallen chunk of bark and lifted the musky old thing to stand along one edge. He pushed it to lean against the mouth of the small cave. It worked, leaving a small gap at either side. Shelter was complete. We had just enough light remaining to gather what we needed to setup for the night.

"Well done." I commended with a slap on the back. "Knew it was there the whole time." I fibbed.

"Of course." He chuckled.

It took less time than I had expected for us to settle in. The little alcove provided a nice makeshift shelter with the improvised wall. Camp was set. We removed the false wall until the others had returned so that our fire would be easily spotted. All that was left was to stoke the fire and wait.

Cas set to work striking a flint over some tender. Within three strikes a flicker of light appeared in the bundle of fibers. Cas placed more fuel around the tiny flame in hopes of it growing. He whistled a familiar tune as he worked, one stuck in my head as well. The sound of our people united in song.

With evening came the promised cool of early fall, chilling the damp air. The moisture enhanced the earthy scents of the forest, intensifying and sharpening the smell of rotting vegetation around the smoky fire. I sat there against the tree with my eyes closed, breathing in the beauty of the forest to still my heart.

I breathed. I listened.

The forest was alive with the transition, as the twilight faded to deep shades of blue and black. The canopy was chattering with a thousand tiny voices. Frogs croaked, insects buzzed, and the birds of the night began to whistle and call.

This humming chorus was that of a peaceful world. My worries began to fade with the light, and in its place I felt something else. I felt the kinship of my companions, both those somewhere ahead on the journey and those traveling with me. I felt a deep sense of gratitude for my brothers with whom I would share not only this journey, but my life as well.

I focused on this line of thought, mind reflecting over the faces of my people. One heart, one life. An overwhelming sense of gratitude rushed over me, as I was hopeful for all that awaited us in the journey ahead. Hope would be the first promise of each day to come, for each step carried the sons of the Dóvai further along the journey of life. There was no single destination of importance; there were many.

My anger melted away, as the familiar sounds of bare feet skipping through vegetation grew closer. My brothers had returned.

"Hey! You're back!" Cas's voice rang out in excitement to confirm my suspicions.

I rose from my meditation to welcome the warm faces of my companions, joy and excitement expressed openly for the world. My legs were not quite ready to move as I shakily made my way to greet them. I laughed aloud as I stumbled and nearly tripped over a thicket of ferns.

"Careful there. I appreciate the sentiment, but there's no need to trip over yourself. We weren't gone all that long." Pol laughed. He slapped my shoulder as he passed by on his way to the fire where Cas stood.

"You're in good spirits." Kori smiled. The trinket given by his beloved was safely back around his neck. "Glad to see it, brother."

I reached out my hand, and his outstretched to receive and embrace it. "No worries, brother. Forgive my anger. Glad you made it safe."

"Saiyu."

Kori responded, placing his hand over his heart as he spoke the blessing of our people. His spirits were much improved as well, his wits restored.

Even Pol seemed to have somehow benefited from the small venture, his chest out and proud as if he and Kori had completed the entirety of the journey on their own. With our brothers returned, the false wall was fitted back into place, completing the shelter. The fire was warm as we ate the last of our provisions.

Pol recounted the details of their hurried errand. Of course, he took it upon himself to embellish the truth with false accounts of beasts that stalked them from the growing shadows. Kori recounted no such threats. The only concern he remembered was finding the gift from his intended.

As we talked and laughed into the night, the sounds of the forest changed around us. The hums of insects faded, and in its place came the calls of the nocturnal creatures waking to greet the night. Eventually conversation faded, and we simply sat around the light of the fire. The light flickered and cast dancing shadows against the tattered bark of the false wall.

Night had fallen, and the forest had grown restless with the change. The sounds of the newly active creatures created a symphony, reminding us the forest never slept. I listened intently, focusing on a familiar tune.

I had heard it many times whilst out with my brother and father. It was a song any traveler making camp in the forest should know. I focused hard and eventually found the somber, almost ethereal rhythm calling out from the trees above. This was the call of the whisperquill.

These small birds roosted in the lower branches, spread throughout the forest. Each bird released a perfectly timed trill in response to the trills around it, creating a vast network of sound. The oscillating wave of their call was like the pulse of the night, echoing throughout the forest in all directions as each bird passed the message along. All clear.

"You reckon you'll get any sleep with those damn birds?" Pol teased, knowing well the importance of their song.

With the laughs that followed, conversation started up once again. The others began chatting away, Kori blathering on about his night with Tiahla for what must have been the tenth time since their return. The twins were more than eager to hear the details, interjecting with bits of their own hypothetical encounters.

This was my queue to turn in for the night. I settled in a nice spot, laying next to the fire. It was my habit to stare into the glowing bed of coals as I waited for sleep to take me.

The swirling colors were hypnotic. The glow offered a soothing sensation, as waves of heat moved over my face. There was comfort knowing the shimmering bed of coals would have life left to it, even after it had provided warmth and safe passage through the hours of darkness, a comfort much like the affection of a mother's hand. I always thought of her in these moments, and her words came back to me.

"Sleep well and worry not my child, for the light of day awaits you. Rise to meet it, with all the strength of the Dóvai."

In that moment the forest was as close to heaven as any of us ever need be, and peace was everywhere. At last, I slipped softly into sleep's gentle embrace.

Krayton the Mighty

The conference room grew eerily quiet. Thaut felt the need to move his limbs and stretched with the break from the story's hold. Subject One had fallen silent, the sadness of his expression deep like the lines of his aged face. He stared blankly into the space before him, eyes glazed as if he might begin to weep at any moment.

"Are you okay to continue?" Thaut asked concernedly, a rasp in his weathered voice from having sat in silence for some time.

"Yes."

Subject One responded, his eyes closing as he breathed deep. A gentle smile rose under his shaggy beard.

"My story grows difficult from here. It was all so long ago..."

"Take your time. I brought water, would you care for some?" Thaut asked. He reached into his satchel and produced a thermos and two small silver cups from a side compartment.

Subject One brightened at the gesture. "Please."

Thaut removed the lid and filled the cups, offering one of the metallic crucibles to his guest. There was a moment of tension as Thaut extended his reach across the table, but it broke easy enough. Subject One slowly reached to accept the offering, his hand bony and thin with age. He placed the drink gently to rest on the table before him. He did not drink.

"Thank you, investigator."

"You must be parched after all that." Thaut drank his readily. He refilled his cup with the tinkling trickle of the cool water against metal. "Good stuff. World's finest."

Subject One laughed. He seemed all the more human with the gesture. Thaut felt more at ease with this, and it seemed to lighten the atmosphere in the room. The numbers displayed on the recording device ticked away, marking the duration of their visit.

"That night I dreamt of all the things my brothers and I discussed around the fire, visions of a future, a future that surely awaited us when the journey was complete." Subject One continued at last.

Thaut eased back into in his seat, eager to hear more. He'd been intrigued thus far, it would be a shame not to hear it through.

"Before I awoke, I saw my mother. It had been years since I'd dreamt of her. She held my head in her lap like she did when I was but a wildling, her fingers running through my hair as I looked up to her. She smiled down, her dark features glimmering by the light of the fire.

"Be strong, Kael." Her words came. "Be strong, my son."

Her loving face was lost to the waking world, as I tried desperately to hold onto the dream. The apparition left me rattled, as I found myself quiet literally shaken from sleep.

"Kael! Wake up!" Came Kori's voice, as he shook me. "Wake up!"

There was an urgency in his voice I had not heard before. I jolted upright, my body rigid with sleep.

"What is it brother?"

He rose, pushing back the large bark slab that it toppled flat, exposing the gray morning light of the forest.

"We have to move. The twins spotted a war party while they were out hunting. It looks like they mean to march on Reisenbough!"

At this news, I was awake. "What?!"

No response came. Instead, he ran to the east, in the direction of the ruined roadway. I ran behind him, stumbling as I tried to keep up in my groggy state. He led the way, winding around the gnarled roots of the Allichene, our steps quick across the rich dark earth and debris.

When we neared the road, he slowed and quieted his steps. With an outstretched hand, he gestured for me to do the same. We carefully made our way up a nearby ridge, where we met with Cas and Pol. They were ducked low in the foliage, looking out over the roadway from the height of the ridge. Their faces were stark and serious, a look most unusual for them. Pol pointed to the southeast.

My eyes followed the direction in which Pol pointed, and my heart skipped at what I saw. There were many armed soldiers scattered around the ruined roadway where they had made their camp for the night. Many were still resting, lazing around several small fires still burning in the early morning light. They wore armor and carried weapons of combat. There was no mistaking their intent, Kori had been telling the truth.

"What do we do?" The words escaped my mouth before I had time to process.

"I say we take them on!" Cas all but growled with an aggression I wouldn't have expected from him. "Save our fathers the trouble."

"Don't be foolish." Kori scalded.

I nodded in concurrence. None of us had seen actual combat, and they were many. Where our forefathers had experience, we had only practice.

"I don't mind the idea of dying a fool, but I don't think I could live with being a coward." Pol snapped, a wicked glare in his eyes.

"I feel you, brother." I spoke low and poignant. "But we shouldn't be rash here. I say we tail them, pick them off little by little, avoid direct engagement."

It was the best I could muster under the circumstance. The twins looked to one another in astonishment.

"Well, that just might work..." Pol chirped in a hushed voice. "They are still a good way from the village, we could pull it off if we are careful. Good thinking, Kael!"

"And even if we don't get them all, our people can more than handle what's left. Kael, it is downright scary to think what goes on in that deep brooding noggin of yours." Said Cas.

The two of them were far too comfortable with the situation for my liking. It was indeed foolish.

Kori said nothing. He too felt the unfavorable odds stacked against us, and worse, the danger for our families back home. This war party was undoubtedly meant for them. There was an undeniable feeling of dread clinging to the air. As we watched the troops begin to muster and break down camp, I all but hoped I would wake back under the tree.

Be strong, she had said.

The armed men took most of the morning to mobilize. We were restless with anticipation by the time they began to move. There was little in the way of conversation, as we each set to work assembling arrows for the bow we had constructed, hoping to use it well in the task ahead. Just as we suspected, they headed north along the road.

We watched from the dense vegetation along the ridge. It felt wrong to prepare for murder, but murder was the intent of this party marching toward our homes. Once we were sure the camp was abandoned, we split into two parties. Cas and Pol continued to monitor the convoy, while Kori and I moved down to investigate the campsite.

The area stank of feces, as we moved through the abandoned camp. Fire pits still smoldered near the center. Heaps of soft broad leaves littered the floor where beds had been made. Several poorly cleaned carcasses remained suspended on skewers, enough meat still clinging to them to feed our small party for days. Such a waste. Kori and I gathered all the roasted meat we could manage from what must have been a strong doe, and set off to rejoin the twins.

We carefully tracked our way along the western base of Mount Yerok, making as little noise as possible as we moved through the vegetation. The higher ground of the slopes provided a good vantage point over the road below, and we had agreed it best in case the need arise to retreat. There was always sanctuary at Yerok's peak.

Finally, we caught up to the twins. The two called to us using bird imitations. They were well hidden in some brush along a small cluster of rocks, nestled between two trunks of Allichene. They were more than glad to see us and happy to share in the spoils we had found, wasting no time in accepting their share of the roasted meat.

"We've counted thirty-seven in total." Pol reported, hungrily tearing at a hunk of roasted venison. "There's also a rather large bearded fellow who seems to be in charge of the lot. And I mean what I say. He's big."

"Big!" Cas stressed the word.

"We haven't seen him in a bit though." Pol continued. "They've slowed pace since the road ended."

"They have archers, but only a few. The biggest trouble is going to be the armor. All of them are wearing armor. Even has the crest of Verda like in the stories." Cas added through a mouthful.

Verda...

Kori and I peered carefully over the large stones to see for ourselves. Down the ridge we saw them. Slowly they trudged their way north through the brush. A few of them paused at a stream, much like the one we had visited the day before. There wasn't much distance left between them and Reisenbough. They could be there by nightfall if they knew the way well enough. If they did, there wasn't nearly enough ground between them and our people.

"So should we start picking them off? These few stragglers at the stream would be a good start." Pol suggested anxiously, reaching for the bow he wore about his shoulder. The two had managed to string it with a silvery strand of woven spider silk.

We had plenty of arrows, some twenty collectively. They were better meant for the hunt, for survival. Even if we managed to take them out one for each arrow, there would be many more left to confront or leave alive.

I began to shiver at the thought of it. Today we would know battle. Today we would destroy human lives. Was it truly a noble cause? I thought myself ready, but perhaps deep down I never truly thought it would come to be. I felt a hand on my shoulder. Kori's eyes met my own, as I snapped from my stupor. To protect my family, I must.

"You alright, Kael?" He asked, his tone stern. His long dark hair was that of his father's. Would this be the day their spirits reunited?

"Of course, brother." I lied.

"That a boy, Kael!" Pol encouraged, landing a heavy slap against my chest with a smile.

Cas wore a sly, devious smile. I hoped their confidence found its merit in the conflict to come.

The four men below chattered as they guzzled at the water they collected. The sounds of laughter accented their idle conversation, as we carefully moved into position through the dense undergrowth of the forest. They were well separated from the others when at last we had them within range. Pol took point with the bow, Cas ready with a bundle of arrows at his side. Kori and I moved closer still, ready to engage if the men moved to pursue or alert the others.

I watched them closely, as I ducked low in the brush only a few paces away. The emblem of Verda was clearly distinguishable across their chest plates. Studying their faces and their movements, I wasn't ready when the first arrow was loosed with a hiss through the air.

The first target was struck hard in the throat, dropping him in his tracks without a sound, just as the men had turned their backs to join the others. A second arrow hit another just the same the moment his head turned round in alert. As the remaining two turned toward the commotion, a third struck and then a fourth.

The four men lay dead. I had no words as I felt my eyes bulge wide and my heart skip. It didn't seem real. I looked for Kori in the brush to my left. His blade was drawn in one hand and his shield gripped tight in the other. He looked ready for battle, save for the ghastly expression he bore upon his face. Long had we trained to be ready to defend ourselves, but nothing could have prepared us for this.

The words of my elders burned through my mind in this moment, as they often did through training. Peace cannot be won through bloodshed. If those words were true, then what was the point in any of this? Just as I had asked then, no answer came. Just the terrified beating of my heart.

There was little time to dwell on my thoughts, as a voice sounded an alarm. The four had not fallen unnoticed. In an instant, several armed soldiers converged on their murdered comrades, their heads shifting all about as they looked for those responsible.

Kori and I both held fast, as still and silent as the towering trees, ghosts among the green. More of the armed men gathered , blades readied, archers with arrows at the draw. My heart pounded, and for perhaps the first time I truly knew fear.

Suddenly, an impossibly large man appeared as if he had dropped from the sky. He was easily the tallest man I had ever seen, standing well above the others. His broad shoulders were nearly as wide as a nearby tree trunk and his girth nearly as massive. His armor was not that of Verda. He carried a large spiked hammer over his shoulder that looked to be an impossible weight. His hair was matted and thin, his beard unruly and battered like his angry face, as he scanned the forest with a hateful glare.

"Spread out! Find them!" He barked and spat in a booming voice. His face contorted with a burning rage.

At once the minions followed his command. They fanned out with the clamor of weapons, treading dangerously close through the bush. The archers encircled their titan commander and aided in his watchful search.

As his eyes scanned in our direction, a strange sensation crept over me. I felt a connection to this man, this creature. It was as if I could feel his presence there. Suddenly his eyes locked on the brush where Kori and I lay hidden. I had little time to ponder this phenomena, as he had surely felt it too. His lips sneered back from clenched rotten teeth.

"There!" He barked with hateful authority, pointing a finger in our direction with his massive left hand.

How?!

It didn't seem possible or likely, but it mattered not. The men began to move in our direction, blades ready, archers at their backs. The eyes of the big man watched over the men he commanded with malice, the eyes of a tyrant.

Survive.

In an instant they were upon us. The soldiers had yet to spot either Kori or me, leaving the element of surprise in our favor. Kori jumped into action, slicing down two of the men in an instant, catching one at the legs and another through the gut as his swing went through and up. He parried a blow with his shield and ran a third through. Arrows began to hiss through the vegetation, dangerously close to my brother as he fought.

"Kael!" Kori called, battering down another man viciously with his shield, the heat of battle heavy on his face.

I turned to see two armed men converging on me. I was stiff with the shock of it all. In a flash, the two were cut down by slashing daggers. Cas and Pol had joined our efforts, and very much saved my life in doing so.

"Snap out of it, Kael!" Pol commanded. "We need you!"

The sight of my brethren in action raised me from my stupor, and I reached over my shoulder and brought my sword singing free of its sheath. I felt my breath leave me in the moment of my decision, to be the slayer this day, to protect my brothers and my family. With the next came the fire from within, as I reached out with my blade and struck down a soldier of Verda. His flesh was thick against my blade, but gave well enough. Behind the familiar well trained movements, it was all too easy.

"Kori! Take the bow and cover us! We're going for the big guy!" Cas called to Kori as he met another sloppy swordsman's pathetic offensive.

When his attentions were freed, Cas tossed the bow to him. Kori caught it and readied himself behind an arrow. We were all well engaged. The dead lay in the forest, their numbers growing.

"Kael! Cover me, brother!" Kori commanded with authority.

I moved close to him, as he set to firing arrows at the archers. I watched as he felled two, the others narrowing their aim with deadly accuracy. I held fast next to my brother, my blade at the ready to cleave through any fool that dared attack.

The twins worked their way toward the tyrant as gracefully as they had performed at the festival, twirling and leaping through the band of hostile men, slicing at limbs and throats as they passed. The tyrant merely watched, a defiant smirk across his hideous face.

They circled him, daggers ready to deliver the killing strike. The giant man stood strong, the ridiculously large spiked hammer still perched over his right shoulder. One strong hand clutched hard at the tattered, dirty bindings of its grip. He couldn't hope to swing such a cumbersome weapon well enough to take on even one of the twins, let alone both. It would soon be over. Perhaps our fathers would never even know of this threat, aside from the stories we would tell upon our return.

Pol went in first, Cas moving to circle the tyrant's opposing flank. With a quick leap he dove for the man's abdomen, but in a flash he was gone.

The giant had brought the hammer down so fast his movement was instantaneous. A crackling sound like that of rolling thunder sounded with his movement, as the mighty hammer shook the ground where Pol had been. He had vanished beneath its mass.

Pol was gone...

I watched in disbelief, my mind spinning to make sense of what I had witnessed. No man could harness such power, move with such speed. This was not a man we faced, no natural opponent.

Cas, outraged by the loss of his brother, dove hard at the man's exposed right flank. His attempts were for naught, as once again the tyrant moved with incredible speed. The same crackling sounds ripped the air with his movements. He swiped the weapon hard into Cas, hitting him with the broad side of the hammer in a crushing swing. The impact sent out a wicked crack, and the crumpled body that was Cas went tumbling through the air and into the trees beyond.

The gifted brothers of Shemah Yen were no more.

"Kori, we have to go! Now!" I shrieked, rising and tugging at his arm, all but dragging him in the direction of the mount.

Arrows hissed around us, as we ran through the trees. Each step was heavy, as if my legs couldn't possibly carry me fast enough. Kori trailed just behind me as we made for the dense green.

Suddenly I heard my brother cry out in pain. I turned to see him stagger forward and fall to his knees, his sword and shield still gripped tightly in his hands. The red tail of an arrow protruded from his back.

"No!!!" I felt myself scream in raging disbelief.

I all but toppled, as I scrambled to his side. The arrow was deep in his left shoulder, the wound already bloody and vile upon his brawny physique.

Not him. Not like this.

The men were closing on us. I grabbed hold of his right arm and brought it over my shoulders, lifting him to his feet. Groans escaped him, as he jerked in pain.

"Just go, brother! You have to warn the others!" He pleaded, pain in his eyes.

"I won't leave you! We go together." I replied, pulling him along as we moved closer to the jagged rocks ahead.

We were near the mines. It wasn't far to the summit pass. We were close to sanctuary, if we could only make it. The angry voices behind us grew closer, urging me onward. I did not feel the weight of my brother, nor did I hearken to the aching in my legs. We would make it. We had to.

Two of the armed men caught us, leaving me no choice. Knowing Kori was in no condition to fight, I quickly pulled the bow slung at his back, and turned to face them. I breathed deep, heart racing, desperation in the arrow fixed toward its mark. I released my hold on the string with the exhale of my breath, steady and slow. The arrow struck hard in the first man's throat, dropping him in mid stride.

The second I met with my sword, sending a hateful stab just below his armored chest, clean through his gut until its crimson sheen shown at his back. He froze upon my blade, surprise and horror on his face. I pulled the blade free, and in the same motion swiped his head free of his shoulders.

Their heavy armor made them slow and clumsy compared to the prodigy of the Dóvai. Our fathers would crush them all, save for the beastly tyrant that led them. We had to warn them of this unnatural foe.

I quickly scanned for more threats, my sword steady in hand. There were no signs of others, but I continued pace as if there were. Move, we had to move.

I saddled the bow across my back, sheathed my blade, and pulled Kori back to his feet. I was frantic, my brother's breath laborious, as we shuffled through the brush toward the cave hidden in the rocks. He was growing weak, blood oozing from the wound.

By the time we reached the mouth of the pass, Kori had grown pale and drowsy, too weak for the climb. I collected a nearby fallen leaf of the Allichene still fresh enough to provide the needed rigidity for a litter, and laid Kori across it. With any luck, I would drag him along behind me.

I grabbed hold of the thick stem and hoisted it up and over my shoulder. As I did, it caught on the gear at my back. For a moment I thought it had only been the shield Sarah had given me. I had all but forgotten it was there in the midst of all the action, and as I removed it I noticed two arrows stuck hard in the wooden surface of its face. I had so nearly met a fate similar to that of my brother, struggling for breath as he lie face down on the leaf.

There was little time to waste on sentiment. I collected the lock of hair Sarah had attached to the inside handle, and tossed the shield aside. I placed the bow next to Kori and reset the stem of the leaf over my shoulder now free of obstruction, and began to pull my injured brother toward the mouth of the pass. Slow and steady, the smooth belly of the leaf hissed against the ground as I towed him up the perilous path through darkness, ascending back to the crown of mount Yerok.

I was well exhausted by the time we reached the light at the top of the path, the beacon which guided our ascent through darkness. Kori's breathing was all that he could offer to let me know he was still alive. He struggled to retain consciousness, as I pulled him up the rocky steps.

Once we were under sky, the level ground of the summit made it much easier to drag him to the nearest cave. I set to work at once, building him a small fire and covering him with a dusty old fur. He was shivering and pale, the arrow deep in his back.

I did what I could, bringing water from the cistern and rinsing the wound. The bleeding had stopped, but he was far from recovery. I carefully snapped the arrow as close to the wound as I dared manage without harming him further. There was no way I could remove it here. I would have to return with help. I had to warn our people!

"Kael... Help me sit up. Please, brother." He struggled to speak.

I helped him slump against the wall of the cave, the fire flickering wildly at my back. It was hard to watch the promising son of Raethos wither before my eyes. My brother was fading.

He seemed all the more pale against the dark wall of the cave, the dancing orange of the fire glowing around us. His eyes rolled under the drowsy blinking of heavy lids. He was all but struggling to keep his head erect as he slumped against the wall of the cave. His hand still clutched tight to his sword. I draped the fur over him in hopes to provide some further comfort.

"Kael, you have to warn them. You have to let them know... what's coming..." He struggled to say as he fought against what I hoped was sleep.

"Yes, brother." I took his hand from his sword and held it tight in my own. "And I'll return with the elders. They'll fix you up. You'll hear of our victory soon enough." I assured him in the most soothing voice I could muster, my confidence a lie.

"Go!" He commanded. "You have to..."

I let his hand slip from my own to fall against his leg with a soft thud. I fought the tears as best I could. I retrieved the bow, placing it against the wall at his side. He was in no shape to fight it any longer.

"Yes, brother. Rest now, gather your strength."

With all the courage left to me, I turned to leave. He called out to me once more.

"Kael! Take the bow. You'll need it."

I smiled, only half turning, unable to face him again. "Then you had best return it, brother."

"May your feet be swift." He spoke low, with all the conviction left in him.

"Saiyu." I uttered in a wavering voice, as I darted from the cave.

I raced toward the path that had brought us up the steep mountainside from Reisenbough. The tears burned down my face, as I descended the hazardous slopes. The sun burned low somewhere behind the trees to the west, sinking like the hope within me.

My feet slid most of the way down the steep path, forcing me to balance my weight low and topple back on all fours at times along the perilous mountainside. My heart pounded, as my limbs gripped for anything to grab hold and guide my reckless decent along the path in my accelerated haste. Fear and desperation wrestled my mind for control, adreniline pulsing through me.

The forest canopy was just off to my left, groping at the rocks below. Night was coming all too fast. Time was precious. I was only halfway down the steep crest, I needed to move faster. The great leaves of the Allichene were so close...

I had leapt from the mountainside without a second thought. My feet thundered like the drums of my people with each step toward the ledge until there was only air. I curled my limbs to my body, ready to spring and grab hold upon impact, fingers and toes outstretched in front of me like claws.

The heavens whirled about me in the longest breath I had ever taken. The breath of a young warrior of the Dóvai. My fingers punched through the familiar, soft tissue of a broad green leaf upon the crash of my impact. I gripped hard, eyes closing with a flash of deep green, as the force shook the leaf violently. I didn't wait for it to steady, clawing and tearing my way to its stem and climbing to the branch.

I worked my way through the canopy in a crazed frenzy, moving with a speed and precision unknown to me. I had little time to reflect. Jumping from such a height had been a daring feat, pushing a familiar concept much further than ever before. My mind was occupied by one concern, my people. Their endurance was the ambition of my thought, their drums the pounding in my chest driving me forward.

I continued along the canopy until I could no longer, my legs weak and burning. Once my balance began to suffer, it was time to return to the path below. This descent was one I had all but mastered, dropping from branch to branch, working my way closer to the forest floor.

I dropped from the lowest branch in the Allichene, catching the top branches of a tall sapling. The small tree bent under my weight, breaking my fall with the resistance it provided as it leaned to the ground. I landed with a roll and was up on my feet. The sapling sprang upright behind me with a snap, as I raced for the village.

The forest was growing dark with the coming night. Time was running out. My lungs burned, my feet and legs ached. My heart pounded. I was almost there, just a little further...

At last I could see the Spirit Gate ahead on the path. A golden glow radiated behind it, a familiar dancing golden glow that would have otherwise been warm and comforting. The smell of smoke became thick in the air, the flames beyond the Spirit Gate too great to come from the burn circles at the center of the village. With dread heavy in my heart, I raced toward my darkest fears.

A deep chilling numb crept over me, despite the intense heat of the fires that burned. The mouths of the stone huts were filled with flames, the small windows like wild wide eyes, faces screaming in horror against the night. Bodies of the dead littered the village, ruin smote upon this sacred place. I did not bother looking over the faces of the fallen. I did not care to see my loved ones perished, my friends and family.

Instead I looked for those responsible, those who had destroyed my home, my people. The flames burned hot, as I set my sights on a band of sniveling marauders. They reveled in the spoils of another sacked home, my life, the life of so many wonderful people. I drew my blade slow and hard, letting it sing its high silver note to gain their attentions, and for the first time I felt the change...

At first I thought it to be my rage, but when the first soldier of Verda rushed at me, I realized a new condition. In the grip of my acceleration, his movements had slowed, as if all the world had become sluggish. Whatever density surrounded them, I was free of it, free to move, free to observe, free to slice through this despot with such speed and precision that the others dropped their sinister smirks.

I watched their faces change, feeling my lips curl away from my teeth. Whatever reserve I had felt for taking life before slipped from me with my humanity. For they were the dogs of war, worse even.

I was upon them with the glint of cutting steel, dealing death before they even knew they had been engaged. To them, it must have been a flash, as not a single one of the group I cut down even managed to ready their guard. It wasn't fair, it was slaughter. But they didn't deserve to die with dignity. That was a courtesy for honorable men, not the dogs of war, those who so readily destroy life.

Onward through my burning home I marched, eager to put my blade through more flesh. The flames were suspended in a slow dance all around me in this new accelerated state. Their roar became a deep rumbling vibration, rippling through the air. The unknown power resonated through me. I was a force beyond the scope of the natural, perhaps born of the woes of a thousand wronged spirits. My skill already made me a formidable opponent, but with this boost in ability I was beyond equal.

One by one, two by two, I cut down the remaining dogs of Verda. I did not wait for them to take notice of me. I hardly even saw them anymore, just glimpses of flesh and blood I meant to cleave to pieces, souls I would send to oblivion.

The village center was mine now, their numbers dwindled to naught. Two archers readied their arrows, but the once deadly projectiles merely slid through the air like lazy wiggling worms. I was upon them, cutting them down before their eyes even saw me.

With the disposal of the archers, there was only one left. I fixed my gaze on him, and though I had no idea what my face looked like in the moment, the terror I saw in him reflected the contortion I felt in my heart.

He had stumbled back off his feet when my blade slid through his gut. He would die slow, feel his life drain from him as the flames devoured my home. It was too good a place for him to die, here with the noble people they had destroyed.

Suddenly, a shape fell from the canopy above. A massive glinting object came down hard at me. I narrowly escaped its path, even in my state of acceleration. It was a mighty hammer, striking with the momentum of its wielder's descent. It hit with a thunderous crack that shook the village. The twisted face of the tyrant gleamed behind it.

He moved every bit as fast as I did, only he seemed much more familiar with his abilities. He swung the heavy hammer about as if it weighed nothing, each swing dangerously close. I had witnessed what it could do. One hit and I would be done.

Swing after swing sent us moving across the village center. For every step I retreated, he advanced. I wanted this one's life most of all. I would have it, but I could do little without a proper opening. He kept me on the defensive, relentless in his attack.

I kept my wits about me, watching his movements closely. The blunt end of the hammer swung right, the wicked spiked end swung left. I waited for the opening I needed.

Finally, an opportunity came. He added a jabbing thrust at the end of a swing in attempts to catch my surprise. I spun around the attack, advancing toward my foe and slashing hard at his ugly face.

The end of my blade caught him just under his jaw and tore up through his left eye, splitting his face agape. A turbulent roar escaped him. His left hand reached for his face as he recoiled from the blow.

I made for the killing strike, all too eager in my lust for vengeance. A massive kick caught me instead, hitting me with crushing force across my chest. It sent me tumbling back and into the tall grass outside the burning village.

I was dazed, my body drained. I felt myself slip from the accelerated state, as the flames quickened their dance and the world returned to its natural pace. My body ached. Were it not for my new strength, I couldn't have hoped to survive such a hit. That mattered little, as I looked up to see the beastly creature standing over me, malice hard in his remaining eye.

"Looks like this is it, boy." The tyrant spat in a deep voice, thundering with hate. "Your head is mine!"

There was little fight left in me, my sword lost in the tall grass. My hands clenched into fists, hard as my defiance. I gritted my teeth and returned his hateful gaze. I would not die a coward.

He raised the great hammer over his head, ready to bring it down upon me. Just as he meant to swing, an arrow struck hard into his right flank, sending him tumbling left. His swing missed its mark to smash heavy against the ground at my side with a quaking rumble.

My eyes scanned in the direction of the arrow's origin. There stood Krayton, the mighty son of Kraegar. His powerful bow readied with another arrow. His face stern and set to his duty. He stood a proud warrior of the Dóvai, ready to face a noble end.

"Run!!" I cried, the tears already creeping into my eyes, knowing he wouldn't even consider.

I watched as the tyrant turned on my father, his bow reset and aimed for the monster. Before the next arrow was loosed, the giant cleared the distance in a burst of supernatural speed. The mighty hammer came down on the last warrior of the Dóvai with a thunderous crash upon the world like the shaking in my body. My heart broke impossibly so. My mind shattered.

"No!!"

I screamed with a thunderous roar. I felt my body ripple with the change, my heightened fury pushing it further. I felt the tension surge, pulling me free of the world, allowing me to move through it as if I were not a part of it, not subject to nature or her law. I lunged hard at the titan's back with a mighty leap to clear the space, my fingers like claws. I would tear him apart with this new power, rip the life from him. Like an arrow shooting through space, I closed the distance.

The brute turned toward my attack just as I set upon him, shock clear in his face. The element of surprise was well in my favor. His throat was mine.

A whirling burst of immense force ripped and whistled through the air around the beastly man. Even in this accelerated state, these strange projectiles passed in a flash, leaving rippling waves in their wake. Just as I reached out for the ugly visage I meant to destroy utterly, a great flash exploded behind him. The force of the explosion sent me hurtling free of my target, the beast tumbling hard as well.

The force of the blast and the impact of my landing shook me from my heightened state once more, a deep ringing in my ears. The flash left me disoriented, as I desperately scanned for the tyrant. My eyes found him not far from where I had landed. He appeared to be avoiding a flurry of invisible projectiles as he made to retreat, leaping high into the canopy and into the darkness above.

"This isn't over, boy!!"

I heard a booming voice call out into the burning night. He was gone. My home was gone. My friends, family, my life was gone. Darkness fell over me, and with it a bleak and dark sleep which I did not resist.

The Witch, the Brute, and the Warrior

Perhaps I had just imagined it. Yes, that was it. It was nothing more than one of my crazy, vivid dreams. I would wake somewhere in the forest, surely. My brothers would be there to tease me for sleeping so late, and we would regroup with the others. All was well. Everything would be fine.

Of course, I did not wake to their faces. Instead my dreams produced exactly what I wanted to see. I dreamt of home, of my family and loved ones. I saw the twins and my brother Kori. We caught up to the others after getting separated. I dreamed that together with the others we reached the first destination of our journey, the cliffs where Hathlanda had once overlooked the great Purge. But that is when I knew for certain I was dreaming, for I had never seen this place.

Such dreams had been a kind distraction at first, and I was all but willing to lose myself to that imaginary paradise. But fantasy did little to ease my spirit, for deep down I knew. That deep certainty struck again and again, for what is known is known. Denial could not save me from the truth it seemed. I knew them lost, and these dreams in turn haunted me, reminders of the glory that was Reisenbough. Memories could never hope to fill such a void. Darkness had claimed that light.

When at last I opened my eyes, a beautiful blue sky welcomed me. The sun was high and warm, partially hidden behind a few white fluffy clouds adrift in the vibrant blue. I was moving, floating along some unfamiliar path. Tall grass whipped in my peripheral. Was this the afterlife? Was I soon to be reunited with the others after all?

I tried to move, but my body didn't respond. It did ache however, letting me know that this was not likely some vision of the world beyond, that I was still very much alive. I tried to move again, groaning in my efforts against some unseen force that bound me.

My movement triggered a response. There were others nearby, their footsteps grinding in the rubble of the roadway underfoot as they approached. Suddenly, a strange shadowy figure loomed over me. A sleek dark mask obscured the man's face. The same sleek material composed the strange dark armor that cloaked him. Muffled words came from within the mask, their meaning lost to me.

In a panic, I struggled to bring the change I had discovered. I felt the familiar surge run through me, but before the change came, the masked figure tapped at a beeping mechanism. The bindings that held me released, and I sprang up at once, stumbling to crash into the tall grass of the field.

I recovered on my aching limbs, taking cover in the grass to asses the situation. Before me floated a small carrier much like a flat bed. It drifted as easily over the path as the clouds in the sky.

There were several masked figures, each dressed from head to toe in the same mysterious dark armor. It fit them tight, making them look scrawny and weak compared to the beastly foe with the hammer. They brandished no swords, knives, or bows. Instead they carried strange devices, one end thick like a stalk and carried tight against a shoulder. The other end of the device was narrow and extended away, a dark opening at its terminal end. Without a doubt, these devices were weapons by the way they held them.

The symbol of Verda was not found anywhere upon their alien attire. In fact, there were no indicative symbols of any kind. Just the sleek black of shadow, the empty stare of the visors, muffled words I did not understand.

My instinct was to run. I considered it heavily, it would have been nothing to disappear into the tall grass of the field. The best I could tell, we were heading east, maybe in the direction of the White Hallow. Easily I could have escaped these mysterious shadows, made it back to Reisenbough. Instead I watched them. They held their ground but did not advance, nor attack.

There was a moment of silence, as the four armed strangers held their positions, waiting for my reaction. Maybe they had witnessed my new found abilities in the fight against the tyrant. Maybe they knew something more about what had happened.

After some time, the dark armored stranger that released me from the floating gurney relaxed his grip on his strange weapon and stood easy. He brought a dark gloved hand up to his shiny, sleek helmet. In a flash, the mask covering his face peeled back, segments retreating into the helmet, revealing the man's face.

He looked young, perhaps only a few years older than myself. His eyes were kind, his smile friendly. This man was no enemy. I felt relief in seeing a human face, but kept my wits about me. Caution remained in the forefront, as I approached this curious band of strangers.

"Who are you? Where were you taking me?" I asked, cutting straight to the heart of matters. I had been detained, and I wanted to know why.

Confusion fell across the man's face. He offered a response in exchange, but his words were unfamiliar, the meaning lost behind his apologetic tone. One of the other men stood fidgeting with a device about his wrist. He spoke with the same strange words.

The man with the kind eyes clicked and tapped at a similar device at his own wrist, and when next he spoke, his words were legible, though they sounded strange and did not originate from his mouth.

"Hello! Can you understand me now?"

The man asked via a synthetic voice that originated from somewhere at his collar.

"Yes." I responded rather coldly, not sure what to make of the encounter just yet. "Why was I held captive?"

Laughter echoed from the helmets of the other three. Two began chattering before the unmasked man shot them a stern look and spat a command in an authoritative tone.

"Lock it up!"

He was clearly the leader of the small band. Watching them, it seemed somehow appropriate that they were dressed in black. The events of Reisenbough began to flood my mind, but I resisted memory. I needed my wits, needed to be sharp and ready.

"My name is Devon." The leader spoke from the voice at his collar. "This is Sig, Creeper, and Scotch."

Devon introduced his crew, pointing to each as he offered their names. Sig waived. Creeper didn't acknowledge in the slightest. Scotch nodded and raised two fingers in what seemed like a friendly gesture. They seemed okay enough.

"We are scouts sent on behalf of his Majesty's Holy Empire." Devon explained. "Our mission is to survey new lands, identify the native peoples, and asses any threats prior to assimilation."

"And what does this have to do with me?" I asked, still unsure of what transpired while I was locked in sleep.

"You were injured, first and foremost." Devon responded. "Typically, our mission objectives prevent us from directly interfering with local affairs, but when we came across the village..."

"Go on." I urged him, hoping to mask the pain in my voice as I fought back the tears.

"He means to say that sometimes following orders is bullshit."

Came a rumbling voice animate with angry passion. The other two snickered and laughed, nodding in agreement.

"No way to justify watching people die like that. After all, we represent the good intentions of his Majesty's Empire, right captain?"

I liked him. I didn't need to see his face to know he had a good heart.

"Thank you, sergeant." Devon responded, glaring at the man named Sig. His smile returned as he shifted his attention back to me. "Sorry we didn't get there sooner. What's your name?"

"Kael." I responded coldly, holding his gaze with my own.

Devon didn't seem to let this get to him in the slightest. "Well then Kael, would you mind traveling with us for a while?"

"Why?" I asked.

"The brute you faced last night was no ordinary foe, but then again you aren't so ordinary yourself, are you Kael?" Devon suggested.

They knew. My heart jolted against my chest with his implications. "What do you mean?"

Devon smiled again. "It's alright, Kael. We mean you no harm. You see, across the world we have encountered persons of exceptional skill, people with powers like yours. Some choose to use their powers for the better, aiding mankind by serving in his Holy Majesty's court. Unfortunately some use it for their own selfish means, like the man you fought last night."

"That wasn't a man." I all but spat in response. "That was a creature."

Devon looked surprised, but merely nodded in concurrence.

"Yes, well... That's why we would like your help. Its difficult to take down a 'creature' like him. They are known as celestials, extraordinary in their ability. Little is known about how or why they exist. What we do know is the best way to fight a celestial like him is with another celestial. He will be hunted down and brought to justice, and if you come with us you can help make that happen."

"I don't need you or the Empire to bring down a dog of Verda." I all but growled.

Imperialistic and vain, I was in no way interested in assisting a culture that swore allegiance, subservience to a man proclaimed as king. Titles like 'majesty' were meant only to divide the hearts and minds of the people. A man was to live by his will alone, and if his heart is just, then he would live that life to inspire greatness and bring peace to the lives around him.

The Dóvai had little need for a governing hierarchy or centralized leadership. That was the beginning of the vice that had corrupted Verda.

If a man cannot govern himself to righteousness, then he is not worthy of calling himself a man, let alone fit to govern others.

I thought of my father in his final moments, the duty on his face, the heat of the flames.

"What manner of weaponry is that?"

I asked pointing to the odd construct in Devon's grip, both desperately seeking to preoccupy my mind against the imagery of my father's death and curious to know what I was up against.

"These are the weapons of the Empire." Devon was more than happy to explain. "This one here is a standard issue rifle, but I've made a few modifications. Gotta make it your own."

Devon activated a switch, and the weapon sprang to life. A bright blue light began to shine from within the thick body where it seemed all the active mechanisms were located. A high pitched oscillating hum churned within.

"Delivers rounds as fast as I pull the trigger, practically no recoil now that I've added a dynamic counter force." Devon continued, his right hand held across the guard, protecting a small curved lever that must have been the trigger.

"With each shot, the counter reacts with appropriated force, perfectly negates recoil, improving accuracy across the board. Burst fire, or even full auto."

"And he still can't hit anything farther than twenty meters." Scotch added. The others laughed. Devon took no notice.

"That's why I carry a cannon, don't have to worry about accuracy. Just have to hit close enough and KABOOM!" Creeper chimed in, pulling a larger bodied weapon from his back. He was quite enthusiastic about this cannon.

"Kaboom."

I repeated, the explosion that shook me senseless and robbed me of my victory was fresh in my mind. So they had been the ones responsible for the projectiles.

"It was a good shot. You move pretty fast for such a scrawny little shit." Creeper retorted.

I couldn't help but smile. It was a relief to know the attack had not been meant for me, though I still did not trust them. At least they had been trying to help.

I looked over the scouts, examining them more closely. Each of them carried weapons similar in design, though only Sig carried a rifle like Devon. Creeper had several smaller weapons aside from the bulky cannon, two at his chest, one at his hip. Scotch's weapon had a longer profile, sleek in design with a small looking-glass fixed across the top.

"Come with us, Kael." Devon pleaded. "We could really use your help. That brute is still out there. You could greatly aid the Empire in bringing him down. There is an outfit for those like you. You could meet others, and better yet, use your amazing potential to rid the world of scum like him."

"Others like me?" I repeated, contemplating the idea.

"That's right." Devon assured, a warm smile upon his face to match the twinkle in his eyes. "The Vanguard, defenders of the realm."

His words were convincing. My vengeance would be realized, and I could learn more about my new capacities, learn more of this Empire. Perhaps I would even find nobility in putting my skills to use in some greater cause. Or perhaps, it was because I realized I had nowhere else to go...

"I will go with you, but I walk free." I responded.

Devon smiled, laughter came from Scotch and Sig. Creeper appeared to be staring at the dirt again, indifferent to the world.

"Fair enough." Devon responded.

He approached the magic gurney still floating at hip level and tinkered with a small panel. In an instant, the platform folded into itself as if of its own accord, smaller and smaller until it fit in the palm of his hand. He slipped the small cube into a case at his belt.

"What sorcery is this?!"

I blurted, baffled by what I had witnessed. Between their strange armaments and gadgets, I couldn't help but wonder what more this Empire had at its disposal. The scouts laughed at my reaction.

"They call it tech." Devon explained. "It's the result of a bunch of big brains working together, pushing reality to the brink of imagination."

"I like sorcery better." Creeper chuckled.

Much of what I thought I knew of my reality had changed overnight, and as I set out with the scouts I tried not to think of the flames that had consumed my home. As my feet scrapped across the hard dried earth of the path we followed, I did my best to focus instead on learning more of this strange new world.

The sun moved slowly west overhead, as the breeze swayed the tendrils of the tall grass in waves across the open plains. The heat of the day was warm, but this late in the season it was mild compared to the harsh fury of summer. Somehow the scouts didn't seem the least bit bothered by it, as we marched east. Perhaps they were immune to the world, protected by the mysterious technology they wielded. So many questions came to me, and Devon was more than happy to indulge my curiosity.

I came to know more of their role. If the Empire was a spear, then they were the path that predetermined its striking point. They had traveled the land, watching and learning of its people. They shared accounts of the barbaric men of the dessert beyond the plains to the northeast, the grand markets of the White Hallow, and Verda, the so called City of Champions.

As the sun drew closer to the forest at our backs, the familiar reds of a great towering mass loomed ahead. It appeared to be a massive wall, comprised of colored stone blocks stacked higher than what seemed possible. I realized at once that this was the Tomb of the Shadjah, the great structure that had haunted fables and captured the curiosity and aspirations of the adventurous young hearts of the Dóvai. Never had I seen it this clearly, and it seemed impossible that it grew larger still, as we drew closer and closer.

I voiced my concern, explaining the myth behind the ominous structure. The scouts had a good laugh, but found my stories little more than entertaining. They assured me there was little to fear in the way of demons or evil spirits.

To them, it was nothing more than crumbling ruins left by an ancient race of giants they called the 'Architects'. They explained that the Architects had long since vanished from the Earth, leaving only traces of their advancements and technologies. The same technologies that the Empire sought and utilized for their advancement. Little was known about these giants, only that they were no more.

This only brought more questions to my mind, though I did not bother sharing my thoughts on the matter. If these giants had vanished, why? How could they simply disappear without a trace?

It also seemed silly to so quickly dismiss the idea of these ruins being a spiritual place. If the Architects had perished, perhaps their spirits lingered there along with their technological achievements.

The path we followed at last came to an intersection. Another path ran north to south along the towering ruins. The tomb was now close enough to touch, though I did not dare. The rough porous stones seemed somehow insidious, stacked neatly atop one another. Regardless of what the scouts thought, it seemed a wicked place, and I couldn't shake an ominous feeling of dread growing in the pit of my stomach. I would be glad to put distance against it once more.

Unfortunately our journey south followed the great western wall of the tomb. The stones radiated heat, as the sun cast our shadows against the various shades of red and dark brown. My anxiety of this place kept my mind well occupied, a welcomed distraction from the reality that chewed at my thoughts.

I vied to keep the conversation alive with a well exhausted Devon to distract me further, inquiring what had lead them to my village. It was far from this place, which much to my disappointment served as their base of operations in the area. A wise choice, as few would venture near it.

Devon seemed less than interested in answering my new line of questioning. He offered very little aside from a vague response followed by a change in subject. After which, he fell silent on the matter.

Sig took up the topic easily. He explained that a secondary objective had been received while they were on patrol. They were to investigate the location where Reisenbough stood, as intelligence operations had reported unusual activity suggestive of celestial presence. It was suspected this activity was the result of a rather powerful celestial, and the scouts were tasked to investigate. Their mission had been to search the area and identify the source if possible.

"I'd say we did a little more than identify the source, two in fact." Sig continued. "We reported our findings while you got your beauty rest. That guy looked strong enough, but he'll fall easy if the Emperor sends the Vanguard, which I'm sure he will. If you want my opinion, his Majesty is concerned with something big. There are rumors that the sorceress herself-"

"That's enough. Lock it up." Devon was quick to shutdown Sig's informative rant.

There had been some tension mounting around our conversations, and the sensitive nature of whatever he was about to divulge was to remain a secret. I didn't care for secrets. I let the silence prevail this time, conversation abandoned much like the trust I had hoped to find in this new circle. Truth is no threat to honest men, nor should it be to the institutions of honest men.

I pondered after his words. Sorceress? Perhaps another like myself. Exactly how many were there in the service of this Empire?

Suddenly I felt distant from my new companions. As we walked along the sun baked wall, the dust kicked up underfoot stirred in the air before me. It reminded me of the smoke rising through the night.

"Hey, you okay there?"

A voice finally broke the silence. I looked up from the dust to see a new face. It was Scotch. His eyes were a piercing blue, his hair nearly as light as his skin. His brows and lashes were thin, nearly invisible. Never had I seen a person like him.

"Yes." I lied. Perhaps I was no better, no more honest than the intentions of the Empire.

"We'll make the zone before sundown." He explained. "On our way, what do you say we get some fresh grub?"

"Grub?" I asked. My stomach was hardly ready for food, despite the length I had gone without sustenance.

"Yeah, food. We'll break from the others once we reach the zone, see if we can't kill something to eat. That's how it's done around here, is it not? Maybe you could teach us a thing or two." Scotch continued. "I haven't fired a shot all day. I could use the practice."

"A hunt?" I asked. This was my element. Though the terrain we traveled was new to me, the hunt was not.

"Well, sort of. It's really not much of a hunt." Scotch patted his weapon. "With this baby, I can lay a target down from a distance farther than I care to hike. I figure that's where you come in." He smiled. "Teamwork makes the dream work."

"Very well." I responded. So I was to play fetch. Eventually we rounded the edge of the western wall, the corner jagged and sharp despite the great size of the stone blocks. The southern wall stretched far to the east, beyond line of sight. The terrain was dry and dusty, the plants few and withered upon the cracked and thirsty land.

Rocks and rubble littered the space instead. Far to the south, the gentle hills of the land rolled into a lush dark green landscape. To the east, a great structure protruded from the ruins, looming far overhead and supported by many great columns. Our new heading drew us closer to this curious structure.

Not long after we rounded the corner, we came across a great door set into the stone wall. The door itself was massive and weathered. There was a gap under this great portal, leading to the dark inner recesses of the Tomb. I was grateful that we did not venture near, as this new discovery made me even more uneasy with the place. What manner of creature had the Architects been?

"That leads to the sublevels of the structure." Sig explained. "A rather odd civilization resides just beyond that doorway."

This I knew from the stories of Balthar. The civilization to which he referred was undoubtedly the metal workers with whom Balthar had studied.

"The Salvek." I muttered.

Sig was intrigued. "Salvek?"

I nodded in affirmation.

"Huh." He seemed to reflect. "Have you seen the way they live?"

"No. They do not often venture from the Tomb. There was one who knew of their ways, but their secrets remain with him." I confessed.

Balthar was lost I assumed. I tried not to think of Sarah. Suddenly I felt as if my heart would drop from my chest. I stopped.

The scouts stopped with me. For a moment we stood, as they waited patiently for me to gather myself. I turned to face the great door. The ancient metal was corroded and rusted with time, yet it stood tall and mighty still.

My body was numb; I felt nothing. For a moment I considered wandering into the unknown confines of these ruins, as my eyes shifted to the gap leading into darkness just below the door. After all, my greatest fears had come to pass. What could possibly be worse than that which I had already faced?

"You know," Devon spoke uneasily, "that door is only about half the size of what is typically found in ruins like these."

I looked to him in my astonishment.

"This was most likely a crawl space or maintenance access or something." He went on. "Who knows for sure? Kind of makes you wonder..."

My eyes went back to the rusted door. Only half the size? A crawl space? I shuttered at these implications, glad to know that whatever race of giants that had constructed these ruins no longer lived within.

The scouts pressed onward, away from the fading daylight. I continued with them, unsure of any other path to follow, unsure of what awaited me with the coming of their Empire. I tried not to think on anything in particular, as my feet kicked at the rough terrain, dry and rocky underfoot.

Shadows had begun to creep toward the east, as the sun blazed lazily over the trees to the west. Soon it would disappear behind the great forest, and shadows would sweep the plains. The mysterious platform structure wasn't much further, and it didn't take long for us to near one of the massive pillars.

It stood a towering height, supporting the weight of the indescribable architectural feat overhead. Long had it been since these structures had been erected, their makers long forgotten from the world. Yet here it remained, a standing testament to an age passed.

The earth became more dry, the dust soft like powder underfoot. There were no plants to speak of, few signs of animal life either. The dank dusty terrain was all but veiled in shadow, stretching on to the east where the last of the great pillars stood. The platform above reached to the south from the wall of the ruins, denying light and rain to the forsaken land below.

"We'll setup camp here." Devon spoke, shaking me from my assessment of the unfamiliar landscape.

"Are you sure this is a suitable place?" I asked, hoping he would reconsider.

The scouts had a laugh. I suppose it would seem funny, save for the remains of a large insect laying to the southeast. Something had enjoyed a meal here, something big and strong enough to break apart the armored shell of what looked to once have been a green beetle.

"Relax, Kael." Devon assured. "We have more than enough firepower to handle anything that comes our way. Besides, we won't stay long, just until our ride gets here."

"Ride?" I asked, unsure of what to make of his words.

"A shuttle will arrive just before daybreak." Sig explained. "It'll take us to the closest Imperial city for some well earned time off. Some commander will be there, same old cliche speeches. Things like 'Great job! Well done, you've really earned it'. Then we drink our faces off. All just to be sent out to some other prospective territory and do the whole gig over again..."

"Beautiful." Creeper rasped. "My romantic dream." He kissed the side of his cannon.

"Creeps, you ain't right, bro." Scotch teased.

They all laughed together like family. Family was everything...

"And where will I go?" I asked, wishing home were an option.

It seemed my question left them stumped, draining the smiles from the moment. Devon was left to take charge, the others looking to him with uneasy shrugs.

"His Majesty will no doubt take favor to you, especially in light of your situation. You have refuge, don't worry kid."

I didn't like his implications. The uncertainty in his response suggested we would part ways upon reaching their next destination. For a moment I considered parting ways well before the arrival of this shuttle, no destination in mind. Anywhere but here. I began to feel lost. Instead of running, I sank down in the dust, my back against the rough exterior of a nearby pillar.

The texture of the pillar was familiar. As I looked closer, I realized that it was cut from wood, one solid piece from the looks of it. My eyes ran up its length. How had this been accomplished? It was as if this pillar had been cut from the heart of an elder tree, the very idea seemed impossible.

Night was falling. The last deep yellow bands of sunlight that burned from the west spilled around the pillar. I sat in the shadow it created, my back to the setting sun. I was hungry, but unwilling to address even this basic need.

"You ready to find some food?" Scotch asked.

I looked up from the dust to see him standing before me with a promising smile, his rifle slung across his shoulder.

"Sure." I responded flatly.

Scotch extended a hand to help me to my feet. "That's the spirit, lad."

He pulled me to my feet. This simple gesture of kindness was a welcome relief from the gloom. The two of us on a hunt was a perfect opportunity to run, yet I reconsidered my thoughts of abandonment. Perhaps a life beyond this land would serve me well. After all, I had longed for adventure, and there was little left to lose.

I had scarcely taken a step when an uneasy sensation creep over me. I had felt it before, once in the forest and again when my village was destroyed. A familiar crackling pop rippled through the air.

"Contact!" Creeper shouted.

Shots rang out from behind the pillar following his call. I felt my stomach churn, knowing well what I would see when I cleared the pillar. I came around the northern corner just as a mighty hammer swung hard at my face. I slipped into the change as if by reflex, ducking under the blow as it shattered through the pillar, sending shards of splintered wood sputtering through the air.

Devon and Scotch reacted, moving to engage the threat. But as I saw them now they moved far too slow to be effective. At this range, they were doomed. I watched as the tyrant turned to them, crushing both in two consecutive blows before turning back to me. The left side of his ugly face was twisted and bloodied where his eye had been.

"I've been waiting for you, boy!" His words boomed.

Another furious swing lashed in my direction and then another. Each heavy swing missed its mark, but it was all I could do to avoid the massive hammer. I desperately scanned the area for something to use as a weapon, spotting one of the scout's rifles to my left.

I lunged for it, not knowing if I would even be able to use the thing. The hammer came down on the mysterious metal mechanism, crushing it to the ground before my hand could clear the distance. The kick that followed sent me skittering across the dusty ground, landing me hard against the great wooden pillar.

Dazed, I sat helplessly in a cloud of dust, my back against the pillar. Splinters of wood lay strewn about the dirt from where the raging hulk had smashed a section of the great beam. I pulled my knees to my chest, righting my weight on my heels, as the angry cyclops closed the distance between us. A hunk of splintered wood lay within reach to my right, about the size of a dagger, jagged with a wicked point.

"This is where it ends, you little runt." He growled, standing over me. "I'll grind you into nothing!"

He raised the large hammer up and over his head, readying himself for the killing blow. I waited until his arms were arched back, and in an instant I pressed the change and grabbed hold of the splintered wood. My heels kicked hard against the earth, and I rose strong into the face of my enemy, driving the jagged piece of splintered wood hard up and through his skull.

His remaining eye went wild. The hammer fell at his back, as the beast dropped to his knees in defeat. The weapon and its wielder hit the ground with a synchronized thud. His hands jerked and twitched as they groped the air. The sharp tip of the wooden splinter protruded through his thin greasy hair like a horn. Guttural choking sounds escaped his lips. His stare was blank and wild with bewilderment, as death surely crept upon him.

I felt a powerful surge in my triumph, and with this strength I retrieved the massive hammer. The ridiculous weapon was heavy, even in my accelerated state. In a rage, I sent the broad face of the hammer against his chest with an awkward swing, laying him flat on his back. He would die at my feet.

I stumbled after the weight of the weapon, righting myself to stand at the ready once more. I squatted low to gain the force needed for the final blow, setting my grip for the final swing. The sharp spiked end was ready to strike. With a fierce roar, I brought the hammer up and over me before sending the large spike down hard, well through the chest of the fallen tyrant.

With a sick splash and a rumbling impact that shook the ground underfoot, it was done. The beast stirred no more. I backed away, leaving the hammer standing in his collapsed chest.

I felt the world resume normality around me, as my power slipped away to wherever it resided. I was spattered in the blood of the tyrant, sore and exhausted from the endeavor. Twice I'd taken a beating, and with little time for recovery.

Aching, I looked around, hoping the scouts had not all perished. The body count confirmed. My new friends had all fallen, leaving me alone once again.

Alone with the dark of night, I wept.

Night had fallen. I lingered in that place of death, my mind silent, my body still. I was at a loss, unable to find the will to continue. The skittering sound of insect wings not far in the distance brought me back to reality. I had to find a safe place to spend the night. I had been correct in my assumptions. This place was ill suited for making camp.

Perhaps it was the smell of carnage that drew them. Regardless, I decided it best to move. With no better direction, I turned to retrace my steps to the west.

As I rose to my feet a glint of blue light caught my eye, reflected from the hammer still erected in the dead man's chest . I rounded the pillar to see Creeper's cannon, still active and glowing with the mysterious light that powered it. Inspiration struck. An idea came to mind, and a plan with it. The Salvek resided just behind the rusted door the scouts and I had passed earlier. Perhaps I could trade this alien gadgetry for food and shelter, maybe even a weapon more suitable to my skill.

The insects were drawing near. If I did not move fast, I would be dinner. With a new sense of urgency, I found the motivation to trigger the change. I grabbed hold of the clunking cannon, hesitating in the moment I felt it pull free of Creeper's death grip. He died a warrior's death, fallen in battle. Silently I bid my farewells. With the cannon in hand, I retraced my steps to the west along the wall.

I moved through the night in complete freedom, the accelerated state carrying me the distance in a fraction of the time. The waning moon was nearly full, and the silvery light added a surreal feel to the night. I moved through the world as if through a dream. The looming wall of the ruins helped guide the way in the dim light, the reds of the stone now like a monochromatic scale of black and gray.

The flashy cannon had almost no weight to it, making it hard to believe it could produce such devastating attacks. Operating the technology was well beyond me, but I felt all the better carrying the weapon in hand. I caught sight of the great rusted door in the wall of the ruins.

My powers dismissed, and the world returned to its normal flow as I stood before the door. The deep dark confines of the ruins beckoned me forth. Why I chose to enter, I do not know. I could have easily traded this item anywhere, yet the Salvek came to mind. They had been proclaimed the best weapon masters in all the land. I would need the finest weaponry to do what I meant to do. Cannon in hand, I made my way under the ominous door.

As I approached the gap beneath the door, the darkness within seemed to dampen my courage. Yet I did not stop, I couldn't. I held the cannon before me, using the blue glow to light my path as best I could, leaving the light of the moon behind me. With each reluctant step I passed further under the great door. Dark obscured the unknown space before me, the air musky and stale.

I had all but considered giving in to my impulse to turn back, when I caught a glimmer of firelight. The flickering yellow light mapped out the shape of the inner contours of the wall. As I drew closer, several figures became discernible amidst the dark and gloom. I continued in their direction, hoping it was the Salvek, hoping they would be hospitable in my time of need.

The glowing blue of the cannon alerted them of my approach. Once I was close enough, three shaggy looking men with torches came to meet me in the darkness. They kept a cautious distance from me at first, their curious eyes fixed on the strange armament I carried. I held it like the scouts had, hoping to make it seem as if I could use it if needed. One of the men approached.

"What brings you here, young traveler?" His voice was bland, his tone less than kind.

"Shelter for the night." I responded in a voice just as cold as his. "I brought this for trade." I trained the muzzle of the cannon at his chest.

The men flinched and cowered back from the weapon when it pointed their direction. They recovered easy enough, sharing a nervous laugh at the excitement. They seemed to know what it could do.

"Fancy work you've got there." The man said, his tone more friendly at the prospect, his eyes sparkling in the light of his torch. "A piece like that should do well enough. I reckon a trade can be made. Come."

He smiled wide, revealing dirty mangled teeth that made his smile almost sinister. He turned back toward the lights of their encampment, the sway of his torch leading the way as he limped along. The other two men were much younger than the one who had spoken.

They had thick black beards and dark colored eyes. They said nothing as they came close, one of them reached for the cannon. I was reluctant to release my grip at first, weary of their intentions and unsure of what to expect. The two of them gawked over the foreign technology, as we trailed behind the elder.

As I followed the three back to the lights of their camp, I pondered how they lived in this dark place. There were few stories of the Salvek. Mystery surrounded their ways, as they had little to do with the outside world.

How could they live without the light of day, the blue sky to remind them the Earth is round like the mother's womb? I shuddered at the thought of a life without the sky. To me it seemed a cursed existence.

Their settlement was nestled in the corner where the western and southern walls met. The dark colored stones towered well into the obscurity of the darkness above. There were perhaps a dozen or so others, most of which crowded around small fires.

Sparks flew through the dark in bursts of orange, as a beastly character pounded at a glowing chunk of metal near the rippling heat of a bed of coals. All had shaggy beards and angry faces. Their rigid stares were the only greetings I received, as their eyes followed me along my path through the camp.

I followed the limping elder towards an opening in one of the great stone's of the western wall, keeping only a few steps between us. There were no women. There were no children. This was no village.

An arched doorway marked the opening in the stone, chiseled through a lighter colored stone block. Light spilled from a well lit chamber, and as we stepped inside I was surprised to see the tidy decor of the space within. The chamber was rounded, the walls lined with many blazing torches. The pale colored stone reflected the light of the flames well enough to brighten every inch of the place.

Racks of fine blades and other works of metal lined the curved walls. The ceiling was dark red in color, the flat bottom of the stone resting above. The sound of whispers reverberated through the chamber, as the men that met me upon arrival presented the flashy cannon to those gathered to see.

A long wooden table with many chairs stood in the center of the chamber. Food was still scattered, leftovers filling the place with the delicious aroma of breads and meat. My stomach churned with an audible growl. At the far end stood what looked to be a throne, and atop this throne sat a squat bearded elder.

He looked to be well soaked in age. His squinted eyes were set deep within his wrinkled face, his body slumped against the back of the tall chair. He wore long decorative robes, dark in color with silver lining. A crown rest atop his head of thin silver hair, many jagged spikes rising from it. I thought him well asleep until his crumbling voice beckoned me forth.

"Come closer, child of the Dóvai." His voice sounded as old as the ruins.

I moved through the warm chamber until I stood before the elder. To his left was another, a silver haired female, draped in scarlet robes much like those worn by her male counterpart. She seemed less than well, her attentions away from the others in the room. A small crucible burned before her as she rocked back and forth muttering to herself.

"Do not worry, young warrior." The aged voice came again. "Our ways may seem strange, but there is no danger here. Not for you, child."

With his words, the muttering of the elder in scarlet robes stopped. Her long silver hair clung to the robes as well as to the air all about her, and it twisted as her head turned to at last acknowledge my presence. Her eyes were as gray as her hair.

She did not see me, yet she smiled as if she had found me in her gaze. Her smile seemed empty, as if it carried no sentiment whatsoever, its only purpose to show her gnarled teeth. She said nothing. Instead, she turned back to her smoldering crucible, splashing it with a mysterious substance that doused the flames and created a billowing smoke to rise from the small dish.

"Delthi, high priestess of the three tribes." The elder spoke from atop his throne. "I am Amos, eldest tribesman. Once a fine warrior, now a brittle bag of bones waiting to pass."

He laughed, raising his left hand from where it rest on the arm of his chair in a slow, simple gesture. The others left the chamber, leaving me alone with the two robed elders of the Salvek. I stood before them. The glowing cannon lay on the tabletop where the men had left it.

"You brought this weapon to us all on your own did you?" Amos asked.

"I did." I responded, saddened by the realization that I was once again alone in my travels.

"And I suspect this means you have felled the one who wielded it?" He asked, a smile following his words.

"No. He was a friend, killed by a monster. His body lies near one of the great pillars to the east." I responded bluntly, unsure of his line of questioning.

Amos let out a crooked laugh. "I see. Sorry for the loss of your friend. This weapon you have brought us, the secrets it holds. We owe you much thanks, young one. What is your name?"

"I am Kael."

"Welcome, Kael..." Amos repeated my name. I saw the glimmer of his ancient gaze, as his eyes fixed on me. "The ones who wield such weapons, they came from the sky. My boy, you could not fathom the powers this Empire has at its disposal. Unfortunately, those who arrived held no interest in trade, and we lost many in attempts to acquire such an item by force. The secrets this weapon holds will usher in a new era for the Salvek. On behalf of the three tribes, we thank you."

He followed his words with the bow of his head. I bowed in turn. Had they fought against the scouts? Surely not. Blades seemed little match against such advanced weaponry.

"You remind me of another youth of the Dóvai, one I met long ago." Amos spoke now with the warmth of pride and memory in his wavering voice. "A strong young man named Balthar. He won the respect of the tribes, warming our hearts and reminding us of the bond between brothers. Stories of his courageous heart have become legend, so many times have I heard them told around the fires of our people. Surely you know him?"

"I did." Pain flooded my heart surely as the truth washed over my tongue. I thought of my home, this time I did not fight the tears.

Amos seemed pained as well. "So it is true then. The Dóvai..." He turned his head and swallowed hard. "A great loss for all the land. I am sorry, Kael."

I had no words. Silence lingered in the moments that followed. Tears rolled down my face as I wept before the elders of the Salvek.

"They are not lost, boy."

Came the aged voice of the lady shaman. She rose with the flutter of her great robes. She collected my attention instantly. Her very presence seemed to resonate through the chamber like the words she spoke.

"Reisenbough is no more, but descendants of the Dóvai live on."

She shuffled closer. The hair on my neck stood on end. "I foresaw the flames of war, the falling of our brethren to the north and the rise of a great warrior, an avenger, a reaper of souls..."

Her words brought a cold shiver to run through me. I was locked on her words.

"For as the flames of anguish burned, the all seeing eyes awoke in the darkness around you, Kael. Their piercing gaze sees only truth. Will they bring peace to the hearts of man or still them in cold judgment?" Her clouded eyes seemed piercing as they remained fixed on me, unblinking, unyielding.

Her words were captivating, holding my interest under self scrutiny. I knew nothing of this strange power I had come to discover, other than what I suspected. They were not of the natural world.

"What am I?" I was compelled to ask the question.

She laughed deep, a weathered smile rising upon a face that had once been smooth and fair.

"A child of the Eons, as surely as you are of the Dóvai. Though you bear the flesh of man, your spirit is as old as the cosmos itself. You are the physical embodiment of the heavens."

Her words seemed ripe with meaning, yet they only confused my thoughts further.

"How? Why?" I asked, desperate for answers to the mysteries within.

Again she laughed, as she turned and began shuffling back to where the small crucible still smoldered. "My visions only provide witness to the energies of this world."

She stooped over the crucible, dousing another rolling flame with a strange fluid poured from a small mortar. A final plume rose from it like my anticipation for her response, as she stirred at the brew.

"I do not posses the answers you seek, but you will find them well enough. Carry your questions with you, child. Understanding is a noble quest for a young mind."

Her voice seemed to resonate in the cylindrical chamber, as she turned and approached. She carried a small silver chalice that now contained the brew she had produced. The contents sloshed with each shuffling step.

"Your path is one as formidable as your spirit, but worry not. Truth will realize you, as surely as you realize your potential- in due time. Your journey is your own..." She offered the chalice, carefully cupped between her bony, aged hands. "Drink."

I approached the steps of the platform upon which she stood and accepted the offering. The murky yellow contents swirled within their silvery confines, emitting a strong scent like that of stripped bark and ash. I raised the drink, the taste of it bitter to my tongue. I made quick work of it, trying hard not to gag. The experience left me all the more ready to depart from the Salvek.

No sooner had I finished the strange drink, than I began to feel a warm flush run through me. Suddenly all worry seemed to leave me, and a great desire for sleep took its place. The world around me seemed unified as if it were a body of fluid, and I was all but swimming in the rainbow colors of the radiant chamber.

Amos rose from the prestigious seat in which he perched, and shambled his way to stand at Delthi's side. "It was a great honor to meet you, Kael of the Dóvai. May your spirit prosper in your days to come."

Their soft robes fluttered around me as I collapsed upon the stone steps at their feet. The gentle touch of soft aged hands met my face, as the crimson of Delthi's robes encircled me.

"When your perceptions align, you will see." The room around me began to swirl in waves of light, as she laughed. "Eyes many like the stars in the heavens, pervading the darkness. They see all... You have only just begun, son of Eons."

Her words echoed with meaning, as it seemed all the lights in the cosmos swirled about me, and soon colorful visions filled my mind. Darkness seemed an impossibility, as I whirled about in a tempest of vibrant energies. There was comfort despite the turbulence, and though I could make little sense of it, I found some glinting hint of a deeper understanding that beckoned to me from obscurity. It remained just out of reach of conceptual thought, as a deep calming darkness lulled me into a dreamless sleep.

The Path to Verda

I awoke to the sifting sound of tall grass whipping in the breeze. The world was painfully bright, my head heavy. My skull throbbed against the light of the sun. As my vision adjusted I recognized the dusty sand colored path. The tall grass danced across the fields in waves, moving like a turbulent sea of green and golden brown.

My back was against the western wall of the ruins. I must have lay there for some time, my body stiff and rigid to movement. I checked myself over as my senses recovered. Nothing out of order. Aside from feeling a bit dazed, I seemed well enough. There was a slender black object left propped against the wall, a small cloth bundle on the dusty ground next to it.

When at last I dared, I rose to my feet and stood over my bounty. The tall slender object leaned against the wall was a sword, held in a hardened case that was in itself a work of mastery. Metal shimmered down the sleek dark length of it, the jeweled handle indicative of the blade within.

Taking hold of the sleek black case, I felt the weight of the weapon. Already I was taken by the marvel. It was a bit heavy, but well balanced and latent with potential. It boasted a slightly longer reach than any traditional blade I had known. It would require some adaptation, but the gilded sheath more than compensated for an effort needed. The metal had been formed with a rippled design, forged well enough that this item in itself was an asset in battle as well as the blade it carried.

Much detail had been put into the design. I traced my fingers over the three symbols that encircled the mouth of the case, where the small squared guard of the blade rested snugly. It was as if the two rested in perfect harmony.

The grip was extended and well suited for two hands. The bindings were of thick darkened leather, warn and soft to the touch as I took it firmly in hand. I felt the unyielding strength of the blade within my grip as I held the weapon aloft, right hand on the handle, left clutching the marvelous case.

Once my hands had studied the weight of it, the blade was ready to break free. I commanded the motion of their separation, and the blade gently hissed from the embrace of the sheath. The high pitched ring it made came naturally, like the bitter sweet lament of lovers divided. The sound of that romance became the feeling in the air, and it won my heart immediately.

Truly I was inspired by this fine work. Devotion had shaped it, devotion would shape our movements together, as I gained a familiarity with its dimensions. As my body moved, energies aligned. The blade sliced through the air as if it weighed nothing, and suddenly it became weightless.

I had entered the accelerated state. This time there had been no danger to trigger it, just a natural connection to the energies within me. I pushed further still, my confidence as radiant as the sunlight glistening off the blade at my hands. So long as devotion sustained, my hand would deliver the blade home at the end of its journey. Two loves reunited as one, with each and every victory.

My eyes closed against the warmth of the sun as I held the magnificent blade before me. I focused on the energy of my heightened state with a new certainty, and concentrated now on calming its flame. Reality slipped over me with slowed tranquility, exaggerating the motion as I brought the marvelous case up to receive the blade.

A promise was made. The blade slid softly back into the case's embrace with a promise kept. Harmony was restored.

As I looked out over the waves of grain, a life of peace seemed a real possibility. The road at my feet could lead me north toward the people of the White Hollow. From there I could return to the Arching Forest. But as my gaze shifted west, the dark shadowy outline of the forest beyond the plain brought another destination to mind, and with it a new idea. An idea considered most unclean.

Vengeance...

I shook this dark notion from my mind, shunning the heat it brought to my heart. Vengeance was not the way of the Dóvai. Had I not already witnessed the price of bloodshed? The elders had been right, peace is not won through violence.

Enough life had been lost already. Grief was in order, not suffering. But even grief wasn't worth holding onto. In order to regain peace, I had to let go completely.

With this noble objective in mind, I decided to travel north along the road. I fitted the new weapon at my waist to sit at my hip. The blade was too long to draw from my shoulder, the case far too useful a tool to leave at my back. I practiced drawing from my hip, exploring various options to find the best way to carry the thing.

In my excitement over the sword, I had nearly forgotten about the small cloth bundle near the wall. I snatched it up, finding a loaf of bread and a canteen brimming with cool water. I was grateful to the Salvek for their aid, but not yet ready to trust another drink. Weapon and provisions settled, I began my way north on the dusty path. Perhaps some new beginning awaited. I need only find it.

The day was warm despite the change in seasons. The earthy smell of dry dust filled every breath, as I walked north along the wall. The sun was slightly to the west overhead, beaming down as it slowly dipped toward the great forest beyond the fields. The wind sighed gently through the grains, as the canteen rattled and clinked against the metallic scabbard with each step.

I wasn't far from the northwestern corner of the ruins, when reluctance began to drag at my feet. My mind seemed want to wander against my will, thinking of that alternate destination and the sinister purpose it sought there. Vengeance was working its way into obsession within my heart and mind, darkening my very nature.

Many times along the way I had to remind myself of my duty to those fallen. If I were the only one left, who else would honor their remains and send them to the beyond? I had to return. I had to send them, to honor them.

This responsibility helped motivate my feet to continue, hoping to face down grief and regain peace. After all, the witch had said the Dóvai would endure, all was not lost. The others would return, surely. We could rebuild.

I came to a break in the path. The road leading to the White Hollow was underfoot, but another road met it from the field, leading west through the tall grass. As I approached the road, I caught sight of another traveler.

He rode upon a rickety carriage pulled by two silver coated akbars. Their large glistening black eyes portrayed their gentle nature, their large fan shaped ears alert to my presence. They slowed, but did not stop.

"Whoa girls!" The man wailed, pulling back on the reigns.

The two docile creatures pulling the open wagon stopped at his command. Their sleek fur shimmered in the sunlight, as they began affectionately grooming one another. Their furs looked soft and warm, much like the darker colored fur I had kept on my bed. I thought of the raid, of the burning fire that consumed my home.

"Hi there, stranger." The rider greeted. "Where you headed out here all alone?"

"Nowhere." My flat tone reflected what little effort I had placed into the response.

The rider laughed. "Well then you're right where you need to be. Nothing around here for a while yet. You headed north then?"

"For now." I answered.

The rider chuckled. "I'm headed that way myself, trying to make it back to the Hollow before sunset. Still have a ways to go though, probably won't make it until after dark. You're more than welcome to hitch a ride. Hop on! Juniper and Daisy here will get us there safely."

"Thank you." I responded, gracious for the offer. My interests seemed to lie elsewhere.

"Where does this road lead?" I asked, pointing down the path from which he came.

"This road here leads to Verda, but I don't recommend traveling it alone, or at all for that matter. The closer you get to Verda, the closer to trouble. Thieves and looters stalk the outer regions around the city. Best to continue north from here, friend." The man explained, concern on his face.

"Thank you, sir." My gracious response did little to ease the worry on the man's kind face.

"You sure you don't want a ride to the Hollow? The festival is only a day away. You're sure to find a good time." The man all but pleaded.

"Thank you, but I'd like to continue on my own." I declined.

By the look in the man's eyes, he knew what I meant to do was no good. He meant to save me from it, but he was far too gentle a sort to press further.

"Take care, lad. We hope to see you again at the Hollow." He smiled as he whipped the reigns, setting Juniper and Daisy into motion once again with the creak of wagon wheels. "Can't miss it, just follow the road north."

I stood at the junction and watched the carriage travel its way north along the wall in the direction of a righteous path. It seemed I was stuck there in limbo where the two roads met, faced with a decision that should have been easy. Yet as I remained there, torn between the two paths, it seemed anything but.

The path to Verda led to darkness, the shadows of the forest beyond the field were deep. The shadows would grow deeper still when the light faded with evening. Again it called to my anger, perhaps the only emotion I had left. I took another step to the north attempting to walk the better path, but I managed only the one.

To what was I returning? Reisenbough and its people had been destroyed. Doubt began to cloud my mind.

Again my eyes turned to face the darkness. I felt as if a sinister energy seethed within that dark forest. A vision gripped me, striking fear as it took form. The dark swirled like a cyclone, pulling to consume the light. Gripped by the illusion, I watched as the energy took the form of a great pale worm, viciously hungry and writhing there in a sea of human suffering. In its greed it groped to consume what it could, leaving only despair in its wake. This creature sought to devour hope and spirit alike.

The vision broke, and I all but screamed. Perhaps I did, but that fear broke to anger once again, and my rage kindled strong enough to set that darkness ablaze. The change broke over me, and I felt my teeth grind hard. A wicked sensation rippled through me. My reason tried to still my anger, reminding me of a greater purpose, but it was no use.

Send them. Send them...

"Avenge them. I must." A broken heart confessed aloud, the voice of mutiny and treason.

My left hand gripped hard at the handle of the blade at my side. My eyes set on the dark facade beyond the field, and I began my journey down the path to Verda.

The air grew chill as the sun began to disappear behind the dark wall of forest to the west. The last of its golden rays lit a clear sky above. I looked back to the ruins behind me. The same golden light crept up the height of the structure with the setting sun. As it shrank little by little, my steps marched me closer to the city soon to feel my blade.

The dark caught me, as night fell over the fields. I had made it some distance, but with the night came new dangers, and there was little chance of hunting down those responsible in the dead of night.

I stopped to await the morrow. The tall grass offered shelter well enough against the chill autumn air, but a fire would have certainly been nice. Cold and alone, I settled down and tried to ready myself for sleep, eating what I could force down of my provisions. Whatever bread they had given was clearly concocted for its nutrition and not its taste.

Sleep did not come easy. Prowling creatures howled, welcoming the night. The stars were brilliant in the sky above, and as I lay awake listening to the world around me I watched them slowly swirl across the heavens. My mind seemed empty, and if I had gratitude left at that particular point, I would have been grateful for such a moment. The grass of the fields danced about in the wind, the soft whipping sounds at last lulling me to rest.

The green of my home was at peace in my dreams. Reisenbough stood intact, as if the flames of the siege had never happened. I saw my loved ones. The smiles on their faces warmed my heart, as they comforted me with their words. I knew it to be a lie, but held to it with all of my being, hoping that reality instead had been the dream.

The faces of my people were somber, as if love and worry surrounded me as surely as they did. My father stood before me, his father next to him. Darius was there as well. Hands reached out to touch me, the familiar feel of family's embrace as their words pleaded in hopes peace would still my heart.

"Do not do this, son. Vengeance will solve nothing. Let go of pain, return to us." My father's words came. His eyes soft and endearing.

"Restore peace in your heart, son. Sow the seeds of prosperity and live well. You can do it."

Came the voice of my grandfather Darius. He had long since passed, yet here his presence was convincing in my mind, his voice full of love and wisdom as it had been in life.

"It's okay, Kael. Everything is okay. Let go." Kraegar spoke in the softest tone possible of such a man.

Their call to peace may have reached my heart, were it not all just a dream. They were lost, and surely as I realized that fact the flames returned to the village around us. The drums of my people surged through me, as their cries rose in my ears like a deafening roar. Pain once again gripped at me in the darkness.

I awoke to the cry of my own voice, as I shook from my slumber. Dawn had yet to fully spill its light over the world. Frost licked at the high stalks of grass, giving the field a crystal white glow in the silver light.

My breath was heavy before me, as I rose to my feet in the chill morning air. I stumbled out from the grass and onto the dusty road once more, still shaken by the elements of my dream. I looked to the west as I stood in the crisp morning, my back to the direction I should have been traveling.

"Sorry father." I whispered to no one, my voice as cold as the air into which it escaped.

He had once told me to not hold back, to share my love with the world. Love and wisdom were to be shared, not pain. Yet as surely as I understood these words, I meant to break them. I would visit my pain upon Verda, sharing with them the ruin of my people.

It wasn't right, but to hell with being right. Nothing I had witnessed was right. That concept burned with Reisenbough, those searing flames the new passion of my heart.

Tears streamed my face, as I turned from the path of my people and continued west. I couldn't retreat to some other beginning, some other lie. Not while the crimes I had witnessed went unabated. That worm would wither before me. Those who returned could clean up the mess. The enemies of the Dóvai would perish, preventing them from ever again threatening ruin upon anyone. With the crunching of the dusty earth beneath each step, I continued down the path toward Verda.

The way was lonely and cold as the sun continued to rise behind the Tomb. By late morning, a soothing warmth crept over the tomb in golden rays, lighting the road I traveled with its radiant shine. The forest grew larger with each step it seemed, as the southern forest was mostly elder trees, massive and towering well beyond the Allichene that grew at their trunks.

As I walked, the dusty path became darker in color with the rich earth of the forest. I looked up to the high branches of the elder trees and wondered what the view might be like from such a height. What would the land look like from the heavens?

I came to another split in the road. The path I traveled met another, running north to south along the edge of the forest. Verda was to the north, and as I stood on this new path I looked to the south, pondering what lie in this unfamiliar direction. It wasn't too late. Perhaps I could just forget everything and wander the Earth, free.

As I looked to the south contemplating my intentions, movement in the brush caught my attention. I turned to face the source, spying three armed men as they moved out from the wood line to approach me on the path. They wore sinister expressions, wasting no time at readying their arms.

Two carried short swords, the other a gnarled club of sorts. The traveler I met near the wall had been right it seemed. Danger lurked.

"Well look what we have here, boys." One of the men spoke in an arrogant tone. "Out here all alone on his way to the City of Champions. Looks like breakfast is served."

The others laughed as they moved in closer. The shortest of the three men circled behind me, sword in hand. The other two stood before me as if to bar my way forward.

"Everything you got is ours now. No need to hand it over, we like taking it all the better." The man with the club snarled.

I smiled wide in the face of this threat. To rid the world of such treachery would be an honor. With a new sense of purpose, I reached for the blade at my side. Finding the center of focus within that brought the change, I willed it forth.

Again I felt the surge and the brief disorientation as my perception enhanced, finding the way much easier this time. It was as if an energy harnessed within pushed away the confines of the physical world, occupying everything within a zone of influence around me.

Time seemed to stutter, and then to drag. I no longer understood the sluggish words of the thug or the demands they carried. The implied message was clear enough, danger. I moved into action.

With a thunderous snap, I drew my blade and struck in the direction of the man closest to me with a wicked slash. The fool held his weapon at guard, but he and his crudely improvised club were no match for the attack.

My blade ran down the length of his awkward defensive, severing every digit from his right hand and horribly mangling his left as it did so. His face had not yet made the dramatic transition from sinister to appropriated terror as I moved my blade to counter an incoming slash from another of the three.

He came at me with a downward slash, his blade falling toward me. Using the force of his own attack, I redirected and propelled his blade far left of its intended target, and drove my shoulder into his exposed flank, setting him wildly off balance. Quickly, I made my way around him, passing the bite of my blade low through the top of his left leg just above his knee as he moved to recover. The leg was nearly severed in two.

I withdrew my weapon back to the ready and turned my attention away from the two wounded, focusing on the third. The shorter man swung his sword wildly in my direction. I toyed with his hopeless offensive, allowing his strikes to narrowly miss their mark.

His eyes were wide with rage, twisting his bearded face. I faded away from his slowed advance, nearing the taller swordsman who had fallen to the ground. His wails were prolonged, as he clung to his gaping leg. I swung high with my wondrous blade, delivering a fatal blow to the man's throat, ending his awful song.

My execution was deliberate and true to my teachings, using only the end of my blade for the assault so that in an instant it was back at my guard. The downed man slipped free of his woe, his severed leg far less damaging than his severed throat. He was finished. He dropped to the dirt, choking on his last moments.

The third man continued his advance, raging toward me in a flurry of attacks. Each a wasted effort, as one by one they missed their mark. I maneuvered around the flailing thug, working my way closer to his remaining accomplice with the missing digits. He shrieked at his mangled hands in petrified terror.

Once I grew bored with the desperate attempts of the flailing swordsman, I utilized one of the many openings in his offensive and sent him to the ground with a crushing kick to the sternum. In an instant I turned to his shock stricken comrade, and with a quick swing I cleaved the gaping fool's head from his shoulders. Their mouthy leader was no more.

Time seemed to slow further still, enhancing the moment. The ringing lingered in my blade from its journey through the man. My heart beat low and steady, like a throbbing distant thunder. My blade continued through the air as if in perfect harmony with the world despite the carnage.

The body of the club wielding assailant collapsed as the head fell independently alongside. The two seemed light as feathers, falling at a reduced rate by my perception. My blade and I moved freely. The advantage was clearly mine. The band of murderous theives chose the wrong victim on this day.

I turned from the fallen leader to the man who's throat I'd cut, still clinging to life despite the amount of blood that had spurted onto the road. I approached him, intent on delivering a final blow. With the new strength at my disposal I stomped my foot down into his chest, crushing it to the ground as one crushes a daisy.

My accelerated state felt amazing; I was unstoppable. With a heavy pull, I removed my foot from the caved chest of the second dead man and turned my attention to the last of the three. He had recovered to his feet, but what his eyes had witnessed in this turn of events inspired a madness from which there would be no recovery. He tossed his weapon aside, and ran north along the road. The battle was over.

As I relaxed the surge ended, and the natural flow returned to the world around me. I watched the coward flee from his intended victim. Even though I could have caught him in an instant, I allowed him to maintain some distance. He was running home, where he felt safest. I would meet him there and drown that last feeling of safety in blood.

The blood he had sought to spill when he and his band of misfits ambushed me, the lives of the brave scouts, and all the blood of my people fueled my lust for vengeance. With the sticky squish of blood and dirt in my step, I followed him. He would lead me to my destination; Verda, the so called City of Champions.

Verda

The battered thief fled further and further along the road, leading our way north along the edge of the forest. I allowed just enough distance between us that he continued to stagger along in desperation. He was quite exhausted and all but frantic when at last we reached the city. The weary fool had led me to Verda, a true metropolis even in its day.

Despite the circumstances, I was awestruck when I neared the ominous city. A great structure stood just within the forest to the likes of which I had never seen. This constructed marvel stood several levels high, and unlike the ruins to the east, this architectural feat was accomplished by the hands of men. The streets around the structure were crowded thick with all manner of people in colorful dress.

The shock of this new place left me baffled and curious. The people all seemed busy to some means, too busy to even notice their neighbors, passing one another with determined indifference. Some even bumped into one another without the slightest acknowledgment.

Vendors lined the streets with their stalls. Items of all sorts imaginable were available for trade. Much to my intrigue, the exchange was not of goods but of small golden coins.

For a moment I lost sight of my query, so entranced I became by the culture of Verda. Colorful linens adorned the common people, draped about them in layers. Others wore simple dressings, less ornate and more practical to their toils. There were also those who wore tattered and dirty clothes, even shackles.

The sounds of a thousand conversations droned through the air. The clamor of footsteps on the stone streets tapped amidst the commerce. Eyes seemed to follow me, suspicion in their glare. My sharp expression deterred their prying curiosity, that or the blood spatter I wore.

When at last I rounded the large wood and stone structure, I saw the full potential of Verda. Deeper in the forest the city grew, mostly built into the trees above ground level. The Allichene had been bound, cut, and shaped to support a floating city of scattered platforms bridged together by grand wooden arches and suspended walkways. Overhead were even more colorfully dressed citizens. Armed guards patrolled everywhere.

At this point I was well distracted. Sight of my target had been lost completely. In a moment of innovation, I explored a new aspect of my capacities. I willed the change, using my heightened senses to search for the familiar profile of the murderous thief.

It didn't take long to find him, as he worked his way through the crowd. He had tried to blend in hopes to disappear in the heavy flow of people funneling into the main entrance of the large multilevel structure. I closed the distance in an instant. The oblivious throng was slowed to a crawl around me with the change. Carefully I weaved my way through the sea of bodies, leaving many startled by the speed in which I flashed by them.

I stopped short of the thief, releasing the change. His face all but twisted in terror as he caught sight of me. He turned and shoved his way through the crowd, pushing through the grand archway. A thunderous roar rattled the great structure, shaking me all the same. It was voices, what must have been a thousand or more. What was happening in this place?

I followed him through, careful not to upset the armed guards that watched the man suspiciously. They didn't seem to take notice of me, their attentions set on the frantic thief. He slipped through a wooden door at the base of a grand stairwell. The guards moved to follow him.

I entered the accelerated state again, eager to catch the man before they did. I zipped through the door the moment one of the guards opened it. His eyes widened in disbelief, as I closed the door between us with a wink.

Behind the door was a wide, poorly lit corridor. The thief stood just out of arms reach before me. I could have ended it there, but I didn't. Instead I slipped from the change. He turned toward the commotion of the wooden door, crying out at the sight of me. With a shriek he all but stumbled, turning to flee further down the corridor.

I let him go, taking time to examine the hall. Light filtered through the dusty air via narrow slatted windows along the outer wall. Wooden beams lined the confines of the corridor like the many ribs along the spine of a serpent.

The thief ran down the length of the corridor, desperate to put distance between us. I could think of no more fitting a place for such a man to meet his end. The wooden door fluttered open behind me.

"You there!" A voice called in a commanding tone. "This area is off limits. What business have you here?"

"That man." I pointed down the hall. "I mean to kill him."

The thief had managed to clear some distance, as he rounded a set of stairs leading up to sunlight. The door opened further at my response, and the two armed sentries moved to enter. Whatever they had intended was too little too late. I made the change and advanced, closing the distance to the stairs in an instant by their perception.

A turbulent roar rattled through the place once more, droning with a reverberating resonance in my heightened state. When the man I followed reached the top of the stairs, I again released the change. Light rained from the sky above, making it seem as if the stairs ascended to the heavens. Toying with the bandit was all too much fun. Making each step heavy, I climbed the stairs behind him with an audible progression. The masses roared, their voices closer, more clear.

His panic rose. He stumbled back from the top of the stairs in disbelief, tired and frantic as he pleaded. I stepped into the light of day in steady pursuit. The place was thick with people, impossibly so.

The thief backed into a crowd gathered around a rail that separated them from whatever spectacle captivated the attention of so many. His back was to the rail, closer with each step. There was a gap in the crowd just wide enough, his hip met the rail, and over and down he tumbled.

Gasps escaped those gathered, as I went up and over as well, dropping the distance to land with a roll on the dusty ground below. The thief had not fared so well, all but broken upon the dust. Gathered around this pit was a sea of people, alive and cheering hard from the rising stands that encircled.

The two armed guards had caught up to us. The bolder of the two called down over the rail, his voice belting through a thick mustache.

"Stop right there!"

The broken bandit stumbled to his feet. Confusion began to spread through the crowd gathered around the scene. The guard with the large mustache blew a shiny whistle. Other guards began to converge on our location.

Two more approached from either side on the dusty grounds of the pit. They were already in place and were the first to respond. Their spears were long and looked wicked sharp. Time was of the essence, it was now or never.

My hand found the blade at my side, setting it free with a hiss. I exhaled with the motion, rippling into the change, powering the motion that drove the attack. The blade traveled through the man as easy as it traveled the air, cutting through his torso with a deep slash. His eyes glazed, as his body slowly fell upon the dust.

I lost myself to that empty stare, watching him fall. He had yet settled in the dust when a sense of impending danger shook me into action. Even in my accelerated state, I narrowly avoided the incoming thrust of a spear.

The motion of the stab moved with me, as I tumbled out of reach. The guard's form was perfect, his face empty with the flow of his motion. His armor was the same as those my brothers and I had encountered in the forest, the same as those that burned our homes.

My blade moved through him quickly, before thought could intervene. Like a hateful reflex, I drove it hard up and through his gut, deep under the heavy armor that protected his torso. I set against the next the same, slashing hard down his side, wounding him horribly.

There were others on the field. Other battles as well, though it seemed I was gaining much attention, distracting from the action already at play.

There were armed warriors, clashing with lethal intent. There were poorly armed men with shackles about their wrists and ankles. There were dead, spread with crimson spatter upon the chalky dust. What was this madness? Nausea took hold with the realization of what had transpired, the feel of it unbearable under the change. I slid from it just as I heaved with sick.

Several more armed personnel entered through a heavy gated doorway. More filled the stands around the dusty center, vying for room amidst the shuffling crowd that gathered to see. There were archers, arrows ready...

Those on ground level were well upon me, circling me with their pointed spears fixed on target. I took stock of it all, wiping the sick and spittle from my mouth, my blade still in hand. The archers would be a problem, but it wouldn't matter. I would kill them all or die trying. Readying myself for battle, I steadied for the carnage ahead. Before I could slip into the change, a voice boomed.

"Enough!!"

I looked for the source of the voice. On the field stood a cloaked figure, his gloved right hand raised with the command. The forces of Verda held their positions in response, looking to the elder as if awaiting further instructions.

The loud voice boomed once more. "Looks like we have a trouble-maker on the field ladies and gentlemen." The source was a large bell shaped spout that hung from a high balcony. "Please allow for a brief intermission while we sort this out. Thank you."

The crowd booed and groaned, as the cloaked figure approached. He was older and rather rough looking. His face was porous and hard like stone, smooth only where scars shimmered in pink accents across his weathered flesh. His dark red cloak draped about his slender form. He looked to me with a piercing gaze, hard as his demeanor.

"Come." He gestured for me to follow as he turned. I did not move.

"You are of Reisenbough, are you not?" He asked.

"Aye." I responded, unsure of this mysterious elder. His accent, his clothes. He did not look or sound to be of Verda.

"Then come!"

He turned and walked in the direction of the same heavy iron gates through which the soldiers had entered. Those soldiers lined the way, his dark gloved hand holding the line. There was a sheen from a jeweled saber at his hip, glimmering beneath the flutter of his robes as he walked.

He had rightfully assumed my origin, meaning he likely knew of Reisenbough's fate. From the authority he held, surely he knew more of those responsible for the attack. Perhaps he was the one who had given the order. The soldiers that cleared our path moved as if it were his dark gloved hand that rendered their commands. Trust was out of the question. I followed, glad to move from the range of the watchful archers, eager to have my answers.

The armed forces obeyed the order to stand down, but looked on with angry faces as I passed by them. The cloaked elder led our way through the iron gate to a dusty chamber within the confines of the structure. Stomps from the people above rattled the roof overhead. The heavy iron gate creaked and shuttered as it closed behind us. My blade remained gripped at my side, bloodied and ready.

The glaring eyes of strangers washed over me, as we moved through the poorly lit chamber. A motley assortment of characters paced, ready for battle it seemed. Many of them did indeed look like killers. Yet, the hardest looks came from the guards, no doubt sore about the loss of their comrades.

A guard stood at either side of a door to the rear of the unkempt chamber. They moved aside as we approached. A stooped servant in tattered clothes reached to open the door. Tension rose as I neared, pride getting the better of the guards' sense of duty upon what they had seen.

The larger of the two wore an angry look on his face, making his mustache appear sinister. His robust frame filled the shiny armor about his chest, and his mean eyes fixed on me as if he meant to advance. He readied the metal tip of his spear in my direction. The other guard was shorter and rather fat. He aligned his squat profile against me as well.

"Lucky punk." The larger man growled through his mustache. His fat companion sneered.

The angry faced guard continued to growl his threats, but in my accelerated state the message was obscured into slurring nonsense. The man's expression was much distorted with active speech, as I advanced around his spear and slammed a hammering blow hard into his face. It sent him back to smash against the stone wall behind him. In the same burst of speed, I turned and landed a solid kick into the shiny armored chest of his chunky comrade, sending the squat man tumbling back and over a wooden bench.

I breathed deep, slipping softly from the accelerated state as I slowly exhaled. The others in the room stood dumfounded, eyes wide in disbelief. The angry mustached man lay slumped against the wall, battered and beaten. The other rolled slowly to his feet, groaning with the effort. The eyes in the chamber continued to watch, but no one advanced.

"Are you done?" The elder all but scolded, not the least bit shaken. "Enough..."

I slid my blade gently back to rest in the magnificent case at my side. "For now."

The elder in the scarlet cloak led us deeper into the confines of the structure, through corridors similar to the one through which I had chased the thief. There were a few armed guards along the way. Some patrolled, others stood posted near entryways. Servants bowed from our path. Fear seemed to cling to them like the shadows in this place.

A spiral staircase led us to another corridor two levels higher. Midway the hall opened into a lavish chamber. Several robed figures stood casually chatting within.

As we entered, the chatter faded. Never had I seen such people. All were dressed curiously, wrapped in soft looking layers of linen, finely crafted and colorful. Gems and precious metals adorned them, the wealth of Verda.

From the many unknown faces, three approached. Two were older men, both carrying themselves with prestige. One was shorter, draped in purple robes. His face was cleanly shaven and almost hateful in the worn expression the years had pressed upon it. Instinctively, I did not like him.

Another of the men was tall and lean. His posture proposed sovereignty despite the shaking he did his best to subdue. His skeletal frame all but rattled beneath his dark yellow robes. Whether the shaking was his nerves or his health, he at least managed a nod in my direction when our eyes met.

The third man stood centered between the two elders. His robes were of a deep red, a dark blue cloth belted the linens about his waist. He stood more steadfast than the rest. His clean-shaven face was younger, his nerve solid.

"Hello." He greeted with a smile.

The voice I had heard boom in the arena was his. My hand found my blade. The guards in the chamber began to stir in reaction, but the man held up his hand to stay them.

"No need for all that. Men can be decent if given the chance." He looked back to me with a sip of his drink.

I released my grip. The cloaked elder nodded in approval, releasing his the same.

"Ah! Now that's the spirit! Well met, young sir." The young man bellowed. His voice was loud even without the aid of the megaphone. "Billy T. Marcius." He offered his name with his hand.

I did not give my name in exchange, nor did I offer my hand. He only smiled softly, a false smile as cold as the marble stone underfoot.

"On the streets people call me Boss, but my friends call me Marci. I hope in time you do the same." His smile brightened as his ego recovered. "So, how should I call you?"

"I am Kael, born of the Dóvai. Son of Krayton the Mighty and surviving member of the house of Dóv. I was there when my village burned, there when the soldiers of Verda laid it to waste, and I am most certainly not your friend." I spat in response.

"Ah," his smile drained, "this discussion will take some time." He turned his attentions to the two men in his company. "My lords, if you would excuse me please."

Marcius bid his tidings with the bow of his head and a sip of his drink. The two elders bid their own partings. The man in purple shot a sinister smirk as our eyes met. The two hastily shuffled through the rear entrance of the chamber, where a grand balcony overlooked the arena. When his company had left us, he turned for the corridor with the gesture of his hand.

"Well then, Kael of the Dóvai. Would you care to join me in my office? We can talk more there."

"Very well." I muttered, as I exited the chamber into the dimly lit corridor. Marcius accompanied.

"If I may ask, why did you kill that man today? The one who fell in the arena." Marcius asked as we walked the corridor. The cloaked elder trailed behind us in silence.

"He was a murderous thief." I responded coldly.

"I see." Marcius sighed, looking at first perplexed and then relieved. "So a just killing, I'm sure. All the better for the arena. The people love to see justice well served. If we'd known, you could have avoided the scrutiny of the guard. They do their jobs well."

"Do they?" I hissed.

"Of course, protect and serve that is." Marcius defended. "What happened with Reisenbough had little to do with Verda."

I stopped. "Explain."

He turned to face me. "Here? The privacy of my office is far better suited. Please."

"And if I don't?" I challenged.

"Well then you'd best do whatever it is you mean to do and be gone. If you're still lingering about when the city watch arrives there will be more trouble." Marcius responded with utter cool.

"Trouble?" I all but chuckled. "What could they possibly do to me?" I gripped hard to the blade at my side, as the possibilities ran through my mind.

"Yes, trouble. Verda may lack certain virtues, but murder is still a capital offense. Swinging your sword about will only make a bigger mess. Be you reasonable in what you have done, perhaps we could work something out in the way of a pardon. For that, I'll need to know more about what led to this event. I have questions of my own, you see. So please, would you care to join me? I'd very much like to finish this conversation in private."

"I have no use for secrets."

"Yes, but I do." Marcius confessed. "Like I said, lacking in certain virtues. Listening ears are everywhere. Trust is hard to come by here, my boy."

I looked him over as I reflected over his words. He seemed sincere.

"Very well."

"Wonderful." He smiled wide. "My office isn't far." He pointed up. "We won't be bothered there. If you would accompany me, I would be most delighted."

He gestured for a servant to open a door near the stairwell. We stepped through into another corridor. The structure shuddered, as another rippling roar shook the place. The sudden burst gave me a start. Marcius chuckled, as dust sifted down from the rafters overhead.

"No worries, my boy. Its only the enthusiasm of the people, swooning over the spectacle below. They love a good fight."

His tone was warm despite his scruffy voice. The walls shook again, the distant roar crested and faded in the black of the corridors.

"What is this place?" I asked.

"Why this is where legends are born. This is the coliseum!" Marcius replied. He spoke as if his words were part of some grand revelation.

"And what makes this coliseum so great?" I asked, following his footsteps as he led us deeper into the facility.

"What makes it so great? Well, I suppose you'll just have to witness the fury of the arena and decide for yourself then, eh?" He laughed merrily. "For better or worse, the coliseum continues to rise as a symbol of greatness across the land. The fight in the arena represents a very primal drive to which all can relate; the struggle to endure despite the odds."

I pondered the depth of his words, searching for reason. I would hear more. "Tell me of this arena."

"Ah, my boy. Of course." Marcius smiled wide. "Right this way."

Torches flickered in the shadows, as Marcius led us farther into the architectural maze. He bragged about the construction and history of the coliseum as we walked, his adoration as evident as the prestige with which this construct was commended. It very well may have impressed me, were it not for the sad faces that retreated into the shadows as we passed. Those who wore simple rags compared to the clothing adorned upon Marcius, those who bowed or kneeled as he passed, making every effort to clear his path. What manner of fear could sustain such sorrow I did not know, but I would discover it soon enough.

What I witnessed deepened the bitter chill left in my being, and my anger began to churn. I no longer cared to hear of the great effort it took to forge such a place, nor for the methods used. I did not care how long it stood or why.

Beneath his words was the truth of it. Vice had built this place. It was forged from the blood and misery of the lesser fortunate, this place where lives ended on display as entertainment. I would destroy it all sooner than pay it praise. The timeline of its glory would end along with Verda itself.

"You're not giving up on me are you?" Marcius' voice pulled me back from the dark. "I promise it's not far now. Right up the way."

He pointed to a short case of stairs. Two armed guards stood at either side, their armor golden and gleaming by the light of the flames as we passed between them. Neither moved, they simply stood statuesque in the flickering light of the torches.

Marcius continued on the history of the coliseum, the significance it held to all the regions. I would have found it less than believable were it not for the crowd I had witnessed, the roar that shook the coliseum. We walked through another short corridor, climbed what had to be the final flight of stairs to arrive at a lavish pair of double doors.

"Here we are." Marcius exclaimed. "My private quarters. Quite a hike from where we started, eh?"

The heavy twin doors were solid. I kept my silence as I looked over the deep red of the stained oak. As we approached, two servants posted at either side of the doors bowed at once and moved to open the way. The doors creaked open with a low groan, light burst forth from a well lit chamber. A caped older man in shinning armor turned with the opening of the doors, his helm tucked under his arm.

"Captain!" Marcius called. The man bowed, duty evident in his demeanor.

"My lord-"

The man stammered for his words, gaze slipping from the man he called lord to me as he stood in the luxurious chamber. He was all but insulted to see me walking so freely next to Marcius. He cleared his throat.

"My lord, this rogue killed several of my men."

"Yes, he most certainly did." Marcius responded, as he crossed the chamber.

Death did not seem to stir this man. He turned from the old guard, fixing his eyes in my direction.

"No worries." He spoke for the uneasy guard. "He's cooperating well enough, we'll spare the council the burden of a trial. Relax, old friend."

"Should I notify the watch then, my lord?" Asked the guard, clearly upset by the easy dismissal.

"Yes, I think that a wise course of action. This gifted young man is no threat to the citizens of Verda. No need to add more casualties. Have medical see to the survivors." Marcius commanded, his back to the guard as he toiled at his robes, removing the outermost layer.

"Lord." The guard responded, his eyes searing as he left the chamber. The elder in the scarlet cloak followed him. The doors closed behind them.

"Make yourself at home."

Marcius offered as he crossed the extravagant chamber to a large well kept desk. He stood next to a shiny black chair that stood nearly as tall as he did. He rested one hand on its shiny smooth surface as he retrieved something from a drawer behind the desk.

"You and I could become great friends. I have a proposition for you, my boy."

"Kael." I corrected.

"Come again?" Marcius asked most confused.

"My name is Kael."

"Ah." He smiled before biting hold and lighting the cigar he had produced from his desk. He puffed a few times before continuing. "Kael it is then."

The herb he smoked was pungent. Sunlight lit the smoke as it trailed through the stagnant air. It was then that I noticed the glass. The southern wall was nearly completely composed of glass panes. I approached it before I had really meant to do so. I had seen glass before, but never like this, never so clear, never so much. I reached out to touch its smooth surface. It was cool and soothing to my fingertips.

"Ah, yes." Marcius rattled as he made his way across the room to join me near the glass wall. "Just as promised, have a look." He pointed down through the crystal clear glass. "You were standing somewhere down there, by the north gate I believe."

It was only then that I saw the grand image before me. Far below was a dusty plane, only a few pillars to mark its terrain. This was undoubtedly the arena of which Marcius had spoke, the same dusty pit upon which I had stood. There were figures moving about, and though it was difficult to discern from the distance, they were no doubt engaged in armed combat.

The arena itself was surrounded by a thick crowd of people. The masses heaved about on seating that rose nearly to the top of the coliseum walls. Bodies littered the arena where the distant figures fought. This was a place of death and ruin.

"I've seen what you can do. Use that talent in the arena and you'll be a star in no time." Marcius spoke low and direct. "You know, you could rule this town. Maybe even the region itself."

I watched as the figures below continued to battle. "I know I could destroy it. I have no desire to rule."

A deep laugh rumbled from Marcius. He puffed at his cigar. "Sure, sounds good." He exhaled a plume of smoke. "Not exactly clean though, am I right?"

"Clean?" I paused, pondering his words as I spoke. "Vengeance is never clean. It is a wicked thing."

He snapped his fingers in excitement. "Exactly! What I mean is, wouldn't you like to leave your mark in a more substantial way? Make a mess, they'll clean it up and move on. You become a villain and the people meet you with hate and distrust. Now respect, that's something of value. They can hold onto that..."

Below in the arena, one of the fighters struck down the other. Only one remained standing as the crowd reeled. Thunderous applause once again shook the place.

"What do you mean?"

I asked, unable to take my eyes from the man now strutting across the arena, weapon and fist held high, thrusting at the sky. He roused the stands, and the walls shook with praise.

"The coliseum is a unifying power for the people of the lands." His tone was now deep and serious as he spoke. "All are connected before the arena, made one in the moment. The cries of men become the thunder itself, shaking the very Earth with voice. Fate is cruel for many on that dusty stage, but for those who survive, glory awaits. Glory that lifts a man beyond all other men, beyond life itself. Here, they become legend."

"Legend?" I asked, half mockingly.

The other half chased the idea, my dream come to life. The Dóvai would endure, the witch had said. I could return to my people, my legend surviving long after my time had ended through the stories they would tell.

"Indeed, Kael. Win their hearts in the arena, and the people of Verda will worship you as a god among men. All the people of the land will know your name, tell your story. All will know your might. You'll command the respect and adoration of all, live like a king if you wish!"

He all but burst with the extravagance of his words. I did not care for riches or power. I did not seek the affections of Verda or its curious inhabitants. I sought revenge, I sought justice for those lost. Most of all, I sought protection for the generations to come. I would give them a legend alright; I would indeed leave my mark. Once they witnessed the spirit of the Dóvai, never again would the inhabitants of this land rise against my people. How perfect it was falling into place.

"Very well, Marcius." A wicked smile crept upon my face as I spoke. "I accept your offer."

"Brilliant!!" Marcius sprang. His face was beaming, teeth gripping the cigar in a smile. "A most excellent decision. I won't fail you, my boy. No, you will indeed be a legend among men for generations to come."

His hand found my shoulder. "You will dine with lord and lady alike, travel the territories, know no boundaries... But of course, we have to plan for it, act accordingly. When everything is ready, you will be unstoppable out there."

I watched as servants scrambled to clear the remains from the arena below. The cheers from the crowd had died considerably. The rumble of their praise seemed to linger in the walls of this place of madness.

"Ready?" I pondered after his meaning.

"Indeed." Marcius nodded, the glowing burn of his cigar glistening in his reflection upon the glass. "There's much more than just killing to be done. It's the spectacle that matters. The people enjoy the sport, and as such, certain traditions and expectations have evolved around the arena. Etiquette, if you will."

"Murder for sport." I concluded aloud.

"Life and glory..." Marcius' voice came stern. "Fate is decided down there. That is the heart of Verda. A man can find redemption down there, or at the very least face a noble end."

His words lingered in the brief silence that followed. Redemption? Noble end? From where I stood it looked more to be the belly of the beast than its heart. Indeed I would overcome this trial. I would know redemption through the hearts of my enemies and deliver Verda to its noble end from within. In time its own citizens would rise, inspired by a new message, a new calling. Freedom.

"Very well." I broke the silence.

A smile brightened Marius' face, a chuckle broke away his somber poise. "That's the spirit!"

The great doors creaked. Marcius and I turned as the elder cloaked in scarlet entered the chamber.

"Ah, Dahl!" Marcius exclaimed with open arms. "Perfect timing, old friend. Come, there's much to discuss."

The stern elder crossed the chamber to stand before us. His eyes met mine with a firm gaze, making their bright yellow all the more piercing. He was indeed hard as stone, both within and without.

"May I introduce Kael. A rather gifted young man, well interested in being the next champion." Pride swelled in his voice, his ambition burning through his smile. "Kael, this man is my most trusted friend and ally, my teacher and mentor. He will guide you well."

He turned to embrace the old man with both hands firmly on the elder's gloved right hand. "My friend."

"Havi." Came the low rumbling voice of the elder. He returned the gesture, then turned to face me.

"Please, have a seat."

Marcius gestured to the open chairs in front of his desk as he made his way around it. He slumped into his large chair.

"Now, to business. You asked me about the attack on your village, about the fate of Reisenbough and Verda's involvement."

He had my full attention. "Yes."

He puffed hard at his smoke, as if readying his words. "Do you believe in fate, Kael?"

"Aye." I snapped, eager for answers.

"Well, I believe fate has led you here." Marcius began. "You see, not long ago an emissary arrived from a distant land. He brought with him news of a grand Empire, one set on world conquest."

I laughed. Marcius and Dahl did not share in my laughter. The air was serious with his words.

"Kael, nothing I can say could express the importance of these events. I know it sounds silly, but surely you saw the big man yourself, the one they sent?" Marcius suggested.

"Did he have a big hammer? Ugly face?" My voice ripe with sarcasm.

"Aye, that'd be him." Marcius rumbled through a plume of smoke.

"Oh yes, a few times. Hammer came down hard on that one. He won't be back." I confessed with pride.

They looked to one another again. It was their turn to have a laugh while I sat with a smug smile.

"You killed him?" Marcius gasped.

"Aye." I felt my expression harden.

"Well, I suppose with your talents..." Marcius shook his head. "All the better, didn't much care for him anyway. So much for the offer."

“What offer?" I asked suspiciously.

"Yes, he told us he was on a mission to hunt down a fugitive, asked for a team of men to aid in his efforts. It seemed a fair trade, we assist the Empire in its objectives, and when it arrives to the area we hold favor and maintain, maybe even expand our establishment in the territory." Marcius explained.

"So my people were slaughtered for trade?!" I nearly sprang across the desk to kill him with my bare hands.

"No! Kael, I swear it. We had no clue they meant to destroy Reisenbough. The man had said he was hunting a fugitive, not committing genocide. Please, Kael. I know it isn't right, but that doesn't mean it can't be righted, as best we can anyway." Marcius pleaded. "This power of yours, I'm thinking it might have something to do with it."

The words of the scouts resurfaced in my mind. The Empire had sent them to Reisenbough for just that reason. The brute that had followed me beyond the village was sent the same. I had thought it was vengeance that led him. Was I the cause of it all? Had that murderous raid been solely intended for me? Guilt drained my anger, flushing through me with the chill of realization.

"My apologies, Kael." Marcius spoke with sincerity. "Never mind my words, think no further on it. It's not your fault. My point is, we are all faced with this same adversary. The big man was clear, the Empire is coming. Forced assimilation. That's how they do things."

This revelation changed everything. I found my thoughts muddled, unsure of my direction once again.

"Then why bother with the arena at all?"

"Why the people of course." Marcius explained. "Align yourself with the hearts and minds of the land, and they will stand with you."

"You mean to resist them, the Empire?" I postulated aloud.

"You got it!" Marcius exclaimed. "Kael, I hate to beg, but you could really add the punch we need. Will you rise to be our champion, fight against tyranny on our behalf?"

I thought for a moment. I was to be welcomed into the fray, thrust into the face of my true adversary. Fate it was.

"Aye."

"Brilliant!" Marcius rose from his chair with the clap of his hands.

"There is much to be done in the meantime. Most of it on your end is patience. You're a fugitive at the moment. I think it's best if you are out of pocket for a while, just until things simmer down a bit. Even with time to prepare, I doubt the people will be ready for you."

He puffed at the cigar before snuffing it in a tray at his desk. "Dahl will escort you further. Together, we might actually stand a chance at this."

Dahl rose to his feet. I followed his lead. Our meeting was adjourned.

"Come." Dahl directed in his strange accent.

"I believe in you, Kael. Be well, my friends." Marcius turned back toward the glass.

Dahl turned with the ruffling of his cloak and led the way through the doors. I followed the stoic elder that was to be my guide. So began my journey to win the heart of Verda, the same heart I meant to destroy.

The Blood Pits

Dahl spoke not a word as he led our way through the dimly lit confines of Verda's great coliseum. When we reached ground level, the deep blue of late evening loomed outside the small windows of the stone corridor. The torches seemed much brighter with the fading light, warming the shadows that danced across the stones as we walked, our footsteps the only sound pervading the hall.

We traveled the length of the great structure, passing through a rather busy port centered on the eastern side. Brawny workers carried large crates heavy with food and supplies. They stacked them sloppily along the interior wall, as they offloaded cargo from several carts.

All manner of beast were kept in rigid metal cages that lined the stone walls. The smell of straw and feces was overwhelming. Many a shady character glanced over us as we passed but paid little mind, lost in the steady routine toils of their work.

Guards armed with spears lazily strolled about the mess. It was fascinating until the clatter of metal shackles drew my attention to a chain of captives being driven into barred cells adjacent to the snarling beasts. Whether they were slaves or people condemned, I did not know. I was glad to leave it behind as we continued further south, down another long corridor.

When we rounded the southern bend, the torches began to shimmer against the shiny smooth surface of polished stone. Before us was a gateway of stature, fine linens of purple draped across the smooth surface of the patterned stone walls. At the rear of this antechamber were two artfully carved doors, smooth and dark with shiny, golden handles. Two finely adorned female servants moved from either side of the chamber to reach for the gilded handles. In ceremonious locomotion, they opened the way to the well lit chamber behind the ornate doors.

Within the brightly lit chamber was a bounteous feast, ready and untouched. The chamber was well decorated and cluttered with tapestries and furs. There was furniture and stuffed bedding that looked soft and plush. This place could have easily accommodated many, yet its luxuries seemed abandoned despite being so well prepared.

"If you are hungry, eat." Came the thick voice of the elder as he pointed to the feast at the center of the chamber.

"Cleanse and renew." He redirected his gesture to a large stone basin where steamy water gently churned in a welcoming pool.

"Rest well. Tomorrow we leave with the rising sun." With a stern shift and rustle of his thick robes, he turned to exit the way we had come.

My stomach churned as I looked over the feast. The smell of it was overpowering. I reached for a cut of meat. It was cool to the touch, slightly warm at its center.

"This was not meant for me..."

Dahl stopped short of the doors. "No."

He turned to face me as he spoke. His aged face was as indifferent and void of emotion as the cool, smooth stone underfoot.

"This is where the champion was to celebrate his victory. Many have risen to claim the right to these halls. Few live to pass that right in wisdom."

His words resonated with the knowledge he shared. I now saw him as a regal soul, ripe in both age and wisdom. His presence here held some deeper meaning. He was a good man, and though I could not be sure, I was glad for the encounter nonetheless. Like me, he was different from this place.

"Partake of these blessings freely. You will not again know them until you earn the right. With morning, I shall return."

He pointed his gloved right hand to a high window on the north wall of the chamber. A grand set of golden doors stood tall between this window and another like it. I nodded in acknowledgment.

Dahl turned and left the chamber through the same dark doors we had entered. Once they were closed behind him, I pounced upon the delicious feast. Hunger had grown fierce within me, like a ravenous force. The ferocity with which I ate made it all the better I dined alone.

After I had my fill, I took a much needed bath in the heated stone basin, trying to forget everything that had led me to this place as I soaked by the flickering light of the torches. The sleek surface of my stone knife shimmered from where it lay tucked in my waistcloth. The braid of Sarah's hair lay with it in the bundle of clothes I had shed. I collected the two and tied the lock of hair around the knife's handle to hang like a tail. I would lose neither.

When I felt I had soaked long enough I ate again, then crawled into the big fluffy bed. Swallowed in the soft linens, I did my best to still my mind. My thoughts rolled over the challenges ahead. When at last I fell into sleep, it was dreamless and deep.

A slow creak roused me from slumber, the sound of a door opening across the chamber. I grabbed hold of my blade and lay still, waiting to see who would emerge. It was early morning, and the dim waking light of the world lit the chamber just well enough that I could see. The door creaked its way fully open. Two young women entered, each carrying a wicker basket.

I relaxed my grip but did not let go, nor did I stir. They took no notice of me, at once setting to work cleaning up after the mostly untouched meal. I remained still and silent, as they tossed food and utensil alike into the straw baskets. They chattered and giggled as they worked.

One of the young maidens was somehow familiar to me. Her smile seemed to light the chamber with joy, her dark locks thick and lush like my own, her eyes the color of the forest itself...

The dark ornate doors opened. I bolted to my feet as Dahl entered the chamber. He looked to me, his face stern and grizzled. His attention shifted to the young women, who broke from their task to kneel and address him.

"Lord." They spoke in unison.

Dahl's face contorted into a grimace at the gesture. He shook his head and waived them aside with his gloved right hand. The maidens smiled and returned to their chore.

My eyes found their way back to the dark haired maiden. The moment came that our eyes met for the first time. She smiled, and the light of the heavens rose within my being. It was as if I knew her, remembering from some lucid dream of long ago.

In my stupor I hardly noticed Dahl call to me for what must have been the second time.

"Kael! Come." He was grinning wide, several shiny metal teeth standing out among those yellowed with age. "Make friends later. Our way is set, we leave now."

Hastily I took the exit, looking back once more to meet her eyes, her smile. There was no doubt that I would find her again, somehow I knew. But that would have to wait. My path was clear, unlike the journey ahead.

Once more I followed Dahl through the eastern corridor, and once more we stood in the busy chamber with the iron cages. The animals stirred with the morning. A hatual in shackles roared as prods pushed it back from the workers attempting to clean its space. Keamett, the demon hatual that killed my uncle, this had been its fate. Never did I think I would feel pity for a monster of legend, a killer of my kin.

The cages that held the people in chains were now vacant. I tried not to dwell on this, looking away as we passed. More wooden crates had arrived. The smell of fresh vegetables mingled with the stink of the beasts.

"This area is known as the east gate." Dahl spoke direct and true, already sounding the part as teacher. "It takes much to sustain this way of life. Supplies enter this gate; refuse and waste are pushed out another."

"Supplies..." I reflected deep, pausing in my step as I chose my next words. "And the people in chains?"

Dahl stopped dead. He turned with the rustling shift of his cloak.

"Some are those condemned, others fated to serve. When we return, you will know the difference."

I did not like his response.

"Do not worry." Dahl spoke reassuringly. "When that time comes, you will be ready. Know this."

He turned and continued through a large open gate, a portal leading out to the world from the coliseum's eastern entrails.

Not far from the noisy beasts of the east gate was a small stable. Several horses lazily chewed grain to their delight. Two had been saddled and loaded with supplies.

"This is Scarlett." Dahl rubbed and patted her shoulder. "She will carry you."

With that, Dahl approached the other creature, an older looking white stallion with dark gray speckles along his face and rump. With one fluid motion, the old man mounted the steed. With the flutter of his cloak he settled atop the horse as peacefully as a feather come to rest.

I stood before the ruddy coated horse known as Scarlett. She was a beautiful creature, and her large black eyes peered into mine with a friendly curiosity. She approached me, her neck outstretched, her soft bristly nose against my face. The smell of her was pleasant, her breath warm and powerful as she sniffed at me.

"Come." Dahl commanded, reigns in hand. He and the stallion moved as one. "Why do you hesitate?"

I said nothing of my inexperience. Instead, I approached Scarlett and gripped hold of the saddle as Dahl had done. Standing at her side I hopped up, hoping to land as gracefully as he did. Instead, I clumsily overshot and fumbled to right myself upon the beastly animal. She jostled and stomped, snorting as she waited for me to situate myself. I grabbed hold of the reigns, again imitating Dahl as how to hold them.

Dahl laughed, but he said nothing of my blundering first attempt to ride horseback. He simply turned in the direction of our heading, working with his hoofed companion as if it took little to no effort. Unsure of how to progress, I sat idle upon Scarlett's back, reigns in hand. After a moment of uncertainty, Scarlett happily followed suit behind Dahl.

I had seen horses in the fields, even watched men ride upon them when visitors came to Reisenbough. But I had not ridden before this, and I was much relieved that Scarlett was happy to go along without a fuss. She seemed to have a genuine, friendly spirit.

Little prompt was required from me, as we trotted north along the same road that had led me to Verda. I looked to the south in the direction from which I had come, where I had encountered the bandits. Remembering the gruesome scene, I was glad to travel farther from it.

To the east, the sun had finally crept over the shadowy silhouette of the great tomb, and its warm golden rays were much welcomed in the brisk morning air. The sky was clear and blue, save for a few puffy white clouds lazily adrift in the peaceful heavens. The dew was heavy, and the dirt road was sticky under the plodding march of hooves.

Our path changed direction ever slightly, as we trotted northeast through the heart of the fertile plains. The tall grains of summer were dry and brittle with the late season. The lush, low growing grasses of winter had already began to cover the earth in a deep green at their roots. Shoots of wild onions whipped about in the breeze, as patches of soft clover looked welcoming under the golden sun. Tiny purple flowers accented the green. A traveler could not ask for better conditions.

I wasn't the only one who took notice of the beauty of the field. Scarlett, who had been well behaved up to this point, decided to break from the trail to enjoy the greenery. As I sat helpless atop her broad back, she strayed from the path and began to gingerly munch on the soft green vegetation. I pulled at the reigns and tapped at her with my heels again imitating Dahl, but with no luck. Much to my embarrassment, Dahl had to backtrack and take Scarlett by the reigns and lead us on.

The sun ascended high overhead, and its golden rays were hot despite the lingering cool of morning. It was nowhere near the heated fury of summer, yet it was as if some part of summer remained strong. The great structure of the tomb was to the southeast. The green of the fields stretched well to the east, meeting the valley of the Veylspring far to the north.

Ahead in the distance a massive figure took shape, rising up from the earth. Wide at its base, I followed the great pillar skyward, realizing that this was a great elder tree. It must have towered well over the Tomb of the Shadjah. My eyes found its great branches, tracing them against the blue of the sky. I nearly tumbled from Scarlett's back, as I followed the closest branches to their distal tips high overhead. Far was the reach of this great tree. This was the legendary white oak of the plains, standing strong and peerless. Below its mass, we would surely find the people of the White Hollow.

We stopped at a small spring. The horses drank deep of the cool, clear water. It didn't take Scarlett long to find the soft green vegetation growing along its banks. She munched happily, each mouthful fragrant and crunchy. The sun had began to sink toward the forest, and the air once more began to cool.

I looked up through the great branches of the white oak. The moon hid low to the east, waning as she cycled anew. Glowing soft against the blue of the sky, she looked entangled in the massive crown of the towering oak. I'd always considered it a good omen to see both sun and moon together in the sky, and it did much to lift my spirits.

"Impressive sight. No one knows why this elder stands alone in the fields. Many legends surround this place, revered as sacred by most." Dahl's voice came, taking note of where my attentions had strayed. "The Hollow isn't far, we will rest there for the night."

"What is our destination?" I asked. It felt foolish that I hadn't asked sooner.

"There is a tribe near the mesa to the east, known as the Kifdah. Soon their young warriors will hold a ritual known as the Hasak. You are to participate, prepare yourself for the challenge ahead. Once I feel you are ready, the arena will be open to you." Dahl explained.

"Hasak?" I repeated. "I am not of the Kifdah. Why should I participate in the rituals of another people?"

I hadn't meant to be rude, but my frustration was building. I was both eager and impatient. Already I felt astray from my purpose. I hadn't traveled to Verda to play games abroad.

Dahl simply laughed. "No, you are not of the Kifdah. This is certain. But your path has been laid before you, embrace it or turn from it. For this truly, is the plight of any man."

A hint of compassion glistened in the old man's eyes as he spoke. He almost seemed soft. Perhaps he was right. I nodded in understanding of his words.

"Come. The Hollow isn't far." Dahl commanded as he hopped atop his majestic white steed.

Scarlett was still stuffing her face and hardly seemed to notice when I climbed on her back. This time when I urged her to follow, she required little more than a few clicks and a nudge. With the sun at our backs and the moon rising above, we made our way closer to the base of the great tree.

The sun had all but disappeared behind the forest, when at last we arrived at the base of the oak. Others were arriving as well, travelers and riders alike, guided by the bright yellow flames of torches that lit the way. Scarlett began to slow her pace in reluctance, as we neared what appeared to be the mouth of a large cave. The path we traveled entered this cave, which led under one of the gigantic roots. I wondered how deep into the earth it reached.

Long had I considered visiting the Hollow, but never had I expected to visit under such circumstances. Scarlett began to drag her hooves on the decent into the cave. Understandably so, I didn't much like the idea of going underground either. The path through the cave was well lit. Once we cleared the descent to level ground, it opened into a grand chamber beneath the ancient oak, a place of light and color, a mutual mixing ground for the many peoples of the land. This was the White Hollow.

Dahl led our way to a stable, far different than the one from which we had departed. This was more a cramped barn dug into the dirt and stone. Dahl exchanged a handful of silver coins with a brightly painted young fellow, who in turn gestured for two rather dirty boys to take our horses by their leads. Dahl and I dismounted and made our way into the crowd, as our horses were boarded for the night.

All manner of ornate costume and exotic fashion alike flooded the well lit streets with splashing color, a vivid blending of the vast cultural differences that gathered there. Language and laughter filled the space of the cavern with a heterogeneous hum of human expression. The flicker of flames reflected off glittery decorated surfaces. The reflective ambiance was familiar to me, the same used in the celebrations of the Dóvai.

I tried not to think of Reisenbough. Suddenly I felt alone and distant from the welcoming atmosphere of the festivities at hand. The excitement of this new experience left me, despite the fulfillent of childhood ambition.

We made our way through the crowded street, passing by numerous kiosks and stalls where overly friendly merchants all but pressed their wares, eager to convert many a casual stroller into a buying customer. Trade was very much alive in this place, be it coin or goods exchanged. I had no currency, nor items for trade. I looked over their wares with interest only, shrugging with empty hands whenever a vendor solicited.

Relief found me when at last we stepped from the bustling street into a well lit entrance carved into a large root. Inside was a comfortably decorated chamber, warm and inviting. Dahl spoke with an elder behind a counter. Her wavering voice was thick with age. When a deal was struck she produced a key, and with the slow shuffle of her tiny feet, she led our way down a corridor lined with rickety wooden doors. Behind one of the doors was a cramped room that was to be ours for the night.

The woman bid us farewell and left with the closing of the old wooden door. The room was small and cozy, just enough room for Dahl and I to move about without bumping into one another. There were two small straw beds and a single candle to light the dim space. Two small windows were open to the bustle of the Hollow, but it did little to stir the musty air.

Dahl unbuckled and removed his blade from around his waist, propping it next to his bedside. I removed mine the same, only I held onto it, just in case. Not yet ready for sleep I lay there, eager for the next day's travel, trying hard not to think of home.

How wonderful it would have been to share this place with my elders, my father and his father, with the twins, with Kori. In a way, I did share this place with them. Through dreams and stories, we are always united with those we love. Desperately, I tried to convince myself this was enough.

"Another day's journey."

Dahl rumbled as he sank onto the straw bed with the groan of age. He sat erect, kneeling on the bed as if he meant to slip into prayer more so than sleep. His eyes eased shut as he settled with a sigh.

I sank into my bed as well, trying not to compare it to the same bed I had known all my life. It was certainly different from the soft bed I had known the night before, which inspired me to question. "The feast last night, why had it been neglected?"

"It was for the new champion." Dahl answered, his eyes remained closed.

"Why did he not partake?" I asked. "Did he fall?"

"No." Dahl sighed heavily, as if I were interrupting his concentration. "The title of champion was won, and the man known as Bryn made his wish heard before the people. He chose freedom over fortune. He and his wife had been taken from the territories to the southeast and forced into servitude. Condemned to the arena for his rebellious spirit, he fought. With his final victory, he earned his right to be called Verda's champion, earned his right to choose his own path. He bargained with the high council, asking that he and his wife be reunited in freedom upon his victory. Together they fled from Verda." Dahl explained. "Such was his decision. It is the way of Verda to honor the wish of the champion."

"For love and freedom." I reflected.

"The true path of the warrior." Dahl replied. He did not break his meditative poise. His energy was calm again. "In the service of others."

As I reflected over the story of the man known as Bryn, my mind began to drift. The way of the warrior; peace, nobility, honor. Verda must honor the will of the champion. Maybe there was something to this plan after all.

"Open the heart before raising the sword; for if you must strike, strike with all of you." I repeated the words of Krayton the Mighty, words he had spoken for my ears what seemed so long ago.

Dahl's eyes opened, a barely visible smile broke upon his stone face. "Indeed. Well spoken."

"The words of my father."

My mind wandered further into the past, remembering the lessons spoken around the fire. My father passed those words, followed with a blessing.

Peace be with you, that you may share it with all. Live well, my son.

"Your father's words are wise. A noble man." Dahl spoke kindly.

I did not stop the tears. "He was."

"Grief is not fitting of a warrior." Dahl offered, concern in his voice.

"No, it isn't." I agreed. I took to my bed, turning away from Dahl.

The sounds of festivity echoed through the Hollow outside the small window. The rhythmic vibrations of music reverberated through the tree like a living pulse. I thought of the drums of the Dóvai, and I wept.

The next morning we departed. Scarlett seemed well fed and lethargic, as she lazily trotted along, head down. Dahl led our way east through the heart of the plains. Grass and clover covered much of the dark soil, the sky bright and blue overhead. The sun was warm, and its golden rays were much welcomed in the cool breeze.

The smooth rolling green was accented with flowers, none as impressive as the large yellow dandelions. They covered the expanse of green, each like a small sun. The tall shoots of feathery seed pods gently swayed, the breeze jostling their white fluffy heads. A herd of antelope grazed to the north. A beautiful day, perfect for the journey well at hand. Silently, I praised thanks under the open sky.

As we traveled further east, the grass grew thick and tall. A junction opened in our path, one fork led northeast, the other continued due east in the direction we had been traveling. Dahl stopped as he considered our heading. Concern was evident in his expression as he looked to the eastern path. It looked barren, the tall grass reaching out to reclaim the naked trail.

"Come, this way." Dahl finally decided. "Best to stay away from the tall grass. Arachnids." He pointed to a fresh line of silk trailing the ground.

I shuddered despite myself. Arachnids were often lazy, but incredibly lethal hunters. Very rarely did they choose to feed upon humans, but an easy meal is difficult to decline for any creature. Even with the abilities of my heightened state, I wanted no part of such an experience and was happy to avoid an encounter.

It was just after midday, and much of our journey still lay ahead. The wind was playful, dancing across the plains in cool gusts as we crossed the open land. Dahl spoke more easily. Perhaps it had been the experience thus far or the conversation we had shared the night before, but his demeanor had warmed considerably. As we trotted along, the beauty of the divine seemed to follow us on this day, and a kinship began to build between us.

Dahl spoke on the histories of the Kifdah. I was to be familiar with their customs, well enough at least to participate in the Hasak. I still didn't care for the idea, but listened as the old man spoke of the people we were to visit. My wits were as light as the clouds above and drifting along all the same.

From what I could tell of his words, the Kifdah were a crude militant race. Boys only became men through bloodshed, living in exile until they earned the right to return to the tribe. The village of the Kifdah was a series of caves, carved into the dry earth beneath a barren stone mesa. The Veylspring gushed from the mouth of a deep cavern at the northern end of the mesa, collecting in a deep crystalline lake. Along the shores of this lake, the Kifdah planted their crops and raised their livestock. The village of the Kifdah was known as Lokdah.

The elders had spoken of this tribe in my youth with warning. Far to the east, across the plain was a great stone mesa, stretching from the Veylspring to the Tomb of the Shadjah. The mesa was considered an eastern border, for all were warned not to cross it and never to mingle with the tribe of the sands beyond. Respect and distance had kept the peace between our peoples, but their ways were much different from our own.

"Are the stories true?"

I asked as our horses lumbered along. The sun was again setting toward the forest far to the west. Light rippled off the Veylspring to the north, where its crystal waters met the gentle slope of the plains.

"Do the Kifdah conquer other peoples as does Verda?"

Dahl laughed a hearty chuckle.

"No, not anymore. In the long forgotten past they did, in the histories of my forefathers." He seemed lost in contemplation for a moment. "But nothing like Verda. The Kifdah do not take slaves, nor do they trade lives or the coin. My ancestors killed for dominion, for territorial right. War was the way of ancient times."

I was relieved a bit, but not yet satisfied. "And of the histories?"

"Not all beginnings are humble." Dahl explained. "In the times of old, there were many tribes in the eastern forests. War was common, and no other tribe was fierce as the Kifdah. Our ancestors had taken refuge in the harsh sands east of the mesa. War was glory to this tribe, manhood gained through lives taken and battles won. Their way was to vanquish men and take what remained."

"And how do they live now?"

"It is different now. Manhood is still gained through bloodshed, but not by conquest. Instead, they slay only the evildoer and the wicked." Dahl insisted, sounding prideful at his words. "The Kifdah protect the land."

"And how do they manage that?" I asked, still skeptical of this people.

"You will see." Dahl answered, looking to me with a devilish grin. "Just as your ancestors saw."

"What do you mean?"

I had heard stories of the Kifdah, though my elders had referred to them as the Stone Tribe. They were told to be barbarians and killers, no meaningful interaction between our two tribes was ever mentioned.

"The way of the sword, where did your fathers learn the art?" Dahl inquired.

"You mean to say..." I didn't like his implications.

"Indeed." Dahl bowed. "The most skilled warriors in all the land shared that knowledge with your ancestors."

Scarlett trotted along the soft hillside, the wind wiping at her mane. "The art of war."

"The way of the warrior." Dahl insisted. "So that they might defend themselves in the western territories. For a time, it seems they did."

"They have." I corrected. "The Dóvai live on."

"Oh?" Dahl smiled at my retort. "Then remember this and grieve not. Death is shared by all, but until it claims you, that is life. Embrace it."

"Or turn from it." I sneered in jest.

Dahl chuckled, a smile cracking his hard demeanor. "Ah! You're learning well."

As we traveled, we neared the Veylspring. Its clear, cold water rippled with the steady current. The last light of day shimmered across the top of the water, as fish began to jump. To the east I could see the profile of the mesa, rigid across the skyline. It looked very much to be a barrier of sorts. As the sun set, the light of fire began to appear against the base of the mesa. Lokdah was not far, and as night descended we made our arrival.

The twilight made this place almost surreal to my senses. The air was moist and fragrant with the smells of the rich earth that nourished the bountiful greens. Mysterious figures herded goats and sheep toward the flickering yellow lights of the village. Dahl rode up to a young maiden who urged a small herd of a sheep along with the tapping of a wooden staff. He greeted her with the raising of his right hand.

"Sahlam, flora bengina." He bowed his head softly.

She raised her hand in the same manner, smiling brightly at his words. "Sahlam, zen adom."

Her eyes moved to me. I said nothing, for I had no knowledge of this language. I could hardly think of what to say in my own tongue, her image having me lost for words.

She stood proud and confident under the fading light. The hide that wrapper her delicate waist held a stone knife taught against her hip. The cloth and knife were all that adorned her aside from many intricate works of ink that colored her skin. Her eyes were deep and piercing, as she stood firm despite the brisk chill of evening. She was quite lovely, and as I finished taking in her profile, I flushed and looked away.

Hearty laughter belted from her at my reaction. She exchanged words with Dahl, and the two laughed again. I did not care to know the nature of their talks. We followed behind the sheep, as she led our way into the village.

The mesa loomed like a great shadow overhead, but somehow this place seemed welcoming as we trotted behind the sheep. Perhaps it was the light of the fire, or perhaps it was the smell of food. A few of the young children had spotted us as we approached, and they ran alongside our horses as we rode. Heads were turning everywhere to see the strangers who arrived with the night.

At last we reached the gate to a small corral. We dismounted and the maiden led the horses into the small corral with the sheep. My legs were like jelly from the long ride, and I was very hungry.

"Ready yourself, Kael." Dahl began. "A large fire burns near the center, that is where we will find the elders. We must pay our respects. You will make your request to participate in the Hasak."

"Very well." I responded. My stomach churned loudly.

Dahl laughed. "Come, there will be food as well. The Kifdah know plenty."

The village was alive and buzzing despite the hour. Fires lit the cozy confines of caves, spilling light out into the night. Many lounged around small fire circles under the mesa, mostly mothers and their young. The light of the fire added a greater depth to the warmth upon their faces. This was a place of family and peace. I might have wept, remembering the same warmth upon the faces of my own loved ones, but I was a young warrior of the Dóvai. It was better I show the world our strength first.

As we continued toward the heart of the village, I couldn't help but notice the daughters of Lokdah. There were few males to be seen at all, save for the old and the very young. A thunderous bout of laughter echoed from the darkness ahead, the voices of men.

There was indeed a large fire as Dahl had said, and despite the size of the blaze I did not see it until we were well upon it. Gathered around were the men of Lokdah. All were well aged. Even the youngest men around the fire were well over my years. They were as subtly adorned as the females, most wearing only the cloth about the waist.

Some wore bands and intricate works of ink. All wore scars. The warriors of the Kifdah were indeed formidable, standing as hard as the mesa. Yet, their yoke was warm around the fire. As we approached, Dahl was welcomed as a friend.

The crackle of the large fire was all I understood, as I looked about the faces of the Kifdah. Their eyes were piercing, but there was no malice or hostility. I saw curiosity, even excitement. There was anticipation, rising like the flickering tongues of the blazing fire. Dahl stood proudly by my side as he spoke with the elders of the circle.

"Sahlam, Dahl." Came the shaky old voice of a grand elder as he approached. All heads bowed in acknowledgment of his stature.

Dahl stepped forward. "Sahlam, Nosh Kilu."

Dahl bowed deeply. The elder was quick to beckon him forth with the excited wave of his trembling hand. He and Dahl exchanged words, as I anxiously waited by the fire. After some length of delegation, Dahl turned and called for me to join them.

"This is the elder chieftain of the Kifdah, Nosh Kilu." Dahl introduced.

I bowed in respect before this great elder. His smile seemed permanently etched into the wrinkled features of his face. The glimmer of his eyes peaked from under bushy brows drooped with age. His energy was that of peace and wisdom. It was hard to believe such a gentle elder could have once been a savage warrior. He gave an approving nod, and spoke enthusiastically in the tongue of the Kifdah. Though I did not understand his words, the warmth of their meaning was clear enough.

"He is pleased to welcome you, son of the Dóvai." Dahl translated, as the elder continued to speak. "The Hasak is a sacred rite of passage, a ritual that requires many years of reflection. Do you believe yourself ready for such a thing?"

"I do, grand elder." I responded.

All my life I had been training, learning and honing my skills for just that, a sacred rite of passage. This was far different from the way I was to go, but perhaps no different from the path I had since known.

Dahl relayed my words to the elder. His smile widened further as he looked to me. He laughed deeply, nodding approvingly. He spoke to Dahl in his strange words, and the two laughed again.

"Permission granted." Dahl smiled. He raised his gloved right fist to his chest and bowed deeply. The elder reached for him, and embracing his friend, they spoke further.

As they exchanged, I felt the eyes of those who patiently watched. The stone underfoot was warm where I stood near the center. The fire lit the figures gathered round in such a way that their faces were silhouetted against the dark of night. By the light of the flame I had known the faces of loved ones all my days. But standing there, it was the faces of strangers who earned their rights as men in lives taken. They were far different from my people. Even still, I much preferred this to the likes of Verda.

Dahl and the elder finished with their lengthy discussion. A smiling Dahl returned to the center where I stood, nodding approvingly. The elder called an announcement for all the circle, which erupted in roaring cheer. Their acceptance brought much relief, and I felt my spirits brighten ever slightly.

"They are honored to share this experience with a son of the Dóvai." Dahl explained. "They welcome you."

I had no words. I looked over the circle one last time, wishing I could think of some way to show my appreciation for their acceptance.

"Come. We have paid our respects." Dahl insisted. "There is food and drink to be had."

Dahl led our way from the men of the Kifdah. I was quick to follow, for I had certainly not forgotten my hunger. We made our way through the village to another fire circle. A feast had been prepared, and though it looked as if most had already had their fill, there was more than plenty remaining. Dahl offered a clay bowl, which I gratefully accepted and began to fill.

There were fire roasted vegetables, breads, rice, fish, and curry. I didn't relent until the bowl was nearly overfilled. Not bothering to even lift my face from my bowl upon filling it, I simply followed the outline I assumed to be Dahl as he found a spot to sit around the fire. I sat next to him, and ate ravenously by the warm light of the flickering flames.

"Were our rations not enough for you, my friend?" Dahl asked before taking a bite.

I had nearly finished, the contents of the once heaping bowl reduced to a few soggy globs of rice floating in curry. Contentment filled me like the food swelling in my gut.

"Thank you."

"Hmm?" Dahl finished the food in his mouth. "Of course. It is good to visit home. Even better to share it with someone who can appreciate it as well. The Kifdah have lived by the mesa for countless generations. Long are the histories of this tribe, strong is our spirit."

Some giggling caught my attention. A few of the many young maidens watched us intently, whispering and snickering to one another. It was clear they didn't see many visitors, and they seemed to find my presence most intriguing.

"Many daughters are born to the Kifdah." Dahl began. "They grow to be all that is Lokdah, to become mothers, a sacred role passed by the life bringing All Mother herself. Each is a physical embodiment of the goddess, her gift of immortality to mankind. The right to the womb is the right to life. Should a daughter of the Kifdah choose you, you may have her. But know this, she and her offspring are bound to the Kifdah. This is the way of our people."

"I am not of the Kifdah. Such matters do not concern me."

I responded earnestly. In truth I found these beautiful young maidens most intimidating. The brute warrior was something I understood. The goddess of the field was still far beyond me.

Dahl laughed. "Very well. I expected as much. A mutual respect between the Kifdah and the Dóvai existed long before my time. Of course, in the way of the warrior the Kifdah are superior. There is no doubting this."

I remained skeptical. "Is that so?"

"I saw Reisenbough in my youth." Dahl confided. "It was many years ago, in the summer before the great sickness."

I remembered that summer well. It was the last summer for many of the Dóvai. I did not think on this too deeply.

"What of Verda?" I asked, hoping to talk of something else. "How did you come to Verda?"

Dahl seemed to contemplate. "In my youth, I did not respect the sanctity of life. I knew only of my own ambitions and selfish ends, a temperament ill suited for the selfless warrior. When I heard of the 'City of Champions', I was drawn to the arena."

"You fought there?" I asked, very much interested in what Dahl had to share.

"I did." Dahl nodded. "Fought my way to the top and remained there until I met Marcius. My goal was different then, a time when my resolve was not strong enough to hold back the dark."

Dahl trailed off, his eyes fixed on the fire. It seemed a sorrow lurked within him, as if a glimmer of that dark still remained.

"It is late. You should rest. Tomorrow, we leave for the sands beyond the mesa."

The day had indeed felt long with our travels. With a belly full the same, I lay by the light of the small fire. The soft fur upon which I lay was cozy and welcoming, despite the solid stone beneath it. Many questions remained. Thoughts of vengeance were far from my mind, Dahl's words resounding with a story much like my own. The sands waited beyond the mesa, as did the ritual of the Kifdah.

Reisenbough crept into mind. Dahl had seen my home in its prime. I wondered if he and I had crossed paths. If we had, I did not remember him. My memories as a wildling were much stained by grief. More importantly, the years had also known much joy and love. I tried my best to remind myself of that fact, lest the dark of that grief overtake me. As I watched the crackling fire, I slipped easy into a gentle sleep.

I awoke to song, a collective choir of female voices joined to fill the morning world with beauty. The fire had reduced to ash and coal, but what little heat remained was most welcome. I looked around for Dahl. There were a few young girls, mothers with children, but no Dahl.

I rose to my feet in the chill morning air. The giggling chatter of the girls made my decision easy. Collecting myself, I set in the direction where we had met the circle of elders, hoping to both reunite with my guide and avoid further attention.

The light of morning illuminated more of the village. The stone of the mesa was rough and porous. I could only imagine the effort it must have taken to carve the many small caves in which the Kifdah resided. They were certainly a prosperous people. Children ran about freely. The wise eyes of the elders and mothers alike watched over their play.

Women strolled about, casually carrying out the day's work with infants wrapped snugly across their chests. The inked designs that covered them were unique more or less. Many wore intricate works covering their right hands. In my ignorance, I had misjudged them. Their customs differed from those of the Dóvai, yet we were similar in ways I could feel. Lokdah was home of the Kifdah, a strong and respectable people.

When I reached the southern end of the village, I found the large fire circle once more. As I suspected, Dahl and the others had gathered there around the smoldering pit. Dahl noticed my approach and beckoned for me to join the circle of stone men. Their energies were particularly jubilant this day. It was as if they were celebrating.

"Welcome, Kael." Dahl greeted. "We are soon to begin."

It was then that I noticed the many young boys gathered at the south end. Nosh Kilu stood hunched over them, the boys looking intently as if he were passing the wisdom of his years. They were scarcely bigger than wildlings, yet they were to endure the world.

The grand elder called to me. I approached the center and stood with the youngsters. The elder spoke further, and though I did not understand I listened.

"He preaches on the sanctity of life." Dahl began to interpret. "Life is to be cherished and defended. To protect life, to respect life, this is the sacred promise of man and his duty to himself and the world. Grow strong, grow wise. May the Great Mother guide you."

With these words, others approached the center. A bold looking warrior carrying a small clay bowl stood next to Nosh Kilu. The others surrounded me. Dahl extended his gloved right hand.

"Your weapons."

I hesitated.

"You will have them again." Dahl assured.

I allowed them to remove both my blade and my knife. The men returned to the edge of the circle once more. Nosh Kilu rounded his leathery old fist, and dipped it into the contents of the bowl. With a fist covered in an inky black paste, he reached out and pressed it upon my chest. When he withdrew his hand, the mark of his fist remained. In the tongue of his people, he offered his words.

"You now bear the rite of participation." Dahl clarified.

Oddly, I felt my pride swell at this. The Hasak was the tradition of the Kifdah, barbaric and violent. Yet, as I stood before the grand elder, it was eerily similar to the ceremony surrounding the Allioht. Even the markings upon our chests were similar, though I would not have received this mark until my return by the ways of the Dóvai. It was different. These people were strangers. The others set to embark with me were but children.

"Thank you." I bowed my head before the elder.

An excited Dahl reached for me. "Come, we wait outside the circle for the others."

We moved away from the young warriors to be as they received the same rite. With the last child marked, the circle erupted into a tumultuous roar. The mesa itself seemed to shudder with the energy of the Kifdah, the entirety of the tribe calling in turn.

As the men cheered and roared, the boys left the circle, heading further south. Cries echoed, as the voices of Lokdah reverberated across the stone. With the sounding of the tribe, Dahl and I followed the boys south along the mesa.

We kept a brisk pace along the stone wall. The cool wet vegetation of the field slapped at my legs as I trotted behind the boys. Dahl kept pace just behind me. I watched the young warriors of the Kifdah that led our way. Already they were strong, much reminding me of the wildlings of the Dóvai, much reminding me of a journey I began with my brothers. I was glad for our quick pace. It left little time to dwell on my thoughts.

A crag split the mesa. The rubble and dusty soil deposited there created a natural incline up the stone face. We climbed the steep mound of rich, silt like soil. At the top of the run was a great cluster of palms and leafy greens. Dry prickly brambles picked at us, as we crawled through the dense green thicket.

We emerged under the morning sun. The thicket hid a natural cleft in the rock. The fine soil and bits of stone completed the incline, providing easy passage to the top. As we continued our ascent, the boys began to sing. One by one, they would chant a verse, others sounding off in turn. Their voices were like those of tiny men, resonating within the cool confines of the stone crevice.

Atop the mesa was a barren waste. The stone rippled as if it had been shaped by the flow of a river. The wind whipped and whirled dust and sand hard against us in furious gusts. The sky was clear above, and the sun just barely shone golden and warm from the east. To the west was sky and the distant green of the land. With the same brisk pace, we continued east across the mesa.

The songs of the group helped keep the pace, as the sun crept higher overhead. As we traveled, Dahl spoke of the legends told by the Kifdah. According to Dahl, the mesa stretched from the Veylspring to the northern face of the Tomb of the Shadjah. They too revered this place as cursed. To them it was a symbol of wrath.

Long ago, Dahl explained, there had been a mountain at the heart of the region. Upon this mount, a great and terrible demon resided. Jealous of the prosperity man found in the garden, the demon would churn the fire within the mountain like the burning hatred it felt for mankind, releasing great bursts of fire and ash upon the land so that it could delight in the suffering it caused.

Crying out to the heavens, the spirits of the people united against this evil. The divine heard their prayers, and the sky opened. A great light descended upon the mountain where the demon lurked. Piece by piece, the mountain was ripped apart, great hunks of it used to build the tomb in which the demon would be imprisoned in darkness for all time. The molten rock and fire was emptied from the mountain, cooling to form the mesa as it crept across the land.

Many times had I gazed upon the massive tomb. Long had I pondered its origin and purpose. I remained skeptical of this tale in light of what I'd learned from the scouts, yet I had no better explanation or legend of my own to offer in turn. Dead giants had built it. Somehow that truth seemed lacking by comparison.

The sun grew warm against the stone underfoot with the approach of midday. Heat began to ripple through the air over the rocky terrain. Ahead was the end of the mesa, or rather, where the eastern edge of the mesa was swallowed in fine white sand. The outlines of others approaching from the east became visible in the distance. As we met the sands of the desert, the outlines became the profiles of several young warriors of the Kifdah.

The youngsters led our way to the welcoming party. Eight strong looking youths about my age met our path. They were painted and bold, armed with spears and stone knives. One of them stepped forth to approach Dahl and me, his expression hard as if he meant to do us harm. Dahl stepped between us and lifted his hand, speaking in the tongue of the Kifdah. Dahl exchanged words with the young warrior briefly, who then returned to address his party.

"They will lead us to the Oasis." Dahl explained. "It isn't far."

Following the youth of the Kifdah, we marched through the sands of the desert. The sun was harsh overhead, and I grew more thirsty with each step. The sands gradually thinned, and the ground became more solid and rocky. When green appeared in the landscape once more, it was a vibrant and beautiful color to behold.

The boys of the Oasis were wild, but nowhere near as savage as I had imagined. In contrast, they appeared to work and live together in relative harmony. The Oasis was a sort of small village. A band of a dozen or so came to greet us, as we walked the small copse of dusty trees.

The older boy that led the troop stood hard like the men of Lokdah, the look of the warrior well upon him. He stepped forward from the rest. Dark paint covered most of his face, his eyes a fierce amber color. Many small bits of bone adorned him, suspended from his neck and shoulders by leather strands. They shuffled with his movements, the hollow twinkling sounds they made crinkled through the air like a ghoulish wind chime.

He approached Dahl, speaking the language of the Kifdah. Dahl seemed to explain our journey easy enough, pointing to the mark on my chest. The fierce eyed warrior laughed hard, shaking and rattling the bones that adorned him as he did. He looked at me most disapprovingly before turning and gesturing for all to follow.

"Come." Dahl ushered. "Our passage is granted. Welcome to the Oasis."

The green was the only welcoming feature, as we entered the strange encampment. Hammocks swayed empty overhead. The wide dusty leaves of the desert palms blocked the direct fury of the sun, golden rays slipping through to light the grove.

All about were the busy hands of the Kifdah. Few lifted their eyes to take notice of their guests. Their craftsmanship was unique, bone seemed to be a much favored material.

At the heart of the oasis was a natural spring. Crystalline waters gushed from the sandy earth, marked by ripples when the occasional bubble escaped to break the surface. Eager with thirst, I turned to Dahl. He smiled, nodding in approval. At once, I made for the spring.

The water was icy to the touch. A shrill shock moved through my body as I splashed, lifting mouthfuls of the delicious pure water to my dry mouth. Never had any drink tasted sweeter. The sun broke through the leaves overhead, and I closed my eyes against the golden rays, feeling the radiance upon me. I praised my thanks for this blessing, my spirit at peace with the moment.

"We should join the others." Dahl spoke softly from the water's edge.

I turned my face against the sun once more. The feel of the wind through the trees, the sounds of the Kifdah all around me... Song emerged, a sound deep with meaning. The ghastly timbre of the notes added a woeful sound to the melody. The drive and power the voice carried through the words was heartfelt. This was a sacred song, without a doubt.

As I listened, the wind became still as a break left a silence in the rhythm. When next the voice sounded, it was accompanied by all who knew it. The Oasis was alive with voice, resonating with the sanctity of the human spirit. Moved by the song of the Kifdah, I stood in reverence, my ignorance abandoned.

One final note resonated through the green desert paradise, and as suddenly as it had begun the song was gone. The stillness that came left only the sound of the wind and the rippling of the gushing spring. For the first time since I lost my home, my heart did not ache at the memory of my people.

"Come." Dahl urged. "We eat."

With a gentle smile on his aged face, Dahl turned and made for the heart of the encampment. Taking one last sloshing mouthful of the cool pure water, I followed.

It seemed that everywhere I looked, the young warriors of the Kifdah were hard at work to some end or another. Even the spry youngsters that had led our way already found their places alongside their elder brothers. All manner of crafts were being honed and perfected as we passed, from the skillful weaving of plant fibers into long coils of rope to the mashing and rendering of wild grains. All about me, the youth of all ages were devoted to learning and becoming.

Dahl and I made our way to a large gathering around a small fire. The meal was simple, but delicious. When at last it was my turn to scoop from the pot simmering over the fire I filled my clay bowl nearly to the brim. The stew was hearty and spiced, served with a grainy bread. The bread was slightly sweet, and together the two were magnificent.

I found a spot to sit on the ground around the circle. Dahl eased his way down next to me with a handful of bread tossed in with a bit of stew. He ate with grace, dipping at the stew with bites of bread. I commenced to feast on my bounty, guzzling down my portions in no time at all. I placed the empty bowl on the ground before me.

"Satisfied?" Dahl asked teasingly.

"Indeed." I leaned back, kicking my legs out before me and rubbing my belly. "A good meal."

"The only meal." Dahl responded, a smile at the corner of his mouth as he chewed.

"Well, at least I know I'll eat well while I'm here." I joked.

We shared a laugh. The hard young faces ate slowly, their portions much less than what I had taken. Their eyes had hardly left the two of us since our arrival. Some looked to me with curiosity, others with scorn or contempt. I couldn't tell which. They could comprehend my words no more than I could theirs, the encounter made all the more awkward with the language barrier.

"We will need to secure a place to sleep for the night." Dahl explained. "Out here one must sleep above ground. The higher, the better. We will negotiate with Dardek, the young shaman that greeted our arrival. The troop seems to look to him for guidance."

A shaman? He seemed too fierce to be spiritual in any sense, too young to bear the wisdom of such a title.

"I'm fine sleeping by the fire." I insisted.

Dahl laughed deeply at my words, as if my suggestion were absurd. "Not for long, I'm afraid. By night, the desert belongs to the Kerr."

I swallowed hard at this. "The Kerr?"

"You will see. Remember, they cannot climb. You are safe up high." Dahl assured.

His response did little to ease my concern, but it would have to wait. Most of the others had finished eating. Abandoned bowls cluttered around the fire. I waited as Dahl spoke with Dardek. The exchange sounded pleasant, as we were redirected to another of the older boys.

He was an angry looking sort, glaring at me while Dahl spoke. A bone spike pierced through his nose, reaching out from either of his huge flaring nostrils. The delegation took some length of time, as I eagerly waited. The sun sank steadily over the mesa.

"Bone Nose says he has space enough for us, says you may stay if you accept his terms." Dahl explained. "He asks a challenge for the trade."

"I accept." My arrogance proceeded reason. Whatever his challenge, he could not possibly hope to best me.

"Very well." Dahl nodded in agreement, a smile on his face as he relayed the message.

Bone Nose was ecstatic at the news, releasing a series of short cries and pumping his fists into the air. Soon the entire camp was alive with cries. The Kifdah led the way to a ring made of light colored dust poured in a circle upon the loose dry soil. All gathered round as Bone Nose and I set to square off in the ring. The challenge was combat.

"Force your opponent from the circle. That is all you must do." Dahl explained, then he stepped aside and gestured for me to enter.

Familiar with the concept, I stepped into the ring to face Bone Nose. The Kifdah began to stomp and clap as they chanted. The rhythm encircled us the same as the powdered stone dust that marked the boundary, the goal made clear.

Bone Nose growled behind his intense glare, snarling and howling like a beast. It was a bit unnerving, but my victory was sure. The greater challenge before me was not simply besting this rival, but to do so without using my ability. Best him, not harm him.

He continued to raise his spirits with the fury of his display; he was ready. We circled one another but once, steps in time with the chants of the Kifdah. Bone Nose moved to attack.

I managed to evade his initial strike, answering his advance with my own. Bone Nose took the hit against his raised guard and delivered another series of attacks, swiping hard with heavy swings. He worked his way to my left, sending a barrage of kicks. I all but danced around the confines of the ring, dodging the blows. With the last kick I went for him, closing the distance and righting my footing as I grabbed hold of my wiry opponent. I shifted with the rotation of my hips, pulling his weight over me and tossing him hard against the sandy ground.

Bone Nose was far from defeat it seemed. His grip had found me in the moment of his descent, and using the momentum of his fall he pulled me down as well. We tumbled and rolled in a frenzied fury on the dust, grappling and vying for control. I struggled to break free more than anything. I was not as skilled in close quarters as my opponent. Taking him down had been a mistake.

Just as I thought he would tire, Bone Nose broke free of my grasp long enough to get the upper hand. In an instant, he had my arm completely compromised. If I did not act quickly, he would force my submission. Desperate and struggling to free my arm, I shifted my body hard and grabbed hold of the only weakness I could find amidst our entanglement, his little toe.

I grabbed and pulled hard in a direction the joints did not bend. Bone Nose yelped and released enough for me to pull free. I broke from his grip, turning and head butting him hard in the face. He backed away, and I rose to my feet.

The Kifdah booed. I placed distance between us despite the advantage now open to me. I would fight him standing.

Bone Nose rose to his feet in a fury. He screamed and stomped in anger, the Kifdah cheering him. It was over. The look in his eyes was that of pure rage; I knew well what this meant. He would rush me again, and this time I'd be ready.

I backed away as If I were afraid, only a step away from the edge of the ring, waiting for the trigger. He took the bait and set to charge. I took a single well timed step into his path, just as he closed the distance. With a trip from my advancing foot and a well timed pull when he stumbled forward, I shifted his momentum in that crucial moment.

Bone Nose went up and over my shoulders, continuing well out of the ring to land hard on his back.

Gasps filled the air followed by silence, as all eyes fell upon Bone Nose. He gulped for air and spat, as he regained his breath and pulled himself up. He rose to his feet, looked to me, then disdainfully raised his fist and cried. The Kifdah burst into raucous cheer. My victory had been accepted. I would have a safe place to sleep for the night. The Kifdah dispersed, readying for the coming night.

"Cheap move, but victory is victory." Dahl congratulated. "Had me worried for a moment."

"That was fun." I confided.

"It is good you think so. There will be plenty more, I assure. Fighting is what they live for. Come." Dahl said, a grumpy looking Bone Nose arriving at his side. "He will show us where to lie for the night."

Bone Nose stood firm with his arms crossed over his chest. He glared my direction, but said nothing. Instead he turned and led our way into the palms. Hammocks seemed to hang in every place one could fit, stringing the trees together the same as would a spider. I shuddered at the thought. He stopped under several hammocks strung between two very old looking palm trees, one with a crook near its base. He and Dahl exchanged words as Bone Nose pointed to the lowest two nets.

"He says we may use these two." Dahl relayed.

Bone Nose continued to speak, pointing to the bottom bunk and back to me. Whatever he had said, he found it quite humorous. As he finished his laugh, I asked Dahl what had been said.

"He says the bottom is for Little Toe." Dahl grinned a bit. "Elders don't sleep on bottom."

"Little Toe?" I asked, mulling over the new nickname.

Dahl laughed. "Yes. That is how they call you now."

"I see."

I was less than ecstatic, and though I didn't share in his laugh, I couldn't help but smile. The name fit our encounter. Very well, to the Kifdah I would be known as Little Toe.

As dusk descended, we lay in our beds. The broad leaves of the palm bobbed with the wind. The stars began to show through the fading blue, and the natural rocking of the trees was soothing even though it reminded me of home. I couldn't weep here, my pride wouldn't allow it.

It seemed wrong not to finish the day sitting around a fire. The dark was empty, save for the stars high above. Their twinkling became a swirling blur as the tears welled in my eyes.

Suddenly, a vibrant chant rose from the chatter of young voices. Silence followed the subtle first notes, then others joined as the song continued. Soon it swept through the Oasis, moving in time with the sway of the trees. My troubles melted. The hammock rocked like a cradle, and I was quickly lulled to a peaceful rest.

Night was well upon us when they came...

I awoke to the skittering sounds of movement low to the ground. The sound seemed to cover the entire floor of the oasis, and once my eyes adjusted enough to see the movement I wished they hadn't. Droves of pale, ghoulish insects patrolled the ground, clicking and grinding with powerful looking mandibles armed with sharp pincers. Each specimen was easily the size of a rabbit, and there must have been a hundred stalking the grove. I now understood why the Kifdah slept high off the ground, why there was no fire circle late into the night.

Sleep did not return to me until just before the morning light. The Kerr had thinned and eventually vanished, and it was only then that I felt comfortable enough to catch my rest. When I awoke, the Kifdah were gathered around a small fire pit. A meal had been prepared and enjoyed already, and many of the young tribesmen had already commenced toward the toils of the day. Dahl was waiting.

"Good morning." He smiled. "Sleep well, my friend?"

"No." I confessed. "Was that the Kerr?"

"Aye." Dahl confirmed. "They prowl the desert by night, consuming anything they find. By day they hide from the sun underground. The entrance to the hive is known as the Blood Pits. That is where the first trial is held, your first challenge."

I shuddered at the thought of intentionally going near the Kerr. "First trial?"

"Indeed." Dahl continued. "In the days of old, the Kifdah would challenge their adversaries, besting them in combat to prove themselves as warriors. War has long since faded from the land, and tradition has changed. The young live here in the Oasis. Once they have killed at the Blood Pits, they pass to the second trial."

"Killed?" This word stung with the reality of his tone.

"Another few days must pass. The warriors of the Kifdah will return, and with them they will bring those to be judged. The fate of all who enter the trial is that of fatal combat. Two enter; one remains. Thus, a young aspiring warrior spills Adem-Reshan, First Blood."

This practice seemed most barbaric in nature. Then again, my actions had already led me down such a path. Already within a fortnight of leaving my home I had killed several. Had my actions not been barbaric as well? How many had I slaughtered? I couldn't even remember.

"This troubles you?" Dahl asked. My concerns must have been evident.

"No." I lied. "Those to be judged, what have they done to deserve such a fate?"

"Most are murders, some worse." Dahl revealed. "Collected by the warriors as they patrol the land, brought as tribute to their rising brothers."

"I see."

I paused to let it filter though my mind. I thought of my encounter with the bandits near Verda, of the gory hole I smashed through the tyrant's chest. The violent imagery turned my stomach.

"So I am to play executioner?"

Dahl smiled. "Yes. The test, my friend, is whether or not you can find it within yourself to accept this path. Such is your first test, the test of action. Should be easy for one as seasoned as you."

I smiled back. Surely he witnessed my bout at the arena, the men I had cut down during my short stay in Verda. If only he knew of the rest...

"Very well." I conceded.

The days seemed to drag along, as we patiently waited for the arrival of the Kifdah warriors. Dahl shared more on the history of his tribe. The others gradually warmed to my presence, and Dahl was soon worn thin of his role as translator.

The Hasak was the way by which a man was born to the Kifdah, and the desert oasis was his cradle. Only the youngest chapter of Kifdah were to be found here, and as each troop graduated they moved beyond the safety of the spring fed haven.

I was far from alone in my waiting. Many would be participating in the coming trial. Bone Nose and his group were next in line for the Blood Pits. The young shaman to be was also among them, though he rarely mingled with the others. As the days passed, enthusiasm waned, and a serious depth seemed to echo with the words Dahl had spoken. When the warriors finally arrived, it seemed all too soon.

I had just finished yet another sparring session with the troop, and I lay exhausted in my hammock, gently swaying in the breeze. My grappling technique had much improved under the study of the Kifdah, and I reveled in this fact.

As I looked out over the bleak landscape of the desert, two figures emerged from the southeast. They did not enter the Oasis. Instead, the two mysterious silhouettes stood a distance away from the patch of leafy green. Their profiles were hard to discern against the bright glare of the sun and the rippling waves rising from the dust. The others were ready for this omen. Bone Nose and his group assembled at once.

"The time has come." Dahl's words came low and serious. "Are you ready?"

The troop had already began toward the figures, running single file into the desert. "I am."

Dahl looked me over. "Very well. We must follow."

Together, Dahl and I followed the troop. The two warriors that awaited remained statuesque, colored in ceremonial paint. The wind rattled the bones and feathers of their simple garb, their spears resting skyward at their sides. I understood enough to know the Kifdah warrior was lethal with a spear, even from a distance.

When Dahl and I rallied, we completed the troop. There were no words. The two warriors simply shouldered their formidable spears and turned to lead our way into the desert from which they came. Into the shimmering heat we marched, a band of killers led to where our victims awaited. I had been eager to prove myself, a commonality I shared with the troop. But faced with the deed at hand, I was conflicted. Each step drew the moment closer, and my heart slowly sank.

We marched to the southeast, the dust swirling in the whipping wind. When I saw our destination, I knew. Two stone pillars rose from the desert, a platform suspended by chains hung between them. As we drew near, the outlines of others became visible atop the two pillars. Bones littered the dust.

The warriors led us to the western column. As we ascended a simple wooden ladder, I wondered how many others had taken this very journey, how many hands had climbed the wooden rungs worn smooth by the blasting sands. Dahl and I were the last to reach the top, above us a weathered wooden canopy shielded the pillar's occupants from the fury of the sun. The platform atop the pillar was well crowded. In addition to the eight others participating in the day's ritual, there were several Kifdah warriors posted as well.

A rather shaky rope bridge connected each pillar to a heavy wooden platform suspended in the center by powerful chains. To the east stood the other pillar. It was crowded as well. Several more Kifdah warriors stood among those to be judged. They were all strung together and bound by a long knotted cord. I contemplated which of the unlucky chosen would face me on the floating arena.

That's when I noticed the whirling, crawling mass of creatures lurking in the shadows below the suspended platform. A large conical pit in the dusty earth writhed with the movement of the Kerr. Their shiny translucent bodies shifted about restlessly, as if they knew of the bounty to come.

A warrior on the adjacent pillar sounded a horn to signal the beginning of the trial. The two warriors that had led our way stood at either side of the rope bridge leading to the suspended platform. One of them stepped forward and handed a crude metal club to the first participant. The boy accepted the heavy weapon and stepped out onto the shaky bridge. The Kifdah erupted in sound behind him, whipping and howling after him to wish their brother well.

As the young Kifdah warrior emerged onto the center platform, his chosen rival stepped into the center as well, prodded along with the sharp tip of a spear at his back. The condemned man was nervous, clutching to a crude metal club like the one the boy held. Though the man looked every bit mean and capable of harming the boy, he seemed reluctant to do so. The boy was smaller than most, nothing to indicate his violent capacity. He simply watched the condemned man as he slowly stepped around the platform, making his way to the bridge that would lead to his freedom.

The man had cautiously worked his way closer to the boy, who moved to bar his path to the bridge. He held his club higher, ready to use it if the boy moved. With the man's next step, the boy sprang into action.

His attack was subtle in its delivery, catching the man well off his guard. A heavy swing tore the weapon from the man's hand and a following back swing drove the jagged mass of the club hard into the man's head. He dropped. The boy swung once more. It was over.

The Kifdah cheered. The boy looked up from what he had done, horror on his face. With the voices of his kin pulling him free of the carnage, he seemed to recover well enough. Suddenly the boy's face contorted with the rage of war. A cry burst from him as he thrust the club into the air.

The Kifdah roared in turn. The boy turned to the dead man he had slain, and dropping the club, he moved the man's body to the edge of the platform and pushed it off into the pit below.

The Kerr were upon it instantly, tearing and shredding as they dragged the body into the bowls of the pit. The boy returned to the pillar and handed the bloodied club to the next in line. And so it went. Again and again the condemned were defeated and tossed into the pit. The sound of the Kerr feasting was more than I could bear.

At last there were only two participants left on the pillar. Bone Nose was before me. He looked back with a smile, as if he were stepping onstage to perform, ready to display his talents for all. When he got to the center, he yipped and taunted. The Kifdah roared. The man that stepped into the arena to face him set my hair on end. I had felt the sensation before, each time I had encountered the tyrant...

"Dahl, something isn't right. Bone Nose is in trouble. Let me face this one." I pleaded so abruptly that I all but startled a heavily invested Dahl.

"What?!" Dahl looked puzzled, almost insulted. "How could you know this?"

"Because..." I didn't really know how to put it to words. "That one is like me."

"Like you?" Dahl laughed. "He should do well enough then."

The insult missed. "Dahl, he will die."

"Then that is the way of it!!" Dahl snapped viciously, the glare in his eyes was unforgiving.

"Very well." I growled, cold and detached.

The deaths of the wicked were difficult enough to watch. The death of a tribal member, a boy, would be insufferable. I prayed I was wrong, but my gut was resolute, steady and hard as the truth.

The man was by no means intimidating as far as his stature. He was short and scrawny, his head shaved down to reveal several scars across his face and scalp. The look in his eyes was indicative of his hollow nature, a wild creature in the guise of a man. A sinister grin crept upon his face as he picked up the metal club at his feet and stood before Bone Nose. My heart pounded as I watched.

The two stood ready, neither making a move until Bone Nose gave a war cry and lunged. I felt the man initiate the change, almost surging into it myself as I felt it. As Bone Nose raised his club to strike, his opponent drove his hard into Bone Nose's skull. It was over in a spray of red flesh. Bone Nose crumpled, limp and twitching against the suspended platform.

There were no cheers, the shock left only silence. The man dropped the club and smiled wide at us. The path to freedom was his, and he gingerly made his way across the bridge and onto the pillar where I stood with Dahl.

The solemn faces of the Kifdah glared hard against the man as he passed, but a path was cleared for his exit. Our eyes met as he passed, I felt the sinister nature within him. He must have felt something too, for he looked back to me again as he descended, as if he knew what would come if I only got the chance.

The troop slowly made their way out onto the platform where the body of Bone Nose lay. A chant broke the silence, as the boys gathered round their fallen comrade. They moved their hands over his broken body, paying their last respects before rolling him off into the hungry swarm below. I looked away, I couldn't stand to see him drop. Yet another friend had fallen. Disgust swelled within me.

"Why?" I pleaded, seeking some justification Dahl could not hope to offer. The emotion in my voice raw and powerful, almost searing.

"In his first steps, man discovers violence." Dahl's voice was heavy as he spoke. "When he grows tired of violence, he contemplates peace as he rests. Returning to the world, he learns to balance the two within his heart. Only then is he ready to protect and guide others along the way. For this is the supreme purpose of man, to defend and serve others. Even if this means he must lay down his life. For a warrior, there is no greater honor, no greater end than to fall in battle."

I felt the deep power of his words, spoken from ancestor to ancestor. How closely the basis of his philosophy mirrored that of my own. I understood his detachment, but I did not share it. I kept his hardened gaze with my own, my resolve like an angry stone mask.

"Very well." I hissed, stepping out onto the rickety bridge.

The Kerr swooned below the bridge of weathered sticks and rope underfoot. They had finished picking at all the remains, and the swarm had slowed. When I reached the platform, my opponent was waiting. I picked up the metal club that had been in the hand of Bone Nose just moments before.

I scarcely even noticed the man that approached. He took the chance and advanced upon me as I stood in a daze, remembering Bone Nose, trying to block the sounds of the swarming Kerr. The change broke over me stronger than ever...

The man's attack was only inches from my face when I regained my focus. I ducked, narrowly escaping the sluggish swing. My heart thundered, my pace quickened and the world slowed further. It was as if the world took on a dreamlike quality. My awareness extended beyond the immediate, and I could feel the other as he fled through the desert. He would die this day.

I centered my focus on my attacker, now at the completion of his swing. The club came to a hard stop over his left shoulder, his body twisted and awkward. He would unwind for the next attack. I took the opening, striking hard with all the fury of my heightened capacities. The club moved through the man's torso as if I were batting a fly. The carnage of what I had done whirled, suspended in time. I closed my eyes hard against it.

I could feel the hurried steps of Bone Nose's killer as he ran hard through the desert. He had bested my comrade and perhaps won his freedom by the ways of the Kifdah. Fast as he was in his accelerated state, he would not escape his desert tomb.

Focusing on his energy, I leapt high into the air, leaving the platform well below me as I soared into the wind. When I reached the pinnacle of my jump, I hurled the metal club with all the precision, might, and malice I had. A thunderous roar escaped me as the club shot through space toward its mark. Following the throw, I descended to land softly on the platform below. In the distance I felt the man's energy spike with the impact, then fade...

My attacker's body lay brutalized on the platform before me. Suddenly I was overwhelmed with the sight of it, and with an outstretched hand I willed the thing away from me. I had done so instinctively, as if I had known I could. The body was jolted over the edge of the platform as if something heavy had collided with it, pushing it off. Astonished at what I had done, I let the change slip away. What was left of my breakfast spewed from me, adding a splash of color other than red to the weathered boards of the platform.

Footsteps rattled the rickety bridges on either side, shaking and rocking the platform. I wished they wouldn't, as I sank down to my knees to ready myself for the next wave of nausea. How had I known I could do such things? I was getting stronger it seemed, or was I just becoming more familiar with my new capacities? Perhaps the most foreboding question I pondered, suspended there above the angry maw of the desert, struck me as my attentions collected on the many Kifdah warriors surrounding me. They looked confused and frightened, some ready behind their spears they were so uneasy. What was I to become?

Dahl made his way through to the center where I stooped, unsure how to progress. He looked to me with sheer amazement.

"How?" He finally managed to stammer.

"I don't know..." I answered earnestly.

"The way you moved... The way you killed that man..." His eyes wide in shock.

"I killed them both." I confessed. “The man who killed Bone Nose is dead as well.”

"What?!" Dahl barked in disbelief. "He was redeemed! You have no right, the way of the Kifdah-"

"I am not of the Kifdah!!" I roared so that all stepped back.

I felt the change erupt, sending ripples through the world around me. I looked into the heated passion within Dahl's dark eyes. Images began to flood my mind, a place where desert cliffs overlooked a deep canyon. I had not seen this place, yet it felt as though it were a memory. Meaning began to take shape around the images... I was seeing into his thoughts.

My heart dropped, and I suddenly felt a deep urge to escape. I shot from the platform with all the speed and power with which I had leapt into the sky and ran hard through the desert. I headed north, where desert cliffs would meet the canyon of the Veylspring, the place I had seen in Dahl's thoughts.

The Monks of the Nameless Canyon

The sun was bright overhead, the wind whirled at the dust. I stood along a sandy stone ledge and gazed in awe. The Veylspring rushed through a deep canyon, the turbulent current rapid as it churned against earth and stone in the narrow passage far below. The sound of the water seemed to resonate through the canyon, soothing in its ambiance. To the east, the canyon widened into a deep valley. To the west, the river was swallowed into the dark mouth of a large cave that lurked beneath the mesa. To the north, more dust and stone.

A cool breeze rose from the canyon, lifting my spirits with the familiar smell of the river. I turned to face the light of the sun, when I noticed the figure of a man resting atop a rounded boulder. He sat upright with his legs crossed, his right hand held before his face with a single finger raised skyward. His eyes remained closed and he spoke not a word as I approached.

Grainy pigments of bright yellow and vibrant blue colored the shaggy man. Serenity surrounded him, a deep tranquility much like that of the coursing Veylspring itself. I looked up as if to find whatever peace he had discovered. The sky was clear and blue, boundless in its depth and beauty. In that moment I felt so small.

Reminded of the world, my burdens became lighter. I breathed deep of it, sitting to rest near the jagged cliffs that overlooked the river. The only path was forward. I could not run from my fate, whatever it was.

Acceptance was the key, mastery of the self my new goal. I had to be ready when the time came, ready for the challenges that awaited my return to Verda.

The sun began to sink behind the mesa, and the dusty stone terrain offered little protection from the dreaded Kerr. The shaggy man slowly roused from his meditation, stretching his limbs over the edge of the stone before rising to his feet. As if in sync, others I had not noticed began to stir as well.

He spoke not a word, simply waived for me to follow before turning toward the cliff. With nowhere to go and no better alternitive, I followed. Trust was yet to be established, but they seemed welcoming enough. Violence did not seem possible in the company of these spiritual beings.

Falling in line with the others, he joined the progression as it made its way down a steep, narrow passage of stairs carved into the canyon. The fading sunlight lit the stone walls with deep yellows and orange like fire. A grumbling roar echoed from the gaping mouth of the cave, as it swallowed the raging water of the flowing river. It was as if the entire place were alive with a natural healing resonance.

The monks led the way to a series of caves above the raging waters of the Veylspring. One by one, they retired. The man that served as my guide showed me to a small cave with a simple straw bed. The colorful holy man did not break his silence. He simply met his hands together before his chest and bowed gently before taking his leave.

The cave was quaint. There was a stone fire pit and enough old driftwood to make a small fire. I found a hollow stick, filled it with shredded bits of straw. With a few shreds from my damaged clothing and another stick I constructed a small bow. Using the bow, I ground the bits of straw vigorously against the dried wood. Smoke appeared in moments, then a flame.

The fire lit the close confines of the small cave. The sun had sank behind the mesa, and the air rising from the river crept into the cave with a chill. The warmth of the fire was comforting, just as it had always been.

I sat close to it, remembering a time when my father and my brothers had sat around a fire much like it. My father's words came to me, a lesson from long ago.

"True mastery lies within the Self. Learn to balance the three pillars; Mind, Body, and Spirit. A man at peace with himself is at peace with the world. Acceptance is the path by which a man may overcome any obstacle, any trial. Be strong, my son, and surely you will grow stronger."

Tears flooded my eyes, but not in grief. A peace extended over me, and with it an allusion to an understanding that remained just beyond my grasp. The way ahead was clear. I was not ready, but in that moment I knew what I had to do. Running would solve nothing, for I could not hope to outrun myself.

The people of the land would need a champion to defend them when the Empire arrived, to show them the way. Verda was only the beginning. I praised thanks for all that was and all that would be.

The next morning I awoke to find a small basket with a loaf of bread and a few fresh fish. Next to the basket was a new bundle of firewood. I wasted no time stoking the fire to cook the fish, eating much of the bread as I did so. The fish scarcely had time to cook before I set to eating them as well. When my breakfast was complete, I tucked what little was left of the bread in the basket for later and stepped out from the cave to greet the day.

The morning sunlight was warm against the chill morning air, casting gentle shadows as it crept across the red stone of the canyon walls. The sky was blue and clear above, save for a couple of white puffy clouds to the north. The river raged its way into the dark mouth of the cave to the west. Above the cave, the familiar figures of the monks lined the rocky cliffs, all facing the rising sun in a meditative state.

I did not wish to disturb them. As discretely as I could, I climbed the stone steps to the top of the canyon. The dust lay settled, the rocks and sandy soil warm with the climbing sun. Barren as far as I could see, the desert over the canyon was a perfect place to hone my strange new skills.

Facing the golden heat of the sun, I eased my mind as best I could and steadied my breathing.

The youth of Reisenbough learned to move in the ways of their fathers by practiced motion. There were many such drills, passed down the generations. It was a tradition that unified the movement of the people in the same way as music and dance around the fire circle. Move as one, feel the flow.

I decided on one of these practiced movements and eased myself into a starting position. Focusing on my breath, I waited for the moment. When I felt it, I willed the change and burst into motion.

Each transition snapped and flowed seamlessly, as I moved at speeds faster than ever, repeating the familiar routine. With increased focus, it was as if I were floating at times. I improvised and added the fury of my intent, pushing harder with each strike, lashing out with the unseen power at my disposal.

The force I released whipped and whirled the dust of the desert landscape over the canyon. To finish the movement, I vaulted hard, aiming for maximum height in my jump. The rush of the air was like ice, the sky clear and welcoming. At the apex of my climb, I saw the distant fields west of the mesa. I saw green in the land to the far north, the peaks of the elder trees of the eastern forests...

I did not look down. I knew better. Instead I steadied myself as best I could against the rush of the moment and focused on the floating sensation I had felt in the fury of my movements. With the ease of muscle memory, I found it within and willed my effort into slowing my decent. When the ground met my toes, it was with a gentle nudge as if I were a feather come to rest there.

I opened my eyes. The change broke, and I dropped to my feet. With a deep breath of the crisp morning air, lost somewhere between exhilaration and contentment, I made my peace against the madness of all that had happened.

"I knew I would find you here."

Dahl's voice came from the direction of the desert. I felt him there just before he spoke.

He stood silent as if unsure how to proceed, the gentle morning breeze pulling softly at his cloak. I stood just as still, just as silent, my back to the bluffs of the canyon. When it seemed he was sure of himself, he stepped forward.

"I brought your things." He offered my knife and sword.

"Take them with you." I gestured as if to push them back. "I will not need them here."

Dahl seemed shocked at first. A warm and vibrant smile soon lit his aged face, a look I had not seen on him.

"You say you're not of the Kifdah. Why continue?"

"I'm not. I have my own reasons..." I confessed.

"Not all choose the way of the warrior. The monks of this canyon, their path is peace." Dahl responded. "If that is what you seek, you will find it here."

He paused. "Should I wait for you?"

"No. Go ahead, my friend." I directed.

"No?" He repeated, concern on his face.

"I will return to Verda in time." I assured him. "But not yet."

I took a moment to look at the gentle deep blue of the sky, the radiant sun overhead. "There is much to be done. It must be done right, or not at all..."

"I saw what you meant to do, saw the fate of your people..." Dahl confessed.

My heart skipped. "And?"

"Many prayers will be answered, many lives saved if you rise to this calling." Dahl continued. "Verda is only the beginning; the ambitions of those in power extend well beyond that vile city. Too powerful has it all become for one tribe alone, and soon all the tribes will be powerless against them. The people need a warrior such as you. I fear the worst is yet to come."

His conclusion was the same as my own, though it held more truth hearing it from another. "The Empire?"

"Indeed." Dahl confirmed. "Emissaries of the Empire met with the court, already negotiating deals on how the land will be governed once Imperial rule is established in the territory. The masters of Verda are soon to grow stronger under a new banner, that of 'His Majesty's Holy Empire'. Yet, I never would have imagined the court bold enough to so readily allow the massacre of the Dóvai."

"Bold?" I did not care for his choice of words. "Foolish... Cruel... Wrong..."

I let my words linger, contemplating my own selfish intentions. So many had already been hurt, lives lost. Who was I to judge so readily?

"Wrong? I began this path with vengeance as my goal. Does that make it wrong to continue? And what if I lose myself again? What if this strength was used to do something terrible? I am afraid." I confessed aloud. The tears welled in my eyes.

"No, Kael." Dahl countered, stern with the certainty of his words. "Wrong is greed, wrong is oppression, wrong is slavery. These great evils have coerced the people under one banner, that of Verda. Verda is just a city, a symbol for the people to see. Those who control its policies and rule its doctrine reside far from that toxic city. Its many vices blind the people, calls them to serve in all manner of villainy, villainy to themselves and unto others. It has become irreparably corrupt, its influence forcibly spread across the region. People are treated like resources to use as well and easy as the land. Don't you see? This unnatural course is destructive, to allow it to continue will bring ruin to the land and its people, you know this. You've lived it. The Dóvai are not the first to suffer this fate, nor will they be the last if nothing is done. Verda is only the beginning. The big man you killed, his death sparked a response from the Empire..."

"What do you mean?" He had my full attention.

"Marcius sent word to Lokdah. The big man answered to another." Dahl revealed. "He arrived with a small band of Imperial troops the day after we left Verda."

Images returned to me, the way the big man had butchered so many of my loved ones. A killer sent on behalf of this Empire. The same Empire had also sent the scouts, the brave men that had traveled the land peacefully and risked their lives for my own. Both were agents of the same Empire, yet they warred with one another? It made no sense to me.

Dahl continued.

"The man appeared for a banquet among the lordship, boasting of the era to come with the arrival of the Empire. The large man you encountered was his second in command. He introduced himself as a Knight serving of the Holy Empire. Apparently he wore his title well, blending with the lordship and impressing the court. He was well interested in the fate of Reisenbough, more so to know the whereabouts of the boy who had killed his associate. That is all I know." Dahl concluded. "Marcius was wise to hide you."

"This Knight..." I contemplated aloud. "He is like the other, like me?"

"Be strong, Kael." Dahl responded. "Follow your path with all your heart. It is the only way. The light is with you. The other, he is far from it. Hope is on our side, my friend."

Dahl taped his fingers over his heart and kissed them lightly before sending off the motion as if ending a prayer. "I believe. I know we can do this, you can do this."

"Return to Verda. I just need a little more time. I won't be long." I promised.

"Very well. So you will help us?" Dahl asked.

"When the time comes, I will do what I can." I assured.

"I will await your return." Dahl placed a hand over his heart and bowed. "Mealocke."

"Mealocke?" I reflected, puzzled by the name. "A new name given by the Kifdah. Word has spread of what you did, the man you killed in the desert. You defied the sacred ways of the people, yet they rejoice that you would face shame to avenge their fallen brother. Already, legend is taking shape over the events. The tale ends with you disappearing into the desert, leaving only blood and tears. When the desert drinks these dry, all that remains is salt. They now call you Mealocke, the Salt King."

Dahl turned to depart on his long journey back to Verda. In the days that followed I focused all my efforts into testing my new abilities, honing both skill and control, centering my will toward one goal: mastery of the self.

I learned much of my capacities in the first two days of my new training. The monks of the canyon were excellent company, despite their respective distance. They were inspiring without words. When I wasn't wandering the canyon alone on my quest, I worked alongside them, weaving straw baskets and nets, collecting fish to be traded for grain with the youth of the oasis, and baking bread to be shared with them as well. There was peace in the ways of the Kifdah, though I still considered their path most radical compared to the ways of the Dóvai. Even so, I was glad for the refuge of the canyon and the people who resided there.

One morning as the sun rose in the canyon, inspiration came to me. I had set out to begin my day in meditation, following the ways of the monks. I could not gather my focus, finding it difficult to silence my thoughts that particular day, and so instead I set out to collect driftwood along the lower rocks of the canyon.

As I worked, I sorted through my thoughts. My struggle remained as to whether my return to Verda was the right path to take. Dahl spoke the truth, and I felt the same. Yet here in the presence of sustainable peace war was a distant darkness, well beneath human capacity.

Human? Did I even qualify under that term anymore?

While I pondered, a peculiar piece of driftwood caught my eye as it moved with the churning water. The current whirled it about as it lapped against the stone of the canyon. It was a lengthy segment of a strong branch, a perfect staff naturally carved by the elements and delivered to swirl at the water's edge before me.

I watched it dance in the whirling current that had collected it there. In an instant, I willed the change and tested a new possibility, leaping out over the water's surface. As I reached down to retrieve the item, I made contact with the rippling current just long enough to quickly bounce away before it broke. Landing again on the rocky ledge I released the change, staff in hand. The water broke, splashing behind me with the sudden release of force.

The staff was strong and light, the perfect tool for my training. The wood was of a tree unknown to the region, a rare find. As it dried it hardened and became feathery light, yet remained strong and durable.

The staff was well balanced, handy for navigating the rocky terrain. For combat practice, I held it like a sword. In length it was longer than a traditional blade, yet somehow I found harmony in its performance. With this simple tool, I practiced and tested my new abilities in isolation, lost between worlds as I ravaged the desolate landscape in preparation for battle. There I faced myself as well as the foes I envisioned, in the rocky desert terrain above the Veylspring, a place known as Stone's End.

The cliffs were jagged and rocky, made treacherous and slippery with the dust of the dessert. I would find no better place to hone my focus, stress my capacities and test new possibilities. The wind slowly pushed the desert off the steep ledge to meet the Veylspring far below, deep within the rocky gorge. The fall was far, and perhaps not even the mighty could have survived it. The river smashed through the pinched stone walls, the great rock faces jagged and broken.

The splashing surge of water gushed into the mouth of the deep dark cave that took it on some hidden course through the mesa. Lokdah received these waters, where the river deepened into a gentle lake. Directly above the mouth of this cave is where the monks gathered, and it only made sense. The prayers of the Kifdah who meditated in the winds at Stone's End were carried home to their people.

This revelation awoke the purpose within me, solidifying my resolve. Defend the people of the land.

Wielding the staff, I learned to focus the unseen force into concentrated action. I could send stone and dust flying, striking with powerful bursts of unseen energy. I could move faster, focusing on my movements, channeling the same strength into the power of my strikes or to harden my bodily defense. Holding the staff as a blade, I soon learned that I could direct this concentration into the weapon itself, so that even the wooden staff could smash through dust and stone alike. Faster and stronger I became with each passing day.

It seemed whatever innovation I conceived, my body and energy could achieve. In meditation, I relaxed from such thought, retreating to refresh and gather. In contemplation, I tested my capacities further. With mind at ease and focus centered, I could feel the flow of the world. I found that if I entered the change with this state of focus, my influence came natural and with ease. I could lift things at will, practicing with the stones of the dessert. When lifting one became easy, two became a possibility, then many...

My greatest limitation was the capacity of my mind it seemed. When comprehension slipped, and what I felt and witnessed became overwhelming to my senses, my control slipped with it and chaos ensued.

The only way to break it was to exit the change and reenter. This I acknowledged as a potential liability. If my opponent remained in the accelerated state, then any instance no matter how brief would leave me blind and vulnerable. The only way was to press on, pushing ever further against these perceived limitations. I knew that I must and did not question whether I could. There were others, like this Knight of the Empire. How strong could he possibly be?

I must be ready... for all.

A breakthrough came one day when I turned my focus inward, intent to lift myself of my own will and take flight. I accomplished this goal, floating just above the ground before panicking and dropping with the loss of concentration. I hit the ground hard, bruising my rump upon the rubble. I had felt as if I were floating out of myself, away from the world.

It had been uncomfortable to say the least. As I groaned with the climb to my feet, I decided it would be some time before I tried again. I did not like the feeling it gave. I felt severed from the Earth herself, as if I would drift endlessly, whirling in boundless vertigo. It left me feeling sick and a bit defeated at first.

My training continued. Though my attempt at flight had been less than successful, it led to a stunning discovery. The weightless experience in the moment of transition could be countered with a quick release and return to the accelerated state. Any gained momentum could be redirected or neutralized with the flux in state. Thus, by rapid controlled bursts I could recover and redirect instantaneously.

The more I practiced, the more lethal my speed and power became. The air cracked and thundered against my movements. The effort was excruciating at first, but in time the nausea became less intense, less frequent as I acclimated to the experience.

As I watched the sun set over the canyon, the moment of decision found me. The battle ahead was my destiny, but it was not to be waged against the people of Verda, nor for the sake of vengeance. I would win this battle where it truly stood, in the hearts and minds of the people. Becoming champion was the first step in my path to realizing this goal. Dahl was right. The Empire was well on its way, revolution would meet revolution.

I shuddered at this, feeling the time for my return drawing near. The world darkened, and I retired to the cozy little cave and stoked a fire. After a simple dinner I lay by the light of the flame, knowing the next morning I would set off for Verda, City of Champions.

Mealocke, the Salt King

The next morning I woke peacefully, rising easy from a dreamless sleep. The coals burned warm as I roused. I ate what I would need for the journey ahead, my return to Verda. The staff that had accompanied me through the depths of my training stood propped against the wall next to me. I felt the smooth surface of the worn featherwood. It had become dear to me, much like the headband that tamed my unruly hair. Yet as I took my leave, I left it where it rest against the wall of the cozy little cave.

The sun had already began to rise through the canyon. Taking a moment to bask in its warmth, I bid my farewells to that sacred place. The monks had risen with the light of day, already making their way to the perilous stones above the river to greet the sun in meditation. They acknowledged me the same as usual, with only a bow. Silence seemed to be their way. I bowed deeply in turn, allowing the entire procession to pass before me as they climbed the stone steps, hoping the gesture expressed the deep appreciation I felt for the sanctuary they had given.

With my farewell to the monks of the canyon, I climbed my way to the top of the mesa to stand at Stone's End, taking a final look over the desert landscape. The sun was bright as it crept over the horizon, the wind cool and heavy with the scent of the river. I offered my thanks and praise to the Great Mother, feeling her love in the world around me.

Resolute in my decision, I turned with the next gust of wind and ran hard across the desolate mesa. The dust and stone were cool beneath my feet. Resolve lifted my spirits as high as the wind, as I sped toward the western edge.

The western face of the mesa was open to the sky. A smooth, sheer drop overlooked the valley below where the land was green, breathtakingly green. There was no path leading down, the climb long and treacherous. Far below was the lake and Lokdah. The height was dizzying as I looked over the edge. Before there was a chance for second thought, I leapt from the mesa.

The warmth of the sun faded behind the rock, as I plunged through the brisk morning sky over the lake. The wind whipped hard, and I struggled not to close my eyes against it, feeling the cool rush of the air across my skin. This experience was more what I had imagined flying to be. I felt weightless and unstoppable, alive like never before. When I felt the cooler air near the lake, I initiated the change. Just before impact, I redirected my momentum to swing in a wide arch over the water and landed softly in the grass of a lush green pasture.

Sheep and goats lapped gently at the water's shimmering edge. Startled by my sudden entrance, the flock scattered in response, clearing wide of my landing. I couldn't help but smile. I took a moment to look back at the top of the mesa where I had stood. It was a powerful moment. I felt invincible.

As I reveled in the feat, a few curious goats returned to the scene, one or two sheep at their backs. The boldest of them approached to sniff at my fingers in search of food. When the brave goat did not find what it had hoped for, the mischievous little thing nibbled at my fingertips instead.

My hand jerked back in reflex. Realizing what had happened, I laughed. So invincible was I, humbled by a playful goat.

Someone approached.

The commotion had caught the attention of their keeper. The same wild haired maiden I had encountered with Dahl stood with the flock. Her eyes were as piercing as the first time we met. The look on her face was that of surprise and astonishment. This time when our eyes met, I did not shy away. I waived the sign of blessing to her, and with a bow turned for Verda.

Willing the change, I bounded with a powerful leap, soaring high into the morning light that spilled over the mesa. The warmth of the sun was soothing against the chill of the rushing air. How beautiful is the world under such freedom.

I traveled the fields at incredible speed, the earth cool beneath my feet. The green of the land was magnificent after being so long without it. I felt as if my heart were full again, as if I could reach up and touch the heavens. Every now and then I had to stop to rest, finding many of the same places Dahl and I had visited on our journey to Lokdah. The moon had phased well and again since then, the morning chill with the season.

The sun had nearly crept its way to high noon when I neared the great white oak of the field. I drank from the cool waters of a nearby stream, feeling much replinished as it flowed through me. I looked up into the dizzying heights of the massive tree. Its crown seemed impossibly lost in the sky. For a living thing to reach such size, it was truly an elder spirit.

In the distance to the south stood the deep reds of the Tomb of the Shadjah. The great oak towered over even that, and suddenly an idea came to light. No sooner had I realized the possibility than I had set into motion like the smile that rose to my face. I focused on the lowest of the great branches. Willing the change, I jumped for the heights of the great tree.

My feet landed on the rough bark of a massive limb, and with a sigh I released the change. The branch underfoot was large, extending well to the south. Below was the swirling greens and yellows of the plains. I could see the dirt lines of the roads below, one leading to Verda, the other along the western wall of the tomb.

The canopy was thick above. Limbs branched in all directions from the tree's massive trunk. I followed the branch on which I stood to its distal end, in the direction of the tomb. The farther I traveled from the security of the trunk, the more the sway of the limb became apparent. The breeze that moved against the large, broad leaves rocked the mass of the colossal oak. It looked alive and swimming in a blue sea of sky.

The limb narrowed and branched into smaller segments, as I neared the terminal bushels over the tomb. The smaller branches left only a narrow path to walk, and my weight was beginning to add to the sway of the vegetation. The surface had become smoother, more difficult to grip than the shaggy bark near the oak's massive trunk.

Below was the north face of the tomb, but I had no time to admire this breathtaking perspective of the monolith. Suddenly my instincts rang with danger, and without hesitation I willed the change and rolled clear just as a large shadowy figure impacted where I had stood.

When I turned, I saw the many legs of the creature shift as it readied for another pouncing attack. The hunter spider's soulless black eyes looked upon me. I was unarmed, save for my abilities. Arachnids were fast, and even in my accelerated state I was gripped with a primitive fear.

Before it could lunge for me again, I struck with a wave of invisible energy, sent from a powerful palm strike. The unseen attack struck the hungry arachnid like an incredible gust of wind, hurling it from the limb. A single strand of silk clung to the bark of the branch. It wouldn't take long for it to climb back up and try for me once more. I took the window for escape without a second thought, vaulting for the ruins of the tomb.

Landing on the unfamiliar terrain of the tomb's summit, I released the change. The surface comprising the tomb's cover was unusual, a black and rocky contour laid in large overlapping plates. It had a gentle slope leading to an angled peak to the south. The roof of the structure had sunken and fallen through in a few places, weathered by the ages.

For a moment I pondered the methods of the Architects, wondered what this place had once been as I looked over the foreign scope. Superstition soon overwhelmed my confidence and curiosity alike, and I decided it best not to linger. Quickly, I climbed to the peak over the western wall.

As I approached the ledge high over the plain, I saw the familiar shadows of the western forests, the leafy greens of the Allichene and the elder trees that loomed over them. Far below was the road I had traveled with the scouts along the wall and the junction that led across the fields to Verda. The sun crept higher overhead, a few puffy white clouds moved to dim its light, leaving golden rays to shine here and there. The blue of the sky was liberating, standing there in the moment.

Judging the distance, I decided to shoot straight for Verda. From the height, I would clear the distance easy enough. Willing the change, I took a few steps back from the edge to get a running start.

Three paces, and I jumped to the west, my heart beating against my chest. The cool rush of the open sky was all around me. Once again, I aligned my focus as I had in the desert when I attempted to generate and sustain lift by will alone. Flight was not my intent this time. Instead, I soared the distance at a slowed decent.

The experience was exhilarating. Maintaining the speed with which I had launched, I sailed over the open plains like a bird gliding on the breeze. Gradually, I completed my decent for the Earth. When I came to rest on solid ground, I was once again on the road that led to Verda. Before me at the edge of the forest stood the coliseum.

I made my way through the crowded streets much easier than I had upon my first visit. Without the distraction of pursuit, Verda was much more alive. The colorful dress and commerce was as much a shock as it had been before. It was as if the people of Verda had not a moment's rest from the toils of life.

Servants followed after their masters, balancing baskets upon their heads. There were vendors and stalls, filled with whatever assortment of things a person could desire. Others begged from the street, dirty rags covering their bodies, as those who walked by ignored them completely.

This was Verda, and I was soon to change it all when I became champion. With that goal in mind, I navigated the crowded streets of the market to enter the arched gate of the Coliseum. The structure shook with the stomping and chanting of the crowd. I smiled wide, if only they knew what was coming.

Not far within the gate was the door that led to the structure's interior, tucked beneath the grand stair where I had pursued the murderous thief. Two armed guards stood at either side of this entrance much like before, boredom evident in their faces. As I made for the door, their spears crossed to block my path.

"Not this way, kid." One of them rumbled. He was thick, nearly bursting from his armor.

"I need to speak with Marcius." I explained in response. "He is expecting me."

The guards looked to one another, confusion and disbelief in their expressions. They laughed.

"Oh?" The thinner guard chuckled mockingly. "Whatever for, kid?"

"I am ready to accept his offer and claim my title as champion." I revealed, speaking as matter of fact.

The two erupted in laughter. I smiled, patiently waiting for them to recover.

"Sorry lad, Lord Marcius is a busy man. Not just anyone is granted an audience, and no one passes this way without approval. No one. Now move along." Growled the larger guard, stern in his duty to defend the wooden entryway.

"And if I don't?" I asked, meeting the brash man's gaze. His smile faded into anger at the challenge.

"Look kid, if you're so eager to die, why not just jump straight into the arena then?" The other guard offered. "That's the only way to become champion anyway. There's no since in it, but at least dying in the arena won't be a total waste. Not like getting skewered here. That would just be foolish, yeah?"

"Very well." I accepted. "Lead the way."

"Yeah?" The smaller guard continued, clearly puzzled by my response. "Well, the next match is soon to start, so I guess it wouldn't hurt.

I can let you through the gate... But I'm telling you, it's suicide. Are you sure?"

The concern on his face was genuine, replacing his snide humor.

"Quite." I responded.

He looked back to his angry faced comrade for reassurance.

"Let'em! Mouthy little runt. Save me the trouble." He spat at the ground, gripping hard to his spear. "Next match has yet to start anyhow."

"Okay then." The guard was hesitant, but he led the way across the crowded stone foyer.

A grand stair led up into the seating from either side of a sturdy iron gate fixed at the center of the hall. Sunlight cooked the dust of the arena on the other side of the tall metal bars. They were thick and strong, like they could hold against anything. The guard produced a key which he placed in a lock at the center of the massive barred gate. With the turn of the key a lever was freed with a metallic click. His hand reached for it, but lingered when he found his grip.

"You don't have to do this, kid." He warned in hesitation, his voice warm with sincerity.

"I must." I assured him. "Like you said, it's the only way."

The guard pulled hard on the lever, releasing the bolts that held the gate in place with the shriek of metal scraping against metal. The door released, groaning as he swung it open. I stepped through the iron threshold, onto the dust of the arena where the sun shone bright over the sea of faces.

"Hey kid!" The guard called as I stepped through the gate. "At least take this with you."

He pulled a short sword from the sheath at his side and offered it to me.

"Thank you. I'll not forget your kindness." I responded.

Taking the blade in hand, I turned and entered Verda's great arena for the first time as a willing contender. The iron gate groaned as it closed behind me. The lock clicked into place.

The thunderous chanting of the crowd was much louder from the arena, and as I made my way to the center I looked over what must have been hundreds of faces. I gripped tight to the blade I held at my side.

Other contenders made their way into the arena. They stood fast against the roar of the crowd, ready for battle. One whooped and flaunted, showboating for the eager audience. He stood stronger than the rest, a bronze helm shaped like the head of the mighty hatual rested atop his head as if the creature meant to consume him. This man was sinister, I could feel it even without the change. I would defeat him first and foremost.

The contenders moved to the center of the dusty arena. Two fighters dressed in black stood back to back, making it clear they were of no threat to one another. The robust man with the bronze helm continued to tempt the fervor of the crowd, raising his double headed ax high and roaring like a beast. A fourth contender kept himself at the ready, his face wrapped and covered, leaving only his watchful eyes exposed. His bare chest already glistened with sweat.

Armed guards moved the last man into the circle. He seemed frightened and well out of place, prodded along by the spears of the guards. Wearing only shackles and rags, he was clearly an unwilling participant. He shook with fear, his eyes wide and frantic. He was a man condemned, though he did not seem wicked in the slightest.

I stood among them, the short sword given to me gripped tight in my right hand. As I waited for the fight to begin, I studied the others intently, looking for any indications of another like me. I had to be sure, ready for anything. Nothing unusual, I was to fight ordinary men for the day's victory. It would be over quickly.

At last a horn sounded with a mighty resonance across the arena, and the fighters sprang into action. The pair dressed in black converged on the masked fighter. Outmatched, he could do little more than avoid the fury of their attacks. Each swing of their blades was perilously close to the mark. He wouldn't last long.

The cowardly man in rags turned from the action, running hard for the iron gate through which I had entered. The man with the bronze helm went after him. I willed the change and moved to intercept.

With impossible speed, I moved between the two. Their sluggish movements left them all but frozen in the moment. Standing before him, I studied the fighter in the bronze helm more closely. Reaching for the same connection I had accomplished with Dahl, I sought to see into him, to read his character. When I broke through, I saw this man. He was greedy, he was cruel.

Many had fallen to him long before he was dragged to the arena, with or without reason. It didn't matter to this sort. Strength and violence were all he knew. He fought for pleasure, for glory and fame of which to boast, for riches and the means to acquire that which he desired. He held no honor, no value other than greed, that deep soul consuming lust for personal gain that forsakes all others.

I had seen more than enough, glad to sever the connection once I found my way out. Facing him, I simply held my sword out before me as if it had been thrust for the man. His eyes met mine as the blade slid into his chest, driving through him as he ran upon it. I reached for the ax in his hand, taking it from him gently. His hand reached for the blade lodged in his chest. Shock and disbelief widened his eyes as the sensations of what was happening began to sweep over him.

I turned to the cowardly man as he fled. Reaching for his identity, I learned he had been a servant before he had been forced into the arena. He had done nothing deserving of this fate, having served with devotion. His insidious master was an empty man, who forfeit him to this fate by way of a losing bet. He was an innocent to be murdered for entertainment. Not today. I would destroy any who tried.

I turned from him just in time to witness the blades of the dark pair cut through the masked man. They had flanked him, rendering him powerless against his odds. I did not bother to read him, for I could do little to help him against such injury.

Instead I turned to his attackers. The two were from a village to the southeast, deep in a river valley within the eastern forests. They fought for the wealth the title would bring, wealth they intended to use to bring prosperity to their home and ensure protection from the forces of Verda. Their cause would be honored, a cause to which I could relate. Verda would not threaten their home, I promised.

Positioning myself in line with the two, I made to strike. With a heaving toss, the broad head of the ax was sent hurtling toward them. It contacted the closest of the two, hitting hard into his chest and sweeping him into the other with crushing force. The man who had taken the direct impact was badly injured, his ribs horribly broken with the impact. Both were still living, but most certainly defeated. The man they had attacked dropped to kneel, bleeding from a terrible slash to his right side. He was done.

My attention returned to the man with the bronze helm, upon his knees in the dust of the arena, hands groping at the grip of the short sword lodged in his chest. The Emblem of Verda shown boldly on the end of the hilt. Reaching for it, I removed his hands to secure my grip. With the same motion, I ripped it free of the man's chest and kicked him to the dust, leaving him to die.

The ill-fated servant was frantic at my approach, looking to me in horror as he desperately pulled and shook at the iron gate. The two guards on the other side stood watching, a smile on the mean one's face. When I was upon him he dropped to his knees as if to beg, his words lost in the droning hum of the world.

I focused my will on the blade and sliced hard through the locking mechanism with a mighty downward swing, cleaving it in two and setting the gate free. With this, I dispelled the change.

"Rise and be free." I spoke, feeling strangely distant from my own words as if they weren't my own.

The man looked confused for a moment, but wasted no time as he jumped to his feet and bolted through the open gate. He ran past the two guards who stood dumbfounded at what they had seen.

"Thanks again." I smiled at the kind guard, offering the short sword to its rightful owner. He accepted it, lost for words.

"Kael!!"

Dahl's familiar voice called to me as he ran across the arena. Much to my surprise, he embraced me with a warm welcome.

"You've returned to us! I knew you would."

He smiled bright, most pleased to see me. It was difficult to contain my own excitement, long had it been since I'd known familiar company.

"It's good to see you, my friend."

"Aye, looks like you've wasted no time in getting started." Dahl laughed. "I imagine you will be champion soon enough. If we have the time..."

I looked over the arena. The man with the bronze helm lay dead, as did the masked man. The servant had fled as instructed, and the pair cloaked in black writhed and moaned in the dust of the arena, dirty and beaten. No one came to their aid.

"So what happens now?" I asked.

"Now we celebrate your first victory." Dahl smiled.

He led me to the arena center. "Stand proud, show the people they have a new champion on the rise, like this."

Dahl grabbed hold of my arm and thrust it up high for all to see. The crowd blasted in response to my victory. Some cheered, others booed. Standing there in the center of it all was overwhelming. The voices, there were so many.

Somehow those that cheered reached me. Feeling their support, my arms raised high with clenched fists as I spun round to show the full devotion of my intent. I would be their champion. They would all be freed from this toxic place.

Coins rained down upon the arena from all around, shaking me from the arrogant stupor of victory. They threw currency to me so easily while others in need begged for it in the streets. The destitute were deemed unworthy, while a killer among sheep was readily exalted. My heart sank at the gesture, my arms dropping to my sides. There was no victory here. Not yet.

"They pay you tribute." Dahl explained. "Come, Marcius awaits."

We met with Marcius in his high chamber, where a fine dinner lay prepared and ready to eat. The smell of it set my stomach to rumble and growl, for I was very hungry. There was fruit, salad, roasted meats and vegetables, and wine. Lots of wine.

"Kael!!"

Marcius bellowed with a huge smile, throwing his arms open as he stood to receive us.

"Welcome back! I was beginning to think you'd reconsidered. Have a sit. Eat!"

I wasted no time taking a seat at the table, reaching out and cramming fistfuls of delicious food into my gullet, completely ignoring the silverware. The food was delicious, long had it been since I'd eaten so well. It brought to memory the feasts of Reisenbough. Suddenly I felt as though I'd had enough, despite my appetite. That familiar sadness had dulled considerably, though it still remained.

"So, Dahl has assured me you will no doubt be our next champion." Marcius continued. "After that performance today, I'd say he's onto something. You're well on your way, my boy. Did you hear that crowd? Already there are talks of the mysterious fighter who vanishes and reappears in a flash. Thunderboy is what they're calling you out there."

He laughed.

"Thunderboy?" I did not like this name. It was fortunate the twins had not been around to hear it.

"You struck down Iron Helm, the big smelly guy. He was on his way to his fifth victory, you know. One becomes champion in seven."

"Seven victories?" I pondered after his words. If the man I had killed was able to get as far as he did, I stood little chance of failure.

"Aye." Marcius continued. "You've won your first, but it was a bit messy. Don't you think?"

"What do you mean?" I asked, a bit taken aback as I sipped at a goblet of wine.

It was strong and bitter to the taste, nothing like the sweet wine of the Dóvai. I did not bother with another drink of the vile stuff.

"Well, it was all over rather quickly, wasn't it?" Marcius began. "The battles of the arena are for spectacle more than anything, a central event to entertain and capture the hearts and minds of the people."

"They find death entertaining?" I felt anger rise at my disgust.

"Not death specifically, but the action, the emotion, the theatrics!" Marcius explained with passion. "You don't have to kill. Today you've proven as much. But make no mistake, when red spills on the dust of that arena, the people go wild. Of course, that isn't the only way to win their affections. You've proven that as well..."

"When I released the man in rags?" I asked, feeling hope and focus return, quelling my lesser emotions. The heat of anger left my face, quenched with my thirst as I found a drink of water.

"Yes!!"

Marcius jumped and pounded a fist upon the table in his enthusiasm, shaking wine to spill upon the smooth cherry colored wood. Dahl smiled wide as his eyes shifted to meet mine.

"Already the streets are filling with chatter. A wild thunderboy suddenly appears, entering the arena at the last possible moment to slay the rising champion and free a common slave?! It's all the buzz, my boy! Well done indeed."

"Oh, this is only the beginning..." I promised. A smile crossed my lips at his words. I took another drink of water.

"Agreed!" Marcius bellowed most radiantly. "Nothing will aid you greater on your rise to fame than winning the favor of the common people. Well played."

He seemed to miss the authenticity of my actions altogether.

"Now, Dahl said he informed you of our visitors, says you're willing to fight all the more. Is this true?"

His eyes were wide and glistening in the candlelight. His face was warm with wine, making him appear genuine where little true humanity was suspect.

"It is." I responded.

"Splendid!" Marcius beamed. "A champion like you is a godsend. Whatever powers you posses my friend, they will be most needed. The people will flock to you when the time comes. Well, actually the time is coming, perhaps here even. And that's what we really need to discuss. I know it's not what you want to hear, but when dealing politics it pays to be ready for anything. Which means we may need to keep you hidden for the time being, much like we did with your little dessert trip."

"Why bother?" I asked, insulted by the idea.

Marcius laughed.

"It's not running, Kael. It's strategy. We can't start a war in the streets, that only gives the advantage to the opposition. The people must adore you, talk about you, dream about you. They must come from far and wide to fill the coliseum just to see you. The more you give them, the more they will come to love you, or hate you depending. This is where it matters how we do this. The Empire must look like the bad guys here, not us. We can't start the war, our role will be that of the defender. The people must side with us, and for that they must believe in our cause. Know what I mean?"

"They've already started the war, attacking my village and manipulating your politics here in Verda." I spat in response.

"Not just here in Verda, not just Reisenbough, Kael. They've done this the world over, set to take the entire planet... That's the scale we're talking here. And yes, they've already managed to win favor among the lordship. Greed is the language they know best, and the Empire speaks it well enough. I must warn you, not all can be won by acts of compassion. You, Kael, are like nothing we have seen in all the years this arena has known spectacle. You have the potential not only to inspire the people, but to lead them as well. The people will all but worship a man like you, and there will most certainly be those who come to resent you for it. There always are..."

Marcius took a deep drink of his wine.

"Let them. I will free even them, every last soul." I swore before him.

Marcius spewed his drink across the table and choked a bit before clearing his throat with laughter.

"Well my boy, wouldn't that be something? Good luck. You'll not be the first to have tried. Right Dahl?"

"Perhaps he will succeed." Dahl reassured. "The champion Verda needs."

Marcius seemed put off by the direction the conversation was taking. "Come now old friend."

He produced a thick cigar and beckoned a servant from the corner of the chamber to approach and light it for him.

"If we must relive another attempt at revolution, best we meet it on good terms. Am I right?" He puffed deep of his smoke. The servant retreated back to the corner of the chamber. "We need to be smart about this, fellas. If the lordship catches wind of what we mean to do, the Empire will no doubt hear of it as well."

"Playing sides? Why not dispatch the lot and be done with them?" I suggested bitterly.

"Hmm, not so much. I like the idea, trust me. But like I said Kael, hearts and minds. If we murder our way to the top, we become villains. People don't willingly side with tyranny for the most part. It'll defeat the whole purpose. Besides, that kind of radical change would definitely draw some attention and give the Empire reason to oppose us openly. Aside from that, how could we hope to know the snakes from the worms?"

"Want me to show you?" I offered.

Marcius laughed. "If only."

"I just don't see how people can be so easily corrupted." I admitted aloud.

"Well try to think of it from their perspective, yeah?" Marcius puffed another cloud of smoke. "You live like a king, have whatever you wish, do whatever you wish. Why on Earth would you want to throw that away? Such power? Such luxury? It's mighty honorable, bub. But they aren't going to go for it, and neither do I honestly. Every man has his price. When you find yours, you'll abandon that dreamy nonsense the same as I did."

Now I was the one who did not care for the direction of the conversation. Dahl fell silent as well. Marcius seemed to take note of the fall-out, standing to signal the conclusion of our meeting. He retreated to admire the view through the large bay windows behind his desk.

"Many lives will be lost in the chaos you'd bring. I suggest you really consider the consequences before you set to swinging your sword around. Believe me, revolution is already underway. Our best efforts would be to solidify and expand what we already have. Trust me on this."

He took another sip of his drink.

"It's how he said it, the knight of the Empire that visited in your absence. He said, 'soon the savage people of the world will be brought to serve under one cause'. He also said those who resist, including any of us mind you, will be 'dealt with swiftly'. It may not be what you want to hear, but there is only one direction; strengthen what he have and hope for the best, play the game. Revolution as you seek it, freedom, is not an option for any of us in the long run."

"We shall see." I responded, my resolve strong like the pulse in my veins.

"Indeed we shall." Marcius conceded. He turned, a smile returning to his face. "Perhaps it's best to call it a day, hmm? I'm sure you're exhausted. I know I am."

He tipped the ashes from his cigar into a small silver tray on his desk. "Dahl my friend, would you show Kael to his new chambers? See that he is comfortable."

He turned to me. "Welcome back. Don't let our differences in opinion sway you. We may not agree on the philosophy of the matter, but together we will most certainly accomplish great things. Rest well, my boy. Tomorrow is a bold new day."

Dahl escorted me to another chamber deep within the coliseum. It was a simple space, a wooden floor that matched the rafters above. The outer wall of the chamber had two small windows, open to the outside world. Across the room adjacent to the door was a large cozy looking bed, covered in finely sewn quilts of vibrant color and piled high with fluffy pillows.

A small wooden stool held a wash basin next to a table along the north wall of the chamber. On the tabletop was a silver tray with several candles and a bundle of tenders next to it. I stepped onto a soft plush rug that covered the floor around the bed. The cushy feel of it tickled at my feet.

"Here." Dahl offered my belongings, placing my sword and knife on the table with the silver tray.

The sleek gilded case was cool to the touch. I took hold, feeling the familiar weight of it. The blade of the Salvek was back at my command, my capacities far greater with my recent studies. The possibilities of what lie ahead flooded my mind, as the sword came to rest at my side. I tucked the stone knife with the lock of hair that bound it safely into the cloth about my waist.

"Thank you."

Dahl bowed gently. "Marcius does not share our vision, my friend. Given into greed and his own darkness, he seeks only to further his entanglement in the political web. He believes that to be the front by which this battle can be won."

"What if he's right, Dahl?" I asked. "If war can be avoided, shouldn't it? I came here to free the land, not to provoke it's destruction."

I thought about those words. In the beginning, that had been my intent exactly.

"Or maybe I did..."

Dahl looked shocked, then laughed. He knew the truth within me.

"My friend, you have nothing to worry about. Win the hearts and minds of the people, and they will follow you anywhere, against all odds. Marcius was right about that. But you don't have to see things his way. The people can indeed be led away from this terrible place and the toxic culture that enslaves them. There is hope. You can do this. You've already won their intrigue, now win them over with your light. Shine with all your heart, lead the way for them to open theirs. You're not inspiring the death of these people, but their inevitable rebirth. Change is coming regardless. We can show them a path worth walking, a chance allowed to us solely in the midst of change."

"And violence, that is the proper way of it?" I asked, casting my doubt once again. "If war results then there will be plenty more violence, spilling blood for sport in the streets as well as the arena..."

I buckled, as if I were waking to some grim realization of all that had led to this point. My knees hit the floor before me.

"Why must I continue the path of the slayer? Knowing no equal, I cannot be the warrior. Even that honor has been taken by fate! How can I ever again know decency?"

I wept like a lost, sulking child. Dahl stood silent for a moment, concern deep in his aged face. He kneeled, reaching for me with his gloved right hand.

"My friend, fate takes no sides. You are that which you are, that which you choose to be. Already you've passed from anger and despair, now you must release the fear that binds you. You have been the slayer, yes. You will most likely slay again, yes. The difference is not in the act, but in the conviction behind it."

"Those who will fall before this cause will hardly number compared to those who have fallen already, those who will continue to fall both in the dust of the arena and to the forces of tyranny sweeping the land. The enemy is not weak, Kael. This burden will not be easy to bear, and for that I am grievously sorry, my friend. It is a lot to require, a lot to ask of you. I believe that you can, but you alone must decide. One day I hope to live in this land as it was in my youth, at peace. This is why I endure, I choose to fight the darkness threatening the land and its people; I give my life to protecting that which is sacred. Life... For that is the way of the warrior, that is the path before us. I stand with you, Kael. As does all the might of the Kifdah."

"Thank you." I muttered.

Moved by his words, I felt foolish for losing my way. I had been so certain until that moment, set out with such confidence. That confidence returned, my doubt dispelled. I thought of my father, how the mighty Krayton had fallen in battle. How he had given his life for my own. They had met their fate well, but the odds had been against the Dóvai. What chance would the people of the land have if I did not stand to protect them? For if the people struggled against Verda, the Empire would take them for sure.

"I am sorry, thank you."

"It is nothing." Dahl stood, waiving his hand in dismissal. "To stand firm in belief, one must be able to weather all doubt. Proceed when your standing is firm and you believe. To overcome what lies ahead, you simply must. Rest well, my friend. Tomorrow is a new day."

Dahl took his leave, and I sank into the cozy linens of the soft bed to try and rest. My mind was turbulent with thought, my body racked with emotion. Memories echoed against the distant dark, as heated hypothetical scenarios sparked and clashed over and over in the foreground of my mindscape. I was beyond anxious. I was exhausted.

I awoke to the warm light of morning spilling in through the windows. The sounds of movement in the room roused me from the numb transition into waking and set me clumsily upon my feet, blade in hand. Across the room stood a woman, robed in the drab garments of a servant. Startled by my sudden burst, she turned to face me, shock evident across her delicate features. It was her! The one from before.

Now we were both uneasy. Sliding the blade back to rest, I carefully knelt to place the weapon at my feet. She breathed a sigh of relief, a soft hand rising across her chest.

"Forgive me, master." She bowed on her knees. "I have brought fresh water for the basin."

She gestured to the corner behind her, where the wash basin had been placed on the floorboards next to the squat wooden stool. A few neatly folded cloths were stacked on the tabletop.

"Thank you." I managed.

She was trying not to meet my eyes, but I had already seen. They held the green of the forest, much like my own. Her dark thick locks spilled from beneath the hood of the robe, framing the beauty of her face. She at last lifted her gaze to meet mine. I couldn't help but step forward, drawn to her beauty.

"Who are you?" The words rippled from me before thought had formed them.

"My name is Liallia."

Her voice was warm and soft, washing over me like the gentle lulling pull of the lapping water at the river's edge. Her lips were lush and delicate like a flower early in bloom, meeting the smooth caramel of her skin with the pink of rose petals.

"I have been charged to your service."

I was speechless. The idea of a servant was grossly unappealing, in direct contradiction with my very objective. When my mind broke free of my stupor I took another step, closing the distance.

"Rise, Liallia. You are a servant no more." I stood bold with my words.

She laughed.

"Forgive me, master. I am grateful for your sentiment." She smiled. "That would be most kind of you."

"Do you not believe?" I asked, confused and far less bold. "And please do not call me master. Among my people, that title comes only with age and wisdom."

"As you wish, sir." She replied. "Your people sound very noble. And I believe your intentions to be true, but you are not the one who holds my bonds."

A chuckle escaped me. "Your bonds do not exist. Rise."

Our roles had swapped. Confusion scrunched her face as she rose to her feet. "Sir?"

"Kael, my name is Kael." I felt bold again. "Son of Krayton the Mighty, born of the Dóvai. By that name, when I become champion of Verda, all such bonds will be no more. So you are free. The lordship will catch up on the details later."

"Kael." She giggled. "That sounds wonderful. But even if you do become champion, how can you be so sure?"

"My word is given." Finality saturated my tone. "I am not your master, nor is any other. The spirit lives free. The people have only forgotten, but I will show them the way."

This time when our eyes met, I saw the depth of the maiden before me. Her warmth was open to me and welcoming. I stepped closer, heart pounding, humbled before this delicate flower of the garden.

"On your word?" She shrugged with a smile. "Good enough for me. So what now? Shall I just be on my way then?"

She turned for the door.

"Madam!" I reached out.

"Yes, Kael?" She turned back. "You said I'm free to go, right?"

"Yes of course!" I fumbled. "What I mean is, may I escort you?"

My courage was gone, the stammering fool returned.

"You're going with me? Aren't you to become Champion of Verda? How exactly will you do that if we run off together?" She smirked with a raised brow.

"Well, I mean to ensure you safe passage." An honorable motif improvised on the spot.

"Ah, noble indeed!" She quipped with feigned enthusiasm. "And convenient. If anyone has a problem with my going, you'll be right there to explain, inform the lordship of the details. Problem solved!"

"Precisely." I smiled reassuringly, and together we laughed.

She stepped closer this time. "That's mighty kind of you, Kael."

I looked deep into her eyes, green like the canopy in summer and tinged with the kiss of a golden sun. It was as if all the world stopped, and I scarcely felt my breath. The door swung open behind her.

"Good morning, Kael!"

Marcius boomed as he burst into the room. He wore a big smile, adorned in purple robes. Dahl entered behind him, stoic and hard as usual.

Marcius took little notice of the servant girl who retreated to the corner of the room, diving straight into the details of the day's schedule. There would be a fight in the arena. The rest was a blur to me, lost in the background. My attention strayed from the conversation despite my best efforts to at least pretend to listen.

Dahl on the other hand, had indeed taken notice. He followed my eyes to the source of their distraction. A bright smile sharpened the lines of his aged face. He nodded approvingly while Marcius continued to blather about the happenings with the council. I felt myself flush with embarrassment.

"Kael?" Marcius called my attention. "You alright?"

"Yes, I'm fine." I responded, flustered and eager to exit the situation. The window had potential.

"Well then, we'd better get a move on. Much to be done before the round, and you'll want to eat I suppose. Hope you have the stomach for it. It'd be a shame to waste a good meal on the dust of the arena." He moved for the door. Dahl followed suit.

Liallia smiled, clearly reading the concern on my face. "I'll be here. Can't leave without my escort."

I was swooning. A brimming smile rose upon my face like a blazing sun rising within my being. I all but floated for the door.

"Kael!" Liallia called after me. "You might need this."

She had retrieved my sword and offered it to me. Our fingers met when I took hold of it.

"Good luck out there, champ." She winked.

"Madam." I responded with a warm silly smile.

"Kael!" Dahl called after me.

"Aye!" I called back.

I had to pry my eyes from hers, and it wasn't until she closed the door behind me that my focus somewhat returned. Today would see my second battle in the arena, my second victory. To have her at my side, I would win a thousand more.

Marcius led the way to a grand dining hall where a feast awaited. Several servants sprang into action upon our arrival. Many others already attended to the dining needs of those seated at the long table. As I watched their hurried movements, I could almost feel the anxiety about them. Fear saturated the energy of the chamber. I wished I could dismiss them all at once, or at least let them know freedom was coming. Six victories remained.

As I drew closer to the banquet, the smell of the food woke my appetite, and my stomach churned with hunger. Guilt at the given circumstance began to ache in my mind like the hunger in my gut.

A pair of servants rushed to move a rather gaudy chair at the head of the long table, pulling it out so that Marcius could be seated. As he sat, the servants began to arrange the space on the table before him. One servant filled a large goblet with wine and a smaller one with water. The other prepared his plate and presented it to him. Marcius took little note of their efforts, as if they weren't even there.

Dahl was seated next to Marcius, servants snapping into action around him just the same. There was a seat open across the table from Dahl to Marcius' left. He gestured for me to join them, servants at the ready.

"Sit, my boy. Eat! You'll need your strength for the day ahead."

I did not take the seat at the table. I was hungry, but I would not be hosted in such a way. Instead I grabbed an empty plate and began filling it at my leisure, strolling about the table to pick and choose. Gasps spilled across the chamber, and the conversation died with the hush of it. For a moment Marcius was as flabbergasted as the other onlookers.

Then with a laugh, a smile replaced his shocked expression. Dahl looked on with a smirk, intrigued to see a wild heart feast among the civilized.

"Prefer to do it yourself, eh?" Marcius teased. "That a boy, a real go getter he is."

His laughter bellowed, cascading down the table. They could all laugh as they liked. Soon there would be no servants, no masters. When they had to do their own fetching and filling, would they laugh the same? I smiled to myself at this, and walked away from the table, shoving tasty bites of delicious cake into my hungry muzzle.

A doorway of glass panes opened onto a grand balcony that over-looked the arena. I retreated to the balcony in hopes of enjoying my breakfast far from the social happenings of the long table. The aristo-crats of Verda were less than fetching.

The late morning sky was bright. Sunshine flooded the stadium, chasing the shadows from the arena with rays of gold. Its soothing warmth was much welcome against the lingering chill of the early hours. I gazed across the seats of the grand stadium. Already people had begun to file into the benches for the spectacle to come. Had I not seen it full, I wouldn't think it possible that so many people would gather for such a thing, murder for sport. Then again, hadn't I gathered with my loved ones to hear the stories of war and carnage by the flame? I pondered the similarity, convincing myself of the differences as I chewed hard at an-other tasty mouthful. If only the truth were as easy to swallow.

A cloaked figure stepped out from the dinning hall, rousing me from deep thought.

"Kael." Dahl approached, offering a goblet brimming with drink. I accepted it graciously.

"You do well. Still your heart, my friend." He reassured.

"Thank you." I muttered, wiping my mouth across the back of my arm. "So when's the fight?"

Dahl chuckled as he sat next to me. "You wake in better spirits. Good. High noon. That is when you fight."

"Contend." Marcius called as he stepped into the conversation. "Sounds much better between friends." His smile was beaming, his face already warm with drink.

I grabbed one last mouthful of food, unmoved by his terms of endearment. He was as false as his cheeky smile, and it was making the food less enjoyable. I washed it down anyhow, with a colorful explosion of tasty fruit juice. Never before had I tasted a beverage like this. One sip, and I downed the rest, unable to stop until the drink was gone.

"Now," Marcius continued, taking a seat upon the railing, "next order of business is to get you properly dressed and looking sharp for your audience. You'll want to stand out, be easily recognized."

"Stand out?"

I looked over my worn hide tunic, dirty and tattered. The cloth about my waist was snagged and torn. The hides bound by it were stained and weathered. It all felt like a part of me, like a second skin.

"Why bother?"

"Winning the favor of Verda will be much easier if they recognize you when they see you. A unique look will catch the eye."

Marcius snatched at the air as if he were catching the very gaze of the people. He all but shook with certainty at his words.

"We get you a solid look, something fetching but practical. Believe me, people will follow you more readily this way. They live for it. They love to watch a champion rise, even if they love to hate 'em. It's their love for you that lifts you. They decide you champion or not long before you manage that final round." His brow raised for emphasis. He finished his words with a drink.

The sun was warm across my skin. Already it had risen above the wall of the coliseum, creeping its way toward the canopy over the city. High noon would not be radiant with light and heat as it was in the desert over the canyon. The deep forest would keep a chill through winter, and the change in seasons would see that chill extend upon the land. Soon it would grow colder, linger further into the day. Better clothing was necessary. Even if I'd been on the path of the Allioht, I'd have had need of them all the same.

"Very well." I responded. Reluctance still swelled beneath my words.

"Excellent!" Marcius swooned. "I've sent for the tailor. We'll get you fitted before the round. Come. We have a schedule to keep."

The three of us traveled through the dimly lit innards of the coliseum once more, arriving at a dusty stone walled chamber near the center of the structure. Sunlight filtered in through a barred gate much like the one through which I'd entered the arena the day before. It was all that separated those in the chamber from the arena itself just beyond.

Armed fighters clamored and rattled their gear and equipment, preparing for battle. Some practiced strikes on imaginary targets. Others sat stooped over a battered old table, the space alive with chatter and banter. There were a dozen or so fighters, five more bound in chains securely fastened to the southernmost wall...

"Ah! Here we go." Marcius proclaimed, outstretching a hand toward a thin elder draped in colorful robes. The old man shambled his way into the chamber, a nervous looking youth at his side. "Right on schedule."

"Lord Marcius, my sincerest thanks for choosing my services once again." The man bowed as deep as his age would allow.

"Of course, Ton!" Marcius nodded with a brimming smile, returning his gesture. "Your skill is mastery, unrivaled in all the land. Now, this strapping young lad here is Kael, soon to be Champion of Verda!"

Ton looked me over, calculation in his age old expression. "Hmm, I see."

He stepped forward, reaching toward the young boy that accompanied him with an expecting hand. The boy produced a thin strip of cloth with marks and notches along its length.

"Let's see. I'll just take a few measurements here. How does that sound, Kael was it?"

"Yes." I responded as he approached with the length of cloth stretched between his bony hands.

He ran the tape along my shoulders first, calling out numbers to the boy who transcribed the digits. He took several more such measurements, having me change position for a few of them.

"That should do." Ton said, as he finished with the length of my arms. "It shouldn't take more than a day or two before I have something ready." He handed the measuring tape to the boy who tucked it away.

"Wonderful!" Marcius exclaimed. "I can't wait to see how it all turns out. Believe me, Kael. This will make a world of difference." He turned back to Ton. "Thank you. Send for me when it's done and I'll deliver payment in full."

"Of course, old friend." Ton responded. He and the boy left the way they had come.

An ensemble of horns sounded over the coliseum outside. The crowd that had gathered to fill the stadium roared behind the iron gates that separated the chamber from the dusty arena. Their excitement resonated through the structure, rumbling it with anticipation. Several contenders moved for the iron gate, a few of those condemned were forcibly led by the shackles and chains that bound them.

"Ah, the preliminaries are about to begin." Marcius was happy to announce. I moved toward the gate.

"No, no. Not just yet, my boy." Marcius gestured for me to stop with an outstretched hand. "The first round is for new entries only. You will be in the next round."

I found it difficult to look away from those led in chains, corralled by spears wielded by hateful looking soldiers, each wearing the same armor as those who had marched against Reisenbough. Six contenders entered with those in shackles once the gates were opened. I watched as they all filed out onto the field, the crowd ripping and roaring.

"Dahl, will you stay with Kael?" Marcius requested. "Assist him through the process."

"Aye." Dahl responded coldly. Perhaps the rattle of the chains had stirred him as well.

"Wonderful. I must take my place among the court. I leave you to it then, Kael. Have no doubt, today will mark your second victory. Good luck." He shuffled his robes about to make himself more presentable before taking his leave.

"Court?" I asked of Dahl once Marcius had gone.

"Aye." Dahl nodded. "Nobles from across the land gather for the spectacle of the arena. It is not unusual for members of the lordship to visit the city, but today many of the elites have gathered. Marcius will most likely swoon under their graces while they remain in Verda."

"I see." My eyes moved over the dusty stone floor. "Are these men worthy of their titles?"

"Not only men, and no, most of them are not. They gather here in Verda for spectacle alone. The only other place you will find them gathered like this is Loughtia, a floating palace reserved as a private retreat for the lordship of the land." Dahl explained.

The match had well commenced in the arena. The fighting intensified as the crowd reeled.

"A floating palace?" I marveled at the idea, reflecting over the night of the festival when I had first heard of such a place. I tried not to think of Sarah.

"Aye. Loughtia itself was built and lifted into the canopy of a great oak that overlooks the marshlands to the south, near the Stone River. Chains hold the floating palace aloft, bound into the flesh of the oak. It is there that this self-proclaimed court of nobility host their meetings, high above the land they control. They are the ones most responsible for the twisted systems gaining hold over the land and its people. Already they seek negotiations with the Empire to secure their hold and further extend their reach."

"And they are gathered here?" I watched through the bars as blood sprayed. The people cheered.

"Indeed. You will likely meet them. Marcius loves to boast." Dahl predicted. The fight was nearing its end, only two remained standing on the field.

"It is tempting, my friend." I confessed.

Dahl agreed with a nod. "Many times have I nearly committed to it myself. But the people must be ready. When the time comes we shall offer our own terms, negotiated by way of sword and spear. For now, we must allow peace. Still your heart, know the path before you."

Dahl gripped the hilt of his blade. The horns sounded once more as the crowd ripped and cheered and booed. "It is time, Kael."

I steadied myself. The blade at my side was ready to draw, ready to sing. The gates opened. Only one man reentered the chamber. Blood soaked his chest where a nasty slash still oozed red. He was soaked with sweat and heaving, a short sword clenched in his fist, shackles about his wrists and ankles. His gaze was distant and empty as the guards roughly detained him, returning chains to the shackles that bound him.

"Dahl..." I all but whispered, unable to remove my eyes from the battered victor. "Are you sure this is the way?"

"To be champion of Verda is to be its king, even if for a day. The people will kneel so long as you hold that title. To conquer the city by force alone would spill far more blood than that of the arena, and the people will become confused, divided. Pity this man if you must, but know that your actions will spare others of his fate. Either way, you will meet resistance. Those who wish to keep things as they are will surely seek your demise. Win the hearts of the people, and even those who oppose you will have no choice but to follow. This is the way of it. Be strong, Kael."

Again he offered his blessing in ritualistic gesture. With his sentiment, I turned to the gates of the arena. This time when those to compete gathered, I was among them. At the command of the guard, we filed through the iron bars of the gate and made our way out onto the dust of the arena.

The sun was blinding for a moment, burning high overhead where it mingled with the edge of the canopy. The crowd roared like living thunder all around, as those to contend made their way to the center. There were eight others standing in the dust along with me.

Three wore the shackles of those condemned. Two were runaway slaves, another a man sentenced to his fate by the master who claimed his outstanding debts. Five were willing participants, driven by their own desires for fame and fortune. Two of the willing contenders whooped and hollered back at the living wave of spectators. The three in shackles stood in silence, while the guards that escorted them removed the chains that bound them. Once they were set loose, weapons were thrown to the dust at their feet.

Battle was soon to begin. As I waited for the violence, Dahl's words resounded in my mind. The message was clear, reminding me of the words my mother had spoken in my dreams; Be strong. The horns sounded, the crowd cheered. I ripped my blade free of its case as I initiated the change in a powerful torrent, whipping dust into the air.

One of the willing contenders advanced, lunging his blade for one of the runaways as he bent to retrieve a weapon. The fury of his movements were sluggish, nearly frozen against the change. His face contorted with aggression, eyes wide with the intent to slay, as the shaggy man in tattered rags bent to retrieve the battered short sword tossed at his feet.

He would not ready his guard in time. The moment slowly played toward a likely defeat for the lesser fortunate. The man was open, his attacker in the midst of a killing blow.

A second free contender advanced on me, only a few paces away, full stride with sword raised at the ready. I moved, slashing hard at my aggressor's right flank. The force behind my blade snapped through the short sword and sliced at his shoulder, as I passed. Clear of the assailant, I bounded in the direction of the shaggy runaway, hoping to reach him in time.

In an instant, I closed the distance with a parry, sliding the blade free of its intended target. Setting my focus on the aggressor, I felt the merit of his character. This man had killed many in his years, most for pleasure. He was a murderous wretch at heart, much like the man I had dispatched the day before. A career serving in the guard had been abandoned for the arena. I ran him through with a quick thrust, withdrew my blade, and stepped away.

The three men in shackles were behind me. The shaggy man I saved had retrieved the weapon at his feet, as did the other runaway next to him. Standing before the remaining three contenders, I breathed deep, focusing on each as I did.

Two were locked in battle, their form perfect. Neither was particularly sinister of character, but willing to kill all the same. The third had witnessed the bizarre display of my movements and stood dumbfounded, armaments in hand. Unsure how to react, he decided to advance, his heart refusing fear before the eyes of so many.

In a flash, I met him with a rising knee, landing it hard into his gut. Spinning clear of him as I landed, I set against the other two with the same force, leaving them defeated without death. One was swept down with a kick, the other struck hard across the ribs under his shield. I retreated back to where the three in shackles huddled in defense, weapons out. Breathing deep, I released the change.

The man that had advanced on the captives spurted blood upon the dust. The thrust of my blade had met its mark, melting the rage of his attack. The scruffy looking man he had meant to kill slashed wildly at his attacker, slapping the blade from the dying man's hand and landing a few swipes across his arm and midsection as he crumpled to the earth. Confusion spread, leaving the survivors wide eyed in panic.

The dying man gurgled his last syllables upon his sand colored beard. The light left his eyes. He was gone. The wounded contender I had slashed writhed and screamed upon the dust, clutching hard to his bleeding shoulder. I had cut him deeper than I had intended, but he would live. The others groaned, crumpled the same.

The man that had taken the knee to his gut gasped for air. Standing before the three captives, I slid my blade back to rest in its magnificent sheath and stood easy, my message clear. No more blood need be shed. Victory was sure. My gesture was well received, as the shaggy haired captive tossed his weapon to the ground. The other runaway followed his lead. The two of them stood with me, silent as the crowd roared. I bowed, my gesture of peace reciprocated in turn.

The crowd reeled with mixed emotion. Boos of disappointment rippled like a wave, as those who wanted bloodshed hissed their disdain. Others whooped and cheered at the spectacle they had witnessed. I smiled at this, for it meant there was indeed hope yet.

Several armed guards made their way into the arena, the clanking of metal chains followed them. They approached the surviving contenders, meaning to return them to captivity. The scruffy man looked into the dust at his feet as if he were facing execution. A guard delivered a strike to the back of his knee from behind, buckling him to the ground.

I reacted before I registered my intent, landing a force palm into the chest of the armed guard who had struck the man. The change had snapped with the motion, the force of my attack smashing hard against the metal chest plate, crunching at the man's ribs before sending him tumbling across the dusty arena. He was badly hurt, but he would keep his life.

I stood easy where I had landed the strike, right palm extended toward the downed soldier. The others stood frozen in their tracks, as I awaited their response. The soldier closest to me advanced, spear ready for attack, setting battle into motion.

With his advance I went kinetic, sidestepping the jab of the spear and lunging up its length to drive a nasty kick into the guard's ribs under his left arm. The momentum sent him into a somersault, and as he flipped through the air, I ripped the spear from his hands and tossed it to land with him.

Once again I stood easy, awaiting the next move. The two downed soldiers of Verda moaned and writhed about in the dust. The crowd flared into furious rancor.

More soldiers poured in from the iron gates surrounding the arena. I waited patiently as they encircled. Archers took positions in front of the crowd, aiming their arrows over the arena walls. The scruffy man I had freed stood with me, his back to mine. The others who had been in shackles with him shivered in fright, knees upon the dust. The man condemned for his debts held his hands up in panicked surrender. He was no fighter.

The circle tightened. I drew my sword, sliding it free with enough speed and energy that they felt the rush of it stir the air and dust. My intent was made as clear as my resolve. Their advance halted with the movement of the blade at my ready.

A voice boomed through the large bronze megaphone system, the big bell shaped mouth spewing reverberated sound over the arena. I followed the length of the apparatus to the private balcony on the third level. My eyes couldn't discern the individual standing before the mouthpiece, but when the voice sounded again, I recognized it to be Marcius. The crowd had grown turbulent under the fever of emotion, some wowing in amazed confusion, others roaring and cursing in anger.

"Well now, folks. That was a quickie!"

Marcius's voice sounded across the arena. The cries of the mob hit a crescendo. Somehow, when next he spoke Marcius seemed to quell the masses.

"It's been some time since we've had someone fool enough to attack the guard. Looking grim, ladies and gents."

Laughter rippled through the crowd. He was winning them. I held the line, blade in hand. The line of soldiers weakened, some began to shake under the weight of their readied spears. The shaggy haired man stood more boldly at my back. The other runaway rose to stand with us, finding his courage at last. The third began to weep, his hands remained up in defeat, knees upon the dust.

"So what'll it be?! Should we cut the guards a break and let this young contender fight another day?"

The crowd erupted into a negative frenzy.

"Hold on now, folks. This here is no ordinary fighter. This here is Mealocke, known in the desert of the east as the Salt King. Give him a chance, you've seen what he can do. Let him show you what he can become, a champion like no other!"

His words were true, but the crowd wasn't buying it.

"Boo!"

"More like Soft King!" Laughter rippled around the quip.

Marcius continued his appeal. "Come now, do you really wish to sacrifice more of our beloved guardsmen?"

As he worked at the viscous mob, I focused on my breathing. Reflecting on the moment, I eased my eyes closed against the sounds of men. The sky felt welcoming above me, and an image came to me of an eye staring into heaven. The elliptical shape of the arena, the circle of surrounding guards at its central point like an iris. In an instant I knew what I had to do. Sometimes seeing is believing, and I would end this quickly for all to see.

"I am going to disappear in a moment." I began to explain to the man at my back.

"What?!" He turned to me in confusion.

"When I do, run for the guards."

"You're mad!" The man shook his head with a nervous chuckle. The other agreed, wildly nodding his head. He was wide eyed and soaked with nervous sweat.

"Just before you reach them, drop and lay low. Okay?" I continued.

"Right. Run at the spears. Got it. How about-"

His words fell short, as I initiated the change and jumped hard for the blue of the sky. The cool rush of the hurried air was familiar and soothing, as I sprang higher. When I reached the peak of the climb, I breathed deep and held myself there of my will, slowing my descent from a fall to a subtle dip.

The view from the height no longer bothered me as it had before. I took it all in, as the two men below ran for the line of soldiers as instructed. A smile widened my face. I was floating in the sky at will, waiting to drop upon my prey like the mighty Shemah Yen. I thought of the twins, how much they would have enjoyed such a moment. They were masters of the double strike combo. This was for them.

The crowns of the elder forest were level with me, my only peers to the blue. The radiant sun was warm against the chill air of the sky. Down below the two runaways neared the spears of the guard and dropped as instructed. As they dropped, so did I.

Falling like a shooting star, I focused my intent, sending a burst of reticulated energy hard against the fast approaching ground with the swing of my blade to channel its direction. As I neared the ground, the energy met with the dust and ignited to disperse. I crashed into it, meeting it hard with another powerful release of energy from an extended palm.

A turbulent boom channeled an explosive wave outward, sweeping the circle of guards hard off their feet and back through the air. A thunderous gust of wind swept through the coliseum, shrouding all in a cloud of dust.

My eyes had closed against the force of the blast, and as I opened them I realized I had yet to reach the ground. Suspended there, I looked over the ruffled audience. The cloud of settling dust gave the air a golden hue. I exhaled gently to bring myself to rest on the Earth once more. Releasing the change, I returned my blade to its beautiful resting place.

As the dust settled chatter and panic resounded through the recovering crowd. The armed guards clamored to their feet, disheveled and banged up. No one seemed too shaken by the attack, though the entire coliseum was frazzled.

None of the guards readied their spears, some even fled. My point had been well received, before all. A raucous audience had been reduced to whispers. All around me were the eyes of the dumbfounded, belief surmounting.

"Citizens of Verda..." Marcius spoke through the megaphone. "Mealocke, the Salt King!"

The audience burst into cheers so suddenly it gave me a jolt from the force of it. The people that had but a moment ago called for my execution now jumped and cheered in approval. I turned all about, looking over the entirety of the dusty coliseum. The guards had recovered, seemingly confused on what to do next. The weeping captive had been blown across the arena and had yet to rise to his feet.

"Thunderboy! Thunderboy! Thunderboy!" The audience boomed.

"What on Earth was that?" Came the words from the brave, shaggy haired man that had stood at my side.

"That was a victory, my friend." I smiled. "A victory for all."

"Thank you!! Thank you, sir." He extended his hand in gratitude. I accepted. "So what happens now?"

In honesty, I did not know.

"You are free, decide for yourself. Go in peace." My words came as fact.

"Aye!" The man was ecstatic. "I'll not forget this. All will know of what you did here."

His dark eyes glistened, the expression on his face serious and hard. He was truly worthy of the chance he'd been afforded, and so many others like him still awaited in the campaign ahead. He turned, gesturing for his friend to follow. The pair made for the iron gate to the north, the same through which I'd come the day before. The familiar shape of an older man in robes came running.

"Kael!" Dahl all but screeched as he ran up to greet me. "What did you do?"

"What I had to." I responded.

"Most reckless. You got lucky." He hissed, catching his breath. "No one has ever stood up to the guard like that. They could have named you an enemy of the state. And worse, if the people had cowered in fear, it would have been the end of our cause, bam! Just like that."

"Relax, old friend." The scolding he delivered lacked the punch of conviction. "That did not happen. Now that they have seen what I can do, none will challenge my assent, none will oppose what we mean to do here."

"You may speak too soon on that..." Dahl cautioned. "Come, Marcius has sent for you."

"Of course." I responded, looking once more over the crowd as we made our way back into the inner keep of the coliseum.

As Dahl and I made our way through the innards of the colossal structure, he lectured me without relent until at last we arrived before a twin pair of gilded doors. Servants moved to pull the heavy things open, and within was a banquet set in a room of lavish decor. The opposite wall from which we had entered was much like Marcius' private chamber, all glass panes with doors open to a balcony that overlooked the arena.

Servants diligently moved about to serve what must have been a dozen well adorned social elites seated around the table, the lordship of the land no doubt. Among them I saw familiar faces. The two older men that had been convening with Marcius when we first met, the bald man with the mean face and the tall skeletal elder. Once again, they wore robes of purple and yellow.

"Ah! Here he is!"

Marcius announced with drunk enthusiasm. His rump all but bounced from its seat at the table, sliding his chair back with a groan across the floor as he stood. He approached and placed a hand on my shoulder.

"The one responsible for today's incredible entertainment, the Salt King himself."

The faces around the table changed, eyes widening.

"Are you mad?!" Came the shrill voice of the squat elder with the mean face.

"Marcius, what is the meaning of this?" Scolded the tall elder in yellow with a shambling voice.

"Now, now." Marcius gestured for them to lower their concerns. "He is here as an honored guest. Peace, my friends. Peace."

"Ha! Peace you say?" The angry faced elder tossed a napkin from his lap onto the table. "I watched him cut a man in two with a single slice before pummeling two armed guards. Pieces more likely."

I smiled at this. He spoke the truth before the aristocracy gathered here, perhaps a foreshadowing of their fates.

"Lord Dophil," Marcius all but pleaded, "he is not some mad killer on the loose. You saw that as well. Despite what he can do he chooses mercy. If he meant to harm any of us, I'm sure he'd already have done so. He isn't here to murder at random. He is here to win the champion title. Right, my boy?"

He turned to me with a friendly smile, awaiting reassurance.

"Right..." I smirked, looking over the uneasy faces of the so called lordship.

"Oh?"

Came the snooty voice of a rather thick bodied woman who sat at the table. Her gaunt eyes fixed on Marcius.

"And you are reduced to selecting your champions now? Most iniquitous. The system as it stands will crumble. What chance has any other named challenger against such a...", she looked me over as she struggled for the word with a sneer, "savage creature?"

"Aye!"

"Here's to that!"

The others barked in agreement, banging fists at the table to solidify their congruence.

"My friends, such concern is most unwarranted." Marcius consoled. "Fair is fair. The boy came to best his chances for arena champion. Yes, his abilities are quite extraordinary. Yes, it is likely that not even your best contenders could stand against him... But at the same rate, it is also likely to assume that none may appose anyone who stands by his side."

"And what do you mean by this, Maricius?" Asked another member of the table.

"Lords and Ladies, I present you the rising Champion of Verda. Never before have we seen this kind of raw talent, this much potential in any previous contender. Stand with us, let his might reflect your own... Or continue to name your own contenders and send them to certain defeat. The choice is yours. I'm asking that you join us, that we all work together." Marcius bowed respectfully with his final words.

"You're making a grievous mistake, Marcius." Dophil spoke from a face red with anger. He looked like a grape ready to burst. I half hoped he would.

"Sir?" Marcius inquired.

Dophil rose to his feet. The back of his chair stood nearly as tall as him.

"Do you really think that just because you flex some new hired muscle you get to call the shots? Expect us to simply fall in line did you? Ha! You've lost it completely. No way!"

"I think you misunderstand, Lord Dophil. The Empire-" Marcius began, but he was cut short.

"I think I understand just fine, Marcius. You'll not cut me out so easily. Enjoy your days at the top." Dophil spat.

"Same to you." My words surprised all, diverting the attentions of the room. "Marius will not be the one to cut you out. That measure will be done by those you exploit to build your cities, those you ensnare and enslave to amass your wealth."

"Kael!" Dahl attempted to still my tongue.

I advanced on the stubby man, my steps slow and heavy on the smooth cool surface of the polished wooden floor.

"This land will soon see a new age, and those who side with me will know the end of tyranny. This I promise. Enjoy your pompous titles, your 'days at the top' while you can, for they are false and empty. Soon all shall witness this truth."

"Kael!" Dahl grabbed hold of me. "That is enough! Come!"

He meant to drag me from the chamber. At first I meant to resist, but my better judgment knew he was right.

"You're right about one thing." Dophil called after us, as Dahl led the way to the exit. "A new age is indeed underway. Change is coming, and the victors have already been decided. Not even you, boy. Not even you stand a chance. Young fool..."

I simply smiled back. The first chance I got, he would fall.

Dahl was most displeased with my actions. As we walked the corridors he reminded me once again what was at stake, all but pleading with me to stick to the plan.

"Those vile people control everything. If you give them any reason to call you villain, you lose the support of the people, it's all over. It'll be war with Verda, war with the Empire. We can't win a war on all fronts!"

"It would seem that path is inevitable. Why play their games? From what I've heard today, even the arena is subject to their politics." My retort caught his attention.

"Indeed, Kael." He confessed. "They decide a great deal of what plays out in the arena, the city, the southern territories especially. This is why there is much suspicion and discourse around your sudden appearance. Those who control the arena, control the heart of Verda and all the common wealth attached to it. They will not relinquish their grip willingly."

"Do not forget, I came here to destroy Verda. What should I care about its politics?" I growled in challenge.

"Because, Kael. The battle truly exists in the hearts and minds of the people. If they fear you, they will not heed your call. They will not follow, they will not believe. But if they believe in you, if they accept the truth about their overlords, then the system will dissolve where it matters most, in the hearts and minds of the people. The lordship will lose influence across the land. Defeat the man, another shall take his place. Defeat the idea, and the concept itself disappears. It is not just Verda, but all the people of the land at risk here, Kael. That is why we must take care in our methods."

"I could defeat the forces of Verda alone!" I roared.

"I don't doubt you, my friend." He placed his hands upon my shoulders, his eyes deep with meaning. "Do this right, and you won't have to."

"But my people..." My emotions got the better of me, tears welling.

"The man who attacked your village was of the Empire, you were told this. He merely hired the soldiers he commanded. Terms were negotiated between the members of the council you saw earlier and an Imperial emissary." Dahl reminded.

"Why?" I asked, trying to fight back the tears. All my loved ones destroyed, the ways of my people lost, for no greater purpose than a deal struck between despots. And I was to be the villain.

"I don't have all the answers, Kael." He confessed. "The council has sought control of mount Yerok for generations. It was not difficult to sway them. As for the Empire and its motives, I know nothing."

"The scouts..." I pondered aloud.

"Scouts?" Dahl repeated curiously.

"The ones that carried me away from the flames of Reisenbough. They possessed powerful weapons, shared knowledge of the world. Just the four of them were able to drive off the big man that attacked me. If the Empire posses such might, why do they play these games? Why involve Verda?"

"Hmm..." Dahl gripped at his beard with his gloved right hand. "A most interesting line of thought, my friend. Why indeed."

"The truth will come in time." My stomach churned with hunger. My powers had left me drained.

"You hunger for truth?" Dahl laughed. "Come."

Dahl led the way to a large kitchen on the base level, a busy place filled with servants hard at work preparing food for the next meal. We made our way through the busy throng of white aprons and busy hands. The delicious aromas of breads, meats, and spices filled the air. In the far corner of the facility we found an old stained wooden table and a few wobbly chairs next to a storage room. Dahl spoke with an older maid, who fetched two bowls of hearty stew and half a loaf of sweet bread.

"Marcius is going to have his hands full." Dahl sparked conversation. "They didn't take well to you, my friend."

"It would seem so." I agreed, slurping at the savory flavors of the hearty stew. "They will cope. Those who survive."

"Getting ahead of yourself. The council controls nearly every aspect of life here in Verda. Their favor is crucial to your rise beyond the arena, and with their efforts against you, that's not going to be easy. Marcius has made a brash move, but perhaps it will work to our advantage. If the council considers Marcius their primary threat, they may focus their attentions on him." Dahl spoke in between bites of bread.

"Marcius can handle the lordship well enough. It is not the first time they have been at odds. But they are less than pleased with today's turn of events, that is sure. If tension surmounts, it is only a matter of time before this all spills over."

"I see." The stew was scrumptious. I had nearly emptied the bowl, dabbing at it with bread as I spoke. "They would do best to stay out of the way."

Dahl laughed. "Aye. Indeed. Not likely though. Marcius has no doubt retreated to his chambers by now. We should meet him there."

Dahl and I made our way to Marcius' chamber. Inside we found Marcius, sitting in his chair, looking rather disheveled. A cigar burned between his fingers, the smoke curling through the air. His eyes were distant. Frustration lingered around him like the cloud of dissipating smoke.

"Have a seat."

His lips were all that moved as he stared into space. We sat as he requested. A strange tension filled the space, as we patiently awaited his next words.

"Well..." Marcius finally began. "That could have gone better." His eyes fixed on mine. "You'll need to lay low for awhile, take some time off. Like we discussed."

"What?!" I nearly jumped from my seat. "I've only just started!"

Marcius flustered. "Look, its not going to be easy. The council is a den of snakes, and they didn't like your implications. This sort of thing doesn't happen every day. The people are buzzing about you more than ever, they're excited. In two rounds you've given them more than they've ever seen."

"Good." I smiled.

"Yes, well that's the good news." Marcius continued, taking a puff of his cigar. "The bad news is the council does not share in this enthusiasm. They consider you a liability, and now it seems I've lost a deal of favor as well. We are a direct threat to the establishment, my boy. The ultimatum thrust at me was to remove you from the arena or step down from my position. I'd sooner die, and considering how they do business, I just might yet."

"Let them try." My smile faded, anger heating my veins.

Marcius laughed. He took another puff of his cigar. "Oh, that they will."

"Ridiculous." Dahl interjected. "Banning a contender is unheard of. How can they?"

"They can't." Marcius responded, flicking the ash from his cigar. "The people won't have it. This ban of theirs will backfire. I give it a few days at most. It's a game of patience now. The people will call for Kael, and the council will have to oblige or loose favor."

He smiled big. "See, my boy? Your victory is merely delayed. Relax."

My anger dissolved, and I felt a bit foolish for my shortsightedness regarding the situation. "Very well. What now?"

"You need to disappear for the time being, take a vacation." Marcius suggested. "You've won twice now, even earned a bit of gold in the process. Go live a bit. This place'll be here. We aren't out yet."

"How long?" I was glad to know there was still a chance, but my patience was wearing thin. I had waited long enough.

"I'd say about a week, maybe more. However long it takes for the council to settle down. Let them think we yield to their authority while we wait for the people to demand your return. It's perfect really. You get to travel, rest, whatever you wish. Return after the break, and I assure you they'll be begging to have you back in the arena."

"Very well." Dahl replied as if he were speaking for me. "Then that is what must be done."

I nodded in concurrence.

"Then we agree. Excellent! A new plan of action." Marcius rose to stand before the glass windows.

It was growing late. Evening was not far. The sun was well hidden behind the blinds of the great forest. Torches began to flicker against the dark that crept across the empty coliseum.

"Of course there is much more to be done to help influence the people, but I'll do what I can to that effect." He turned to face us once more. "Matters are getting a bit more complicated. Dophil has managed the favor of the Empire. Or at least he claims as much. No doubt he will seek to use this resource to his advantage if we aren't careful."

His eyes fixed on me again. "Listen to me, boy. Dophil is a greedy scoundrel, but it would be far from wise to cross him at this stage in the game. I know little of the Empire or its capacities, but I know it's less than ideal for us should they get involved this soon. Be smart on this one, work with me. Understand?"

"Aye."

The response rumbled from me in such a way it sounded less than affirmative. I understood, but I cared not for this political squabble.

"Good." Marcius turned back to his view from the window. "It's getting late. That will be all for today. I'll continue to do what I can to pacify Dophil and convince the council. Rest easy for a bit. You leave tomorrow, just to be safe. Dahl, escort him to his chamber if you will."

Dahl began to shuffle to his feet, but I stopped him.

"I'll find my way, thank you."

He looked uneasy at this.

"Worry not, my friend. I understand what must be done and how." I assured.

I took my leave, thinking hard on the long walk through the corridors to my chamber. Feeling much defeated, I was far from ready for sleep. Why should I play their games? I was certain I could overcome anything the council was likely to throw my way. But then again, wouldn't it be the very people I sought to aid that would suffer in the fallout? My mind raced as I reached for the door to my chamber, happy to retreat to the privacy within.

Candles lit the gloomy confines of the room, casting shadows along the profiles of new furniture. What had been a simple, empty chamber was now filled with all manner of tables, ornaments, pottery, and flowers. I removed my blade from my side as I walked along a couch centered over a plush fur rug.

I looked over the new decor as I made my way to the bed. There was another couch adjacent, a small table between the two. As I neared, the quilts that covered the comfy bed suddenly rose, sliding down to reveal the beauty of feminine form.

It was her! Surprised by the reveal, I stumbled back over the arm of the ridiculous couch and toppled onto the floor, dropping my sword and scooting the table next to it hard with a screech.

She laughed. "As easy as that, I've toppled the champion himself! And I didn't have to lift a finger."

Embarrassment was an understatement, as I clamored desperately to my feet. "I'm not champion yet."

The words fell from my lips with no conviction, shock still hard upon me. She laughed again, rising from the soft, comfy bed. She was beautiful, truly a goddess upon the Earth.

"Oh?" She smiled, dragging the soft quilt with her across the space between us to stand all but nose to nose with me. "That's too bad. I've been waiting for the return of my champion..."

She drew close, her arms enfolding me with her in the warm quilt. Her touch was soft against my skin, her eyes deep with the colors of the forest, gold along the edges like the morning sun. Her scent lit a fire within me, as if I breathed the essence of life itself from her.

"Your champion?" I rattled.

In truth, my words were as distant from me as past dreams. I ran my hands up the smooth curves of her back, my fingers enmeshing in the thick dark mane of her hair.

"Are you?" She asked, her voice low with the drive of her desire.

I pulled her close to me as our lips met. The depth of this collision seemed to transcend all existence. The world that encircled us seemed immaterial. There was only this moment. Nothing had ever felt more right.

"Always." I pledged to her, as we collided in passion once more.

When our bodies met, I felt as if I'd plunged back into the Veylspring. Only this time it was warmth that flooded over my senses, a warmth like that of the summer sun. Adrift in darkness, a powerful spark ignited with my own. She was the part of the cosmos I'd been searching for without direction or knowing, my Lady Starlight..."

Knight of the Order

Day had faded from Paeon, as night gently covered the land outside the conference hall. The natural light of the world had been replaced by the iridescent glow of the busy port below the chamber, as Thaut waited patiently for Subject One to continue his story.

Thaut poured another round of drinks and reflected over what he had heard thus far. He contemplated a way to nudge life back into the conversation.

"Love..." He proclaimed as he finished refilling his guest's water. "Powerful stuff, that."

The old man's face lit with a smile, the crinkled lines of age exaggerated the expression. He didn't at all have the demeanor of a killer, nor did he seem particularly threatening to anyone, let alone to his Majesty's Holy Empire.

"Powerful stuff indeed." Subject One agreed.

He fell silent again. For a moment, he looked almost mournful. The picturesque view behind him had faded with the daylight, deepening the mood in the chamber. Thaut shuffled about in his chair to get comfortable. He followed a sip of water with a sigh.

"Well, you have me hooked, sir." Thaut confessed. "Adventure, romance, and even drama? This is by far the most enjoyable case I've ever worked."

Subject One laughed.

"I am glad." The gloom seemed to melt away, returning the weathered old man to something resembling contentment. "It's been a long time. Thank you for this, Investigator."

"Not at all." Thaut chimed. "The honor is mine. Ready when you are."

"Of course." Subject One responded.

"She and I were as one. Our affections carried us deep into the night. The candles burned low, as we shared in one another. We talked about life, the past and the present. She told me of her village, a small farming community nestled along the foothills of the southern marshland. She told me how she had fallen into servitude and come to Verda, taken forcibly from her home. Her life claimed to settle a debt that was not her own.

Passions ignited several times more before I told her of my home. Suddenly I found myself telling her everything. Fortunately my adventures hadn't been all bad. She laughed when I described the silly banter of the twins and my fight with Bone Nose of the Kifdah. She listened to the fate of my people, the falling of Krayton the Mighty and my defeat.

She spoke little of her own experiences leading to our union, and it seemed she had her reasons for that as she lay upon my chest by the warm light of the candles. The brisk night air crept in through the window, making the warm bed all the more pleasurable. The chill in the air told of autumn. The warmth in my being was that of spring. Together we were an island adrift, shining of light and hope, radiant with life and love. A peace embodied this union, a familiar feeling, much like returning home after a long journey.

It grew late. When sleep came, I did not know. Already I felt as if I were dreaming.

The next morning my eyes opened to the sound of a knock followed by the creak of the door opening. Marcius and Dahl entered in typical fashion. I sat up against the wall of pillows that lined the headboard.

"Good morning!"

Marcius smiled as brightly as the sunlight that peaked in through the shutters. He did a dreadful thing and opened them, letting in the full might of the morning sun.

"What do you make of your new accommodations? Not too shabby, eh?"

I looked around the chamber, seeing the new decor in the light. Lil lay next to me, one delicate foot kicked out from under the blankets and a fluffy mass of gorgeous dark hair planted in the pillows.

Dahl had already taken notice of the mess around the chamber, particularly the garments that did not belong to me. From there his eyes moved to the foot, to the hair. He smiled wide and stepped out from the chamber with a chuckle.

"What's got into him? Usually the man's a stone. Humor isn't really his-" Marcius stopped short. "Ah. I see."

He turned and politely made for the exit as well.

"We will talk over breakfast then? Bring your guest if you'd like." He shot a wink over a cheeky smile as he followed Dahl out the door. "We'll be waiting in my office, don't be too long."

The door closed. We were alone. Lil sat up with a frantic look around.

"That was Lord Marcius wasn't it?" Her eyes were wide and beautiful, even in panic.

"Yes. Well, Marcius anyway. You don't have to call anyone lord anymore if you don't want."

Embarrassed, she turned back to me. Her hair was everywhere, alive with the motion. A warm smile melted away her concerns when our eyes met. It was then I realized I was smiling too, like a lovestruck fool.

"And suppose I do? Then what?" She teased, chin bobbing about with attitude and playful mockery.

"Then by all means do. Woman..." I glared and crossed my arms, aloof in the moment with her. Together we laughed.

Laughter led to stretching, stretching led to play, play led to passion, and passion left her snuggled against me with her hand on my chest, one leg over mine. This embrace was powerful, compared only to the strongest submission holds I had encountered over the years. My arm beneath her was forfeit, her hand gently laid upon my chest with immovable weight. Yes, she had me pinned against the world, a world I had all but forgotten, lost there with her.

By the time we managed to crawl out of the cozy bed we were late, to say the least. As we scrambled for clothes, she began to second guess accompanying me among the lordship and thusly began to protest.

"What if they don't approve of our union quite as we'd like, my dear?" She asked, arms flat at her side as if she poised the question in defeat, concern across her delicate brow.

I forced her robes down over her head.

"Nonsense." I reassured her.

She was a mess, her hair hopelessly tangled with the tattered clothes around her neck. She sighed in defeat, laughing when her hands moved to fix the tangled robes, fitting them down over her shoulders.

"Well, here goes nothing I suppose. You're trouble..." She smiled warm, almost deviant.

"The best kind." I kissed her softly, my beautiful mess.

By the time we finally arrived at Marcius's office, they had well finished eating and sat about the dimly lit chamber. There was a somber tone about the space. Boss sat slumped in his tall chair, something like defeat in his eyes as they stared through the slow serpentine trail of smoke that rose from his idle cigar. Dahl sat comfortably upon a small sofa along the wall by Maricius's desk. Concern marked his face.

"Nice of you to join us. Come. Have a seat." Marcius didn't stir from his daze.

Lil was noticeably uncomfortable. I took her hand.

"Relax. All is well." I gestured toward the comfy furniture where Dahl sat. "Wait for me?"

"If I must." She managed a smile, as she nervously drifted toward the cozy corner.

Dahl bowed and welcomed her to a space across from him. I took the seat in front of the large desk.

"Well my boy," Marcius began with a deep breath, "things could get ugly from here. It may take some time before we can continue this campaign."

"What?!" I all but exploded. "Why?"

"Looks like trouble." His eyes remained glazed with whatever held his mind.

"Trouble?" I inquired, all but numb with anticipation. "You said it would only be a few days."

"Aye." He responded, rousing from his slouchy trance and becoming the sly gentleman once more. "Things have changed. According to a little birdie, it seems someone has sent word to the Empire about yesterday's unusual performance in the arena."

Dophil.

"And?" I urged him further, hoping the heat that flushed through me was less than evident.

"Not good." Marcius drifted a bit. "If they actually do posses the influence to spur Imperial interest, probably best you not be here when the hounds arrive."

"So what then?" Frustration began to rattle my voice. I wouldn't surrender. I'd come this far.

"It's not forever, just a break like we discussed. Nobody is giving up. Take some time off, go on hiatus and travel, maybe see a bit more of the world before you jump headfirst into the grinder. Right, my boy?" Marcius chuckled a bit, a smile following a nasty puff on his cigar.

"Hiatus? You mean hide." I sneered.

"Gasp!" He feigned with laughter. "No, not at all, sir. We don't cower before the challenge of an adversary! No! Rather, we go on holiday at a critical time, avoid any entanglement with Imperial forces altogether if possible. They can't fight us if they can't find us."

He smiled again. "Just for a bit, until this all blows over. Breathe. Live a little. I mean, it's a nice chance for a honeymoon." He looked at Liallia then shot me a wink.

I felt myself flush. Both Dahl and Marcius laughed.

"Tour the countryside with your lady friend, live a little. Find victory any way you can. Let them chase their tails while you enjoy the good life. You win, they lose. Am I right?" Marcius smiled, much more himself at the confidence of his words.

When my eyes found hers, I was flustered no longer. It was an excellent idea actually. "Very well, then."

"Wonderful!" Marcius rang like a bell. "Dahl will accompany the two of you as well."

He rose from his chair, prompting the rest of us to do the same. He made his way from around his large desk.

"I've sent orders for a caravan, but it will take some time to prepare." He took a sip of his strong drink. "Make yourself hard to find in the meantime. Just in case."

"The market." Lil suggested.

Marcius reflected for a moment. "Yes, it's booming by now, no way you'll be spotted in such a crowd. Hiding in plain sight. Excellent, my dear."

He reached into the waistline of his robes and produced a small purse, tossing it my way. I caught the thing. Heavy metal coins jingled inside.

"Treat yourself." He winked with a smile. "Now I really must be off, already running a bit behind waiting for you two lovebirds. So much to be done in a day." He shuffled his robes and fixed his collar. "Dahl my friend, I'll send word once we are clear."

Dahl simply nodded in affirmation.

"Good luck all!" Marcius left the chamber.

"Kael, we will depart from the east gate. Do you remember the way?" Dahl inquired.

"Yes." I responded. No way I could forget such a rotten place.

"Good. Don't be long." He instructed.

"Aye."

And so we went our separate ways. Dahl left for the east gate, Lil and I for the markets of Verda. She led the way through the busy crowd outside the coliseum. As we walked, she told me much of Verda. Better yet, she showed me. Together we walked the busy common areas, the bazaar outside the coliseum was only the beginning.

Deeper into the city, the Allichene hid the sky overhead much like back home, but unlike the trees of Reisenbough these had been bound and manipulated to support the weight of the upper levels of the city. The great boughs of the trees looked to have been bent and intertwined at great lengths until the entire canopy had become a floating village.

At first I was awestricken by the sight. Never before had I seen such a thing, nor considered it. I marveled at the size of it all, as we ascended a wide stairway leading to the upper level.

Reisenbough had been a fraction of the size. Shops and homes were carved into the hearts of the sacred trees, others built upon the branches where they joined their stalks. There were even structures suspended to hang alongside the wooden bridges and platforms that made the streets of the upper levels. An intricate system of rope bridges connected it all as if it had been constructed by a colony of arachnids more so than people.

All around us were the citizens of higher Verda, lavishly dressed in colorful robes. Beads and jewelry jingled and sparkled. Accessories of all manner and fashion suggested the citizens of higher Verda did well for themselves.

The common footwear was unique to the region. The women wore open shoes made of elaborately woven leather straps leading up the soft curves of the calf. The men wore a more simple version that tethered about the ankle.

We had missed breakfast, and the smell of food was everywhere, churning my guts with hunger. As she walked, I followed the fluttery rise and fall of Lil's beautiful dark hair, tangled in a chaotic mess of tight curls. The forest came to life when she turned to tell me more of this place with a vibrant smile like the moon herself. Once we were in range of a food stand, I stopped her immediately.

The vendor was a rather large fellow with a skimpy mustache. He seemed friendly enough, his round face making him look all the merrier. The hat that clung to the top of his head looked a bit small for the job, yet somehow it complimented the Verda experience.

"Good day, travelers!" The man greeted us.

Lil and I snickered to one another at his assumption. Close enough.

"Welcome to a full flavor experience! Fresh seared steak, skewered with the finest produce, shipped daily from the south roads."

Juicy hunks of seared meat pressed layers of sliced vegetables tight along the length of each flame kissed skewer. The air around the stand was savory with the spicy smell of seasonings. I eagerly collected two handfuls. The man's face bloomed with excitement.

"Wonderful! Smart thinking, lad. Feed her well, keep her happy." He chuckled with delight. "Have you got coin?"

"Aye." Liallia took over the commerce, as I gnawed at the skewer closest to my face.

"That'll be three pieces, please." The man smiled, his hands patiently crossed before him, resting on his round belly.

Lil produced the coin from the small purse Marcius had given and handed it over to the man, tucking the rest into the confines of her tattered robes.

"Thank you! You two have a blessed day! Enjoy your visit." The man waived.

I offered a skewer to my lady. She snuggled in close with a tight hug, pressing the sharp ends of the skewers at my face as she squeezed. I dodged the skewers and adjusted, righting myself against the impact of her loving embrace.

"This is all too dreamy." Her eyes were piercing. She kissed me with a quick peck on the cheek then bit into a skewer.

I leaned in between the tasty skewers and planted a greasy kiss on her brow as she chewed. The world and all its troubles seemed distant. As it did all the days she was with me.

We had our fill of the tasty skewers as we continued our tour of Verda. A lengthy bridge connected the two greater chapters of the city's upper level. It had little to no sway, solid and wide as the street below. Thick, powerful ropes held the structure intact, woven together with incredible tensile strength. Below the streets were busy with the commerce of midday.

Traversing the bridge landed us in the canopy of the tree adjacent to where we had ascended. The familiar stroll of the well dressed citizens along the wooden decks lined with shops completed the scene. Lil turned west, leading deeper into the forest, further into the innards of Verda.

"We should return soon." I reminded.

"Of course. There's something I want you to see first." She reached for my hand. West we went.

Her steps became lighter, as we hastily made our way along the rows of vendors and their trinkets. The shops began to thin. More and more the structures took on the windows and thresholds of private homes. Ahead was an intersection of sorts. The path leading further west met with a bridge leading south to another chapter. Next to it was a stairway leading down to the lower levels.

As we neared the corner of the last shop on the stretch, a weathered old voice called my name, or something like it.

"Master Kael! Young Sir!"

It was the tailor from the coliseum. Ton, as Marcius had called him. He hailed from the doorway of a shop across the way. I grabbed Lil by the hand and together we crossed to meet the man, if for no other reason than to prevent him from shuffling the distance himself.

"Ah, young master." He greeted us with kind warmth.

"Kael." I dismissed the title.

"Kael." Ton smiled. "Lucky day, seeing you here. You saved an old man a trip across the city."

He chuckled as he turned for the door of the shop and shuffled through. "Come, come."

The small shop was cramped with all manner of linens and materials. Dozens of shelves lined the cozy walls, stacked high with folded cloth and rolls of colored threads. The very air smelled soft, tinged with the musty smell of tree and age. Several outfits were modeled upon static displays that somewhat resembled human form. Behind a counter, the boy who had accompanied Ton the day before watched us with a vacant expression.

"We finished a bit earlier than expected." Ton explained, working his way to the counter. He pointed and the boy recovered a parcel from beneath the counter. "Young hands work faster. Another fine apprentice will survive me yet."

The apprentice opened the wrappings of the parcel to reveal the attire the two had made for the Salt King. He offered forth the trousers.

"Young Sir. Do have a look for yourself." Ton insisted with both pride and confidence.

The fabric was soft to the touch, dark and faded, a dull black in color. It was thick and durable, yet light in my hands. I commenced to donning the outfit then and there.

The trousers fit nicely, perfect for mobility. I wrapped the waist cloth that would hold them in place. It was the same soft material, a bit lighter in color.

"I used the best possible materials for the job. This is by far my finest work in years. The material is light but strong. You will be swift, protected from the elements. The material breathes a bit, and the fine thread prevents the garments from clinging to the environment, reducing snag. Black, for stealth, but also so that the dust of the arena adds a chalky look to it, really solidifying the salt theme. As for the silvery threads of arachnid silk used to reinforce the major seams, your bones will likely give before they do." He boasted with a hearty laugh.

Next the boy offered a pair of stained hide boots. I slid them over my dirty bare feet with ease. They were a perfect fit, tethered and laced with the same fine leather that made them. The design was much like that of the Dóvai, worn in the cold of winter. So similar in fact, that it caught me for a moment.

Only the caliber of craftsmanship, the quality of the materials used set them apart. They felt great. Ton was indeed a master of his craft. He continued to boast as I fastened the tethers to fit over the bottoms of the trousers, creating a blousing effect.

"Ideal for just about any terrain, light and comfortable. The thicker, more dense sole still bends with the foot, allowing for stealth when needed. Much like the hunters of old..."

I shed the last of my soiled attire, the worn hide tunic that had protected my broad shoulders from the heat of the sun. I took care not to disturb my headband in the process before tossing it to lay with the rest. The smooth feel of the new tunic was cool and tingly as I slid it over my body. It was invigorating. I felt as shiny as the silver threads that shimmered in the light, woven to contrast the dark material they bound.

"This last piece really ties it together."

Ton himself stepped forward to present the final item from the parcel, as I finished fastening my blade at my side and tucked away my knife. He held a squarely folded bundle of dark cloth. Taking hold of the thing, he unraveled it to reveal a dark hooded cloak.

"Protection from the elements, and a touch of class." He smiled warmly as he placed the cloak about my shoulders and fastened it into place with two silver clasps.

The cloak was soft and thick, hanging down just above the knee. Fluffy tufts of black fur lined the hood that laid at my back. Never before had I adorned garments as finely crafted as this. I felt refreshed, anew. Marcius was right. It had indeed made a world of difference.

"Your eyes bear the color of the old blood. Reminds me of a time when there was sense in this world. Perhaps the rumors sweeping the land are playing tricks on an old mind, but I felt inspired upon meeting you, young sir. Forgive my curiosity, if I may ask, but is it true? Do you come from the northern tribe?"

"Aye. Your wisdom has not failed you, master craftsman. I am Kael, son of Krayton the Mighty, the last warrior of the Dóvai."

For all I knew my words were true.

"My boy." Ton reached to embrace my hand in both of his. They were leathery with age. Tears welled in his eyes. "I am sorry for your people. Know that the hearts that are left to this land are with you. It is an honor, young sir."

"Saiyu." I spoke the blessing, returning the elder's embrace. "An honor shared. Thank you."

Ton smiled, a single tear caught in the gray of his beard. He retreated behind the counter with his less than enthused apprentice. Lil wrapped her arms around me under the cloak. The sentiment of the moment caught her as well, her eyes sparkling like magic.

"This suites you well, my dear." Lil cooed, as her hands explored the tunic under the cloak.

I took her in my arms, the cloak swallowing her against my chest. Her robes were still those of a servant. Rags could never hide the beauty of her grace. She was fit for majesty, those things of the Great Mother that a man could not hope to thread.

"For my lady." The thought escaped my lips. Lil giggled.

"Young sir?" Ton questioned after the ambiguity of my words.

"Do you have anything fitting of her?" I asked.

"Ah!" His face lit with excitement. The old man erected from his stoop over the counter to shuffle our way. "Of course, of course. How silly of me." He laughed. "A dress for the lady? Not a problem at all. Excellent suggestion."

"Kael, I-" She began, but I hushed her with a kiss.

"Our journey awaits. Anything you wish, my dear."

Ton and his apprentice assisted Lil as she browsed through the cramped shop. She looked over a few before she found the one she wanted. Violet in color, it all but shimmered in the light.

Ton refused to take payment for the item. Marcius would settle things later according to their agreement. As we departed from the little shop, he insisted Lil take a knit shawl as well for the chill of the season to come. The encounter had been wonderful. Ton shared more than just his craft. He shared the light of kindness, proving that it existed even here where it was needed most.

Much time had passed, and surely we were due for departure. From the shop, Lil led the way back to the intersection we had approached before Ton hailed us. Rounding the corner, we descended the stair passage to the lower level of Verda.

Gone were the lavishly decorated doorways and monuments of the upper world. Down in the gloomy belly of the city the people wore simple tunics and trousers, far less expressive in color and craft. The air stank of rotting debris and feces dropped down from the world overhead. Crudely constructed shelters replaced the finely carved and constructed marvels of the upper city.

"These are the citizens of Verda I wanted to show you." Liallia led our way east through the filth littered streets.

A dead man lay among the trash piled along the street as if he'd been tossed there all the same. Hunger. Pain. Disease. How could this be, in a place with such wondrous possibility? Shame, that was all this was. For any people that did not care for their own, it was shame.

"Change is coming. We can help them." My grip tightened on her hand as we walked.

Suddenly my garments didn't feel as great. The food in my gut was heavy with guilt, as we passed the sad faces of hungry onlookers. For the cost of a few coins that hunger could be stopped, the same coin thown at my feet in tribute for the spectacle of violence in the arena. When at last we stepped into the busy main street of Verda, I was most glad to leave the darkness of the back streets behind.

We emerged near the coliseum. Vendors stood along their carts and wares. The crowd was colorful again. This had been my first impression of Verda, yet I could not see it the same.

As we neared the coliseum, the crowds thickened. The vendors called to us along the way. Anything one could desire, garments and jewelry, knives and flints. Even colorful works of art were open for exchange. The forest above had thinned, and the smell of people was ripe as the midday sun blazed overhead. We had nearly reached the main entrance to the coliseum when a hollow dark face caught my eye.

It was a mask of sorts. There were many others set along the display, but this one appealed to me, drawing me closer. A squat elder approached, a little old lady with a kind face. She greeted Lil and I as we looked over her wares. The face of the mask was black, though the pale colors of the wood from which it had been carved peeked through the dark, giving a textured accent to the woeful expression it wore.

"Ah, that one is unique, even for my collection." The elder spoke in a soft welcoming voice, as she reached to remove the mask from its resting place.

"I found this one while traveling the southern forests. My husband and I meant to see all the land in our youth. I'd say we did well enough." She chuckled warm with memory. "This is known as the mask of souls."

She offered it forth with both hands. "Far to the southeast is a nomadic tribe known as the Bhedwii. The warriors of that tribe wore masks like this in battle. They believed that the spirits of their ancestors would allow them foresight and see them to victory in defending their people."

I took hold of the spooky thing. It was lighter than I had expected. The inside was smooth to the touch, well surfaced. Lil awed at the elder's story, as I gawked over the mask.

Worn by warriors? It was perfect. I put it on, feeling the hard wood against my face. I looked to Lil and playfully swooped at her while making my best phantom sounds behind the mask.

"Oh, no!" She playfully pushed me away. "Take it off, you creep! Stop!" She giggled as she playfully struggled to get clear.

"It lifts my heart to see such love, so young in the bud." The elder smiled, her soft dark eyes glazing as if lost in the reminiscence of days past.

"Trade, madam?" I asked holding the mask in hand again.

Her smile brimmed, as she chuckled softly. "What would you offer, young sir?"

I produced the pouch of metal coins, but when I offered it forth she gently pushed it back to me. "Take care of her always, lad. Let this promise be your trade."

"Aye, I will madam. Thank you." I bowed in the way of my people, deep as my gratitude.

Lil hugged the old lady, leaving a few of the gold and silver coins on her cart despite her protest. I secured the mask, and we continued for the east gate where Dahl waited.

The east gate was not as busy as the last time I had seen it. The smell of dung and spices thickened the air, a confusing aroma that assailed the senses. Disgruntled workers moved crates and woven baskets, heavy with produce from the southern territories. The large iron bars of the cages held an assortment of living creatures, some to the likes of which I had never seen.

A roar shook the open confines of the smelly place, at its source was the mighty hatual. The size of its fangs as it roared seared into my memory. Many times had I heard the story of that legendary battle, but now I had new context to go with those tales. It sent shivers down my spine.

Adjacent to the cell holding the hatual were the terrified faces of those enchained. They huddled in the corner furthest from the creature's angry reach. The cramped confines of the cell left little room for error.

I tried not to look further into this cell as I passed, lest I do something rash. They would be free, the cycle of tyranny broken. I promised this in the tongue of my ancestors as they faded from my peripheral. Lil held tight to my arm.

We found Dahl waiting near the stables outside the gate. He paced, his left hand upon the hilt of his saber, his cloak folded back over his shoulders as if he were expecting battle at any moment. A well loaded carriage awaited its passengers. A team of horses kicked and snorted, ready to move. The sun shimmered over their shiny coats.

"Kael!" Dahl approached in haste. "We mustn't wait any longer. The Empire is here in Verda! We leave now."

No discourse followed, though I felt a familiar defiance swelling within me. I did not like the idea of running from my enemy.

I helped Lil into the carriage, then climbed in after her. Dahl took to the stage and manned the reigns, sending the horses forward with a heightened vocal command and the crack of a whip. The horses surged forward, and the carriage began its bumpy voyage along the southern road.

"What is it?" Lil consulted. Frustration must have been evident on my face.

"Just my pride." I admitted.

"Is that all?" She giggled.

Neither of us truly understood the dangers manifesting around us. It didn't matter. Her hand in mine was real. That was all that mattered.

"I'll take care of that ego." She teased, kissing me softly.

I felt better. Yet, as the carriage bumped and rolled down the dusty road alongside the Coliseum, the images of the day reflected in my mind. The hungry people hidden in Verda's dirty underside, those enchained in the gross confines of the east gate. The unknown threat from which we fled... I looked to the solemn face of the mask at my side. Impulsively, I sprang into action.

"Stay with Dahl. I shall return." I kissed her deeply then climbed from the carriage to make for the sky.

"What? Kael-"

She called after me, but it was too late. I initiated the change and bolted high. My destination was the arena, where the Imperial guests had no doubt gathered for the spectacle held at high noon. They would certainly get a show this day.

I fitted the mask of souls over my face, as I bounded up and over the high walls of the Coliseum. The crowds filled the seats. The lordship stood colorfully along the railing of the high balconies. Several figures battled on the arena below, as I pulled the hood up over my head, landing hard at its center, stirring the dust with the flutter of the cloak.

The moment lingered, suspended with the change like the dust that whirled in the air. With the smooth flow of my breath I released the change easy, and the tempo of the world returned. The whirling dust settled about me, chalky against the soft dark fibers of my new clothes. I threw the cloak back over my shoulders, revealing the shimmering scabbard and the magnificent blade at my side. The timbre of the crowd flared and roared.

"Thunderboy! Thunderboy!"

I smiled wide beneath the mask. If dreams came true, I was certainly on the path to this realization. Let them try and stop me, I gloated.

The excitement of my intrusion interrupted the match underway and brought the battlefield to a standstill. There were only four contenders left standing, one of which was wounded and bleeding. The confusion cleared, and the moment was over.

Three of them moved to encircle me. The wounded man kept his distance. Standing at the ready, I waited patiently for the three aggressors to act. The crowd roared and stomped until the very Earth shook with anticipation.

I looked them over. My vision was somewhat limited, peripheral sight all but lost to the mask. Luckily, with my heightened abilities I would not need to rely so heavily on sight once combat initiated.

The wounded man paced a bit slower than the rest, maintaining his distance. His face was blank, his breath heavy. Now and then he would spin a short sword as if to keep it ready, holding his shield hard at his side. It did nothing to hide the blood spilling down his left flank. He had already begun to shiver a bit. He wouldn't last much longer.

Those still thirsty for combat circled. One brandished a strange metal blade to the likes of which I had not seen before, like a dagger in the shape of a sickle moon. No doubt the weapon held intrigue, coupled with the straight dagger in his other hand, its razor sharp tip ready to plunge into any opening. The two surely made for a lethal combination.

There was a thicker man, strong on his feet, a mean face behind the shielding of his helmet. Sweat poured down his thick, hairy gut. He carried two spiked axes, one clutched tight in each hand. Either of which seemed more than capable of delivering a fatal blow. The others gave him plenty of space as they circled.

The fourth and final contender clutched tight to a long pointed spear. A cloth obscured his face, his eyes void of all but purpose as they set upon me. No doubt he was fast, but undoubtedly not fast enough.

The circle began to tighten. A grin rose to my face beneath the mask. I steadied myself. Almost...

Suddenly the man with the spear changed his footing, the signal I was waiting for. He lunged his spear hard. Before the wicked point neared its target, I initiated the change and pulled my blade free with a mighty swing. The added energy behind the force sent my attacker reeling through the air, splitting the spear like a twig.

The other two attacked in turn. I dipped under the heavy swings of the big man and his axes, driving the hilt of my sword hard into the right side of his large gut. Somewhere under his blubbery belly, his liver took the hit. He would be down momentarily.

The bleeding man backed away, his sword and shield at the ready, panic on his face. He looked faint, weak from the blood he'd lost. While my attention was set on the injured man, the combatant with the daggers threw the strange curved sickle hard at my back.

Had it not been for my abilities, this attack may have been my defeat. Reflex set body in motion, and I moved clear of the flying sickle before sending a powerful gust attack his way with the swing of my blade. The release of energy sent him tumbling through the air. When he hit the dirt, I was there, a soft stomp to his gut to finish the attack. He was hurt, he was done.

The man with the long spear had righted himself back to his feet, looking to his broken weapon with astonishment. The large sweaty man had buckled to one knee. The shock to his liver had caught up to him. The bleeding man had scarcely moved, trying desperately to keep up with my movements in vain. The man with the spear advanced again, this time charging forth ready to skewer me with his splintered weapon. Moving with the energies at my disposal, I became one with their flow. Whatever had inspired this shift in me moved with peace, like the flowing waters of the Veylspring.

Though I bested my opponents with ease, I did not slay or harm them beyond defeat. I countered the incoming attack, redirecting the jagged tip of the spear to a safe direction. Maneuvering around the advancing spearman, I propelled him clear of me with a stern kick to his backside.

He sailed wide and crashed hard into the large man doubled in pain. There was blood, but neither would perish. I released the change.

I turned to the last man standing, raising the end of my sword to point intently in his direction. He shook violently. His eyes widened then rolled back as he fell limp upon the dust. I lowered my blade, and the crowd went wild. This marked my third victory in the arena, bringing me closer to claiming the champion title.

A series of crackling pops pervaded the air, setting my hair on end. A figure appeared through the dust across the arena. I had not seen him enter. He stood proud and crisp, his clothes sleek and black, ornamented with many shiny metal rivets and buckles.

A cape draped about his profile. His smile was sinister, lips curled back into a wicked expression. A new challenger then? I initiated the change. There would be blood for the finale.

Scarcely had I initiated the change than an outstretched hand reached for my face. I drew back in surprise, but the fingers had already clutched hold of the mask through the eye holes, pulling it hard from my face as I withdrew. Much to my astonishment, the caped figure had cleared the distance faster than I could react, even in the accelerated state.

"Ah Zami boy, so good to see you!"

The fiend spoke, his accent thick and heavy. I couldn't explain the dread I felt, as if I knew him, as surely as I would know defeat if I faced him now.

"Shall we?" He asked, releasing the clasp of his cape.

He stepped away from it as it slowly dropped away under the change, revealing the wide metal guard of the rapier at his side. It was coupled with a dagger, a formidable setup I somehow recognized.

The rapier hissed like a vile serpent as it pulled free. My blood ran cold with terror. I all but panicked, as he surged into motion. This time I saw him move, and still it was all I could do to avoid the hissing slash of the rapier.

No longer was the change advantageous. I felt slow, locked in fear. The fury of his attacks knew no relent, no restraint. I had to think of something quick, I had to escape. I parried a blow from the rapier, the force of it far greater than the blade should have withstood. The power of it set me off balance. The next attack nearly met its mark, tearing at my cloak.

He was far more knowledgeable of the change, far more skilled. My heart pounded in my chest. His smile was that of a madman. I was far outmatched and bound to fall.

In a moment of desperation, I released a burst of energy hard at the ground, kicking up a whirling cloud of dust, focusing a sandy gust deliberately for his face. In the same movement, I shot skyward in hopes of finding cover in the canopy above.

High above the structure of Verda's coliseum, I clung to the stem of a broad leaf in the crown of an elder tree. I released the change in hopes of better hiding myself. Rigid as the trunk of the elder tree, I didn't dare move, quietly swaying with the wind.

Nothing.

Had I lost him that easily? I thought of initiating the change and focusing my senses, but as surely as I could sense him he would sense me in turn. Instead, I waited a bit longer just to be sure. When I felt it was clear, I moved along the canopy as swift as I could, reserving my abilities to avoid detection. Liallia became my only concern. How very foolish I had been to deviate from the plan.

I found the caravan easy enough, still riding south along the road not far from where I had encountered the bandits on my first trip to Verda. I ran alongside the carriage, opened the door and hopped inside with the flutter of my cloak.

"Kael!" Her eyes were alive with concern as her hands reached for me. "Where did you go?!"

I returned her embrace and kissed her deeply. "Somewhere I shouldn't have."

The steam flushed from her soft face, as her fingers found their way to my hair. "Don't ever leave me like that again."

"Aye, love." I replied.

Exhausted from the ordeal, I buried my face in the soft material at her lap. With her at my side, the world fell away. I felt there was nothing I could not endure. She was all that mattered. How foolish it made my ambitions feel, my pride, my selfish desire for revenge. We could run from the Empire forever for all I cared. Feeling her there, I drifted into an uneasy sleep.

Gan Levan and the Stone River Valley

I awoke to the sound of Dahl's voice, as he yipped and commanded the team of horses. The carriage groaned to a stop, rocking with a sharp sway as Dahl disembarked. Liallia had fallen asleep as well, her delicate features angelic in the soft light that peaked through the pulled curtains. She woke with the commotion, a smile rising to the subtle curve of her lips well before her eyes began to flutter.

"Welcome back." I brushed her cheek with the back of my hand. "You were sleeping sound."

Her smile brightened, she rocked with a giggle. "Me?! You barely said a word before you began to snore."

There was a knock at the door before it squeaked ajar. "We stop to rest. Long enough to water the horses, then we leave."

My body was stiff from the long ride in the cramped confines of the cabin. With a stretch and a groan, I toppled from the coach to meet solid ground. The shiny scabbard banged clumsily about the doorway behind me with the drop.

"Save it for the arena, will you love?" Lil teased as she playfully kicked at my backside, waiting for me to move.

No good. My legs were still asleep and wobbly.

We were in a small village, mostly mud and straw huts with a bit of stonework here and there. It seemed to be a farming community of sorts. The gentle golden sway of grains and leafy green sprouts outlined the village in rows.

The soil was dark and moist, almost squishy underfoot. The ferns grew thick among the other plants, mostly soft leafy varieties. The smell of rich soil and damp rotting vegetation saturated the air. Peace lilies seemed to flourish naturally upon the landscape, the white bells accenting the leafy greens.

High above were the branches of a great elder tree, the massive bulk of its trunk to the southwest. Far to the north were the faint outlines of what I assumed to be the Tomb of the Shadjah.

"What is this place?" I asked, turning to lend a hand to Liallia.

"The eastern most village of the marshlands, Gan Levan." Dahl explained. "We can rest here for a short time. Stay close."

"Gan Levan?" Lil repeated, as she stepped down from the carriage. "Been a long time."

"You know this place?" I asked, half distracted by her grace as she looked around, spinning in the violet dress. She truly belonged among the flowers.

"I know the land." She smiled, closing her eyes against a memory. "There are other small villages much like this. Would you believe me a farmer's daughter?" She laughed.

I took her hand once more. It made perfect sense to me. This place where life flourished, where the Mother provided nourishment for all to grow. The peace. The lilies...

"Did you notice?" She pointed to the canopy.

The shock of what I saw jolted me back to reality. High above the greens of the land was a great structure, hanging from the boughs of the elder tree. It looked to be a palace of sorts, suspended by several massive chains.

"They call it Loughtia." Lil explained. "The nobility of the lands gather there. Not just anyone with a title, lordship only kind of thing. Rumor has it that all the wealth in Verda is manipulated and controlled from right up there, far away from the city. If Verda has a heart, that'd be it."

"Meh. A nest of vermin, held aloft." Dahl spat with a grimace, his hand waiving in dismissal.

"Marcius has a lot of friends up there, so I hear." Lil smirked.

"Just long enough to tend the horses, then we leave." Dahl reiterated, ignoring her implications. "We've made it through the marshlands. From here we go south to the Stone River, make camp by sunset. Best to avoid settlements."

He turned to make his way to a small stable where a man waited. No sooner had Dahl stepped away than Lil turned to me, her eyes glowing with fury.

"What happened back there?"

I felt the smile drain from my face, panic flush through me. "Failure."

"Failure?" Her face scrunched a bit in confusion. Even in the midst of interrogation she was beauty. "Kael, what happened? What did you do?"

She was serious, concern evident on her face, evident in her voice, her eyes. The sick churn of foreboding gnawed at the truth like a stone in my gut.

"I met my match in the arena." I admitted.

"The arena?!" She all but gasped.

"Aye."

"Kael!" She belted in a voice as hushed as she could manage. "Why?!" Fire lit the depth of her eyes.

"I don't know." The truth continued to escape my lips. "There was another. He must be with the Empire. He's like me, only stronger maybe."

"Stronger?" Lil repeated, her eyes grew dark with worry. "What does that even mean?"

"Kael!" Dahl's voice called from around the carriage. "The horses! Food and water."

"Don't worry." I whispered as assuringly as I could, taking her gently in my arms and kissing her on the cheek. My hand accompanied hers to her side, our fingers meshed together.

"Nothing will ever keep me from you. I promise. Champion or not, I'll always be yours. And from now on, if I feel like running off I'll just stay by your side instead. Less trouble..." I winked.

She laughed. Locked in the hold of her eyes, the world brightened with her smile. "You better..."

"Kael!" Dahl called again.

"Aye!" I shouted.

Dahl spoke with the stableman while I fumbled with the horses. Luckily, Lil knew how to care for them far better than I. Taking the reigns, she guided the lead horses to the stables. They went along without the least bit of fuss. Dahl stepped in to help with the last two, my performance indicative that I was less than suited for the job. Nonetheless, the horses were tended successfully.

Lil and I strolled through a nearby grove of lilies while the horses got their fill. A break was much welcomed against the events of the city we had left behind us. Once the horses were fed and rested, we got the carriage back in order. Dahl waived a farewell to the stableman, and with the fading light of evening we departed.

Worry loomed in the silence of the cabin, as we turned south along another bumpy road. I laid back against the wall of the coach. Lil lay with me, curled in my arms, her poofy hair tickling at my nose.

Through the shuttered window across from us we caught glimpses of the passing world. As we descended into the river valley, a stone ridge rose to the west like a sandy red curtain. I watched the changes in the stone and rock between quick naps.

Rest did not come easy. I snapped alert at the slightest disturbance, each time the carriage bumped or Lil stirred in my arms. Paranoia had me, the joys of life on the run.

Eventually, the smell of the river crept into the cabin. The stone of the ridge met the rough bark of a large oak grown at its southern edge.

The dark, rugged bark was an instant contrast to the reds of the stone. It stood tall with the elders, though it was younger and not nearly as heavy in girth. Its crown blended with that of the other great oaks high above the carriage.

"Run away with me." Lil shifted in my arms. Her eyes did not open. She had woke with the thought.

I sighed, breathing deep as I pulled her close. "If only."

The terrain outside was at a sloping descent for the river as we continued south. The stone wall of the ridge was replaced by dense vegetation, leafy and green in the fading light. The river was close. Soon we would make camp.

"We're free of Verda and well off to a good start. Let's just keep going. Never look back." She smiled, her eyes peeking open to reveal a glimmer in the light.

"Yeah." I ran my fingers through the thick locks of her hair, finding this idea much preferable to the alternative. "Maybe we should."

As we neared the river, the carriage slowed considerably. The change was enough to stir Lil and me to shift from our cozy recline. Something wasn't right, and we both peeped through the curtains to have a look.

Thump. Thump. Thump.

There came a sudden knock against the wall of the coach. A small panel slid open, the stage on the other side.

"Boy!" Dahl's voice came low and stern. "You two jump. Head west along the river to the village, I will find you there."

"Where?" I asked in desperation. "Why?"

"Imperial troops. I've never seen anything like it..." His voice trailed in disbelief.

"Let me-"

"No!" Whatever emotion rattled his voice shook me as his stomping had shook the cabin. "Go! Now!"

"Kael, let's go."

Lil had no trouble following his instructions. She kicked the door ajar. The leafy greens of the world behind lit the greens of her eyes.

Hunched in the doorway of the shaky carriage, I pulled her close. She wrapped her arms around me, the look in her eyes as uneasy as the moment.

"Hold onto me. Tight." I insisted, kissing her gently on the brow.

Despite the experience gained along my journey, I had not tried anything like what I meant to do. I was nervous to pull another into the accelerated state with me, let alone my beloved.

Before I could lose my nerve to reason, the change swept over like a wave, in the space of a blink. As my lips left her skin, her voice sounded, but the words were lost, lost in the droning hum of the world. I embraced her carefully, and together we lifted free of the carriage and shot for the cover of the forest. Flying with her there next to me was magical, yet it wracked my nerves considerably. I kept it steady, sweeping low for the cover of the green along the river basin.

A glimmer of colorful lights caught my eye. It was only for an instant, obscured by the leafy greens. It was a blockade, soldiers dressed and armed much like the scouts had been. There were many of them, surrounded by flashing strobes of color and strange equipment. The oscillating lights slowed to a crawl under the change. Most astounding of all, there were flying machines!

Lil shifted in the moment of my distraction, forcing me to adjust and setting us both off balance with the loss of concentration. We tumbled for a brief instance before I recovered. It was enough to get my heart racing, and I set down in some brush next to the river.

The forest was around us, the leafy brush providing excellent cover. The deep shades of late evening darkened the thick greens of the vegetation, hiding us further. We had distance as well. We were safe. I released the change.

"What the hell!?" Lil was frantic.

"It's okay." I assured us both, helping her steady herself.

"Like hell!" She heaved, her eyes wide. She breathed, looking around at her new surroundings. She laughed nervously. "Kael, where are we?"

"The forest..."

She laughed again. "Thank you. Hadn't noticed all the trees."

"Anytime." Her smile. "Shall we, my dear?"

I offered my hand, turning west in the direction of the river's flow. Night wasn't far, and I wanted as much distance as we could get.

"Deeper into the forest?" She took my hand.

"He said to follow the river to the west." I explained, leading our way through the dark leafy blinds.

The terrain was rocky along the barren stones of the riverbed. A stream of water trickled as it spilled down its path through the stones. This was the Stone River.

"What are we looking for exactly?" Lil asked.

"I'm not sure." I admitted. "Dahl said he'd meet us there."

"It's getting dark."

"I know." A plan already forming in mind. "I can get us there much faster if-"

"No." Lil objected.

"Lil, please." I insisted. "Once more and we're safe for the night. Away from it all..."

The stone trough of the river basin provided a clear path, easy to gain some distance if nothing else. Relying on Dahl's word, knowing no other way to go, I offered my hand again. This time she accepted, though she was much reluctant.

"Kael..." Concern heavy on her delicate features.

"Don't worry, love." I assured. Gently I pulled her close and wrapped her in the cloak, raising the hood up over her tangled locks. "Just hold onto me, stay close. Nice and easy this time, yeah?"

"Okay." Her eyes like the forest, alive like the stars. "Let's do this."

She kissed me with a quick peck and buried her face against my chest.

Holding her there with me, I willed the change. Peace veiled the world as we slipped from it, my Lil safe in my arms. Night was falling, time was precious. Together we rose to move with the fading light.

This time we traveled much more smoothly. Nice and easy, we followed along the river, hovering above the water's surface. We traveled far. I was about to set down to make camp for the night, when a familiar glow emanated over the rocks in the distance ahead, lighting the forest in the way that only fire can.

As we neared, the basin dropped into a small valley, revealing a quaint village of mud and straw huts. The silhouettes of people were discernible around several fires. A sparkling lake reflected the light of the fire over the rippling shimmer of its rolling surface. We set down in the soft lush grass of the lakeshore, not far from where the river spilled over the rocks to cascade into the rippling water.

The change released, and the night filled with sound. Music and laughter echoed from the fires of the village. The deep pounding of drums, the light wispy whistle of pipes, the rattle of shakers, the chanting voices of the people...

Lil stumbled with a gasp, clutching at me to right herself. "Wish I enjoyed that."

"We made it, my dear."

"Where are we?" She asked, her eyes sparkling with the shimmer of the water. "A village?"

"The Ireah." I assumed aloud.

A warmth lifted me from within, a smile rose upon my lips. A great honor it was to stand there, to discover the truth of my ancestor's words. To share this moment with her, greater still.

"Legends passed in the words of my elders tell a story of this peaceful tribe. In a time of great need the Ireah aided my ancestors, teaching them the ways of the land so that they lived. To be here... To see this..."

"Well then." Her eyes were warm against the distant light of the fire. She reached for my hand. "We should meet them."

Together we walked into the warm light of the dancing flames, toward a circle of strangers gathered round in that familiar way. Perhaps a tradition that united all the tribes in practice, a time of peace shared each night under the stars. In this time of peace, we were welcomed by the Ireah.

As we neared, the drums stopped. In an instant we were surrounded. Their words were lost to us, as neither Lil nor I knew the language they spoke. Everywhere there were smiles on curious faces, the friendly exploration of a dozen hands. The soft material of our clothes seemed a delight.

We had interrupted festivities of sorts. Some of them wore elaborate costume, dressed like birds with silly faces. Others wore simple hides and furs, much in the way of the Dóvai. Indeed they had shared much with my ancestors.

A squat elder appeared, ushering the others back as he began to speak, stroking at his stringy gray beard. He looked us over intently. His words were lost to me, but the warmth of his expression was enough to know we were accepted. With a generous smile and a greeting, he bowed. Lil and I bowed in turn.

The elder took his place around the fire. All followed, returning to their song and dance. The music revived in the night. Those in ornate costume resumed their performance, moving to the energy of the drums.

Again and again, Lil and I were approached by members of the tribe. Communication was limited, but their gestures were friendly for certain; food, drink, warmth and light. Song and laughter filled the night, until at last we two drifted gently to rest by the flickering flame.

Many such days passed with no word from Dahl. Lil insisted that we should abandon Verda and the revolution, the known lands altogether if need be. She wanted nothing more than to flee together, to disappear along the river to whatever new beginning awaited.

"We should leave it all together, just the two of us." She must have told me a hundred times. She was right, we both knew it.

There was little to argue. This place was like heaven, the lush greens of the valley, the flowering vines that crept up the roots of the elder trees along the steep walls of the basin. We spent most of our time either walking together along the crystal waters of the lake or getting to know the tribe. Eventually I accepted her proposal. What an adventure it would be, to travel the world together in complete freedom.

Lil traded her dress for attire more worthy of travel in the forest. The soft violet material was indeed well crafted and made for an easy exchange. She was outfitted with hides and furs, rugged materials born of the land. With her hair bound back, she completed the transformation. She was ready to brave the wilderness, my wildflower in bloom.

On the morning that we were to leave Dahl appeared, riding the freckled white stallion. Seeing him safe was a relief, and I welcomed him with excitement. Lil did not share my enthusiasm.

"Kael..."

He sounded grim, looking worn and shaken. He all but dropped down from the stallion, righting himself as he met the ground.

"What did you do?"

"Failed." The words stung with truth. My confession did little to ease his spirits as it had with Liallia.

He looked at me hard, as if his heart were breaking to hear what he surely knew. "You have no idea..."

He had my full attention.

"Your stunt in the arena triggered exactly what we meant to avoid, the very reason for the escape was to avoid the Empire, not entice them! What were you thinking?!"

"I wasn't." I admitted, wishing Lil had not been present to hear it all. "It was impulsive. Wrong, terribly wrong..."

The words sent shivers through my bones.

"Damn right!" Dahl roared with the same fevered passion he had at the blood pits. "They've taken Verda! That blockade we encountered was one of many, set to find you."

"Why?" This revelation shook me.

"No one knows." Dahl sighed. "They've occupied the city and continue to search the land, all for you. The leader is a madman. He's obsessed, eager to find you."

"The city?!" Lil gasped.

"Their leader." I thought of the man I fought in the arena. "You saw him?"

"Yes." Dahl nodded, his face serious. "Yierkohl. It is he who commands the Imperial forces."

It was him, without a doubt. A name to go with a sinister face.

"And the City?" Liallia asked concernedly.

"The entire city is under watch day and night." Dahl explained. "So far losses have been kept to a minimum. Marcius is doing his best to reassure the people. Yierkohl is keeping him close, right under his boot. Peace is relative, so long as Verda is compliant."

I turned away, taking several steps toward the leafy green foliage of the wood line. The glistening waters of the crystalline lake seemed too beautiful to accompany this truth for which I was responsible. Two paths lie before me, and I felt lost in deciding the better way.

Should I return and try to liberate Verda? After all, my resolve had once been the destruction of that vile city. Even if I could, should I? Could I? War with the Empire would be inevitable down this path. Perhaps Lil was right. We should just run from it all and disappear, leave Verda to its fate...

"So then, this is how it ends?" I asked aloud, seeking some kind of solace from my companions.

There was an eerie crackling sound, accompanied by the familiar zing of a weapon drawn free of its sheath, that metallic ring that stills the heart...

I turned to see Dahl drop, blood oozing from a slash to his abdomen. Lil cried out as the man I'd fought in the arena held tight to her, his shiny dagger far too close to her delicate features.

"Not quite." Yierkohl beamed. His smile was sinister, his eyes wild with abandon. He was pure villain.

"Let her go!" My voice rattled low, like rolling thunder before a great storm. The energy collected within me, ready to explode with the change.

A wicked smile contorted the man's face. He laughed with the timbre of madness. "Or what exactly?"

"I'll destroy you." My words fluttered with truth, a small surge of energy escaped, sending a ripple that crackled through the air.

His wicked laugh shot into crescendo, like grit between clenched teeth. "Challenge accepted."

He pulled at her roughly to entice a cry. It was all I could take, bursting forth with the fever pitch of the change. It felt as if I might tear the world in two, the fury with which I drew my blade.

Scarcely had I made the bound forward than two figures converged on me. Luck was with me, as the ambush missed its mark. The commotion caught my attention, and I turned to see two more with powers like my own.

They were not as capable, not as fast it seemed. But their strength was in numbers, in strategy. They were three, and the strongest had my Lil. The advantage was theirs. The dark one alone was problem enough, the odds surmounting against me.

The first attacker swept through the space behind me as I moved, his blade hissing through air only inches from me. The second attacker had corrected, his blade driving hard at my left flank. My guard redirected just in time. I surged forth with a flurry of fatal slashes, but my aggressors withdrew from reach. It was clear the two were skilled in combat. They meant to take their time.

The two lesser swordsmen retreated into the leafy brush. The cover was futile. Using my heightened senses, I felt them there. As I did, I felt the stronger presence of their leader as he moved higher, more distant... I looked in the direction of the sensation to see Yierkohl lift away with Lil clutched in terror.

I shot to intercept, taking to the air. The two rushed with the opening, attacking from below. It didn't take long for me to realize I was no match for them in the air. My demise was sure if I remained airborne.

Furious, I seized an opening and dropped back to the Earth. They followed suit, forcing me to repel an onslaught of double attacks and combinations. The fight drove me further from my Lil, further into my fury, further away from reason and the focus of my concentration.

They could no more touch me than I them, yet this stalemate would indeed come to an end. This game was familiar to me, even the most fierce of beasts wears down with persistence. The odds remained against me. Helpless to intercept and desperate to save my Lil, I tracked the madman as he stole her away. Their energies faded to the northeast, in the direction of Verda.

My attackers continued to assail with slashing sweeps from all sides, leaving no room for error in my movement. The hiss of their blades came close more than a few times, as I scrambled for a way to gain the upper hand in the fight. Survival was paramount, I had to save her. I had to.

One of them released a burst of energy, catching me well off guard. The other moved to capitalize as I staggered. I released an energy burst of my own in turn, instinct allowing much more force than I knew I had. The two were certainly pushed free of me, small limbs snapping from nearby trees, plants uprooting, dirt whirling.

Inspired by the opening created, an idea came to light. I shot high for the open sky above the forest, reaching into my waistcloth for the stone knife. I cleared the treetops, higher I went into the blue. I could feel them behind me, one in front of the other as they shot for the canopy in pursuit. Focusing my senses on their energies, I waited for the right moment to strike.

In an instant I changed direction, diving headfirst at my opponents. I threw the knife to shoot like a bolt of lightning, just as the lead aggressor broke through the trees. The lock of hair trailed behind the knife like the tail of an arrow, as it struck him hard in the chest. He fell limp with the impact, dropping back into the green of the trees. The other charged around his fallen comrade to meet me hard with his saber.

Focusing energy into my blade, I sent it forth with a slash, much as I had done to cleave the stones in the dessert above the canyon. He would have to evade. I rained down upon him with the slashing wave of energy.

The burst ripped through space, forcing him to redirect. The opening was made; I set upon him, sinking my blade hard down and through his core. In a burst of strength I withdrew and slashed again, slicing him clean. He fell down through the trees in pieces.

No time to lose, I shot through the sky above the canopy in the direction of Verda. The air felt like it would break around me, as I pushed well beyond the comfortable levels of my capacities. I would save her. I would.

My heart beat like the drums of that final ceremony, driving my mind against primal desperation. My focus was aligned, set to that frequency that stole her away. I tore through the leaves of the Allichene, plummeting down through the dense layers of forest. Like a falling arrow, I descended upon the familiar dusty arena of Verda's Coliseum.

Death's Awakening

He had her there, centered on the arena. His dagger aimed and ready. I slowed as I met the dust, releasing the change. Fanfare swept through the audience gathered to fill the stands. So many had come to see this battle, to witness the atrocity about to unfold.

"Kael!" She cried out, tears welling. "Don't!"

She struggled against the monster's grip. He shifted, grabbing a hard fistful of hair and forcing her to her knees between us. Steady was my intent, but my emotions had already conquered reason. I lunged, only to entice the point of his dagger to pierce the distance toward my Lil. It stopped when I did, dangerously close to my beloved's soft throat.

"Excellent!" Yierkohl rejoiced at his cruelty. "The stage is set. No better way. This, old friend, is how it ends."

"Release her!" I commanded, stirring the very air with bridled rage.

"You know, it's quite sad. I catch your pretty little companion here, and you arrive promptly to your own execution. She really is quite lovely by the way."

He leaned in close to her as she struggled against him and breathed deep of her.

"Ah, like a rose in heat." He laughed menacingly at his vulgarity.

My blade was ready.

"I've cut you down so many times over the years, yet you just keep coming back. You're like a weed that refuses to die off, ever pervading the garden. Such tenacity! For that, you have my admiration." His eyes wide with malice, his smile wrong and cruel.

"Who are you, villain?" I had to keep him talking, wait for an opening.

He laughed, clutching tighter to Lil as she struggled.

"Rude... Well, if you must know, I am Sir Yierkohl Dravricht, First Knight of his Holy Majesty's court and commander of the Vanguard's Crimson Wing."

"Quite a title. It'd be a shame to throw it away." I reasoned. He laughed hysterically, his grip tightened on her beautiful hair. "What does any of that even mean?"

He shook his head with a grimace, as if in disgust of my ignorance.

"To keep it simple, think of his 'Holy Majesty' as a gardener, me as the trusty shears at his hand, ever trimming and shaping. My objective is to hunt down and eliminate any threat, ridding his majesty's 'Holy Empire' of that which cannot be tolerated. The dirty work if you will. That which is necessary to maintain the lands. You see, the connection between the garden and the gardener is intimate. In the course of my work, I've really gotten to know you, both of you, time and time again..."

The better part of me attempted to ignore his implications, but my anger, ever my adversary, spoke for me.

"Awful lot of words to describe the role of a servant. Good as being a dog, worse even."

A mad chuckle rattled from a toothy smile. "You have no idea... If only we had time for a chat over tea. Maybe next time, if you behave yourself well enough. Hmm?" He laughed again. "I really must kill you both quickly and be on my way. There are rebellions to quell, people to kill. Duty, if you wish to call it that. It's okay, really. Been fun!"

"That's not going to happen." I objected.

"Oh, but it is." Yierkohl insisted. "I mean, you'll come back eventually. The same story repeats. When you come back, I'll be here waiting. You see? Completely acceptable way of coexisting. We'll do it all over. Over and over... It's maddening!!"

The world was rippling. I struggled to hold back against the change.

"Then why?!" I growled. "Why not release her and just go?! What does she have to do with any of your nonsense?!"

"It's like you said, I am a servant. In truth we are all servants. We all serve a greater purpose, Zamil. You, me, his Majesty... The Emperor only thinks he frees himself of wickedness by pawning it off on others. The price of his conquest is corruption, and it echoes through the shadows left in the wake of his self-righteous campaign. He is a false god, long since deluded and lost to his own ambition."

"Then take that up with him! Let her go!" I demanded.

"Ah, the plan exactly! You see, I cannot best him in battle, nor am I meant to. My role eternal has been to bleed man by way of his own corruption, his ambitions, his greed. Thus, his greatest legacies fall by and by, keeping him ever humbled before creation. The fool doesn't know it, but he's only ensuring his destruction in his attempts to avoid it, and I've been here to help move it along at his behest. Sewing the seeds of destruction at his bidding, patiently waiting for the finale."

"Spare the theatrics. There's no need to harm her." I all but pleaded. "I'll fight him, a thousand times over. Let her go. Please!"

"Unfortunately, that's not how it works. You, old friend, will either die here today, yet again, or deliver me to my end." His dagger nicked the soft skin at her throat.

"Gladly..." I thundered.

He bellowed with mad laughter.

"That's the spirit!" He smiled wide. "Try with all your might, all of it! You've only just begun, but don't worry. I'm about to nudge you right along your path of destruction."

I saw what he meant to do. Lil cried out.

"Kael!"

Sensing his attack, I released my hold and entered the flash state with a power like never before. The world distorted in a shattering burst around me, and I lunged to close the distance and place myself between them before he could harm her.

But he entered the state as well, the aim of his dagger set. His capacities were greater than my own, driving the dagger as it plunged for her. The distance between us felt like it took a lifetime to cross.

Taking her in my arms, feeling her there...

I felt the sting of the blade as it shot through her and into me. Together we lingered there, his dagger uniting us in the moment of connection only to slide away. Together we fell. Dying there in my arms was my world. Her, there upon the dust of that cursed arena.

"Lil!"

The tears spilled out like the emotions tearing from within. Blood choked from the lips of my darling love.

"Stay with me, please. I'm so sorry, I'm so sorry..."

She choked on her last moments, her time was over. Tears dropped heavily down from her eyes, those two heavenly portals through which the garden sprang to life. Her light faded from that vessel. Death lifting her there, from my very arms.

Numb and shattered, I held her close as the monster moved to attack. I felt it coming and willed myself into the flash state, pushing further than ever hoping to keep my eyes on the fading spark of her eyes. Even as the instant slowed to the brink of an impossible crawl, it faded all too fast.

He too had accelerated, his attack coming quickly. I released her as gently as I could. His blade hissed across my cheek, and a kick landed hard sending me skittering across the arena. It was all I could do to recover, narrowly avoiding his next onslaught of slashes.

I righted myself and turned toward my attacker, blade in hand. I expected rage to come, yet I felt nothing in that moment as I squared off with the villain, numb even to my own resolve. He smiled wide as he tore away his cape and tossed it aside. He drew his rapier as well and readied himself for another attack. Once more he lunged at me, a blade in each hand.

Lil lay upon the dust. My beautiful Lil.

Forced into battle, I broke. Reason was gone. It was pure rage that drove me forth, the change pressed farther than ever with searing wrath.

The world about us faded to black, lost in my peripheral as we clashed through the air, across the ground, even smashed into the stands. Many died, but I did not feel them there. The world was immaterial. He was all I saw, his death my only resolve. Anger consumed me, the better man I could have been lay dead upon the dust.

He was fast. He was skilled. His rapier hissed and scratched, lunged with torrents of jabs and volleys of powerful lightning fast slashes. Parry was not an option, his dagger ready like the sting of the scorpion, ready to finish its prey. His wicked face was tormenting behind his offensive. How badly I wanted to destroy him.

Blood oozed from my wound, and I was steadily growing weak. Mad rage kept me animate. I had to finish him quickly, even if it meant death. My teeth gritted, lips curled back. I felt the rage reverberating through me in a primordial growl.

Gripping the gilded scabbard in one hand, I swung hard for him, my blade ready to attack in the other. His guard met the clubbing blow of the beautiful sheath, shearing down its length and sending shards of precious metal glittering through the air like jewels. My blade shot for the dagger, slashing it hard from his hand.

I had him.

The dagger removed, I slid in close through the guard of the rapier, driving an elbow hard for his face and slicing through the arm holding the blade. In the flow of my motions, I spun around to face him with a furious downward slash.

The attack should have cleaved him in two, yet it did not. It was as if the blade had met the side of a mountain, snapping with the force of impact. The blow sent Yierkohl plummeting hard into the dust, the broken end of my sword trailing down after him.

His laugh resounded, as I looked at the broken weapon in my hands. He had recovered, his left hand bloody, his right missing. Blood poured down his face where my attack had made contact with his scalp just above his forehead. As I watched in disbelief, his body began to recover. I felt the energy resonate, gather...

Desperation drove instinct into action, and I dove for the rapier, then for Yierkohl. I couldn't allow him to regain his strength. At full speed, I drove the weapon hard for his core. He stood before me, eyes wild with madness, face contorted in that wicked smile.

A bright flash ignited, just as the tip of the rapier neared its mark. A ghostly blade materialized at his hand to deflect the point high and wide of its target. It was another rapier, made of an eerie light. The properties of this weapon were unknown to me, but instinct warned of its destructive capacities.

The rapier descended in a slash. I responded with a burst of energy, pushing hard against him. The luminescent blade came down for me through the burst, slicing through my left shoulder, leaving a shallow wound searing with pain. Yierkohl was driven back with the impact, allowing only a brief moment to recover.

The rapier I held was red hot where it made contact with the mysterious blade. There was no doubt it would be of little use in defending against such an unnatural weapon. Yet, I had felt the changes in energy, the healing flow like that of a stream when Yierkohl had regenerated himself. The sudden concentrated burst like that of lightning, when the celestial blade had appeared...

"Zamil old friend, you've gotten soft." Yierkohl taunted, shaking his head in disappointment. "Fall here this day, knowing it marks the best fight you've given in ages. Maybe next time, kiddo. Something to look forward to."

He laughed menacingly, lunging forth to attack. His advance carried the intent of his final strike.

Confused. Broken. Lost.

His words... No! Never again would she fall to this creature! Never again!

All my will, my body and might unified under this singular purpose. Deep within, some hidden restraint broke, revealing a network of connectivity. Pathways long forgotten returned to me. The power within tapped this accessible knowledge with all the distal familiarity of reflex.

The blade Yierkohl held as he advanced upon me had been summoned to hand, and I had felt the way, the way now open to me. I focused as if to flex an imaginary muscle. In response, energy began to spark and flash, manifesting into form at my hand.

By will alone I conjured forth a mighty blade, which took physical shape in a burst of reticulated energy. I felt it ripple like cold pulsing shocks throughout my palm and fingers, as the hilt formed at my grip. The energy traveled up the hilt, creeping like a dark flash that sucked and pulled at the world of light. A shadowy substance unraveled at my summoning, revealing an ominous dark blade.

I brought the weapon up hard, smashing his flimsy attack aside with ease when the weapons met. Energy hissed and sparked in the moment of contact. His midsection exposed, I slashed and chopped and jabbed with the shadowy blade. It was all he could do to avoid my advance. He broke away.

"Excellent!" Yierkohl cried. "A most welcomed development! The cosmic tool of undoing, Death itself!"

He was right, the very concept seemed to resonate through the blade. No other weapon came close in comparison. It was total perfection.

End to end it was easily as tall as my father had been, yet it wielded as easily as waiving a finger. The smooth dark surface of its length looked to be carved from stone. Hexagonal in shape, the sword was like a razor sharp double wedge. A sea of intricately patterned eyes ran down the breadth of the blade. Their menacing gaze trailed down the length to where it tapered to a sharp ovoid tip.

Both hands held at its lengthy hilt, gripped to the soft dark bindings that wrapped this perfect work of symmetry. It moved as I moved, our flow exquisite. Energies aligned, I was one with this weapon of the heavens. Together, we were Death.

He rattled with wicked laughter, madness piqued in his eyes. "Rise, Zamil! Serve your purpose and destroy!"

Thunder boomed as we clashed, shaking the coliseum around us to ruin. Energy arched and flared when the two spirit blades met. Sparks ignited, twinkling like stars as our battle raged through space. The world was at a standstill, frozen and adrift in a whirling blur. Direction and orientation lost much of its relevance. Running him through was my only resolve.

I cut him.

He faded, rolling with the injury and countering with a volley of energy bolts. They shot for me like arrows, rippling through the world along their path. I could feel this energy as I evaded, sharp, concentrated, angry. In fact, I could sense a great deal further with this blade in hand, the depth of sensation pervading the world...

Redirecting high, I cleared his attack and closed the distance. I lunged for him again, postured for a downward slash. The moment his guard began to rise, I redirected my momentum as I had practiced in the canyon, and with my new orientation sliced laterally instead.

He fumbled desperately to right his guard in time, but to no avail. My attack swept through his midsection, severing him just below the ribs. It was as if I had caught only the air...

A burst of energy struck me hard as I cleared the swing, sending me tumbling back. His counter was too late to save him. My blade, unstoppable. The blow was struck.

I righted myself in time to see his torso falling for the dusty ground below. I shot for him, thunder shaking in my wake, my blade pointing the way for his heart. We connected with crushing force.

He tried to block with his weapon, but it was shattered in a grand release of sparks. My blade plunged through him, and we plummeted to the Earth. The force of the impact shook the world and sent the dust whirling.

Pathetic and broken, Yierkohl lay pinned beneath my blade, gripped in the clutches of Death. As he weakened, I felt him there. The years of torment and ruin, the cruelties of war ripping through the ages.

He had stood by the Emperor in the beginning much as he'd said. A campaign to unite mankind had indeed become conquest, and Dravricht had indeed earned his title as commander of the Crimson Wing. A title earned in bloodshed. The delight he'd taken in it all, indulgent until the twisted role he played finally snapped his mind.

He gurgled a laugh, my blade driven through his chest.

"Well old friend, seems you finally managed to do it. Took you long enough." His body tried to recover, his will sustaining. "End it, fool."

Natural impulse, like the spasm of muscle memory, activated with a building charge that surged through the blade in a luminescent glow. The eyes radiated along the sleek length of the dark blade, and Yierkohl began to shimmer with it. As the intensity grew, Yierkohl began to dissipate, sparks and flashes of light scattering as the energies of his being released. In a brilliant flash that ignited the nearby stands of the coliseum, his majesty's First Knight, mad dog of the Imperial court, was no more."

The Fall of Verda

Night shrouded the world outside the conference hall, dark as the turn the story had taken. Subject One was silent, breaking from his tale. His eyes remained fixed on the past, as he stared into whatever dream world held his recollection.

Shadows darkened the chamber, the air chill without the harsh summer sun. A sharp buzz broke the silence, as the evening lights hummed to life, illuminating the shadowy chamber to a more comfortable brightness. The change was immediate, and much needed. The gloom had made the grim account all the more haunting. The record rolled, the time blinked as the minute changed. It was 2105.

"So accounts of a devastating fire that swept through the city..." Thaut reflected. "Did it spread from the coliseum?"

Subject One chuckled softly, a smile stretching beneath his gray beard. "You have been most eager for this part, Investigator. Yes, I suppose it did."

"I see." Thaut nodded. "So the damage caused by the flames had been inadvertent, collateral if you will?"

"No, Investigator. That fire was small, only igniting the surfaces closest to where he fell. It was I who burned the city."

Thaut stiffened, his heart dropped. "So you attacked Verda?"

"Yes." Subject One admitted, shame in his voice.

"Let me guess, now comes the unfortunate part?" Thaut suggested with the creaking of his chair as he shifted.

Subject One sighed. "Yes, indeed. I share this with you in reluctance, but it must be told. Truth is absolute."

"Absolutely." Thaut agreed. "Your influence on the region has proven substantial. And conflicting, I must admit. Modern Verda dismisses the events as legend, a fairytale of a demon to scare people into walking a righteous path. To the west, the people of Emtsa Aur differ substantially in their accounts, considering the events to be of a natural order. To them, the entity in question is revered as a spirit of the forest, a protector that smote the wickedness of Verda to liberate the people. Poetic, the verses they recite. The conflict between these two perspectives only furthered my intrigue, and it wasn't until I encountered a tribe to the south-"

"We will get to all that in time, Investigator." Subject One interjected, assurance in his tone. With a sigh the smile faded from his weathered face, his eyes lost again to that faraway time and place.

He continued his story.

"Yierkohl defeated, I returned to my beloved. The dark blade dispersed with the release of the change, and I dropped to my knees at her side. My fingers traced her soft lips, the smooth features of her face.

Violently, the sobs escaped me.

Those who had not fled in panic cheered from what remained of the stands. They cheered. My precious Lil lay dead, and they cheered.

Imperial troops encircled the arena, what was left of Yierkohl's command. Their uniforms reminded me of the scouts. How different their message had been.

Their numbers converged on my location, closing on the arena along the broken stands. Their weapons were trained and ready to engage. Among them were those of the ascended ranks as well, the lesser celestials of the Vanguard. I held her there, crumpled and broken upon the dust.

The troop nearest me barked in a commanding tone, his words lost to the numb that gripped me. Even after all they had taken, still the

Empire meant to do me harm. They destroyed my home, murdered my sweet Lil.

And the people cheered...

Reason broke, as a raging storm of emotion swept my mind from all decency. I lay my Lil gently upon the dust. My humanity lay there with her, my heart as cold as my darling love.

Rage rippled through the air with the change. I rose above the arena, the sounds of the people distant, slowed to that crawling slur. When I had centered midway up the height of the coliseum, I released a tumultuous burst of energy, smashing the remaining structure with a devastating blow and crushing many of those directly exposed.

Numb with furry I slaughtered the last of the Vanguard forces, starting with the remaining celestial agents. They were more than outmatched even with their numbers. Driven by madness I cut them down with the dark blade, whether they advanced or fled.

Under my will, the ethereal weapon sliced through all elements of my surroundings with the ease of cutting through thin air. It was my sharp disdain that honed its edges, my fury that gave it momentum, and my hatred that set its mark. It became my center, my body seemed to merely be the vessel of its conduction. Drifting along its path, we two were death in motion.

The change pulled me further than ever. The world faded from sight, replaced by a brilliant network of interconnected energy systems, bursting forth in radiant light and color. It was blindingly bright. It was as if I could feel the very fabric of reality, see the living pulse of the natural world.

Further still, I could feel them there, each and every living being. All experience known, no secret was safe from me. None could hide.

It was as if the sun itself were burning within me, and I became like a blazing fire, condensed to the familiar shape and parameters of a man. That powerful light burned with shining glorious warmth, rippling and contorting the air about me like the heat of summer upon the land. Easing my eyes closed, I used my accelerated state to feel beyond the glare. It was as if all the world were made of light, I could feel it all, sense all...

Following this new connection, I moved through space, floating like a specter. Concentrating my efforts against a blinding din of revelation, I first sought all those in league with the Empire. Those closest fell by my blade. Those who fled were met with reticulated bursts of energy that snapped into flame, consuming them in fire.

It was all too much to describe really. Feeling so much at once, my comprehension became much flooded. In torrents I perceived the shinning lights of each life force, saw and felt each and every living creature connected to this frequency, for we were one. These perceptions came in rhythm, ebbing and flowing like the oscillating rise and fall of a wave. As the waves crashed, I felt each and every spirit, each of the thousand souls of Verda.

The light radiated from my core, and like a hot tongue of flame flickering from a raging fire, the wicked of Verda were struck as if by lightning. The light gathered within them, burning so bright that all bonds holding their forms were broken instantaneously, releasing all their energies back into the world with a burning flash. One by one they faded from the spectrum, in supernova bursts of radiant energy, igniting the city and the forest that cradled it.

While the many nimble tongues of the flames blazed, I moved with a destructive power unrivaled in the natural world. Most perished in the radiance of my dreaded energy before they met the swift torrents of my swinging blade. Screams filled the air, and the despair of this ill begotten corner of the world united the people in a symphony of terror, agony as its conductor. The corrupt writhed to a melody more true to their nature, as I lay waste to the wicked hearts of Verda. Gripped with flames, Verda was no more. I drifted back through the burning city, returned to where she lay. Taking her in my arms, I fled that ill fated place, leaving the survivors to scurry to the wind."

His Holy Majesty, Emperor Haben Rashawn

Tension filled the room. Thaut was speechless for a moment, as he reflected over Subject One's testimony. The implications thus far correlated with the lore of Irvahem. He now understood the concern in his Majesty's voice when his orders had been given.

"I see." Thaut managed. "Where did you go from there?"

"To the marshlands. To the lilies." Subject One whispered. "Instinct directed me there. At first I didn't understand, but as I returned to myself it became clear."

Tears slid down his face as he uttered the last syllables, in what was perhaps the most human gesture Thaut had witnessed thus far. He reached into his satchel and produced a packet of tissues. There was always something comforting in this exchange, as if the gesture somehow established a neutral connection despite the awkward imbalance of emotional involvement. How the little things make a world of difference.

"Thank you, Investigator." Subject One smiled warmly, tears trickling down his unkempt beard.

"And I thought I had it hard coming up." Thaut teased.

Subject One chuckled softly. "Each to his own journey. The path to becoming is one of endurance and growth. You have endured much as well, I'm sure."

"Rainbows and sunshine. All my days." Thaut fibbed over a sip of warm water.

Subject One laughed, his smile returning.

"So you crushed the top knight of the Imperial court and sacked an entire city. Not bad to hit all that in one go, spectacular really. Is there more you'd like to share?" It was growing late, but Thaut could easily signal the others for time if he needed.

"Yes. There is a bit more I think. Don't worry, I won't keep you much longer." Subject One promised with a smile.

"Very well." Thaut reassured. "Continue. Please."

"Nothing was made right by what I had done. My people were gone. She was gone. The tears slid down my face, as I held her there in a grove of lilies. The earth was dark and wet, the mud thick and cold. Gray darkened the evening sky as thunder rumbled to the west. Droplets began to fall. The air was alive with the smell of rain, telling of the storm to come.

I ran my fingers through her thick black hair. Her shining green eyes had been like the forest, surrounded by the gold of sunshine. Those eyes were closed now, her perfect feminine form cold as the rain. Her creamy skin had been soft as the clouds on the breeze, blush full lips that had kissed me. Her form was that of the Great Mother incarnate. And so, to the Great Mother she would return.

Holding her there, embracing my last moments with her, the mud broke open at my will. Gently, I slipped her down to rest in the murky confines of the dark landscape from which she had come. Down she sank, slowly swallowed in the depths of the marsh.

The leafy greens and delicate flowers slid softly over where she lay when the muddy ground settled back, embracing her resting place in all the natural beauty with which she had brightened the world I knew. It wasn't a world deserving of her. The true beauty of the flower was lost on the people of that world. This was the natural world, every bit the garden of creation that welcomed her, body and spirit. She returned to that world now, a flower to rest in a garden tomb, as I let her go.

Thunder rumbled low in the distance. The air began to stir. A chill swept in with the coming rain. Numb and shivering upon the wet earth, I wept.

High above where I lay in the grove of lilies, the branches of the great oak swayed. The sheer size of the elder tree was captivating as its smaller distal branches danced with the restless winds. As I watched, I caught sight of the many chains that held Loughtia.

A wicked thought crept into mind. The heart of Verda, ripe for the plucking.

Many had died. Wasn't it enough? I tried to dismiss the idea. No amount of vengeance would bring her back to me.

Yet as I lie there shivering in the grip of that chilling numb, cold as the muddy soil at my cheek, my attention was drawn to it. Voices, laughter, music, and all the sounds of festivity collected upon my ears without my intent. Focusing further, I drew more of the distant experience vicariously through the senses of those who witnessed the lavish dress and decor of the aristocracy, the feast and drink.

They lived in bliss, far detached and above those who suffered under their rule. Want was unknown to them, title and privilege paramount. Lives were ended, bought and sold, fates decided, atrocities committed to uphold those titles, maintain that privilege. Many had died. Wasn't it enough?

A wicked smile crept upon my face. The change upon me, I reached out with that unseen might and gripped hard at the heart of Verda. I would bring them down to sink in the mud below. This gem-like palace hanging so arrogantly by a few threads would soon come crashing down like a fallen star, alive with the sounds of ruin as it carried its screaming inhabitants to their murky grave.

I surged forth my will upon the structure, targeting the first link in one of the great chains that held the palace at its distal anchor point. With a screeching groan, the massive ring of metal popped, cracking like an egg when at last it gave.

When the link snapped, the air was filled with the eerie screech of metal. Thundering clanks followed, as the massive weight of the falling chain was caught by the anchor that bound it to the palace, shaking it violently before it broke free to fall upon the land.

Growling with vile intent, I shook the structure further, rattling it until another of the heavy chains snapped and crashed into the east wing of the palace. Rubble rained, spattering in the mud of the Marsh.

Concentration broke from Loughtia, as instinct brought me back to myself. My guard met an incoming attack, deflecting a burst of energy as it struck in an arching bolt. Sparks ignited, swept away by the angry winds. The storm was upon the land.

"That is enough!" A heavy voice boomed. "Leave the people of this world in peace, vile spirit!"

He was large of build, brawny and dark. Gold and precious stones adorned his simple garb. His dark hair was short and neat, his beard the same. The piercing depth of his eyes set upon me with cold, humorless severity. Suspended against the flashing storm, he looked every bit the deluded false god Yierkohl had described.

"Why?" I growled the word like a challenge, the dark blade gathering at my hand.

"Your quarrel is not with the people of this land, I demand-"

I shot for him like an arrow from hell, wicked and angrily intent for the core of his being, the razor tip of my blade leading the way. A shiny burst of light moved forth to counter the stab, sparking in that familiar way as the two energies converged. A mighty ax had met my attack, the spirit weapon of his Holy Majesty, Emperor Haben Rashawn.

He swiped wide and heavy, the golden ax but a blur against my anger. Fixed upon him, my assault knew no relent. Nothing to lose, mad with wrath, my slashes ripped and tore at him.

"Why?!"

I spat viciously, assailing with slash after slash, chasing him through the stormy sky. Space was irrelevant. I would pursue him the world over.

"There is no reason to be had with you, spirit. Be gone!" The Emperor roared, belting forth a golden bolt from the ax.

It nearly struck its mark, catching me by surprise. The air rippled as the energy flashed through the stormy sky, only an arm's width from catching me in its jagged path. Furious I advanced, locking him in close.

The fight exploded through the angry skies above the land. We clashed, the rain falling heavy. The lightning flashed, but the thunder that boomed was that of the epic battle that raged across the turbulent sky. The winds whistled, the heavens roiling with all the fury of my intentions.

I braced my blade down the fullness of my left flank to steady it against an incoming strike. Flipping over the attack, I carried the strike through and clear of me, turning with the same momentum to deliver a downward slash. He managed to evade the furious slash and the flurry of jabs that followed, retreating once again. Yierkohl foretold of his defeat at my hand. If this was his best, he would surely fall.

We fought with the strength of gods, the raging sky alive around us like an angry symphony to parallel my wrath. He began to try and reason with me, though I would hear none of it. The hiss of my blade as it moved through the night my only revelry, as I sent torrents of powerful swipes and slashes at his majesty. So furious was the onslaught of my offense that he could do little more than evade. He had no chance to strike back.

He fled, moving in close to the trunk of the small oak southeast of Gan Levan. He attempted to utilize this terrain, placing branches between us for cover. Nothing would stay my wrath. I sliced through all, sending branches free with a flash of orange sparks. He continued to escape me, remaining just beyond my reach. In a moment of anger, I sliced through the body of the great tree itself, severing its trunk in two with a mighty swing of released energy.

The great tree creaked and groaned. The world rattled with cracks and snapping pops, as the unfathomable weight of the great tree lurched and crashed down upon the Stone River Valley. As the massive body fell we battled along its length, slashing and cutting as we shot up and through the branches.

Suddenly he broke free of my advance, striking the mass of the tree with a bolt of energy that sent a blinding barrage of orange sparks hissing through the air. Capitalizing on the opening created, he counterattacked using the same redirection technique I had used to defeat Yierkohl.

As his ax swiped for my torso, I roared with all my fury, pushing my opponent and the rain with him far away with the force of my unseen power. He had almost ended the battle. So close I had come to falling by my own technique.

The storm raged and the winds tore at me. I eased my eyes closed, the last image of my visual perception that of the proud Emperor righted and ready for the next clash. I felt the rage within me crescendo. The pain of anguish gave me a reason to push my capacities beyond to that next level, that state I had used to lay waste to Verda.

It was as if the world moved without me, as if I were in balance with the stars and the swimming darkness beyond. My capacities were building, my strength growing. Eventually I would consume him. This is what he feared most...

This was my purpose, our shared destiny.

With my eyes closed, I reached out with all my capacities, sensing beyond the narrow scope of my vision. I felt with all the awareness of the physical world, delving into spectrums well beyond my comprehension. It was like being born anew, like seeing for the first time.

Even with my eyes closed I perceived all. It was as if I were an endless body of eyes sailing the endless body of the cosmos. The experience was overwhelming at first, and I all but cried out, losing sight of the battle at hand.

Yet my rage steadied me, somehow allowing me to focus on my target despite the new world overflowing with indescribable sensation and detail. He would die here, the proprietor of my demise over the ages, the insidious lech that stole my Lil.

The power within me surged to such an extreme that my foe could not hope to counter my next attack. This was to be the finishing blow. Focusing my energies into the dark blade, I surged at him with a might that left the drops of rain suspended like tiny worlds drifting through space.

A flash of lightning lingered as if the sun itself were upon us. My blade was ready, low to my right. It shimmered with the reticulation of the energy gathered there, ready to deliver death upon this false god, just as it had when Yierkohl dispersed.

Scarcely half the distance was closed when a voice pervaded my thoughts. A female voice that called from within my being.

I am sorry, Kael.

Memories began to flood my mind, tearing me from reality. Regret swelled like the tears in my eyes, as precious moments replayed in torturous imagery and sensation, the experience heightened due to my elevated state. My concentration was shattered, and my advance lost its focus becoming sloppy and misdirected. I was helplessly caught in the grip of a powerful illusion.

There was another on the field below, I felt her there. Following the connection that ripped at my consciousness, I caught a brief glimmer of her mind as well.

Lady Everret, the one known as the sorceress. From her thoughts, I saw it all. The Emperor truly believed he had no other option than to destroy me for the sake of the world.

In the wake of all that had happened, it was hard to argue otherwise. He saw only what I would become, what I could do. He saw a monster. And she sat next to him throughout the ages, the hound that sought me out each time I was born into the world, helping him accomplish that which must be done...

The connection was severed. My rage broke as I desperately struggled to rediscover myself. I was no longer in the fight, even as I felt the oncoming attack.

Energy had been gathered, massed at his disposal. It rippled about him as if it would tear away the physical world. I sensed the power behind it, but my will had been broken. I no longer cared, as memories continued to flash through my mind.

Liallia was gone from me. Avenging my people had not returned them. Instead, I had shamed them. How many had I destroyed in the arena, slaughtered in their homes in my self-righteous fury? I had abused my power, forsaken the gifts bestowed to me.

Rage melted away, revealing a shattered heart. I crumbled before the truth I had so desperately sought to escape. Perhaps this truly was the better path for the world, my resistance both futile and selfish.

The soft feel of the sheets, her there in the morning light. She was gone. I held tight to the soft leathery hilt of my blade and continued my advance directly into the attack that awaited me.

It struck hard, like an unseen wave of fire, crushing down upon me. The intensity burned away at my clothes, my flesh, as it carried me along its descent. In a blinding blur of blistering heat I rocketed down to Earth, feeling the wet scratching slap of the canopy before I met a dead impact in the dark stormy forest below. Darkness took me.

The Peace of Slumber

There was nothing. When I attempted a return to consciousness, the searing pain was overwhelming. I was burned, battered and broken. A sapling had snapped under the impact of my hard landing and run through my torso. The agony returned my senses to the dark, awareness fading back to black.

I grew weaker, but somehow the strength within me held onto life, much like Yierkohl had at the end. My wounds were great, the pain greater still. Suspended in agony, unable to affect my fate one way or the other, life clung to me.

Time was a blur, the surroundings of the world were lost. It felt like ages, though it must have only been a day or so. Voices rattled somewhere nearby, hands began to move about my tortured flesh. The pain. I groaned and shifted, catching a brief glimpse of what was happening. Was I to be saved after all?

Three men stood over me, my heart sinking as they tore at the precious metals that lined what was left of my garments. A hand reached into the linens wrapped about my waist to find the coin purse there. He found my anger with it, and I gripped hard at him with a fleshy burned hand.

His dagger plunged into my chest, but it was too late. My grip tightened, I pulled him close, wrapping around him to ensnare him, to ensure his fate. In what I consider my greatest act of wickedness, I began to pull from his flesh that which I needed to restore my own, healing the injuries my body could scarcely sustain. The man writhed in pain and shock as he withered.

His two companions fled, leaving their comrade to his grim predicament. I held tight to my host, his life dwindling as my vigor returned to me. My flesh restored, I rose to my feet, removing the dagger from my chest and tossing what remained of the withered man aside like an empty husk.

The dark blade materialized at my hand, and I shot like an arrow for the closest man as he fled, impaling him from behind until the bindings of the hilt were at his spine. He bent forward with the impact. I planted my feet against his shoulders and shot skyward, pulling my blade free as I lifted. From above I released a hateful burst of energy, much like the attack that defeated me, burning the site in a blistering flash of heat.

The attack drained me, and I fell most of the distance back to the ground, righting myself before splashing down into the mud with a splat. The impact scattered ash into the steamy air. Flames licked from smoldering surfaces, singed from the hateful attack.

I rose to my feet, standing somewhere in the southern forest. My feet sank in the freezing cold mud left from the impact of my defeat, surrounded by the ashes of my rage. Perhaps for the first time, as I looked up the towering giants of the forest made the sky seem so impossibly distant in the gloom above.

My hand moved over my chest where the broken tree had been lodged. That tree now smoldered, broken and fading. So many innocents had been caught in the crossfire of warring powers.

To what purpose did those like me belong? What purpose did the Empire serve upon the face of the world? What purpose could ever sustain the indifference required to treat the world as a plaything to be claimed, its people to be collected and maintained like crops?

And I was the worst of all. I had truly fallen. Blinded by pain, I had become selfish and empty. I had lost sight of the immensity of the world and the sanctity of all that is natural, above all the value of life. How vast existence was beyond myself.

At least Rashawn meant to unify mankind, even if his intentions had lost their purity along the way. I had only meant to destroy it wherever I turned. Avenge my people, I thought. Punish the wicked, make them pay for what they did. Wrong I had become, lost in a self-righteous fury, lost in my own pain.

I had forgotten the world, forgotten the wisdom of the elders. Maybe it was better they were gone, honor intact. My legend was not fit to be told by the fires of my ancestors.

My gaze shifted to a pool of water forming at my feet as I bowed my head in shame. The sound of tiny impacts quickened in tempo as the rain grew steady, coming down over the world once again. It doused the hissing flames around me like a cleansing force, washing away all that had come to pass.

I returned my gaze skyward, the dark blade at my side. The clouds had thinned just enough above the canopy that the gloom brightened ever slightly, more than enough to inspire hope. In that moment the flame in me quieted, and peace returned to the world around me. My eyes eased shut as the rain washed over me, and acceptance found me. Lost and broken.

The pain to which I chose to cling was irrelevant. I was not a man, nor would I ever be. I resembled him out of familiarity, but some unseen metamorphosis had changed that. My passions remained with the people of the world. Unfortunately, I found myself unable to resist my capacities, and until I mastered the depths of my ability and overcome the vices of men, I could not hope to use my greatness in their favor.

I did not dismiss my blade. Instead, I drove it gently into the soil at my feet until it could stand without my aid, and I sat to rest behind it with my back to the trunk of the battered tree that had impaled me.

Tranquility eased over me as if it were carried by the rain. I came to rest against the small tree as if it were just as comfortable as the straw bed I had shared with my family in my oldest memories.

I reached out with my right hand, tracing the eyes that ran down the broad length of the blade with my fingertips. Its surface was hard and smooth, and the rain made it sleek and cool to the touch. We were partners, meant to reap the very heart of discord. Together we wove a poignant symphony, bringing disharmony into crescendo before abruptly silencing it from the world. We moved as one, swift and elegant beyond compare, unrivaled and unmatched.

And I had wrongfully meant to subject so many to sanctimonious rage, transgressions of the self forced upon others. I was buried under the weight of my broken heart, consumed by the sway of that burning flame.

"My beautiful Death. Until I am worthy again, my dear."

And together we slept.

Time lost all meaning. I moved between dreams and darkness at first. The earliest of my dreams were haunted by those I had lost. This was comforting at first, but I could not escape the realities that crept in as I failed to save them again and again. It became so torturous that I was grateful for the dark void between intervals.

Eventually the pain grew less, and the places and people of my past faded. In the place of my memories I dreamt of open fields barren of green, where the earth cracked in thirst. Nothing on the horizon but dust and ruin in all directions, the dry air heavy with the scent of a thirsting world. There was nothing but the howling wind that carried the dust in its lament. It was a world of total isolation, and I was utterly alone.

I came back from the darkness. A dull heartbeat pulsing through me still, the world a whirling blur of sensation. The peace within me had accepted defeat, but I would rise again. I would endure. Somehow I knew.

I grew far too weak to maintain consciousness, and in my desperation I focused on the warm life still pulsing through me. In the darkness of my mind it became a warm flowing light, a reminder that my existence was certain. This light became my refuge, and I willed it to continue, to grow stronger. Once I had gained the strength I needed, I willed the change.

It took great effort to push through to the newly discovered heights of the change, but I might have perished if I lost concentration in such dire circumstance. Once again the energies swarmed through the world around me in rippling colors, in all degrees of radiance and sensation. The magnitude of it was difficult to bear, until I found my center. That warm steady rhythm of life, flowing from my core.

I felt it pulse in all directions where it met the world around me, and the energies of the world reverberated through me as well. In time I felt harmony and all fear subsided in a way it seemed impossible to ever know the emotion again. I felt as if I became rooted to the earth, as if billions of tiny tendrils were pulsing their way further and further outward.

The state only grew stronger, going well beyond the physical. Reaching through, I experienced more and more of the world as never before, as I could have never dreamed possible. Yet it all seemed so familiar, as I drifted farther into this new condition.

I lost myself, seeing through the eyes of many instead of relying solely on those most familiar to me. I drifted through it all, the sensations of all living things. The expanse of it driving me to such joy that it seemed I would burst with warm tears of gratitude, my physical body long since transpired into colored bursts of radiant laughter.

At other times it was dark and cold, but always serene. A feeling of oneness overwhelmed any feelings of despair or toils of the past. There was only eternity, boundless and surging with ever greater potential in the floating void of possibilities, like an empty canvas awaiting the work of a grand master.

I felt myself transcend the solid fibers of reality, pursuing further the divine splendor of that unifying state, that sense of oneness with all things. I haven't the words to describe it. Everything was both known and unknown, beyond fathom. I felt the warm glow of the universe, as it all became light and energy.

All was made clear, yet meaning no longer held relevance. Peace surged in waves, bringing an understanding I could not harness. This state was incredible, and I followed it far from the world as I knew it, lost to the depths of the cosmos.

For the longest time I forgot myself. I thought perhaps I was a tree in the fluttering moments where consciousness flirted with the physical. My body had maintained itself in the absence of my presence.

Utilizing new capacities, which perhaps I dreamed into action, my physical body sustained itself by manipulating its surroundings. I grew with the tree in a kind of hyper-symbiotic relationship. It provided protection, growing into a great elder with me at its core. We shared a connection to the physical world, and in my slumber I nurtured it well beyond natural expectation.

My subconscious mind, as it would seem, intermingled with the natives of the area. I only caught fragments of these interactions, lost in the roaring din of the cosmos. It was nice to feel the sense of gratitude in their hearts at the brief positive influence I offered.

Those who sought guidance through hard times, or perhaps answers to the perennial questions of life climbed the great elder tree where whispers carried the truth hearts would seek. To them, I was a spirit of the forest. Seemingly impossible were these experiences, vague and fleeting as it must have been. Still, it was a grand improvement over the ash and ruin of my previous life, planting the seed of hope that I could someday return to the world without fear of subjecting it to my darker side.

Time had no meaning, as the ages passed. On I slept, until the young sergeant happened across me, another of celestial talent. We met when his ship crashed into the tree, shaking me hard from my slumber.

He sensed me there, and I him. Sergeant First Class David Esau is how he introduced himself. A promising youth with a bright future, he became my pupil and I his teacher in the months that followed. The time had finally come for my return, for me to finish what I began, to fulfill my purpose."

New Dawn

It was getting late. Lights flickered in the night sky over Paeon, ships moving like shooting stars as they traveled the dark. The traffic continued around the busy port below the hall, shuttles arriving as others departed. Subject One seemed to have finished his tale. The device on the table dinged, alerting Thaut of the hour, 2200.

"Simply amazing." Thaut exclaimed, reflecting over all he had heard. "So what does that leave for tomorrow? What I mean to ask is, should we expect more incidents like the one that shook the Higbey farm?"

"Yes." Subject One responded earnestly. "I accept full responsibility, for it is my duty, my purpose. I will do my best to keep my influence minimal, well away from the common people. Conflict is inevitable, but the events at the Higbey farm could have been avoided had I taken more direct action. My apologies. When the events unfolded, the task was not meant for me it would seem. For the better in fact, my pride as a master would not have had it any other way."

"Well the Higbey family was certainly shaken. They may not be so quick to agree with you."

"Most unfortunate. Of course, it would have also been unfortunate if the knight had been left alive to continue his assault on the indigenous people of the eastern forest. You see, quelling rebellion has long since taken precedence over the fair and equal treatment of the world's citizens. The knight worked from the shadows of the deep forest beyond the river, intent to either frighten the indigenous into compliance or destroy them."

"Are you sure? The goal of the Empire is to defend the people." Thaut suggested.

"And so it has, thanks to the Empire's very own Sergeant First Class David Esau. A clean kill in the end and another victory for the Empire as well as the people." Subject One assured.

"Victory? Eliminating a defender of the realm is hardly a victory. The knights are sworn to protect."

"The knights of the Empire must fall." Subject One disagreed. "Too long have they aided his majesty in subjecting the people, lost in conquest. Too long have they lingered here in the forefront of this world, upsetting the natural balance. Miguel was following orders to the very like, quietly snuffing out the voices that dared say no. Far easier to manage than a messy invasion of troops. Like Yierkohl said, the dirty work."

Thaut considered his words. "So the young sergeant is an agent on your behalf then? A sort of righteous third party hero fit to enact your version of justice?"

Subject One laughed softly. "Not quite. More like an agent on behalf of mankind. But that chapter has yet to come."

"What chapter is that exactly?" Thaut pressed.

"Exactly what you suggest, investigator. Change. Evolution to a new beginning. It is up to humanity to determine where the next chapter leads. It is not my story to tell, but yours."

"Is the Empire not exactly that? Why bother, and please correct me if I assume too much, to upset that institution any more than necessary?" Thuat proposed.

"The Empire is failing, lost to the vices that accompany long standing politics. Already the people revolt, their cause catching fire across the providences. Most gather in secret. Some quietly wish for it in their hearts. Others have amassed in guerrilla forces, engaging in a fruitless battle against the military might of the Empire. The current institution is strong enough to keep them in control for now, but at the expense of freedom, imposed by godlike interference. For better or worse, it remains tyranny so long as it is done in this way. Mankind will respond with resistance; war is inevitable in this current direction."

"There must be some other way. Won't you at least consider talks of peace? Reason with his majesty perhaps, aid mankind in a more constructive manner?" Thaut pleaded.

Subject One nodded in consideration, but then shook his head with a sigh.

"Humans have always rejected peace in favor of strife, each to their own degree. This is the struggle at heart, to seek dominion through knowledge and understanding, fueled by an ambition to improve that which is viewed to be imperfect in the natural world, bending it to selfish will. The innovations of a creative mind cannot be bridled, nor confined by reason. The utopia you wish to build has been tried many times and never has it endured, nor is it to likely. For it cannot, change is necessary. Humanity craves adversity, the very force that pushes it forward along the evolutionary path."

"You sound so absolute. I wonder, what gives you the right to determine the fates of so many?" Thaut challenged.

Subject One laughed. "That is an excellent question. In truth, I hold no such right, nor does your Emperor for that matter. I have no intentions of setting anyone's fate outside the parameters of my task. In the beginning I was lost. The way has become clear. The denizens of this world will be free to meet fate on their own terms."

"I see. Very well."

Thaut hesitated before his next question. He finished off the contents of his cup to clear his throat. With a deep breath he proceeded to ask, itching to know the answer.

"And what of the celestials? Those like you?"

Subject One smiled wide. "The energies that exist beyond your perception are eternal, churning in the ever changing progression that is the cosmic day. Some energies are consistent, manifesting again and again over the cosmic cycle. Others transcend, first within, and then without this cycle. I am beyond man in my capacities, yet equal to him as a part of the whole. Those who know this truly, are no threat to anyone. They live in peace among you."

"I see... And where do you fit in?" Thaut pressed.

"Unbound, my essence drifts about creation, scattered like the stars themselves. When it becomes necessary, I collect and manifest in a concentrated form. Such is my devotion, such is my purpose."

"Your purpose? what is that exactly?" Thaut was on the edge of his seat.

"To restore balance, to protect the sanctity of life. Of the energies that are consistent, not all choose the divine path, not all respect the beauty of creation or the fragility of all that lives. When these forces rise, they often become too great a burden for the natural system to efficiently correct. Thus, I emerge. This is how I came to be born as Kael, son of the Dóvai."

“A righteous destroyer then?”

“In a way, perhaps. More so, I simply redirect the course of evolution that it should remain on a natural pathway. Though my spirit is great, I cannot destroy the energies created. If they will not redirect, I merely scatter their essence, removing their influence from the field. Does this answer your question?” Subject One bowed.

"Well enough, thanks."

Thaut was overwhelmed as he reflected. He reached for more questions. Surely there was much more to know.

"Do not worry, investigator. It would not be the first time humans have been purged of their more superficial achievements. Wonderful how it never seems to hinder their ambition. Humanity will endure, my friend. Make no mistake. But it is to endure on its own terms, not under the conduction of false gods. In freedom humanity will choose its own path, that is the inherent right of all."

"So you favor mankind after all?" Thaut brightened.

"Yes, I suppose I do." Subject One smiled, as he continued. "The people of this world are not necessarily evil. They simply have a natural capacity for it, being the only creatures who truly do. This in itself is a blessing, the gift of true freedom. Even the dark is needed, you see, the churning flux of light and dark the very force that drives evolution into kinetic development. Growth and advancement are the driving life of the natural world. It is unfortunate that people should infallibly succumb to the excess of this drive and the lesser of their attributes, greed."

The way Subject One said the word brought chills to Thaut's skin. He continued.

"That corruption once again threatens to swallow the hearts of man, as the Empire has grown beyond its capacities for integrity to remain intact, despite noble intentions. Not even Emperor Rashawn, with Lady Everret at his side, can stop it now, having fallen to vices of their own."

"And what saves you from yours?" Thaut questioned.

"Nothing. Nothing at all." Subject One laughed. "I too have my flaws. You've already seen a few of them."

His chuckles made him seem warm where he had been rigid and cold.

"Restraint seems to be an issue. My perception is hardly limited, and try as I may, I sometimes cannot help but catch the occasional glimpse. For I can gain the perception not just through one's eyes, but through the mind's eye as well. I didn't mean to catch sight of it, but it was droning in the background for so long earlier, as you passively rehearsed the movement."

"Pardon?" Thaut sat up.

"Your daring plan for escape, sir. The experience would be quite exhilarating..."

Thaut stiffened, his pulse quickening. He was officially uncomfortable with the change in tone. He all but bolted for the glass.

"One can never be too careful in unfamiliar company. Old habits die hard." Thaut smiled nervously.

Subject One smiled gently. "No worries, friend. I mean you no harm. Not now, nor in any of your days to come. My purpose is to destroy, but

I reserve that right for the wicked, those who would abuse their power and influence to bring suffering."

"So we have no secrets then?" Thaut reflected, looking down at the dusty surface of the table.

Subject One smiled. "In spirit we are good friends, you and I. Secrets are darling reminders of one's own character, this is why we share them so selectively. Your secrets are safe with me, investigator. While there are indeed many archetypes lost in the sheep, you are far from being the wolf you think you are."

"I'll be the first to admit there is certainly a wolf or two hidden throughout the flock." Thaut all but hissed with a sigh of relief, regaining his gentleman poise. "And worse still to say a few swine as well."

"So bitter, Investigator." Subject One teased warmly. "Had we met years ago, we might have spat at the world together."

Thaut chuckled a bit, rather enjoying the conversation with the shift in tone. He felt safe and welcomed, his fear conquered. The evening was drawing to its inevitable close. Mission accomplished.

"Maybe I have become a little bitter with the years. It's been a ride. Pulled my share of crazy stunts in my time." Thaut was proud to say.

"Indeed you have, Commander Thaut." Subject One nodded in concurrence.

"That'll be enough spoken of past titles, thank you kindly." Thaut was quick to object.

"Of course." Subject One bowed respectfully. "Just know you have lived your life well."

"Ah, well. Damn good of you to say." Thaut said, sounding rather indignant with sarcasm.

"Life is the greatest of adventures, and your life is the only adventure that solely belongs to you. It is your story. Live your story, share your story, as I have shared mine." Subject One concluded as he rose to his feet, prompting Thaut to do the same.

The lengthy interview had at last come to a close. Thaut saved the files on the device and stowed it back in his satchel with the rest of his belongings.

"I appreciate your time. I really can't thank you enough." Thaut made his final adjustments before making his way around the table to offer a handshake. To his delight, the gesture was received.

"One last question, off the record." Thaut requested.

"Of course."

"How did your tribe best the Malekaur?"

Subject One smiled warmly. "A brave hunter found a way to see beyond the illusions they created. He closed his eyes and aimed his bow at the heart of the thundering hum of wings, releasing arrows until the hum stopped at his feet. The shell of the Malekaur was strong, but the hunter's will was stronger."

Subject One stood with his arms crossed at his back. His simple cloak and tunic made him look like a vagrant, with his bare feet and unkempt appearance. Yet he stood before Thaut a being beyond the scope of human perception, a warm smile suggesting humility despite that fact.

"You know, you really should." Subject One suggested, stopping Thaut as he made for the door.

Thaut looked puzzled.

"Jump. You'll regret it if you don't. Besides, my apprentice awaits you on the dock below. I have sent for your team as well. Please accompany him out of the providence if you will. The remaining knights are searching for him. If they find him, there will be trouble."

"You want me to smuggle a fugitive of the state?" Thaut gasped. "Sounds like a fantastic opportunity to further my report."

"Indeed. A favor for a favor. Fair trade, is it not?"

Subject One winked with a smile. He closed his eyes and offered a simple bow in gratitude, his beard shifting with the dip of his chin.

"Stay strong, my friend."

"Stay strong." Thaut responded with a hint of sentiment. What a wonderful evening this had been, truly a remarkable adventure.

Thaut's heart seemed to drop in the moment of his decision, as he turned from Subject One and took his first running steps toward the glass. His legs powered him as if he were weightless, veteran heart thundering low and steady.

He felt limitless in the instant his right shoulder impacted the glass, smashing through into the night sky. He turned with the fall, his eyes met Subject One a final time. A smile flashed from his friend, and then he was gone.

The sounds of glittering shards twinkled around Thaut as the air rushed around him, high above the docks as he fell. His eyes were closed against the wind, but he caught glimmers of the lights below as he soared toward them in his plummet through the night. He had never felt so alive. Subject One had been right, life was to be an adventure worthwhile.

As he tumbled through space, he felt all the vigor of his youth return to him. The air roared around him as the lights below grew brighter, closer. Suddenly, it felt as if Subject One was near, sailing through the night at his side. Only for an instant, or maybe not at all, then it was gone.

Thaut had reached optimal altitude, and soon the ride would come to its finale. He felt the tech in his boots activate, and he responded by curling into a ball. His descent began a rapid deceleration, shards of the window brushing by as they continued to fall at normal velocity.

The roar subsided as the rush of the air lessened to a cool breeze. Thaut opened his eyes in time to see the last bits of shattered glass smash into the brightly lit surface below. He managed to upright himself just as he descended the last few meters, landing softly on his feet with the thumping click of his boots on the metal grating. He stood on the East Docks once again. A strong youth with powerful eyes approached.

"Ah, David. Good to see you again, lad." Thaut confessed with an excitement reminiscent of his youth. He felt more alive than ever before, and the surprise on David's face made it all the better.

"Investigator." David replied with a nod, quick to recover from the sight of an old man dropping from the night sky amidst a shower of glass.

Thaut scarcely had time to brush himself off before a response crew arrived on the scene. Thaut quickly broadcast his credentials, but he offered little explanation for the incident.

"Sorry chaps, my footing's not as good as it used to be. Could have been a real doozy there. This one's with me." He added, nodding to David.

He activated his communicator, hailing Major Hapford. It wouldn't take long for his crew to arrive with his shuttle.

"So young man, where to?"

LEGEND OF KAEL

First Printing, 2025